THE
TRUE
BLUE
REVOLUTION

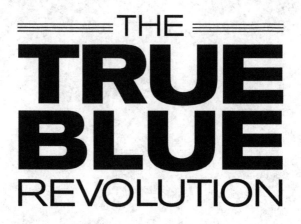

THE
TRUE
BLUE
REVOLUTION

JERRY WILLBUR

The Leadership Mentoring Institute
Vancouver, Washington

For questions or permission requests, **email jwillbur3@aol.com**

The Leadership Mentoring Institute
4909 NE 142nd Street
Vancouver, Washington 98686
United States of America

Library of Congress Control Number: 2017961324
ISBN: 978-0-9993951-0-3 (pbk)
ISBN: 978-0-9993951-1-0 (ebk)

Edited by Ruth Matinko-Wald and Douglas Spangle
Cover and interior design by Machele Brass

Printed in the United States of America

A special thanks to my editors, Ruthie Matinko-Wald, the human sparkler, and Doug Spangle, the mayor of Poetlandia! Also thanks to Machele Brass, the magician. To my friends Dennis and Rose who read my work in process and encouraged me on, a special thank you. And, as usual, a big thank you to my wife of many years, Sherrie, and my sons and daughters: Ryan, Laila, Kevin, and Verna. Finally, I especially dedicate this book to my grandson, Fitzgerald. May this help your world be even better!

"He has brought down the rulers from their thrones but has lifted up the humble. He has filled the hungry with good things but sent the rich away empty."

Luke 1:52

≡ Prologue ≡

As Rey Maxwell Newly started another unexceptional day on the assembly line at the small manufacturing plant called Pipestone Metal, located in Pewamo, Michigan, little did he expect he would soon be the top fugitive on both the FBI and CIA Most Wanted listings. In his wildest dreams, he never expected to fill the most powerful executive position in the world. He never would have done anything purposely to put his family at such perilous risk. If he had known his children would be stolen from him and endangered, he never would have considered getting involved in such a wild, unimaginable plot, no matter what wealth and power were promised to him. He never would have done any of it, especially had he known he and his family would soon be stalked by the deadliest predators on earth, cold and callous killers without remorse.

Looking back on it later, it was so obvious, but almost no one saw it coming. It sounded too preposterous. But that was the idea all along. Make it sound so ridiculous, so "developing nation," so out of bounds, no one would believe it until it devoured them.

For now, however, Rey begins another unexceptional day, unaware of the role he would soon play in America's and his own potential demise, everything seeming boringly normal. And so go the vagaries of American politics. Nothing and nobody are what they seem.

Let the Game Begin

The psychopaths were ready to rule the world. Everything was in place. For many years, they had been content to lurk furtively in the background, pulling all the levers of power, controlling the economy and government to their liking. But now new portable and affordable brain scanning technology was coming online. Using new high-resolution visualization tools, brain researchers were finally able to see there was a whole group of powerful individuals who were totally unencumbered by conscience or compassion. The parts of their brains controlling empathy and controlled impulses were empty, literally dead zones. They could be quite charismatic and excellent communicators, bold risk takers, but the ability to care was not only absent but seemingly unwelcome. To be technical about it, their brains were wired differently. They looked down on vulnerable people who worried about weaker people. They knew how to get what they wanted, and they went out and got it. Now their cover was going to be blown. The game wasn't over, but it was moving out into the open. Technology had finally caught up with the hidden power behind the American throne. It was time to openly seize that power.

The so-called Republican arm of the National Association of Psychopaths (NAP) had the perfect candidate ready for their upcoming primaries. He was brilliant, an eloquent extemporaneous speaker, with well-coifed movie star looks. He was teleprompter ready. He had only a few discreet, sordid, skillfully hidden flaws, supposedly known only to the NAP Republicans—and, of course, to himself. This gave the unscrupulous NAP team the strong leverage they needed to completely and viciously control him.

Then disaster struck. The Democratic arm of NAP knew it was their agreed-upon turn to lose the upcoming U.S. Presidential election. They had selected an unbelievably weak and unsuspecting candidate and should have just sat back and watched the slaughter. But the wide-open opportunity to sting their suddenly inexplicably vulnerable fellow psychopaths was too irresistible for the impulsive rogues to ignore. Even though they could have saved it for an October surprise, they impulsively decided to throw their Republican co-conspirators into disarray right before the important primaries, thinking this could gain them some leverage of their own for the upcoming political season. Their expert hackers had recently found some well-hidden videos of the presumptive Republican candidate their Republican brethren were hoarding just in case they eventually needed some salacious leverage on their own candidate. Soon the nasty snippets were gleefully released to the controlled mainstream media and were rapidly going viral.

A last-minute solution was needed. After a quick social media search, with rushed and minimal vetting, an unsuspecting but suitable replacement candidate was found. He would do. He would be made to do. If there was one thing NAP was good at doing, it was making people do things whether they wanted to or not. The complete control of the most powerful national economy and military the world had ever seen were the stakes. Let the game begin!

≡ CHAPTER 1 ≡

An Unsuspecting But Suitable Man

Reynard "Rey" Maxwell Newly had never even dreamed of becoming president of the United States or of becoming number one on the CIA and FBI most wanted "dead-or-alive" listings. He was having a rare, relatively decent day working on the assembly line making hinges for toilet seats and oven racks at the Pipestone Metal Company. Being a frustrated ornithologist, a "freaking bird lover" as his unsupportive wife and father-in-law called him, Rey was thinking of yellow-bellied sapsuckers and scarlet tanagers to occupy his brain while mindlessly pounding away on his spot welder when Thornton Nithing exploded into his vision and life. He caught a glimpse of a huge, wild-eyed man, followed by several other gigantic men in black suits, hurtling through the production lines heading his way, unexpectedly bellowing Newly's name over the din of the machinery.

Thornton Nithing was a huge man, built like an NFL lineman going to seed, but still nimble and light on his feet. He was dressed in a long, dark overcoat despite the more than 80-degree heat outside and much warmer in the plant. The distinguishing thing Rey Newly first noticed about Nithing, besides his immense size, was his air of intensity. "This is a very focused man," he thought. Indeed, Thornton had the electricity of an exposed live wire crackling about him, as he scattered people and materials while barging his way to Newly, after a co-worker pointed him out.

Rey was too shocked to move. As the big man drew closer, he could see Nithing's deeply pored, sweating face and more clearly hear the growling voice bellowing Rey's name again over the clamor of the shop. A fringe of black hair around Nithing's bald head had one wildly waving strand as he moved briskly toward Rey. He was huffing and puffing and smoking a very large cigar, giving a very good impression of a volatile volcano, ignoring all the non-smoking signs festooning the walls.

"Newly? Ralph Maxwell Newly?" Nithing bellowed, the soggy, stinky cigar bobbing in his mouth with each syllable. "How does it feel to be the next president of the USA?"

Rey nearly choked at the audacity of such a prank. It wasn't the first time his erstwhile workmates had tried to humiliate him. "First, Mister Crazy Man, the name is Reynard or Rey, not Ralph. And second, I have work to do," he grumbled, trying to frantically wave the man away before he got in trouble with his supervisor.

Rey's only previous presidency was that of the Pewamo Ornithology Society of Southern Michigan, and he had been fired after a very brief term of service for not being political enough. He had a degree in ornithology from Southern Michigan University, always wanted to just study and teach about birds, but realized a guy has to make a living. So he did the best he could, distractedly daydreaming about birds while the wheels of industry spun around him and life plodded by.

Thornton Nithing was not one to be ignored. He did the unimaginable. He reached over and shut down Rey's spot welder. Stunned, Rey realized production would be lost, as hours would have to be spent recalibrating and aligning all the welds.

"Didn't you hear me?" Nithing spluttered. "I'm Thornton Nithing of the Michigan Republican Party, and I'm here to tell you something sensational. You've been nominated for the presidency of this country. And, by the way, you will win."

"Look, Mr. Nothing," Rey said through gritted teeth, already ruing the lost production time and probable reprimand from supervision, and starting to get angry, wondering who was pulling this idiotic stunt on him, "A joke is a joke, but you're gonna get me suspended or fired."

"The name is Nithing, not Nothing, and I'm serious. I admit this is a bit of a surprise to both of us. I had to do something quickly, so I searched for local leaders and somehow pulled your name up on social media. You'll make a spectacular candidate!"

"I don't do social media, and I am not interested, Mr. Nithing or Nothing. I just work to barely support my wife and kids, and I'm about ready to punch you out for messing up my production total for the day."

Suddenly Rey's attention was drawn to what appeared to be several local and national TV crews and news reporters dashing his way with cameras flashing and voices shouting questions. His fellow workers again stopped their production, pointed at Rey, and then scrambled to get out of the way of the rushing entourage. Now Rey knew his butt was going to be fired, as the disruption was spreading everywhere throughout the Pipestone plant. Nothing short of a national disaster could do that without severe repercussion.

"Just play along, Rey, and I'll make it worth your time," said Nithing, meanwhile shoving large wads of bills, which surprisingly appeared to be real, into his unsuspecting hands. The shocked Rey could quickly see it was more money than he made in a year. It would go a long way toward buying his twin boys braces and his wife a new car to replace the old, broken-down beater she incessantly complained about.

"Just let me do the talking," Nithing growled at him.

Reporters began screaming questions at him as they swarmed Rey. He would have been crushed except for the cordon of black suits Nithing's burly accomplices formed around him. "Remember, let me do all the talking. You just smile," Nithing growled into his ear again. He gripped Rey with a powerful hand the size of a catcher's mitt and turned him to face the press.

And Nithing talked. Rey listened in confused awe as Thornton Nithing wove an amazing story that mixed Rey's real past with some dazzling twists. No, make that preposterous twists. He made Rey out to be a decorated war hero of epic proportions, and decorated he was, though hardly a hero in his own eyes. He made him out to be a successful labor leader, although his fellow workers had lustily voted him out after less than one year when he attempted to take an ethical stance regarding a safety issue. He was lauded as a community organizer, though this was limited to a brief stint as the president of the now defunct Pewamo Ornithology

Society. He even found out he had graduated from a prestigious school, though he had never heard Pewamo Community College or even Southern Michigan University described that way before. He was admittedly a married father of two adorable children, though the "happily" adjective Nithing added about his marriage was unfortunately most questionable. About the only true thing said was his twin boys were adorable.

Whenever anyone asked Rey to talk, Nithing pushed the microphone away from him and took control. "He will have lots of comments later at a press conference. He's a committed blue collar working man, who happens to be half Pewamo or Pockatoo Indian by the way, the other half Irish. He just wanted to humbly finish his last day at work before preparing to hopefully take over the Oval Office in January. Yes, and he is the real deal, a real working man of the people and for the people! He is good for all of us and good for America!"

Put off by Nithing's attempt to end the supposedly impromptu press conference before it barely started, a riled-up reporter shouted at him, "But your team alerted us he would be here!" Another cheeky member of the media blurted out, "And the party conventions haven't even been held yet!"

"An unfortunate tactical oversight by my staff, letting you know where he was, and a small technical error by me about having the candidacy before the primaries and convention. I meant to say 'when he wins the primaries and convention,' and, as far as the general election, he already leads that Democratic Party candidate, the wretched J. Wrenfield Boguiden, spoiled son of a crooked billionaire by the way, by twenty points in the latest polls. Clear the way," he bellowed. With his black-suited, menacing team forming a wedge for him, he hauled the shocked Rey Newly out of the plant by the scruff of his neck, shoving him into a huge expensive-looking black car, part of a lengthy cavalcade of similar massive vehicles.

The only good thing about this whole episode, as far as Rey could see, was the stunned look on the face of P.T. Pipestone, the owner of Pipestone Metal, Rey's irascible father-in-law, as the caravan of official black vehicles pulled away. Losing his job was almost worth it!

Finally, away from the ear-numbing noise of pounding machinery and the press, Rey could focus on the huge, sweating mountain of a man named Thornton Nithing sitting next to him. He started to get some of his spunk back. "Come on, level with me. What is this really? Clearly not a joke! This car alone costs big bucks, and the little show with the media was insanely impressive if not massively short on the truth."

"Number one," Nithing said, holding up a plump finger with a big, multi-carat diamond ring almost as big as a trashcan on it, "Nobody cares about the truth. This is American politics. Everyone expands on the old resume a bit. Number two," he said with a penetrating gaze at Rey, "Do you, or don't you want to be President?" He said this last while punctuating each letter with a stab to Rey's chest with the slab-like hand still holding the smoldering cigar. "And I would suggest you do, as we probably just got you inconveniently canned from your current day job!"

Rey found himself nearly speechless as the brutal reality of the situation began to sink in. No job; what would he do? "There have to be some primaries, a convention, an election, Electoral College gimmicks, whatever," Rey stuttered, trying to remember his political science classes from years ago and the sequence of processes a representative republic supposedly went through.

Nithing looked at him in utter disbelief. "I love it. How quaint. Leave it to the people. Ha! A complete political naïf! Number one," he said, stabbing with the sickly looking, soggy cigar again. "Americans think they have a democracy if you give them a choice, and we will give them a choice. I mean, come on, if voting mattered, we wouldn't let them do it! Number two. We control the choices. Number three. There is way, way, way too much power and money at stake to let Joe Six-Pack and his soap opera-watching wife make the decisions. It comes down to you or that loser, scumbag, preppy spoiled do-gooder J. Wrenfield Boguiden. Believe me. It will be you, if you know what is good for you and your family." He added this last in an ominous voice that shook Rey to his bones.

"Wait a minute. Why does it have to be me of all people?" Rey spluttered. "Seriously. Everything I try seems to end up a disaster. I try to be decent and kind, and I get stepped on. I don't mean to whine, but I think I am getting set up to be used and abused again, and I don't like it one bit." Then Rey lowered his voice menacingly. "And don't threaten my family."

Nithing looked at him with disdain, not the least bit rattled by Rey's threatening tone. "Losing is for losers, Ralph. I make winners. America likes winners, wants winners, demands winners—and since when does being kind and decent have anything to do with winning? Maybe we can teach you something about real winning. So, stop being a loser, loser."

"Number one," Rey shouted back at him angrily in complete frustration, holding up one finger and vigorously waving it to mimic Nithing's favorite counting gesture. "My name is Rey or Reynard, not Ralph, so get that right. Number two. Maybe I am kind and decent, but I don't take to being bullied. Number three. Either you let me out of this car, or I will bust you in your big, fat, bulbous nose. And, believe me, it is ugly enough already without being broken in several places."

Nithing just rolled his eyes, lifted his hands in fake surrender, and then belly laughed a thunderous bellow that sounded like a wounded bear. He obviously wasn't intimidated or taken aback by Rey's sudden surge of anger or threat of force. It took him a while to get control of himself as he wiped the tears of amusement from his eyes. Finally, he gestured at the car ahead of them. "Okay, forget the numbers, Rey. Just look in the rear window of the car ahead of us."

When Rey looked, he was stunned to see his identical twin boys. Milton and Morton were smiling with their sweet, little, innocent ten-year-old faces and excitedly waving at him, giving him the thumbs-up victory salute. In front of them he could see the silhouette of his wife of twenty years, Prissy Pipestone.

"Right now, they are enthralled their loser dad is suddenly and miraculously a big shot. The wife knows better, having been married to you way too long. Let's keep them all happy. Otherwise, if you refuse, well, let's say the stakes are too high to have people babbling about how we do business, er, politics." Nithing smiled a particularly menacing and malignant smile, revealing a row of repulsive cigar-stained teeth that Rey found quite chilling. They looked disturbingly like the fangs of a demented, slathering carnivore.

"That's called blackmailing," Rey seethed, but in a more guarded voice, suddenly aware of his family's presence in the clutches of this volatile ape.

"It's called leverage," Nithing snarled back. "And don't you ever, ever, ever forget it."

He fixed Rey with a ferocious look, his small, black, piggish eyes giving Rey the feeling that possibly snakes and other ugly evil things moved behind them in those deep, dark pools. "Let me make this perfectly clear. You and your family mean nothing to me, absolutely nothing. But they mean everything to you. And I could eliminate them without a single thought, just like this." He snapped his fingers to make his point. "The end justifies the means, Rey. That is what we say and what we mean. Everything is permissible and everyone is expendable. That's our motto. We can because we can. Power, dominance, control—and then the big bucks flow. Those are our rules of engagement, so get used to them." Nithing stopped to catch his breath.

After letting the chilling reality sink in with Rey a while, Nithing continued. "This is all you need to know. You are now willingly or unwillingly part of the machine that runs this big, wonderful country we both call home. Now let's not talk nasty to each other. Instead, let's talk nice. This is going to be a big money maker for you, bubba. Fame and fortune, my man! You are going to be famous, maybe even win a Nobel Prize or two if we play it right. Millions of dollars in books and media rights alone, amazing retirement benefits, and all you must do? Just play along like a good Eagle Scout."

Rey was lost with all the talk of millions and machines. The only millions he vaguely knew about belonged to other people, and the only machines with which he was familiar manufactured hinges, refrigerator parts, and oven racks. "But why does it have to be me?" Rey asked again, not liking to hear the weak and plaintive sound of his own voice. "There must be many much more qualified people out there, eager to do anything for your bucks."

"Well," Nithing mused, lazily stretching out his huge form, like a big predatory cat. Rey suddenly realized Nithing was at least six and a half feet tall and well over three hundred pounds. Although Nithing was fat, Rey could also see hard muscles rippling in his bulk.

Once comfortable, Nithing continued: "You weren't our first choice, I admit. That's for sure. Boguiden's people got to our first guy. We thought we had him scoped out and ready to roll, and they found some real dirt we thought was well hidden. And, Rey, I agree you aren't much, but you don't seem to have any major dirt we can find. Damn, it is our turn and the blasted Democrats blew our original winner out of the water. So, we had to get a complete unknown at the last moment. Baby, you fit the bill. A blue-collar, factory-working college grad, a good ethnic mix, and—I still can't hardly believe it— but an actual, for real, effing Eagle Scout, a do-gooder, decent family man!" He followed this with a hideous snicker. "Plus," Nithing added, roughly gesturing at the car containing his family, "speaking of family! Lots of leverage for us in case you don't want to play along." Nithing smiled smugly, giving Rey a look that reminded Rey of a predator looking at wounded prey. "Believe me, Rey, everything is going to be okay. Us Michigan Republicans stick together, for a better America!"

Soon the caravan of sleek black cars pulled up to Rey's

modest suburban Pewamo home. He was amazed and alarmed to see a huge moving van loading up his meager, tattered possessions. There were two menacing black helicopters hovering overhead with a well-armed S.W.A.T. team rappelling to the ground, surrounding his place, keeping his neighbors intimidated and shut up in their houses. Other discreetly armed and dangerous-looking big men in black suits were already everywhere around the property, but they deferentially made way for Nithing to escort Rey and his family into his house, where he was immediately accosted by his wife.

Prissy glared menacingly at him. "Okay, Reynard Maxwell Newly! What did you do this time? You never tell me anything and then go get us all goofed up. You never told me we're moving or changing jobs," she hissed as she led him off to the side and away from Nithing. Prissy had been prim and pretty at one time, but now she was a little stocky, with mousy brown hair tinged carroty red from a beauty shop disaster. Her hair now carelessly tumbled down around her face.

Prissy was the youngest daughter of P.T. Pipestone and his long-suffering wife, Theta. Her round face was now drained of any color—either out of fear or anger, or maybe both. Deep lines from constant frowning and nitpicking at Rey bracketed her mouth. She had a deep V etched between her green eyes. All her life, Prissy had been scrutinized, found wanting by her parents, and shown up by her stunning older sister, Paula. Now she viewed her whole life as a balancing act between dismal and disastrous. Being married to Rey certainly hadn't helped, he readily admitted, and he felt a pang of guilt knowing he could never match up to her expectations or help her feel good about herself, as his own disasters in life had only deepened her low self-esteem. She was seemingly born with a tendency toward pessimism, and her life with Rey up to now was proving her right.

"Believe it or not, I didn't do anything this time," he said apologetically. Then, to her surprise, Rey handed her the big wad of money Nithing had earlier stuffed into his hands, at least quieting her accusations for a minute.

Eagerly eyeing the money, and licking her lips as she salivated at the sight of all the large denomination greenbacks, she hissed again at him, though a little softer this time. "Well, keep it up. Don't blow it this time. It seems like your 'doing nothing' trick is finally paying off."

Abruptly cutting off any response from him, Prissy turned and smiled at Thornton Nithing, who was a few steps away, some of her old charm showing through. "Oh, and the charming and thoughtful Mr. Nithing considerately informed me we will be flying tonight to Washington, DC, of all places, to begin working on your campaign. It's all a little unexpected and overwhelming. I wish I would have been told in advance," she added, glaring at Rey again. "The boys are so excited their dad is finally, I mean, is going to be recognized for his … whatever."

Prissy got a perplexed look on her face and started to walk away. Then her face lit up again as a new and glorious thought blossomed in her mind. Turning to Rey and Nithing, she smiled her most disarming smile while waving the wads of money. "I am going to need a completely new wardrobe to wow Washington."

Clutching the cash, she walked off to make some calls or

perhaps some purchases on her computer. Rey decided not to bother asking if it was all for a better America. He was just happy she was temporarily happy—and out of the way.

As his boys came bounding over to eagerly hug him, a part of the bigger picture started coming into focus. They competed in their chirpy voices to share the good news with him. "We entered you in the Best Dad contest on the Internet to win busts of the great presidents, and somebody named Mr. Goggle or Google picked you."

They had filled out a profile on the Internet and, of course, innocently edited out specific details about their beloved Dad, details that would have eliminated him from winning almost anything. Nithing looked on seemingly charmed by their adoring chatter and obvious devotion for Rey.

"Ah, I can see a great campaign video here. The 'missus' is a little sour, although warming up, especially with cash in hand. But the boys are just natural, charismatic little charmers."

"I haven't said I'm running yet," Rey reminded Nithing, and then he cringed as Nithing clumsily patted both Morton and Milton on their heads with his big paw, nearly causing one of them to bite his tongue.

"Leverage, my man, always remember leverage. Besides, you are a lock to win. Once you cruise through the primaries and convention, you will be running against that big-time loser, Lying J. Wrenfield Boguiden, a spoiled child of rich parents, a do-gooder preppy snob. Granted, he is supposedly actually another humble, kind, and decent man—totally unfit to run this country. 'A useful tool,' the DNC boys call him. A well-intentioned loser, an idiot at best, I call him."

Suddenly Rey remembered where he had heard the Boguiden name. "I saw a piece in the Washington Wall Street Weekly about him. They said he was 'intelligent and nuanced,' I believe."

Nithing just harrumphed. "Intelligent, nuanced, and nice people are what the cunning eat for lunch. The so-called Good Book says, 'Be gentle as a dove but wise as a serpent.' My Good Book says that the serpent eats the dove and gets even wiser."

Nithing ignored Rey's attempted snide comment about never having read that book. "You are the real ticket, man," Nithing exulted. He repeated his earlier mantra of Rey's qualifications again. "You are the total package. Let's see," he said, ticking off things on his fingers again. "A blue-collar, factory-working, college-educated man. Part Irish and Indian, Pockatoo or whatever. A fracking war hero. And, heh, even an effing Eagle Scout, for God's sake! I keep forgetting to tell the press boys that. You are almost too good to be true." Then he added as an afterthought, "But, don't worry at all. No one gets to see anyone's real records anymore."

"But I'm neither Republican nor Democrat. I'm Independent, at best," Reynard said, not even remembering when he last registered or voted, or for whom he voted.

"Better yet, dude! And don't forget it! Independent minded as a trait polls well with the voters," responded Nithing. Seeing Rey's frown, he continued: "Don't blow a good thing. You'll get the best food money can buy, swank vacations to hot tourist places, limos, even hot women if you want them, a great house, top education for the boys, and Secret Service guys with big, loaded guns always watching over you and your dear family every minute—if you get my drift. Just learn to play the game and read the prepared script. We write and put on teleprompter everything you're to say. Foolproof. No-brainer. No sweat."

Rey finally gave up trying to convince Nithing of anything and went over to talk to Prissy while they waited for the packing to end. "I'm sorry if you think I have messed things up," he said apologetically, reaching out to touch her shoulder. But she pulled away and fixed him with an accusing glare. Her deep green eyes snapped angrily.

"Since when haven't you messed things up?" Prissy spit as she angrily stalked away from him to sit on a couch the movers hadn't yet taken. Suddenly, she smiled. "I'm waiting for a limo Mr. Nithing arranged in advance to take me shopping before we go to the plane. All this junk goes into storage," she said, gesturing to their furniture and boxes of accumulated trivia. "We get all new stuff," she said dreamily to no one in particular, or especially not to Rey. "If you had told me in advance. . . . Oh, never mind. I wouldn't have believed you anyway. Please just go away and don't ruin the moment. It might just be a dream, and I definitely don't want to wake up!"

Rey took the shunning with his usual aplomb and started reminiscing about how he had come to this pass. A clean-cut, stringy but strong kid with lanky, long arms, he had been a football and basketball hero in his small-town high school. Somehow, he had finally attracted the attention of Prissy's older sister, Paula, who was in his class at Pewamo High.

Even then, Rey knew a Pipestone was way out of his league. Yet he had loved Paula since first laying eyes on her in fourth grade. Every touchdown the Pewamo "Rocket," as he was called, scored was scored for Paula. Every basket he made was for her. He was completely smitten. And no wonder; Paula was a stunning beauty, physically imposing at nearly six feet tall in heels, and with a Victoria's Secret model body before people knew what Victoria's Secret was. Her legs were long, shapely and strong; her hips flared into luscious curves and then plunged abruptly into a narrow waist. She'd had cleavage before any of the other girls even knew what it was, and she knew how to enhance every one of her already enhanced features. Her eyes were so green they didn't look real, and her raven black hair always was in a carefully designed tumble around her heart-shaped face. Her only flaw were her eyes. Paula had her father's eyes—fiercely piercing like a hungry eagle looking at a lamb for lunch. She always got what she wanted. And for a little while in their junior and senior years, what Paula wanted was Rey.

Several hot dates and clumsy adventures in the back seat ensued, but the torrid romance was doomed from the start. Her father, P.T. Pipestone, a multi-millionaire and by far the richest man in Brewer County where Pewamo was located, was the founder and sole owner of Pipestone Metal. He couldn't have approved less of Rey. Despite being raised poor himself, and proud of it, Pipestone had bigger plans for Paula—especially because his own son, Joshua Preston Pipestone, better known as J.P., was a dull-witted sluggard (in P.T.'s own, often very publicly and loudly repeated words) and his younger daughter, Prissy, was merely average (at least by the high P.T. Pipestone standards). So, Pipestone tolerated Paula's fling with the Irish Indian, as he derogatorily called Rey, but his dislike intensified each time he saw Paula and Rey together.

P.T. Pipestone was no man to have against you, no matter who you were, let alone a poor, blue-collar kid. P.T. was a self-made man, partly because no one wanted to take credit for him. Using guts and a vicious intolerance of any competition, he built Pipestone Metal up from a small, garage-based business to a hugely successful and very profitable company in a highly competitive market. He designed and built his own house and never allowed the family to move a single piece of furniture, because it was all planned and organized to his high specifications. P.T. was all about dominance and control. He would walk into a room, ignore everyone present, walk over and straighten a slightly ajar picture, and then walk back out still ignoring everyone. In fact, he described himself as a cold-hearted bastard, and was proud of it. He was hard on himself and on everyone in his family. He was an "awfulizer," able to pick out the slightest minuscule flaw in a near-perfect picture—or person—and then magnify it in his mind until it was all he saw. He believed in very little praise, saying it spoiled people, and seldom spoke an encouraging word. He made his money the old-fashioned way: He had worked hard for it and then stole the rest. He wasn't going to let a young smart aleck like Rey wreck his precious dreams for the prized Paula.

When the time came after graduation, if for no other reason than to get him away from his daughter, P.T. did try to persuade Rey to attend a big-time college and get an engineering or business degree. But Rey was nuts about birds, of all things. Even though he had good grades and great athletic skills, and could probably have received a scholarship to a big school, Rey went to the local Pewamo Community College. He decided to stay home and help his widowed mom, Suzanna "Swan" Newly, and two younger siblings with the family's farm after his dad had been killed in an industrial accident at Brewer Creek Brewery during Rey's senior year in high school. Meanwhile, Paula went away to a hotshot eastern school and joined a big-time sorority at the behest of P.T. They continued to see each other during summer breaks, but it was increasingly clear Paula saw him as just a summer distraction at best.

On the other hand, Rey unknowingly mesmerized the younger sister, Priscilla, better known as Prissy. Even then she was a little chunky but busty, and she maybe too obviously tried to make herself look good when the goofy and oblivious Rey came around looking for Paula. Rey hardly noticed her then, and that only added to Prissy's feelings of rejection.

It all ended with Paula when Rey entered the armed forces with the plan to use his service pay to help pay for the rest of his education at Southern Michigan University when he finished his tour of duty. Because of his athletic ability and tested high intelligence, Rey was soon wearing a green beret. Before long, he was leading a Special Forces patrol on some God-forsaken, bird crap-encrusted little island in the South Pacific when disaster hit. Rey was trying to get his guys to stay off the beaten track and plow through the tall elephant grass. "Never take the easy way," his mind told him, but they were tired, footsore from stumbling around the volcanic landscape, and they wanted to get back to their base, off the desolate island. They were the only recon group on the island and saw no hostiles. They were supposedly looking for commie cannibals, but the locals seemed quite friendly and maybe just a little confused about why the US military was there again. They mentioned that another bunch of Americans had been there earlier and found nothing of concern.

All the natives wanted was Spam, gum, coffee, and cigarettes. Rey could only give them R.T.E., ready-to-eat snacks, some instant coffee, a few sticks of gum, and a few cigarettes he bummed off another reluctant soldier. Interestingly, Rey found some of the locals had learned a little English in the unlikely hope of luring American tourists there to see all the birds.

As they tramped around the rugged island unsuccessfully looking for hostiles, he began to admire the tough, but gentle islanders and started liking the jagged peaks and the rest of the rugged, rocky island, with all the exceedingly abundant bird life. He treated the natives with respect and didn't expect to have any trouble. He was even trying to figure out why they were sent to such a friendly, poverty-stricken place—when everything fell apart.

Rey was intrigued when some of the islanders told him that they had previous contact with the US way back in World War II and that they liked having the Yankees on the island then. Somehow a local chief-cum-politician got the idea that, maybe, if there were an insurrection, the Yanks would come back and bring good stuff again. They had made a mock plane and a fake runway, hoping the planes filled with goodies could be induced to land again if they behaved.

Rey recollected reading about such a quirky thing called the John Frum Cargo Cult, but everything else was a blur in his memory. He had noted earlier that there was a crude mockup of a US plane on a pockmarked runway on the isthmus connecting the two parts of the island. They were going to look at it when they had some time, after investigating the rest of the strange island to determine there was no threat. He thought he might even question the natives about the cargo cult and its origins and objectives. "Weird stuff, man," was all he remembered saying, thinking about the mock plane and the cargo cult.

And then it happened. One of their team stepped on a land mine. As it exploded, Rey suddenly remembered the vague warning in the debriefing that an earlier visiting team might possibly have set some mines to get suspected hostiles. Unfortunately, despite all his repeated warnings, his tired and bored teammates were breaking all the rules, bunching up too close together. For the last time, they had taken the easy way along the beaten path, all of them but Rey.

When he finally woke up, Rey was on a hospital ship. His right leg was in a cast as was his right arm. He had lots of internal injuries and shrapnel everywhere from the belt down. He was just far enough off the path to have missed the main blast that shredded his team. Multiple concussions kept his brain in a fog. From the extent of his injuries, it was painfully easy to see his football and military days were behind him, but he was luckier than the rest of his team. Their various parts that could be found were flown home, and then immediately the island was intensely carpet bombed, for reasons never explained to Rey, by huge, high-flying B-52s.

While still in a coma, Rey was awarded several medals. He couldn't remember much of what happened, which seemed to please the leadership involved. He was sent home a hero, a broken hero, but a highly decorated hero nonetheless.

He had hoped Paula would come to see him. Even as he recuperated during the Christmas holidays, when he knew she was home, she was too busy to visit. Prissy, however, was there every day, as he swam in and out of a drugged daze at the Pewamo General Hospital. She never said too much that was negative, although one day, while looking at his shattered leg and scarred arm, she started to cry. "Paula can't understand why you ever joined the military. She says you could have gone to any big-time school you wanted. But, no, you had to be an Eagle Scout and a war hero."

"I am an Eagle Scout," he muttered, but she only looked away, saying something low under her breath about only getting Paula's rejects. That should have been enough of a warning for him, but he was too drugged to care and still too smitten by Paula.

One other time, Rey woke up to hear Prissy muttering that "Paula really loves you, but Daddy won't let her have you. She would lose everything." Another time he swore he smelled Paula's perfume and felt tears fall on his face. When he finally fought his way out of the haze, however, she was gone.

As usual, only Prissy was there. He wondered where his sweet mother was and was finally told she had suffered a nervous breakdown upon hearing of his heroic actions and near fatal injuries. Sadly, she was institutionalized and never recovered. They told him she died of a broken heart, having lost her husband and then nearly her oldest son within such a short time.

Prissy stayed by him. She helped him walk again and

seemed to be there whenever he woke up. Finally, though he was still on heavy medication, drifting in and out of a drugged and dazed state, probably suffering from post-traumatic stress disorder, and still in love with Paula, he found himself married to Prissy Pipestone—over the somewhat muted objections of P.T. Pipestone. Rey was always suspicious that maybe P.T. felt it was probably the best Prissy could do and conveniently and permanently removed Rey from Paula's life.

P.T. grudgingly got him a job at Pipestone Metal, but Rey's heart just wasn't in it. His severely wounded body continually ached from the hard labor. The place was hot as a cauldron, with flying sparks and molten pieces of steel; it perpetually smelled like grease and burning metal, a little Hell on earth. Moreover, he hated the way Pipestone Metal skirted safety issues at the expense of the workers.

Pipestone Metal was known as a "blood iron" shop that ignored safety standards and eagerly took hazardous but profitable jobs that other companies wouldn't touch out of safety concerns. He cringed as fingers and hands were lost to get orders out on time. His buddy, Henry "Silk" Wilkes, the best basketball player Brewer Creek high ever turned out, lost three fingers on his right hand, but they got the order out. The fact he wouldn't play basketball again didn't seem to faze anybody but Henry and Rey. Little Larry "The Canary" Birdsong, a boyhood friend who could imitate any bird Rey could mention, fell into a dangerously exposed vat of acid used for plating metal while hustling clumsily to get an order out. He was burned over most of his body and died slowly and painfully, but they got the order out.

Finally, Rey had had enough. He stood up to P.T. and

protested the horrible safety practices at Pipestone Metal. It was a heroic but misguided move. He was busted down to the worst factory jobs. He was routinely assigned the dirtiest, most physically demanding, and most dangerous work. P.T. said he wasn't good enough, not tough enough, and wouldn't make it.

Rey stuck it out and was eventually voted union representative. But when it was obvious P.T. would rather shut the business down and lay everybody off than give in to Rey and the workers on the safety issues, the union members quickly rolled over and voted him back out, in the fine American tradition of shooting its leaders. Rey sadly realized the union wasn't so much about worker safety or even unfair management any more. It was more about making the buck, job security, and protecting unproductive workers at the expense of anything and everyone who got in the way.

"Why did he stay at Pipestone?" he often asked himself. He was admittedly stubborn. He couldn't get a good reference for his years of work at Pipestone, and jobs were very tight in the area. There were also his two younger siblings left orphaned by his mom's death, and now he needed to support Prissy, too. Mostly, though, he was just stubborn and wouldn't let his old nemesis, P.T. Pipestone, defeat him and chase him off.

So Rey just kept his nose to the proverbial grindstone. He finished his degree in ornithology at night and then kept plugging away at his job as the years added up. He found jobs for ornithology majors were even scarcer than most endangered bird species. At least he could protect his brain from the monotonously repetitive and mind-numbing assembly line work by picturing all the free-flying birds in his mind and dreaming what it would be like to fly free.

Now, like a bolt of lightning out of the clear blue sky, came this unexpected, life-changing . . . what? Was it an opportunity or just a chillingly real threat to his family? He was sorely tempted to show old P.T. that he could achieve something other than just pounding hot metal his whole life. He also knew Paula would be shocked if he succeeded. And, even though Prissy was sure he would screw it up, she would be impressed if he pulled off winning the most unlikely election ever.

Counterbalancing all this, of course, was the mockery of Thornton Nithing calling him a loser. The more he was around the guy, the more the hackles on Rey's neck went up. The thug could be downright charming one minute, charismatic even, and then in a volatile flash, Nithing would be brutally ruthless the next. He could be extremely persuasive, but, when that approach failed, he would just abruptly and coldly crush the opposition.

At times, Nithing was brutally honest and nakedly aggressive with Rey, rudely exerting his power and leverage. Then the next minute, he was very charming and convincing. Rey had to admit he seemed to have everyone else convinced purely on its merits, and with a little judicious use of psychology, that this was a great deal.

Alarmingly, Rey saw Nithing win over Prissy with a stark appeal to her greed and her desire to gain approval from her dad. He won over the boys by telling them what a wonderful man their dad was, a true Eagle Scout war hero and all-around good guy. Nithing even won over P.T. by telling him how easy it would be to get government contracts with a devoted and influential son-in-law in the White House. It would make P.T. powerful and dominant in the industry, able to even some old scores by gleefully crushing his opponents. Nithing seemed to be able to unerringly perceive each person's innermost desires and craft a perfect pitch to win them over.

Even though Rey knew he was an accidental hero at best, and most definitely not presidential material, even he found himself easily sliding into agreement with the smooth-talking Nithing—until he caught himself.

When he accused Nithing of lying, the snake said he preferred to think of it as the art of mendacity. If Rey pushed more, Nithing just said the American people are so easily lied to because they prefer the lie. The bigger the lie is, the better. They deserve getting lied to. "But I still prefer to think of myself as mendacious, not a liar. Mendacity," he said stretching out all the syllables in the word, "I really love the sound of that word."

Several other things bothered Rey. He was swamped by last-minute phone calls before they left Pewamo. Everyone had essentially said the same thing: "Remember me," and admonishing him with: "Why didn't you tell me you were such an important man?" Most of the people he hadn't seen in years, and some he didn't remember meeting at all. Worst of all for Rey were the local papers, the Pewamo Prattler and the Brewer Creek Enquirer: "Dark Horse Sweeps into Lead for Presidency." But it wasn't the headlines that got to him. It was the reports that followed that were full of flattering inaccuracies and flat-out lies. He had no doubt who had manufactured the flowery press releases. On top of it all, the news made it sound as though his election were going to make both Pewamo and Brewer Creek overflow with government largesse.

Mendacious or not, Nithing proved to be a fantastic arranger. He soon had all their items packed away and put in storage and the whole family ensconced in a luxurious private jet. It was the largest one Rey had ever seen. It was almost the size of Air Force One. "First class all the way for my man Rey!" Nithing pronounced.

Prissy, Morty, and Milty were spellbound and speechless for once. Even P.T. was impressed. When Nithing announced the whole family was going, he didn't let Rey know that meant P.T., Theta Pipestone, P.T.'s wife, and even Paula Pipestone, who, to Prissy's jealous dismay, mysteriously showed up at the last minute from a hugely successful East Coast business engagement of some sort. Prissy had wanted this to finally be her shining moment. She did not want to be upstaged by her glamorous sister.

Nithing was beside himself with delight. An attractive Midwest industrial family was a winning part of the ticket, according to the chortling Nithing. "This will push all the buttons," he said. "Americans love entrepreneurs and self-made men like P.T." Turning to the preening, vicious old industrialist, Nithing added: "Humbly allowing your son-in-law to work in the factory from the bottom up while earning his leadership stripes was sheer genius, P.T. It is a brilliant move and a great American story. And now I find you also have another lovely daughter," he smoothly added, swooning over the smiling Paula.

Paula's only comment on the flight was to sneak up be-hind Rey, poke him sharply in the ribs, press her delicious-ly ample boobs up against his back, and whisper harshly in his ear, "You could have easily had me, you idiot, if you had played your cards right."

This seemed like more than a card game to Rey. It seemed more like playing Russian roulette with several bullets loaded in the chamber. With the malevolent Nithing threatening him and his family on one side, he was sure Nithing's opponents on the other side would be just as ruthless.

P.T. leaned over and unctuously gave him some unsolicit-ed advice. "You look worried, Rey. Listen, son," he said in a disturbingly patronizing voice. "I always found worry to be like a rocking chair. Gives you something to do but doesn't get you anywhere." Smiling at his own sagacity, he went on. "This Nithing is a doer. He reminds me of me as a young man. He believes in the ruthless pursuit of one's dreams. Let's ride this pony for all it's worth," he added, with a wink that reminded Rey of a sated crocodile on a riverbank.

Rey sensed this was anything but a pony. It was more, he thought, like the Chinese proverb about riding the dragon: It gets you places fast, but there is Hell to pay when you final-ly try to get off! Rey was beginning to fear it was his family that might feed the beast. If he had known what was lurking ahead in the wastelands of Washington, DC, he might have jumped from the plane, no matter how sumptuous the vehicle and food. As dangerous as dragons are, the human predator is the worst predator, and he was going with his loved ones, and some not-so-loved ones, into the mouth of the beast!

CHAPTER 2

The National Association of Psychopaths (NAP) Convention

Somewhere in the Darkest Depths of Washington, DC

As Rey and his family winged their way to Washington on the sleek, private jet with Thornton Nithing and all the Pipestones in tow, the National Association of Psychopaths (NAP) annual conference was underway. You didn't have to be a genius to join NAP. Just being unscrupulous and nasty earned you a look. Dirty money helped. Glib and superficial charm was quite a common trait among the group members. They were all unapologetically manipulative and cunning con artists. A grandiose sense of self-worth was just expected. Pathological lying was so common you could tell the truth among this group and no one would suspect it. Lack of remorse and lack of shame or guilt, all marinated in a deep-seated rage, prevailed among its members. Other people would point out traits such as shallow or fake emotions, incapacity for love, a huge need for stimulation, and no compunctions about hideous cruelty as shortcomings, but these tendencies were valued assets to this menagerie of predators. A tendency to live on the edge and relish mayhem were other traits of this unsavory but very successful group. In short, they made excellent politicians and actors, exceptional lawyers, newscasters, journalists, and, in some cases, business leaders, if the industry called for ruthless competition. It was all about power, dominance, and control, how to get and keep power, dominance, and control at any cost.

Achor Nithing fit in not only well, but he proudly felt he exceeded the worst of the worst. He was these things and much more. Achor, Thornton's older brother, was an undoubted genius with a stratospheric IQ and ego to match. He was a star news anchor. "Not just a part of the 'mean-stream media,'" he liked to say. Instead, he was the crown jewel of the "attackerati." When Achor spoke, America listened.

Now Achor Nithing was addressing the annual NAP gathering and didn't doubt he could soon capture their rapt attention. This was the time he would announce the culmination of years of planning, the implementation of the grand plan. As usual, everyone was masked, with each face covered in the visage of a predator. Eagles, hawks, tigers, lions, all stared avariciously at Achor Nithing. He knew the masks were part of what some scholars called the Lucifer Effect. You could become your true self behind the mask. People in uniforms or masks felt and, more importantly, acted like different people than they did in everyday dress. It was a way to literally transform yourself. Properly masked or uniformed people would do things in a crowd they normally would never think of doing by themselves.

Achor Nithing liked the Lucifer Effect and used it for his nefarious purposes. He glared out at the cavorting group as they groped each other and howled. Even though most, including Achor, remained cloaked behind their masks, no one could mistake Achor Nithing's booming bass voice they so often heard as he brought the chaos to sudden order.

"My fellow psychopaths," he bellowed, and the sound reverberated around the cavernous hall, bringing everyone to attention. "All is under control for another glorious election. Both parties, under our usual wise, guiding hand, have selected their candidates. The DNC has J. Wrenfield Boguiden." Nithing paused as raucous hissing, hooting, and growling resounded from the left side of the group. Wagging his finger at the frustrated DNC partisans, he continued. "It is your turn to lose and you know it."

Turning to the right side of the audience, he continued. "And, after some slight difficulty up in Michigan on the Republican side, we have a candidate." There was some snide snickering coming from the left that suddenly stopped when Nithing glared ominously at them. Even with a mask, his eyes seemed to flare with an evil fire, threatening to consume any who wanted to stand in his way.

Everyone knew Achor's usually capable and highly efficient, if sometimes overly zealous, younger brother Thornton had been responsible for the previously mentioned and temporarily botched Michigan operation. "Despite some conniving by certain DNC perpetrators, whom I personally will make sure are punished," he added with a cold dagger of a tone, "we have our man. Ralph—no, excuse me—Reynard Maxwell Newly." Whipping out some small note cards, he continued, "An Eagle Scout, believe it or not! A decorated but bumbling war vet, who, believe it or not again, stumbled into one of our own mine fields, permanently messing up a leg and an arm, along with some other unnamed body parts. An unsuccessful executive, and an unsuccessful union leader, busted back down to factory worker. Overall, just an unsuccessful bumbler. Decent dad, but fairly rotten husband, loyal to his spouse or, at least, very discreet." Flipping note cards nonchalantly over his shoulder, he continued. "Oh, and Irish and Indian and ornithologist, whatever that last bit means. But who the hell cares? He is a perfect loser, our loser, whom we can and will control."

After a tremendous round of applause and more hooting, Nithing launched into a prepared speech that would go down in NAP annals as one of the greatest of all time. You could say it was from the heart, if Achor Nithing only had one.

"My fellow psychopaths, our time has come. We are the future of mankind. We, in fact, are the real ones everyone has been waiting for. I believe it was Mark Twain who said, 'It could probably be shown by facts or figures that there is no distinctly American criminal class except Congress.' I stand here to humbly correct Mr. Twain. We are proudly that new class, and we are also the new Congress as well, for the most part. By the way, I have no problem with the word criminal, if it means protecting the poor, misguided fools of this country from the harm that lurks out there just waiting to devour them! I have no problem with the word criminal if it means maintaining order and a smoothly working country! I have no problem with the word criminal if it means beating back the Chinese threat to our economic welfare! I have no problem with the word criminal if it means protecting our borders from those who hope to destroy us, if it means boldly making this country the most powerful nation in the world. We are the tax our fellow American sheep pay to keep the other international predators at bay! I believe we are the ones ordained to rule!"

As the roar of approval finally died down, Achor Nithing continued speaking, his body posture and tone of voice producing a powerful magnetic affect, drawing the crowd in. "I don't know why we have been chosen to be the ones. To quote another politician, 'That's beyond my job description.' I do know, though, that the laws of the universe are uncannily calibrated to make us possible. We are the ones designed to rule. In this intricately fine-tuned universe, with an equally fine-tuned solar system and planet, only a few of us have the will to ruthlessly rule. Look around at the way evolution works. It is my conclusion that God, if there is one, is a psychopath, too, and that He has ordained the survival of the fittest. And we, my friends, are the fittest!" The crowd roared in agreement.

Nithing continued: "It is our right to rule. Just like the lion has a right to hunt and devour the gazelle, and the cat the mouse, the strong and vicious rule over the weak, we are the fulfillment of the natural law of survival of the most fit and ferocious."

He paused again to let the applause and hurrahs die down, his eyes glaring out of his mask, nearly melting the front row of spectators with intensity. "Just look at this nation, so blessed with wealth, but wallowing in ineptitude. There is too much at risk, too many dollars and resources, to let the sheep run the show. Look at the creeping disconnection from reality, for which I've had to coin a new word just to describe the process, stupidification, of a people hysterically upset when their game shows and reality TV series are cancelled in favor of holding debates on national security or the economy. It is disgusting. Without us, the simpering sheep would be dead meat before the clamoring hordes of the Middle East, Russia, and China! Our control will be the tax they pay for us to defend the USA. Nobody in their right mind will attack us when they know we are such bad ass, cold-blooded killers who would just as soon see them bleed to death as breathe!"

As the bloodthirsty roar died down again, Nithing continued, "Is deceit such a bad thing when the end justifies the means? I say no. The flock is so easily deceived because they love the lies. They want to believe. The bigger you can make the lie, the better. Reality is too complex and confusing for them to comprehend. Malcolm Muggeridge, a great man even if he wasn't a psychopath, once said, 'People don't believe lies because they have to. They believe lies because they want to.' And believe this with me, America wants to believe our lies!"

Nithing paused for effect and then he bellowed out like a water buffalo in heat, "We want to give them what they want!" Letting the applause die down again, he started out masterfully in a near whisper so the crowd again had to lean in and strain to hear. Then he let his voice slowly rise with each word. "And, by the way, what is wrong with power? Just study history. You can have communism, you can have socialism, egalitarianism, any ism you want, but sooner or later the cream will rise to the top and you will have a hierarchy. Hierarchy always prevails. Even chickens have a pecking order, and the biggest, meanest peckers always win!"

This led to another huge uproar and ovation. "Only stupid people are constrained by honesty and integrity, by an idiotic commitment to the truth when lies and deception serve better. We have no such constraints. Yes, we are liars. That is the truth. But the public can't handle the truth. I say that proudly. We want power, dominance, and control. We deserve power, dominance, and control, because we have seized it. I say in Latin, nil medium. No middle ground. We are here to dominate and control. Whatever is possible is permissible. Everything is permissible, and everyone is expendable. Use or be used. The end justifies the means.

"Some have asked me why are we coming out in the open now? I ask, why not? You have all read about the startling advances in brain-scanning technology. We can now potentially be identified in early childhood, because our superior brains are wired differently from the cowering compassionate set. Once they identify us, they can imprison or control us out of their fear of our superior powers. Fortunately, due to our diligent work in the past, we are now so deeply and powerfully embedded in politics and the media that we can prevaricate and digress and the public, easily distracted by shiny objects, will lose attention. Keep them in comfort, and they act just like the sheep they are. We are the ones destined to rule. It is the new Golden Rule. We have the gold and we make the rules. We aren't fooled or ruled by compassion. We are designed to rule, and rule we will!"

With the crowd now in a screaming frenzy, Nithing quieted his voice again and, once more, skillfully drew them in. "Some say we are not religious. I say we have a religion. It is politics. To paraphrase H.L. Mencken, politics is where the jackasses worship the jackals. We are worthy of worship, because it is we who have made this country great and will continue to make it great. Let the people believe it is a representative republic or a democracy. Let them sleep while we rule and run the show. Let them bask in debauchery while we do the hard work of government and world domination. The so-called psychologists may call us disturbed, but what disturbs me is letting soft-willed idiots run the country. They may call us snakes in suits, but at least our snakes are snakier than the other countries' snakes, and we will dominate and rule. They may call us intraspecies predators, but I call it culling the herd of the weak and useless to make the rest of us stronger. They may say we have delusions of grandeur, but is it a delusion when we run the greatest country on earth? When we are the smartest, the greatest, the strongest? Let the sheep sleep. Let them believe they run things. Give them bread and circuses, reality shows and soap operas, and they can give us blood and money."

The NAP horde was on its feet now, howling like wolves at the moon as Nithing roared, "We are the strong. They are the weak. There is no value in guilt or remorse. I pity those that value such weakling traits. Stay hungry, my friends. Stay hungry. The greatest feast is to come."

As Nithing left the podium followed by thunderous waves of applause, he peeked at his cell phone. The text was from his brother, Thornton. "Hocus-pocus, the bogus P.O.T.U.S. has landed!" Achor only shook his head at his brother's glib text. P.O.T.U.S. was the acronym for President of the United States. Only crazy Thornton would think of something that appropriate. "Let the bloody games begin," he muttered to himself as he arrogantly swaggered to the exit.

CHAPTER 3

Washington, DC, Here We Come!

As they flew over Washington, DC, Thornton Nithing regaled them with colorful descriptions of the town. "You are now flying over the town with 'the best government money can buy,' to quote Will Rogers, I believe. It was built from a malarial swamp by slave labor, and basically nothing has changed."

P.T. Pipestone spoke up. "No disrespect, Mr. Nithing. But aren't you being a little harsh? I mean, this is the USA."

Nithing smiled a smile that reminded Rey of a cobra about to strike. "Mr. Pipestone, with all due respect, sir, the great American entrepreneur you are, you will soon learn this country was built and is maintained by people such as yourself, people who respect control and disdain weakness, not the bumbling bureaucrats huddling below." P.T. began smiling again as he saw the obvious merits in that argument. Thornton Nithing continued: "The town needs strong leaders, men like you and Rey, and beautiful and brave women like your Pipestone beauties. Mutatis mutandis, we say in Latin."

"Changing those things that need to be changed," Rey commented before Nithing could interpret, "or the necessary changes must be made."

"Exactly," Nithing continued without missing a beat, but casting a wary glance at Rey, the supposed bumpkin from Pewamo, who obviously knew some Latin. "They call a group of lions a pride, a group of geese a gaggle, but do you know what they call a gathering of baboons? They call it a congress of baboons, believe it or not. How appropriate! The current Congress puts the word funk in dysfunctional. They are a bunch of blathering idiots. They put the tick, as in blood-sucking tick, in the body politic. Speaking of ticks, they are like starving ticks on the lazy carcass of a fat dog. All they want is money and perks. We," and here he embraced P.T. and Rey by draping his massive arms around their shoulders, "are going to change and rearrange things."

Taking a deep breath, Nithing rattled on. "And then there are all those bureaucrats. Oh, my goodness! Huge herds of bucolic bureaucrats, content to graze in fields of forms. They are constantly slowing things down just to protect their own jobs. I call them job justifiers. That is going to change, too."

"What about the incumbent, President Sedgewick Sewell? Didn't he try to change things?" Rey asked sounding innocent enough, at least to his own ears.

Nithing's return glance was a glare of defiance. "You mean old Simpering Sedgewick Sewell? Him, are you serious? He didn't just crater, he Jimmy Cartered. He was so beaten, bloodied, and bruised that we'll be carrying him out in a wheelbarrow. He tried logic. He tried appealing to the 'better angels of their nature,' to quote Lincoln, of all people. With this Congress, you might as well try to bring down and beat up a cape buffalo with a baseball bat. Put a little more delicately, you need to grab them in the wallet and squeeze so hard their brains fly out like popping a zit. With the new spending 'guidelines' we'll put in place and our slick legal minds, we can fund or not fund campaigns depending on how loyal they are in toeing the party line. We'll have them in such a tight vise-like squeeze they will be singing first soprano in our little boy's congressional choir."

"Is that legal?" Rey asked again, in as innocent a voice as he could fake, startling himself with his own newfound acting ability.

P.T. jumped in this time. "Come on, Rey. Get real. Get out of the sandbox and into the real world. Mr. Nithing would do nothing illegal. You don't get planes and cars like this and ten grand suits like his by getting caught doing illegal things."

Rey failed to see the complete logic in P.T.'s argument, but he could see that he, Rey, was agitating Thornton. That was good enough for him. "Well, I still believe in the Constitution. I read an article by J. Wrenfield Boguiden, and he made some good points. The Constitution . . . "

Before he could finish his point, Nithing was within an inch of his face. The blue veins in his bulbous nose looked like the little squiggly highways on a roadmap. His eyes had a savage, demented look. "Get this straight, Rey. It doesn't matter what he or you believe. The only good point he had is on his head. He's a loser. Have you seen him? He looks horrible. He is a pencil-neck geek loser, and he will soon know it."

"How do you know he's a loser?" Rey shot back.

"I can tell you every winner in every county, in every state, and in every race in the upcoming elections right now." The sudden look of dismay on Thornton's face told Rey he slipped in anger and revealed more than he wanted to.

"It's all rigged?" Rey choked, not feigning any innocence this time. "What about the will of the people?"

"People, sheeple. How quaint. I told you before that too much money and power is at stake to leave it to the people—who are more concerned about their football games, soap operas, dancing, and singing contests. And, by the way, almost all of those are fixed, too. The college and professional football and basketball games, even the imbecilic reality shows. Anything that can be wagered on is fixed. Everything is intricately scripted to provide maximum excitement and high drama. It's all a big business, Rey. Even high school sports will be fixed if the money is right. Billions of dollars are wagered. We control all of it, for the good of the country and a nice percentage to us, of course. Nothing is left to chance. What's good for America is controlled order, not chaos."

Rey glanced at P.T., who looked as though he were going to have a stroke. Rey hoped P.T. finally saw through Nithing's scam.

"Why was I never told all of this?" P.T. thundered, but then broke into a hideous, greedy smile. "What a great idea! All this time I have been worried, and, instead, you real pros got it under control! I always say, 'Eliminate risk and maintain control.' Now I learn it's been going on my whole life right under my nose, and I never saw it. This is sheer genius, Thornton, sheer genius."

Rey was now doubly stunned. "Doesn't any of this bother either of you two?" He was vaguely aware the Pipestone ladies and his boys were coming back to the main cabin after snacking on the amazing spread of expensive goodies in the front area of the huge plane, so he lowered his voice.

P.T. was ecstatic. "Rey, just think of all the money this means we can make. Think of all the power. I can dominate my entire market and win all my bets. Right, Thornton?"

"If Rey plays along, the sky is the limit, Mr. Pipestone, absolutely the limit," Thornton snarled, fixing Rey with a threatening look. "Your whole family can prosper."

"Oh, he'll play along, if he wants to keep a happy family," P.T. chortled as he grabbed a startled Prissy and gave her a bear hug and a loud, smacking kiss on the cheek. Rey realized he had never seen P.T. do that in twenty years. Prissy was so shocked she almost fainted. "My little Prissy Poo is going to be First Lady. And I will be first father-in-law. Isn't that right, son?" P.T. jeered at Rey.

"I see you are another connoisseur of leverage, Mr. Pipestone," Nithing said with an ingratiating and grateful smile, not giving Rey a chance to respond. "And a man who appreciates how things ought to be done."

"Call me P.T., friend, and let's make sure you get to know my Paula while we are in DC. I think you will find her not only alluring but a stimulating intellect as well, with a sharp business mind. She has a degree from Harvard Law and an MBA from the University of Chicago. She is certainly not a bird-brain," he added unable to pass up an obvious swipe at Rey.

As they wandered off chatting, taking their seats for landing, Rey could see an unholy alliance being formed. Paula immediately came over to him and somehow managed to snarl while flashing a breathtaking smile. "If you hadn't been so eager to bed my hot-to-trot little sister, it could have been you with me, loser." With that said, she swayed her staggeringly gorgeous rear up the aisle and daintily plunked down next to Thornton, revealing an expanse of gorgeously tanned thigh. She immediately put her head on his shoulder and gazed longingly into his eyes.

As the plane landed, Rey thought he was well over his "loser" quota for the day. He was supposed to be the winner, but everyone kept calling him loser. It only got worse once the plane had landed.

Thornton came over to him, using a massive finger to point in his face, accompanied with the usual menacing scowl. "Rey, another not-so-gentle word of warning: The traits I find admirable and so charming in myself, like cunning, stealth, stinging intellect and versatility with the truth, well, I loathe it when I see it in losers like you. Stay transparent and stop trying to act so innocent, you moron. You tricked me into saying more in front of P.T. than I planned, but it ended up beautifully. That older daughter of his is amazing," he added, smirking, "as I know you know all too well. And, Rey, always remember the key word, leverage, you loser. Leverage!"

As they left the plane and headed for a luxurious hotel, a huge crowd of people thronged the road leading from the airport, craning their necks and holding up their children to see Rey and his family. When they saw them, they smiled and cheered. He saw countless "Newly is Good for America" signs and others that called him "a man of the people."

Rey was shocked and at the same time awed by the crush of people wanting to greet him and his family. Since it was beginning to appear unavoidable, maybe fame and fortune wouldn't be so bad after all, he tried to tell himself. But the massive cloud of doubt failed to go away. He was afraid for his family, especially the boys.

Ignoring the crowds who waved signs he and his team had carefully supplied, Thornton Nithing filled Rey's family in on their busy agenda. "Tomorrow we are going to go shopping for expensive gowns and doodads for the ladies, tuxes for the guys. We will purchase dazzling new stuff to wow the Washington elite." Prissy visibly glowed at this news, excited to have the chance to add to her already well-stocked wardrobe. "We will be attending the military-industrial complex convention first thing tomorrow night and then the religious-industrial complex gala the next night. In between, we will be keeping Rey at the teleprompter doing campaign ads, after he gets some acting lessons and perhaps a little attitude adjustment." He added emphasis to this last comment with a furtive glare at Rey and then a reassuring glance at Rey's assembled family. "We will definitely want Morton and Milton in an ad talking about their Eagle Scout, war-hero dad. My plan is to get all of you involved, as this is a great American family story. I guarantee you will all be easily recognized household names soon."

"You mean like Wombat Toilet Cleaner and Left Guard?" Morty asked innocently in his tiny little boy voice, trying to name the only household items he could think of.

"Sort of," Nithing smiled beatifically at the small boy, "but I meant your names."

"Ha, Morton Toilet Bowl Cleaner!" Milton shouted. Soon the boys were tussling, and Rey had to gently break them up.

"Come on, guys! You've got to start acting like first kids," he said hugging both boys, as they left the car, becoming aware of a photographer already snapping pictures of the action. So much for privacy. We're all in the public eye now, he thought glumly.

"This is Grover 'Snapper' Melville," Nithing said while nudging Prissy and the boys forward to stand beside Rey for a family photo. "He is the son of one of our top NAP, I mean top backers, and a great photographer and trusted assistant as well. Prissy, he is going to work with you first on makeup and color coaching, to enhance your natural beauty." Prissy beamed back at him, eating up the flattery, no matter how insincere it sounded to Rey.

Snapper Melville was about as nondescript a person as could be. He was medium height and medium weight, with mousy brown hair clipped close to his head. The only thing that stood out on Snapper were his big, sad-looking brown eyes. "My dad got all the looks in the family," he jested.

Suddenly, Rey realized his dad must be the one and only dynamic Groover Melville, handsome star of business and media. Seeing the familiar look of startled recognition, Snapper continued. "Yeah, I get the same reaction all the time. Compared to Dad, my lack of looks helps me be unobtrusive, kind of like a chameleon, so just forget I am around, and we'll get lots of spontaneous shots. We want to chronicle this story of a beautiful all-American first family coming to their new home."

"And this beautiful lady is Zara Tallaree," Nithing said, gesturing as a glorious young lady emerged out of the shadows. She was breathtaking, and everyone involuntarily stopped and stared. She had soft, golden skin and luxurious, blond hair. Every man present sucked in his breath in an audible gasp when he saw her; every woman squinted and backed up in an unconscious competitive reaction. As nondescript as Snapper Melville was, she was a unique beauty. She had a slightly Asian look to her eyes, but the irises appeared to be almost purple. On any other face, her nose would have looked too big, but on her it was exquisite. Rey found himself instantly attracted without wanting to be. While Paula was pure kinetic sex appeal and Prissy motherly at best, Zara had a brilliant but gentle smile and grace that set you at ease while instantly turning you on unless you were dead. Rey noticed there even was a delectable fragrance wafting from her body that set his nerve endings tingling.

"She will be your acting coach, Rey. So, stop gaping and start learning," Nithing demanded.

This time Rey did feel like a loser, especially when he caught Priscilla looking at him with a hurt expression. Paula just had a knowing smirk, seeing a worthy opponent.

Pleased with his successful and painful jab, Nithing continued: "You may recognize Zara from various award-winning movies and Broadway plays, maybe from some of her earlier modeling. But now she is the full-time Newly First Family acting coach."

Zara Tallaree seemed to glide like a lithe and graceful lioness as she strode confidently front and center and started to speak in a forceful, but mellow voice that was more like a purr. "From now on, everything must be carefully scripted and choreographed. While Snapper and I are to be trusted, any other people must be carefully screened and cleared only by Mr. Nithing. The mainstream media belongs to us, but they still like to sneak around trying to get any juicy tidbit or salacious story. We can't afford anything but the carefully manufactured truth to get out. From now on you are a loving, caring, sweet family, supporting each other and yet flourishing in separate careers. We have a profile for each of you. Study it and know it upside down and backwards. Only Morty and Milty can be themselves, as they are fine young men. The rest of you will need some work." She said the last of this laughingly, which could have been construed as negative if spoken by anyone else, but she said it in such a tactful and sensitive tone that everyone, even the egotistical P.T. and Paula, shrugged shoulders and agreed.

Only Theta Pipestone appeared ill at ease with this observation. She had remained silent all through the trip up until now. When she spoke, it was in a little, bird-like voice that startled everyone with its clarity. She had always reminded Rey of a little sparrow, with bird-like arms and legs, always residing in the shadow of P.T. She was the only Pipestone, other than Prissy, who had ever treated Rey politely, and even seemed to like him. He knew she mostly remained quiet because of P.T.'s utter control and hectoring on everything she did or didn't do. Sadly, quite a bit of booze also probably added to the dazed look she often displayed.

Now, however, she startled everyone by speaking up. "Young lady, I am sure you are a professional and a good judge of people," she said in her thin and wavering, but crystal-clear voice. "But Rey is also a fine young man. I have known him since he was nine years old, and he is as honest, humble, kind, and gentle a lad as I have ever known."

Suddenly, Theta seemed to realize she was speaking out. She quickly stepped back and seemed to fold like a flower in the night chill. P.T. started to stalk toward her, but Zara deftly stepped in front of him, discreetly cutting him off before he could reach his wife. Rey thought he was the only one to see that smooth maneuver by Zara. He found it intriguing.

Zara went over to Theta and gently lifted her chin to gaze into her eyes. "I am so glad you said that, Mrs. Pipestone. I can see that you and Rey both are great just the way you are." She ended this comment with a small, quick smile to Rey that sent shivers up and down his spine and drew a frown from Prissy.

Nithing would have nothing to do with this touching scene. He rudely stepped forward, trying to nudge Zara aside, but suddenly he now somehow found himself tripping and only at the last minute avoiding an embarrassing fall by grabbing hold of P.T. They both staggered, awkwardly hugging each other, not quite falling. Only Rey had seen the quickly darting foot of Zara knocking the brute Nithing off balance. Zara saw Rey's knowing look and smiled quickly again. The deeply embarrassed and normally agile Nithing looked around but couldn't figure out what he had so clumsily tripped over.

"Enough of this," he coughed, trying to regain control of his composure and the group. "Everybody will work. We will play some, but very carefully. Control is the word. If we plan and execute this right, unbelievable money, fame, and power will be ours."

Nithing started handing out extensive individualized schedules on electronic note pads. "These are secure devices. Use only them and nothing else for your email and other communications. Always assume your communications are being monitored," he warned. Only Rey seemed to notice he didn't mention monitored by whom. He was sure Nithing and his crew would be listening and watching their every move and word. "Now everybody to your rooms and get a good night's sleep. We start early tomorrow morning shooting ads and taking lessons. Rey, you will also be studying policy reports, so, if the teleprompter goes down or a rogue reporter somehow gets to ask you a difficult question, you will be ready with the correct, approved response."

As Rey and his immediate family started toward their room, he noticed Prissy staring strangely at him. "I wonder why my mom said such a nice thing just about you?"

"Maybe she meant it," Rey said gently without any reproach.

"But she never, or at least rarely, speaks out when P.T. is around. And she only mentioned you," she said this last with a wistful voice. Rey reached out and softly touched her shoulder. "I am sure she meant you, too, Prissy. I have just been hogging the spotlight. I'll try to make sure you and the boys enjoy all this and get some well-deserved attention, too."

She looked with a surprised expression at his hand still touching her shoulder and smiled. "Rey," she said in a gentle voice he hadn't heard in years, "they shoot presidents, don't they? And I know you," she continued, speaking a little more rapidly and forcibly. "You are always sticking up for people and doing the right thing. This is going to get us all into big trouble. I just know it," she said with tears forming in her eyes.

He tried to comfort her, but the fleeting moment of long-forgotten tenderness was gone. For just a minute, he had seen the hidden Prissy, the hurt little girl who just wanted to be loved and appreciated. He realized this was the Prissy who had attracted him when he was alone and hurting and feeling unappreciated himself. He vowed in his heart to somehow protect her and the boys. He needed to get his own leverage, he realized. He was intrigued by Zara's actions that he had surreptitiously observed. She was much more than a beautiful young lady. Maybe she could help him and his family. Somebody sure needed to.

The next day was filled with grueling practice in front of a teleprompter, learning to read even the most stilted verbiage with feeling and proper pacing. Rey also was grilled by several of Nithing's assistants on policy statements. Even to his own surprise, Rey was a quick study. He always was a big reader about birds, science, geography, and the like and had a great ability to retain facts, especially in subjects he found interesting. He realized he hadn't lost much from school, where he was known for his quick mind and a good memory. Even Thornton Nithing seemed impressed, despite himself.

A few things did disturb Rey. His advisors noticed his slight limp and scarred arm and asked him to exaggerate both a bit in the media pieces. They insisted he mention his Purple Heart. When he hesitated, Nithing just lip-synched "leverage," glancing over at his family, and Rey grudgingly complied.

Watching the outtakes, he had to admit he was a pretty convincing actor for an amateur. He thought they overplayed the decorated, injured war hero too much, but since his memory of the day was a little sketchy, he couldn't argue too much when they made him out like the next coming of Audie Murphy, the great World War II hero. He enjoyed working with the twins, and he noticed a lot of warm and encouraging smiles from Zara at the natural interplay between the three of them. She also was the only one of the crew who didn't find his being an Eagle Scout somehow ludicrous. This made him a little mad at the rest of the crew, who didn't realize how much work and dedication went into becoming an Eagle Scout, and enabled him to add a bit of fire to some of the ads they shot. Zara smiled and was very complimentary: "You are a natural at this. Usually we must do a lot of takes to get one good one. You are giving us a ton of good stuff to work with," she added with a sensuous wink that made his heart pound despite his best efforts to control himself.

Rey was embarrassed to admit he found her praise exhilarating, intoxicating even. She was not so positive about her sessions with Prissy. Zara asked him point blank about her and her "invisible vultures" that seemed to be circling around in dark clouds over her head. It was an unusual description, but he could see how it fit her gloomy demeanor. Zara went on to describe Prissy as being like a wet blanket in the linen closet of life.

Rey was surprised to find himself becoming a little defensive: "She comes from a hostile home environment. Growing up, nothing was ever good enough for old P.T. When I first met her, she was five and I was nine. I was already mesmerized by her sister, who was my age. Prissy was a sweet child, quite intelligent, with a ready smile. But already I could tell she was being beaten down by the people around her." He saw Zara was listening intently, with understanding in her eyes, so he continued. "I hate to be so negative, but P.T. was constantly hammering her and her siblings. He can be a very discouraging man. He was and is a control freak and the one to always be the center of attention. To this day, almost nothing she ever does is good enough for him. She soon became like a mouse in a house full of hawks. Everybody criticized everybody else, and she was made to do the same, whether she wanted to or not. P.T. said he was brought up like that and that it worked out great for him."

He could tell Zara was genuinely concerned. "Horrible. It's horrible to do that to a child or anyone else. Maybe I am being too hard on her. But you mentioned she had siblings, plural?"

"There is a brother, J.P. His full name is Joshua Preston Pipestone. P.T. also constantly beat him up psychologically, maybe even worse than his sisters. He finally went into a deep depression, supposedly had some drug problems, and was sent to Pewamo State Home. Then he disappeared. Nobody talks about him. I know Theta feels horrible about it, misses him immensely, and attempts to contact him. The funny thing is, you talk to P.T., and he is utterly convinced he is the world's best father. His kids failed him; he didn't fail them. And, of course, his shining proof is Paula and his own millions of dollars. As he says all the time, 'Cream rises to the top.'"

"So does scum," Zara shot back in a scathing voice, surprising Rey, her purple eyes blazing like sparkling lights in a sapphire. "But Paula survived somehow."

"Yes, she did," Rey agreed. "She is a most resilient if

sometimes extremely unpleasant person."

"She is also one impressive lady," Zara opined. "However, my reading is she is extremely unhappy and unfulfilled, still trying to please Daddy, but wanting to get it on with you."

Rey choked on the coffee he was drinking, spitting it out all over the carpet. "You don't mince any words, do you?"

"I call them as I see them. So, I will be even more direct. How did you end up with the mouse instead of the hawk?"

"I guess I was suffering from post-traumatic stress disorder. I was feeling depressed after nearly losing an arm and a leg. Having shrapnel in my head and multiple concussions probably didn't help. I felt I had failed my team who all died in the same minefield that nearly got me. Then I unexpectedly lost my mom to a nervous breakdown and subsequent heart attack. Paula was off doing her sorority thing and dating Ivy Leaguers, too busy for me, and Prissy stayed by my side. I guess I always saw the hidden, hurting little girl in her. There is a very nice lady hiding in there. However, since you are so perceptive, you have probably noticed our relationship has been on the rocks. No matter what I do, it never matches up to P.T. or the Pipestone standard, and I am just not an Ivy League type of guy. Prissy always nitpicks anything I do, but I think it's because it's all she knows how to do. On top of everything else, old P.T. detested me from the beginning, and she still wants desperately to please her father, too, as impossible as it may be, so the attitude rubs off."

"And old P.T. set out to destroy you," Zara added emphatically. He could only stare at Zara with a deep look of confusion. "You won the hearts of all the Pipestone ladies, even Theta, and threatened the head stag of the herd. He has always been and always will be an alpha dog, a top predator. You were dead meat from the beginning, bubba."

"You are awfully perceptive for an acting coach!" Rey said, shaking his head.

"Don't forget humble and beautiful, too," she said. "Now, get serious! Here comes Thornton, another alpha dog wannabe. If we're not sweating, we're not working, in his mind."

Nithing came strutting up, dressed to the nines, moving with the agility Rey always found surprising in such a massive bulk. He called everybody together. "Wrap it up team and let's be ready to go in a little over two hours." As he did a quick pirouette worthy of a ballet master, addressing Rey, he continued: "Look at me and weep, you miserable hunk of man-flesh. This is the dress code for tonight. I know you ladies won't have to work to be beautiful!"

He did look rather dashing in the tuxedo he was wearing. Rey could see with a little work, maybe a lot of work, old Thornton could be a stud, but he shouldn't be flaunting it.

"We will be going to New Xanadu to meet the leaders of the military-industrial complex. These are the huge campaign donors, the movers and shakers, so everybody must keep a close watch over what is said. Loose lips sink ships, to use a nautical expression," he said as he scooted everybody off to get ready, dismissing the staff.

Motioning Rey aside, Thornton took him into another room for what he said would be a brief meeting. Thornton began: "This is Bylow Bellwater, our 'image' man. He may not look like it, but he is a genius in how to present people just right to the public and make them fall in love."

Bellwater didn't look the part. He was a skinny, little, storklike man with a big beak of a nose and geeky, black glasses with Coke-bottle lenses. His bulging eyes swam behind them in watery pools. Sensing Rey's disconcerted thoughts, Bellwater just grinned at him and said, "It's not me people have to look at, thank goodness. We've got to spruce you up big time, boy," he said, clapping Rey on the shoulder. He looked down at Reynard over his thick glasses. "We've got to conjure you up an image. A dashing and debonair leader-of-the-people mystique."

Bellwater warmed to the task. Stalking stiffly up and down the room while studying Rey, framing him with his hands like a picture, he hemmed and hawed, making mental calculations. He exuded a calm confidence surprising for such a weird-looking person. It was obvious he knew his stuff. "We've got to make the American people want to follow you, to think of you as a father figure. We want them to see you as a wise, trusted, and honorable leader. I read the preliminary press releases. Not bad. And I saw some of the outtakes our luscious Zara did. Those are very good. It all makes you look good, but now we are going to make you look even better. We are going to make you look great!"

He paused and looked down at a screen. "I looked at your background. Decorated war hero, Eagle Scout, business and labor leader. Not bad. We can definitely work with that." Then he sharply looked up at Rey. "What the hell is this ornithology stuff? That doesn't sound very all-American."

"It's basically the study of birds," Rey began, before being rudely cut off by Bellwater making a crude, squawking sound.

"Birds?" Bellwater exploded, screaming in a high-pitched

voice at Thornton. "You send me a backwoods birdman and want me to make him a president? At least Sedgewick Sewell was an engineer of some sort, maybe a sanitary engineer, but, at least, a frigging engineer."

Reynard felt all his pent-up anger boiling up and strode forward to confront the startled Bellwater. "I never asked to be President, pompous prick! But suddenly it looks like I am going to be," he said. Then he added in a nail-hard voice, punctuating each word with a thrusting finger just like he had observed Thornton doing: "But know this. When I am President, I will remember who helped me and who didn't."

Bellwater jumped back, and his face went paler than normal. He started trembling. Nithing of all people saved him from Rey's ire, stepping between them. "I love it, Rey. You could get used to this power, dominance, and control thing. Bellwater," he added turning and talking to the still quivering man in a withering tone, "Don't ever insult the P.O.T.U.S., or me either for that matter, ever again. Now get busy and glamorize this bird-loving Boy Scout, or start looking for a career outside government, and maybe even outside the USA, assuming you live. Rey, you can go and get ready," he added, dismissively waving his hand.

Later when Rey read the profile Bellwater worked up, he was stunned. He recognized almost none of it. "But that's not me," he protested loudly. "It's even more distorted than the usual stuff you were spouting. People who know me won't even recognize me."

"Thank goodness," Thornton Nithing responded with a smirk. "Don't worry," he then added in a placating voice. "Look, this whole thing is sort of like a reality show. You just behave yourself, you go down in history as a hero. It's all very simple, so don't blow it. One way or the other you will go down either as a winner or a loser." He then added with the menacing tone of voice he seemed to relish using, "And others will go down with you."

———

As Thornton dashed off to alert everyone else and get the necessary limos lined up, Rey got ready for his big premiere performance. Rey knew enough celebrity buzz to realize New Xanadu was Groover Melville's beyond palatial home. It was rumored to be worth well over a billion dollars, with artwork another billion at least, and set out on Star Island, a manmade and moated safe zone. It was a heavily fortified and guarded location, a secure lair for elite billionaires like Groover.

Groover Melville was both a media man and a real estate tycoon. He produced movies and invented high tech weapons systems. If you bought his spiel, all this was due to his intelligence and hard work. Those in the know claimed he hired great help, paid them the best wages, and then terrorized them, wringing everything out of them and claiming it for himself before callously discarding them. Under everyone's breath, Melville was called the "king of humiliation." Rules were for everybody else. He parked in handicapped spaces and, if his expensive sports car was towed, he just bought another one while his attorneys got the previous one out of hock.

Melville was justifiably proud of New Xanadu. Glowingly

called by fawning society reporters "a crowning monument to democracy and capitalism," the whole place was said to be bigger than ten football fields, was composed of multiple stories, and contained over a thousand rooms, with an immense flat-screen TV in every room. It even had a one hundred thousand square-foot attached garage to house his fifty million dollar-plus collection of cars. It was rumored the garage itself had a forty-foot waterfall in it that Groover had originally seen in a five-star elite hotel in Japan. He had the original designer and construction team flown to the USA to install it and was so pleased that he added an even higher one in the entryway to the main home. Also, New Xanadu was said to have more toilets than the Queen Mary cruise liner, and, if you flushed them all at once, it would use almost as much water as Niagara Falls. Melville humbly said it was a true shrine to American ingenuity, mainly his. He even had a fifty thousand square-foot treehouse built behind the main house, because he always wanted a treehouse as a child, but the grounds of the orphanage in which he was raised in a poor section of New York City didn't have any trees!

Groover Melville would boast he was born bad. He liked to say sharks are born swimming, and he was born to swim with the sharks. He had learned that most developmental psychologists say almost no one sets out to be bad, or even views him- or herself as villainous, but there is a small faction that makes being purely evil their goal and revels in the result. He felt he was one of those purely evil ones. He also had heard that there is a line between good and bad that runs right down the middle of the human heart. By personal choices, people divide themselves into the two races of mankind, the ones who are decent and the ones who are indecent—like him. Groover claimed he never had the two-part heart problem. He said he had no line in his heart. It was pure evil. He had malice for all and good will for none.

Groover also had heard that evil is not always recognizable at first glance but can grow out of a series of seemingly meaningless small acts. A small act here, a small act there, and slowly and imperceptibly the wall comes tumbling down between good and evil. Groover claimed for him it was not a slow process. He went full bore for the brass ring, ferociously knocking down any wall. He bragged that at ten he was already running numbers out of the orphanage. By twelve he was providing pleasure girls from the orphanage to visiting businessmen. By fourteen he had a rap sheet a mile long. His only saving grace was he was a charming and glib genius, and, before long, he got to be too smart to get caught. He was proud to say his slogan was, "It isn't illegal if you don't get caught."

Those in the know said Groover Melville did not possess a conscience; probably one of the few things he didn't possess! He divorced his first wife, Snapper Melville's mother, Tallulah Melville, once a glamorous actress, while she was dying from cancer. When she started to miraculously recover and wanted a measly billion-dollar divorce settlement, he purportedly ran over her five times with a million-dollar Italian custom sports car until her tongue stuck out her ear. Then he complained she had made a mess of his car and tried to sue her estate for damages. He told his legal team they were very highly paid and brilliant people so they could figure out how to get him out of the rap. Somehow they did.

All this was running through Rey's mind as he was being driven to the military-industrial complex dinner gala at New Xanadu. At least Morton and Milton were left at home under the watchful if not so sober eye of Grandma Theta and a large squadron of discreetly, but heavily armed special Secret Services people assigned to him and his family. Prissy clutched his arm nervously as they came across the heavily guarded causeway and approached the biggest house either had ever seen. Melville loved to boast it was based on the French summer palace of King Louis XIV of France, Versailles, with minarets and other garish touches added, just because he liked them. He did copy the meticulously manicured lawns and gardens but had not yet added his dubious touches to them.

Rey also was informed they would be meeting the famous Salvatore Solomon Samms, better known as "Superman" Samms, reputedly under consideration to be his running mate as Vice President, if all the money crunching worked out and he was the top bidder. He was another close ally of the Nithings and another multi-billionaire, and the only question tonight seemed to be whether two egos as large as Samms' and Melville's could both fit under one roof, even one so large as New Xanadu.

Besides these two billionaires, Rey also was going to meet Senator Hiram Festerwart, the Senate Majority Leader and key defense supporter, as well as Admiral Nathaniel Futtock, the Chairman of the Joint Chiefs of Staff, along with a host of lesser notables. "All the people who want to be players in the new regime will be there," Thornton assured him. "They will pour tons of money into getting you elected and then, voila, we will provide them with plum contracts. It's the way things are done around here." He shot a menacing look at Rey and continued, "So don't rock the boat or you won't stay afloat!" Rey was starting to realize that Thornton perversely enjoyed making such threats, whether Rey looked rattled or not.

"Now is your time to shine, big shot," Nithing grumbled at him under his breath as they entered the dazzlingly decorated gates into a manicured courtyard with backlit fountains and past what looked like Buckingham Palace guards. Then, in a surprisingly friendly and soft voice, Nithing told Prissy, "You look incredibly beautiful tonight, Priscilla." She beamed and blushed under such unexpected praise, and Rey had to admit she hadn't looked this good in years. He just wished he'd thought to say it first, before oily, lust-bucket Thornton Nithing did.

"Remember," continued Nithing, staring pointedly at Rey, "avoid Boguiden and his wretched wife and daughter. He is just a malleable do-gooder the DNC is throwing out there as a milksop for the public. Believe it or not, he thinks he is running in an election. What an idiot. He will try to get you in a debate—as if facts mattered. Jeesh, he is such a preppy geek."

As they entered the huge entryway of New Xanadu itself, with the sixty-foot waterfall and a diamond-encrusted chandelier larger than his whole house in Pewamo, he saw Groover Melville standing beneath a huge portrait of, whom else, but Groover Melville. Beneath it was Melville's Latin slogan "nil medium," no middle ground.

All around the room were large statues and portraits of

predatory beasts and a lot of stuffed carnivorous animals that were possibly hunting trophies. As Rey approached him, Melville broke away and stalked up to him, extending his ring-bedecked hand. He was known far and wide as a savage, smart, unscrupulous, but, above all, successful person. He was the consummate conman and manipulator.

His hair was shiny and black, long on top, with a tendency to flop into his eyes, as if he couldn't afford or find time for a decent haircut. With wide shoulders and narrow hips, and with a habit of obsessive-compulsive exercise, he still had the body of the world-class athlete he once was. But he had a steely-eyed, dagger-like stare people often commented on behind his back. Indeed, the big thing people noticed besides his booming bass voice and movie star bad-boy looks were his eyes. They were deep set and startlingly blue. Very cold, opaque, and lifeless, like a shark Rey had seen at the aquarium, or, as he suddenly realized, like the eyes of all the stuffed dead beasts surrounding him.

Melville crushed Rey's hand in an iron grip. Rey was aware of this attempt at intimidation and tried not to wince. Except for those sinister eyes, everything about Melville was straight out of prep school: long hair, deck shoes without socks, sharply pressed pants you could cut a finger on. Everyone else was in a tuxedo, but Groover Melville looked like he was ready for a day on one of his huge yachts. It was his house, he liked to say, and he set the dress code for himself.

"Mr. Newly, so pleased to finally meet you. I will be your biggest supporter," Melville announced in a surprisingly pleasant voice with a distinct New York accent. "I always say, 'If it is going to be, it is up to me.' I will make things happen for you."

"There is no 'I' in team, Melville," said a soft and very oily voice from somewhere behind Rey.

"But there is an 'I' in win, Sally, not that you would know," Melville retorted, his voice suddenly bristling with aggression as he gnashed his teeth and frowned over Rey's shoulder at the person behind him.

Rey turned just in time to see Salvatore Solomon "Superman" Samms sauntering from the doorway. He was flamboyantly dressed in head-to-toe white fur, probably a polar bear, knowing his garish preferences in garb. He was a long, lanky man with a ponytail and a huge gold earring dangling from his right ear. He was quite handsome when he smiled, but, after a while, more perceptive people were alarmed by his quick, furtive eyes. They darted everywhere and missed little. Some people confused him for an aging hippy, but those people didn't last long around him. One eventually realized his rhythm of speech and bearing was a little too jumpy, out of sync with his surroundings, like a ferret on steroids, and he was too quick to argue to the death over a dime.

Samms always had to be right. While Groover Melville was smooth, Samms was silvery quick. Under the fur coat he also had on the most dazzling white tux Rey had ever seen, the buttons were diamonds, and he sported a ton of expensive-looking jewelry on all his fingers and both wrists.

"The name is Superman Samms, not Sally, as I am sure you of all people are aware, Melville, and what you know about winning I could put in my hat," Superman sneered.

"Well, since your hat has to be the size of Texas to fit that swelled head and ego of yours, maybe it's not such an insult.

And while I'm at it, you garishly jeweled dweeb, I already have a glittering globe over my dance floor, so I don't need another glistening blob, though I would be only too happy to hang you up there and watch you spin," retorted Melville.

"You will just have to bask in my reflected glory right here before you. And you are a big basker, I'm told," Samms shot back, perhaps not at his eloquent best.

Thornton Nithing lithely jumped between the two before the repartee could get too heated. He was much bigger than either of them and was obviously eager to avoid a scene. "Gentlemen, gentlemen, gentlemen! I refuse to let us start out badly on what should be a night of celebration." They were still bristling and fuming at each other when he rolled out the big gun. "Achor will be very put out if he finds his two key players are jousting in front of his handpicked candidate. May I present to you Mr. Reynard Newly and his lovely wife, Priscilla." Rey was quick to note that, at the mention of this Achor Nithing fellow, suddenly both Melville and Samms backed down and clammed up.

Nithing quickly escorted everyone to tables, with Samms and Melville purposely on different sides of Rey. Prissy was sitting next to her dad and sister and some Hollywood types at another nearby table. Rey recognized some of the stars as people who advertised as well-paid spokespeople for big weapons manufacturers when they weren't doing anti-gun public announcements.

Thornton spent his time scooting between each table, orchestrating the conversation. Soon he also escorted Senator Festerwart and Admiral Futtock over to meet Rey, each accompanied by extremely well-endowed women who Rey first thought were their daughters but then found out were trophy wives. He already knew from his briefing that once he was elected, these two would be key men he would need to work with to get things done.

The enthusiastic Thornton was reveling in his role as host, and Rey was once again impressed with how fast and fluidly his moods and appearances could change to meet the situation. He was like mercury, shiny and attractive on the surface, but slippery and leaving a toxic mess behind.

Seeing Rey eyeing him closely, Thornton misread his scrutinizing look as worry. "Don't be nervous, Rey. Just relax, but whatever you do, don't be yourself. Be the new Rey Maxwell Newly we are grooming you to be. Everyone else comes here and lets their hair down, if they have any, ha, and takes their masks off, so to speak. Just remember your briefing and don't blow it."

Rey had been worried that the people at the table might quiz him on policy matters or foreign affairs, but both Samms and Melville stuck to their favorite topics, themselves, bragging about new acquisitions and victories, trying to one-up each other. Rey tried to draw out the Senator and the Admiral, but both men were obviously stunned and awed to be in the presence of the two richest men in the world, more so than the next President, and were content to pour drinks and bask in the boasting of the two, while not so discreetly ogling each other's wife, all the while ignoring Rey. This was obviously the VIP table, as Nithing kept bringing people over and introducing them to Rey. Every military weapons industry was represented, and the women wore so much jewelry that Rey assumed the crown jewels of the United Kingdom has been rented for the night.

Even J. Wrenfield Boguiden with his lovely wife, Halita, made their way to the table to meet Rey, but it was made painfully obvious they were not wanted there. Melville and Samms both fixed Boguiden with frosty, arrogant looks and openly sneered at the man. Boguiden certainly had the stuffy prep school look about him. One nasty reporter said he looked like he had never farted. Others complained that he had not one single redeeming fault. Still others said he was too good to be true and poor press to boot.

To Rey, Boguiden seemed another honest, humble, gentle, and kind man, although admittedly somewhat preppy and stiff, with a lost, solemn look in his eyes and a sad face that said he had learned the hard way that the world doesn't care much for honest, humble, gentle, and kind men. Halita, his wife, once a stunning beauty, was still quite attractive in a demure and matronly way, but it was their daughter, Jacqueline, that caught everyone's eye.

Jacqueline's hair was cut in a severe buzz cut, with a few blazing red strands left to curl around her head like flames. She had a body that was tensed like a coiled spring. Rey heard later that there was a well-founded rumor that several martial arts were reputedly named for her. In fact, she was a black belt in nearly everything that offered black belts. She also was active military, serving as a Special Forces personal combat instructor.

Jacqueline carried herself with supreme confidence. Seeing how they were treating her parents, she just sneered back at Melville and Samms, unfortunately including Rey in her flinty look. To Rey's shock, the two billionaire bullies cringed.

"Three dinky men, little dorks with big mouths," she snarled haughtily at them under her breath, so that thankfully only Rey and the other two startled targets heard her. Then, not concealing her contempt, Jacqueline took the elbows of both her parents and briskly escorted them away from the cold reception. Rey was dazzled. He couldn't even say if she was attractive or not. It would be like saying a deadly tigress about to eat you alive was attractive.

There was one seat that was left vacant for half the night, until the room went completely silent. Sweeping in like a sleek fighter jet came a dashing man with carefully crafted hair and a long aquiline nose. He was closely accompanied by two of the most stunning and efficient-looking women Rey had ever seen, except for the just-met Jacqueline Boguiden. It was obvious they were bodyguards, scanning right and left and standing behind him. They had earbuds, and Rey could see the bulges of heavy caliber handguns in their tight uniforms. Thornton promptly scurried over and deferentially pulled the seat out for the man. "Rey, this is my older brother, Achor Nithing, CEO of Nithing Entertainment Enterprises. I am sure you have also seen him as the host on his award-winning mainstream media news show called 'Nithing Notices.'"

Rey felt like a butterfly pinned to a sheet of paper, about to be chloroformed, as Achor Nithing assessed him in mocking silence with his unflinching gaze from yellow-flecked, wolf-like eyes. Finally, the older Nithing broke the silence, speaking in a smooth, well-enunciated baritone. "You will do. Thornton tells me you are a quick study and a man who fully understands the concept of leverage."

Rey nodded and was surprised that he had to struggle

to find his voice, the man's up-close presence was so imposing. "It has been clearly explained to me, Mr. Nithing, and your brother is a very apt teacher. I will not let you or my family down."

"A very good idea, Mr. Newly. A very good idea," Achor Nithing repeated, in a deep, chilling voice that resonated from his barrel chest. He then went completely still, ignored Rey, and thoroughly scanned the hall with disconcerting eyes, as though he were checking names off a mental list. He gave a quick nod to his brother, and then spoke seemingly to just himself. "Everyone we need is here. Now it begins."

The rest of the evening was anticlimactic. The food was superb, as one would expect from the best American chefs who knew their reputations were at stake and their budgets unlimited. The wine was exceptional, as would be expected from Melville's self-ordained largest wine cellar in the world. Except for some now more-genial jousting between the two billionaires comparing their respective palatial homes and the sizes of their portraits, the evening went well. Only once did tempers start to flare, when Achor Nithing addressed Samms and berated him for his tacky dress. When the ponytailed Samms tried to redirect the comment by pointing to Melville's lack of formal dress, Achor Nithing quickly quelled the debate: "You are to be Mr. Newly's Vice President, not his pimp, Samms. Mr. Melville will be Secretary of State, and I am sure he will be properly attired when addressing foreign heads of state."

Both men bristled momentarily, and then quickly wilted as Achor fixed his ferocious gaze on them. It was obvious to Rey that here was the real power behind the throne. He would soon come to find out Nithing was the real thing, evil incarnate, as cold and unemotional a human being as he would ever meet. He also noticed the older Nithing assessing Paula and even Priscilla, then resting his eyes briefly on P.T., before coming back to rest on Rey.

"Attractive family, Newly," Achor said. "I hope you are all ready for the glare of the spotlights. Thornton assures me you will be at your best." He fixed his laser stare on Rey again and pontificated: "Our country is at a pivotal time of testing. We have gone from uncontested world power status to near collapse in just seventy short years. We have clumsily accomplished in such a short time what it took Rome seven hundred years to do. In fewer than three generations we have nearly squandered a unique opportunity. Complete world domination, Mr. Newly, on a scale never seen before. We can still grasp it, if we have the will. Do you have the will, Mr. Newly?"

Rey answered back faster than he thought possible. "Since my family's life and our nation's survival depends on it, sir, I will not, I cannot fail."

The elder Nithing continued staring intently at Rey with a penetrating gaze, seeming to read his mind, and then nodded. Shortly thereafter the dinner came to an end. On the way home, Thornton was like a puppy, all giddy and gushing. "You impressed him, Rey. He saw your steel, man. The Eagle Scout war hero came through! I knew it all along. You're the man, Rey! You're the man!"

Later in the privacy of their own room, Prissy looked over at Rey carefully with deep concern in her eyes. She commented to him that Paula was nowhere to be found. "I think Paula found a more interesting conquest than the future president,"

Prissy muttered, more to herself than to Rey. "That Achor Nithing sends chills up and down my spine. He is so cold, malignant, and calculating, not at all like his nice brother, Thornton. I guess Achor is probably a good match for my super-bitch sister."

Rey was stunned by her comment, never having heard Prissy utter a cuss word in over twenty years together, let alone refer to her sister that way or to the obnoxious and vile Thornton as nice. Most of all, though, he was stunned by Paula hooking up with the Achor Nithing. "A little miffed there, baby sister?" he gently chided her. But she only continued shaking her head, her concern showing even more in her face.

"We are all in way over our heads," she said sadly. "P.T. thinks his gravy train finally arrived, and Paula thinks she met her perfect match. At first I liked the new clothes and all the attention. Now I just want to go home to Pewamo with my boys. All three of them," she added, with a soft smile and a brief gentle touch, totally taking Rey by surprise.

Later, when Priscilla had dropped off to sleep, Rey found himself unable to do the same. When he did briefly drift off into fretful sleep, he dreamt gigantic shadows were lurking all around, threatening to jump out and snatch him and his family. It startled him awake. He knew it was just his imagination and that he was probably being paranoid, but he also realized, if he slipped up, those threatening shadows would become real. He suddenly realized he wasn't being paranoid if everyone was out to get him should he fail. He shuddered, almost waking up Prissy, then took a deep breath and settled himself down. He could not, no, would not, let his family down.

The next night was the big annual religious-industrial complex gala and dinner. Rey had never seen so many expensive suits on smug and slick-looking people in one place, even making the gaudy military-industrial complex crowd look a little shabby, if that were possible. He had hoped the attendees would look like Billy Graham, sort of like Old Testament prophets. Instead they looked just like the people from any big elite suburban country club, only way richer and not as physically fit. He considered himself somewhat of a believer, but he found the negative whining about the moral collapse of the nation quite aggravating. They appeared to be more concerned about the degrading music, movies, and morals of the current generation than they were with the homeless and the hungry the crumbling economy was churning out in ever greater numbers. They also kept complaining about the new, fast-growing "dangerous" church. It seemed the big institutions and established churches and national congregations were losing people and influence at a rapid rate to the new living gospel "dangerous" churches springing up all over the place. It seemed the new churches didn't want much to do with rituals and rules, only a relationship with a revolutionary Jesus.

The living gospel churches played loud raucous music and even showed movies to make a point. They went into bars and invited disreputable characters to their services. In short, they were giving the established church a bad name. Many were complaining that some guy they referred to as Reverend Louie Pastore of the Church of the Lost Children was even saying church membership didn't matter, wasn't in the Bible, and the key was loving the poor and down-and-outers. As unchristian as it sounded, they would save people and baptize them the very same day with no membership classes or discussion of by-laws.

It all sounded kind of exciting to Rey, and the Pastore name sounded familiar, but he was warned firmly he couldn't afford to offend any of the puritanical flock. Nithing informed him they were critical donors to the campaign.

Later in the evening, a strange thing happened. An out-of-place, slightly shabby-looking guy sidled up to Rey and whispered in his ear. At first Rey thought he was a waiter asking permission to refill his drink. Then he saw the guy was wearing an official-looking nametag with another name scratched out and one reading Reverend Louis Pastore scribbled in. Aha!

Fortunately, Thornton had his back to Rey and was enthusiastically addressing some natty-looking evangelist with a pile of fancy, puffed-up TV hair. As the newcomer talked in a low voice, Rey thought he might have met him before. Rey had to strain to hear him say: "I try not to judge these guys, the big church business boys, leaving that job in the caring and capable hands of the righteous judge of the whole earth. But I do admit I see them as pew-sitting, prune-faced, pucker butts, whose frown would make a great advertisement for atheism! I do fear for many of them on Judgment Day when they tell all they've done for the big guy in the sky and all they hear is 'I never knew you.'" Rey nearly spewed his drink over the back of Thornton Nithing as he choked back a laugh.

Rey realized they were being studiously ignored by all the

big movers and shakers, and some of them were even pointedly moving away as if they smelled a rat, so he hazarded a closer gaze at the man and asked, "Do I know you?"

"I'm known to my flock as Reverend Louie. Many years ago, I shepherded a church in your hometown of Pewamo. We built it ourselves brick by brick, up from a little tractor barn into the biggest church in Brewer County. Then the sharks in suits in the big shiny cars from the parent denomination showed up and forcibly moved me on to a bankrupt church to bail it out."

Rey didn't remember the incident, being maybe four years old at the time. But he remembered his sweet mom, Swan, being very upset when a new, smooth-talking minister came in, replacing the founder, and destroyed the church in no time, using it as his own personal playground and piggy bank.

"Yes, Rey, I'm afraid the twin poisons of toxic legalism and greed have corrupted some of the body. I tell people greed sits on the street corner of life like a stripper and seduces us toward the dark alleyways and away from the light," Reverend Louie said. He shook his head in despair. "For the most part, we act like a mirror reflecting all the bad things back, instead of like a window on good showing the world what it should be." He glanced furtively around before saying one last thing that stuck in Rey's mind for a long time: "I believe it was G.K. Chesterton who said something like, 'Coziness between church and state may be good for the state, but, in the end, it is like a fat sheep sitting down to dinner between two hungry wolves and then voting on what to have for dinner.'" He smiled again sadly. "And they call us the dangerous church!

Over ninety percent of their churches are shrinking and dying, only five percent growing by transfer growth, and only our small five percent are bringing new people in—the lost and broken people. Just wanted you to know we will be praying for you and your family." With that, he swiftly moved off into the crowd just before some rough-looking men appeared, eyes darting everywhere.

"Was anyone bothering you, Mr. President? We heard there was an unauthorized guest here, some homeless guy. We have absolutely no clue how he penetrated our security. Thank God he didn't harm you." Rey smiled at the divine reference and assured them he was unbothered and unharmed and that the person was a registered guest and quite friendly. Much relieved, they returned to their posts.

As the evening crept along, a smarmy-sounding guest speaker was talking about a missionary trip to some communist-infested cannibal island. Another speaker excitedly talked about changing to a new and better marketing image for the mainstream churches, avoiding the scandalous overtones, and sanitizing the scriptures. He claimed there was too much emphasis on death, poverty, and the like.

Rey couldn't follow all the theological discussions and the grumbling about moral decay. He always believed the Church should serve as a moral compass to keep the world on track, but it seemed like these people had lost their bearings. It was enough to almost make him miss the sarcastic bickering from the night before between the egomaniac billionaires Melville and Samms.

When Achor Nithing finally showed up at this dinner, he quieted all the grumbling. "If you want a place in this government, gentlemen and gentle ladies, deliver the votes and the money. Let these scruffy, do-gooder dudes you call the dangerous church take care of the homeless, broken, and hungry. It will mean less money and fewer resources our government has to squander on these useless people."

To smooth any troubled consciences his brash comments may have ruffled, he added: "But, of course, we respect the freedom of religion. I am sure, with your financial support and wise insights, our legal and legislative team can find a way to certify, regulate, and tax these unregistered bodies, these so-called dangerous churches, while leaving you undisturbed to do your own good works. We can't have just anybody teaching religion to the American people."

The established church people were at first slightly shocked by such bluntness, but not so shocked they didn't eventually see the light and agree to get behind the Newly campaign.

The weeks that followed were a blur of coaching and video production. Rey and his family were kept secluded and had very little contact with the public or press. It was all a carefully orchestrated and calibrated effort to support the image Bellwater had conjured up. Rey knew he had to keep to the script and he did so, all the while trying to find some leverage on the Nithings, but to no avail. He desperately knew he had to find a way to extract his loved ones from this dangerous situation. Each day, it felt like they were sinking deeper, into quicksand that would soon choke them. If he thought they were in deep now, he would soon find out just how deep and dangerous it could get.

Thornton Nithing was a genius at execution and implementation. Everything went like clockwork; the primaries went smoothly, with Rey easily smashing the token opposition. The convention was merely a great coronation, with Samms a popular choice as Vice President. As the Presidential campaign began, the polls already showed Rey with a commanding lead over the woefully inept and stiff Boguiden. Boguiden and the reluctant DNC kept calling for debates, but only the DNC candidate seemed to have his heart in it. The DNC itself knew it was their turn to lose and be the loyal opposition for four or eight years. They had already incurred the scorching wrath of Achor Nithing for messing up his first candidate and were still licking some severe wounds. Now they had to settle down, play along, and accept their lot. As Thornton so indelicately pointed out, "Everybody gets a turn at the trough."

Even P.T. had to be reined in a few times when he got a little overzealous. He just couldn't wait to deal with some longtime rivals, and several times he had to be threatened with a little leverage to calm him down. "Be patient. Win first. Then you can stomp and destroy to your heart's content," was Thornton's savage but sage advice.

Morton and Milton were without doubt the stars of the campaign. They were sturdy little campaigners and refreshingly and genuinely big fans of their dad. Snapper Melville's camera loved them, and it was obvious that Snapper, Zara, and everyone else did, too.

Prissy dutifully, if somewhat reluctantly, played the role

of the supportive spouse. Zara kept trying to draw her out and find a cause she could enthusiastically get behind. Finally, because Prissy loved to read, they decided a literature campaign would be great. It was hoped Prissy wouldn't appear too bossy or negative, while encouraging people to read to their own kids. The boys helped, as they still loved to read and joyfully made the project a smashing success by sharing their favorite books Dad and Mom read with them. This also greatly humanized them, as Thornton pointed out.

Paula seemingly disappeared into the mysterious Achor Nithing camp, and little was heard from her. When asked her whereabouts, P.T. said she was making good business contacts, so leave her alone! Rey could only imagine what type of contacts she was making, but he also knew she was a capable and smart adult who could handle herself—and probably a Nithing or two as well while she was at it.

Everything was going almost too smoothly. Two days before the election, Zara Tallaree discreetly slipped Rey a note to read right before one of the rare times he was to be alone. The note was quite mysterious. Some guy named Poger Reinbolt wanted to talk to him about a matter of deepest national security. The note cautioned, if Rey valued the lives of Zara and his family, that he should not tell the Nithings or the other staff about their meeting. Rey was to take his usual nightly walk on the enclosed hotel grounds and wait by the big walnut tree in the garden. He would find a cell phone hidden there under a bench with an untraceable and unmonitored line. Rey was unsure what to do.

With only days to go until the election, and no usable leverage on the Nithings or anyone, he felt uneasy. Then he saw letters slowly emerging from invisible ink, probably triggered by interaction with his warm fingers. It simply read: "We have your leverage."

≡ CHAPTER**4** ≡

The Eyes Are Opened!

Because the exclusive hotel grounds were not only fenced in but heavily secured, it was not unusual for Rey to take a solitary stroll in the garden after dinner to unwind. He often wrestled with the boys beneath the big walnut tree during the meager daily free time they were allowed, so he knew the location well. He wandered unobtrusively around the grounds and then sat on the bench beneath the tree. Except for occasional flies and bees buzzing through the grounds, he appeared alone. Then he heard the faint chirping sound of a phone coming from beneath the bench, and the soft whisper of a voice.

"Don't move, Mr. Newly. We are observing you from a long way off. Just scratch your right ear if you are hearing this clearly." Rey scratched his left ear, then quickly recognized his mistake and switched ears.

"My name is Poger Reinbolt. I know you are wondering if you can trust me. All I can say is I work with Zara and Snapper. You don't have any other options. It has taken us years to get key people into the Nithing's inner circle, so this is a great risk for all of us, including you and your family."

"Understood. You mentioned leverage," Newly whispered

softly, with nervous anticipation, barely moving his lips in case he was being clandestinely observed. "Let's cut to the chase. Through no fault of my own, my family and I are now at great risk. I desperately need leverage on these animals."

"Okay, and we plan to deliver that," Reinbolt responded. "But to use the leverage, you need to thoroughly understand our mutual enemy. Like the great Chinese tactician Sun Tzu said, 'You first need to understand the enemy before you can destroy him.' This is going to take some time, so be patient. First, I need to give you a detailed background on the group the Nithings lead called NAP, the National Association of Psychopaths. If that's okay, don't talk. Just scratch your head." Rey eagerly scratched, not having to worry about right or left this time.

"This will take a while. Please be patient. You need to get the full picture. I assume you know about psychopaths, people completely unencumbered by conscience or compassion. Well, both the Nithings, and, I hate to admit it, myself, are psychopaths. Brain scans would indicate our amygdala is injured or undeveloped, and it is the amygdala that controls emotional reactions and emotional learning. Possibly there has been damage to the prefrontal cortex, giving us less grey or white matter than normal, and this often results in poor impulse control. I could go on with all the neuro-psychological blather, prefrontal, temporal, limbic, blah, blah, and blah. Just know this. All of us can be stone-cold killers and cold-hearted jerks. Often we are very charming and intelligent, loaded with superficial charm, but we also can be relentless snakes. We have no remorse. Guilt trips never trip us up. Fortunately for me, my father recognized what he was and the damage he could do, so he imposed family and cultural factors to help mitigate some of the genetic mess. He brought me up with a strong moral code—Tikkun Olam—Hebrew for 'healing the broken, chaotic world.' I still struggle with some residual anti-social personality disorder, but I am not a predator of the helpless. Instead, I am a predator of predators. I hunt down psychopaths and control them. With me so far? Scratch your forehead with your left hand." Rey scratched, fighting the urge to tell the voice to hurry and get on with it.

"So what is happening is this. Any created political position, no matter how noble or benign its original intent, no matter how gentle the original occupant, will within a very few years attract psychopathic predators like sharks to blood in the water. The unreformed psychopath lusts for power, dominance, and control. Some experts say we psychopaths make up only one percent of the population, but others estimate it is now as high as four percent, with the breakdown of families and the desensitization of people through violent video games, excessive screen usage, and media. While a small percentage of the general population, we psychopaths represent about twenty percent of the overall prison population and fifty percent of the most violent incarcerated criminals. However, the smart ones catch on early and don't get caught. For example, you've met the elder Melville and Mr. Samms, both successful psychopaths. They are brilliant and caught on early. They learned to fake the real emotions normal people have. They have no remorse, no guilt, and feel only disgust at those of you who do. They are ruthless, their personality severed from their soul. Still with me? Just nod your head once if you are. And, don't worry! Our night sensory vision tells us you are still alone."

Rey started vigorously nodding, then caught himself so he wouldn't alert any potential watchers, despite the assurances from Reinbolt.

"So why are there psychopaths? Some think psychopathy might serve an evolutionary or genetic purpose. They refer to it as the warrior gene. It could provide a competitive edge to a tribe or people in constant competition. We can be fantastic close combat warriors suffering no PTSD or post-traumatic stress disorder after killing the enemy. I know you are all too familiar with PTSD. It devastates many normal soldiers who kill up close or see killing. It doesn't bother us psychopaths. Maybe it's okay for elite Special Ops people who need to do the necessary dirty work, but psychopaths just loose and un-restrained in the general population can pose a big problem. We are intraspecies predators, if you will. For example, not all psychopaths are serial killers, but almost all serial killers are psychopaths. What about me? I am a member of Shamar. It is an old Hebrew word that means 'guardian or keeper.' We are reformed or controlled psychopaths dedicated to being guardians or protectors to make amends for the damage we historically caused society.

"This brings us to the current problem. As I mentioned earlier, there is a nationwide group called the National Asso-ciation of Psychopaths, better known as NAP. Almost every town of any size has a chapter. They have remained hidden behind the scenes, always lurking in the shadows, wanting the country to stay asleep while they infiltrate and run everything. Over the last one hundred years, they have stealthily seeped into the government and media as the general populace slumbered. The Nithings, Melville, and Samms are all long-time leading NAP members. There are many others scattered in key positions throughout the country. They like any jobs that involve power, dominance, control, and the potential to prey on the weak. They also like police work, teaching, social work, and even the ministry. They make excellent politicians and lawyers because they have what is called 'serial lying syndrome.' They will tell a lie even when it would serve them better or be easier to tell the truth. They also can compartmentalize, separating their lives and lies, almost like having several personalities. I am sure you have seen this in Thornton Nithing. His brother Achor makes him look almost angelic in comparison. Are you still with me? Nod your head."

Rey nodded but desperately wanted to speak. He whispered softly, "This is all fine. A few weeks ago, it would've been hard to believe, but now I've seen it up close and personal. But get on with it. What can I do? They hold my family, and their grip is getting tighter."

The soft voice came back: "Quiet now. Listen closely before someone approaches. This is our leverage: If a big enough event happened, something very visible and shocking, we could loudly blow the whistle on NAP, with the intent of waking up the country before NAP commands all the levers of power and is completely in control. We have people strategically planted in the media who could make sure the news gets out. We also have a plan to permanently remove the psychopaths after they are revealed and the country accepts the threat. Psychopaths are attracted to power like a moth to a flame. What we need is a bug zapper system. With all the new, rapidly improving portable and affordable brain-scanning devices, they know they won't be able to remain hidden. This is the reason why they are making this final big push, coming out from hiding to seize power. They know the tipping point for them to consolidate complete power and safely gain control is at hand. Your sweeping the election and gaining a mandate is the key. With you as their 'useful idiot,' please pardon the phrase, they can complete their takeover and not worry about detection."

Rey looked around for any one approaching or watching, but he could sense or see no one. He whispered urgently, "So? Again! What can I do?"

"Get elected. Win a massive majority. Become a beloved popular hero. Then we will kidnap you." Sensing Rey's shock, the voice hurried on. "We will hide you. The country will be stunned. Then we will reveal the real you when the time is right, with your explaining the whole dastardly NAP conspiracy. Everyone will be watching, and NAP will be thrown off their stride and put under the spotlight of public scrutiny."

Ray could only choke out: "But my family. . . ."

"They will be protected. They are highly visible and already immensely well liked. We have a lot of other leverage collected over the years. Trust us."

Rey was stunned. He started to throw up his hands in abject frustration and then realized someone was approaching. It was Zara. A beautiful fragrance reached him well before he saw her moving gracefully toward him through the dim light of the garden.

"Thornton sent me out here. He is looking for you," she said hurriedly, reaching a soft hand out to touch his, and whispering hurriedly. "Don't worry. Snapper and I will coordinate the kidnapping. The less you know, the better. Get elected, and then they can't blame you or easily replace you. We will use the leverage we have built up to protect your family. Then our ransom or leverage will be that we know all about them and can expose them, and they will still want to remain hidden a while longer until they can try to completely consolidate power." She started to explain more but then suddenly she lunged for him and kissed him tenderly on the lips, pressing her body against him. The startled Rey began to reluctantly pull back and then heard a snide laugh.

Thornton Nithing had somehow stealthily crept up behind them. He was now looking at Zara in Rey's arms. "Why you two-timing barn cat, Rey Newly! Not that I blame you. You've got all the Pipestone beauties and now Zara, too. Maybe I should run for President!"

Zara finally detached herself from Rey's embrace and angrily waved a fist at Thornton. "Rey and I are both adults. We can do what we want. And I wouldn't touch you even if you were President."

Thornton just snorted dismissively: "Just don't let Boguiden's people get a whiff of an idea this is going on. Rey's golden if there is no dirt. Just two more days, Rey, so keep it in your pants." He giggled like a teenager and then danced off doing his favorite move, a pirouette, looking like a 300-pound ballerina as he faded into the darkness.

"Disgusting! Now he has more leverage!" Rey complained. "Not that I minded it, of course," he quickly added. "And I meant he was disgusting, not the, you know, body contact."

Zara just shook her head. "Rey, I am really sorry. He is unbelievably stealthy. I didn't hear him coming and couldn't have him think we were conspiring. It's all I could think of doing."

"Quit smooching you two and get moving," said the whispered voice from beneath the bench. "Somehow he blocked our night vision gear, maybe because he is so cold-blooded, but now there is another much warmer person coming."

Zara hurriedly moved back several feet and then Prissy appeared. "Oh," she said in a startled voice. "I thought Rey was out here by himself. Thornton just said he was."

Rey tried hard to look innocent, but, still befuddled by what had just transpired, he found all his newfound acting skills deserted him right when he needed them most. He knew he was fidgeting like a kid with his hand caught in a cookie jar. And no doubt he had the scent of Zara all over him. He hoped it was dark enough that neither woman could see him blushing.

Prissy's look of disgust just made him fidget more and feel worse. He sensed she could see he was still blushing. Anger and hurt flooded her face. "First it's Paula and now her," she said, thrusting her chin disgustedly at Zara. "Why can't I ever be good enough for you?" she cried, and then spun on her heels and ran back to the hotel, leaving the wordless Rey staring at the calm and cool Zara.

For some reason, Zara now seemed put out with him as well. Shaking her head with disgust, she looked at him and said: "Men! One-track minds! Just get elected. Then we will handle the rest."

"Over and out," said the whispery voice from beneath the bench.

Rey didn't find it hard to believe that it was, in fact, over and out. He watched Zara leave. He was ashamed to admit it, but he still could smell her fragrance and feel her presence in his arms, and he liked it. He couldn't help but reflect that Zara had said it was all she could think of doing, which, of course, could be taken several ways. But then the crushed look on Prissy's face came flooding back to him. He supposed he should go to Prissy and say he was sorry, even though he was innocent of doing anything wrong. However, he was sure he still smelled like Zara, and he doubted he could face Prissy and lie about being sorry. Well, he was sorry—a sorry fool. He did, however, have one good thought: Feeling this much guilt and remorse, and not able to tell a lie, at least it meant he wasn't a psychopath!

≡ CHAPTER5 ≡

On Being P.O.T.U.S.

(President of the United States)

The next few days went by like a blur. Then the election, if in honesty it could be called one, was over. It was a massive majority vote. A complete sweep. An electoral tidal wave. Wrenfield Boguiden was mercilessly clobbered and was squalling like a cat with its tail stepped on.

The Nithing team was sorely aggravated with its brother DNC operatives for not controlling Boguiden better. Somehow the loser just refused to lose gracefully and wanted to contest what he called the sham election. Trying to keep a low profile with a whiner like Boguiden around was difficult. If possible, the daughter was even worse than the dad, making allegations that sounded ridiculous to anyone except Rey, who knew she was telling the truth. It appeared she was the only non-psychopath, beyond him and a few others, to see through the smoothly conducted ruse.

As far as Rey's life went, not much changed. He was still under intense around-the-clock surveillance, watched "for his protection" by the Secret Service. With the constant scrutiny and crammed schedule, it was hard for him to see how he would be kidnapped. He was hustled to one highly orchestrated press conference after another. He dutifully read his teleprompter with a modicum of feeling. People were referring to him as a cool, calming factor as he adamantly refused to be dragged into the whole Boguiden sore-loser fiasco. "Go along to get along" became his mantra.

There were a few accidental glitches, though, no matter how hard he attempted to stay out of trouble. One day he led his two sons, along with a phalanx of Secret Service guards, on a walk to see their soon-to-be new "white" house. Morton immediately thought they should paint it blue, and Milton was yammering for a bright red or yellow, when they noticed an odd commotion. They heard a muffled yell and looked over to see a pudgy little white-haired man being hoisted in a recliner out of the White House side entrance by two very muscular and mean-looking men, surrounded by another squad of frowning Secret Service types. They were loading up a big, unmarked moving van.

As the men sat the chair down, the small man stood up to what looked like a full height of only five-foot-two at best. Rey didn't realize he was looking at the former president, Sedgewick Sewell, until one of the attendants yelled: "Sit down, Sewell, before I knock you down."

The pathetic-looking man quickly plunked his plump butt back into the chair. "But I need my glasses and my elevator shoes," the old man whined. Then he turned and looked, squinting at Newly with his myopic eyes. "You're the new big shot. Tell them to get my glasses and shoes."

Rey found it hard to realize this was Sedgewick Clayton Sewell, the supposedly six-foot-two golden orator. Elevator shoes, lots of makeup, tight corset, teleprompter, Reynard could see how it could work. "Show him some respect!" Rey said sternly, pointing at the group assembled around Sewell.

One of the muscular guys who had been carrying Sewell started to give Rey the finger, when one of Sewell's accompanying Secret Service guys gave the offender a karate chop on the arm and then conked him a good one on the head. He obviously thought at least his new boss should be treated with a modicum of respect.

The rest of the group stared down the remaining muscleman accompanying the ex-president and then gently assisted Sewell into the van after finding his glasses and giving him his shoes. They all then saluted the departing Sewell, as they drove him away. One of Rey's guards said in a sober voice. "Nithing is going to be really pissed when he finds out you saw this."

"Then don't tell him," Rey snapped, putting on his best Thornton Nithing imitation. "And don't use words like that around the boys."

"We won't tell, Dad," Milton said. "We don't want that mean Mr. Nithing getting pissed at you either."

Oh, great, Rey thought. Now I will be in more trouble with Prissy when we get back to the hotel and the boys uncork their new vocabulary.

Again, trouble just seemed to find him like iron filings to a magnet. He was trying to find his way around the Executive Office Building and came upon a heavily guarded room. Figuring, 'I'm President and have the highest possible clearance,' he started to enter the room. The military guards stopped him and then nearly fainted when they recognized who he was. He politely thanked them for doing their job and then opened the door and eased himself in.

Quickly, Rey realized this was a high-powered group discussing the formation of, all things, his new cabinet. He recognized from the military-industrial complex dinner the Senate Majority Leader, Senator Hiram Festerwart of Festerwart County, Mississippi. He recalled Festerwart was called the great grey lion of the Senate, but he looked like a sleepy lion to Rey. He was also known as Filibuster Festerwart, from when he once set a filibuster record with the help of a banjo, a compact disc player, and a list of his favorite opossum pie recipes. He was in the middle of explaining why he looked so sleepy, blaming it on his frisky new buxom assistant, when he realized Rey had just entered the room. He stopped short and started to splutter, as if he were filibustering again without the accoutrements and recipes.

Rey also recognized Admiral Nathaniel Futtock, the head of the Joint Chief of Staff, from the military-industrial complex dinner. How could he forget the thick, pouty lips and protruding eyeballs plastered in a fat, squinty face, making him look perpetually incredulous? Rey not so fondly remembered he had the personality and body of a beached whale with a gastric disorder and had been a real suck-up to Melville and Samms, ignoring Rey all night. He, too, seemed startled to see Rey.

Everyone gaped in stunned silence until a very shrill, almost girlish-sounding third voice spoke up and asked, "What are you doing here, Mr. President?"

"Obviously, I am missing an important meeting," he responded, trying not to be flippant as he noticed a whiteboard with cabinet positions listed as well as a list of ambassadorial openings.

The owner of the shrill voice seemed unconcerned about his interruption of the meeting. "Well, do you have any friends or relatives to whom you would like to offer a position? Not all of them require campaign donations, or, I should say, even extensive experience. Do you have a brother or brother-in-law you want to send overseas to get out of the way? A large donor we should honor? Usually we just divvy these up ourselves, but we would be happy to entertain your suggestions. Perhaps P.T. Pipestone for a position in Commerce?"

Rey was openly perplexed. "And who are you, sir?"

The man seemed offended but equally perplexed that Rey didn't recognize him. "You don't know who Busby Marsh is?" he asked. He was obviously talking about himself in third person, but to remove any doubt, he placed his own thumb on his chest. "I am the third-richest man in the world, behind Melville and Samms, at least so they and their stooges at the big business magazines claim. Achor Nithing has asked me to chair this committee and parcel out the spoils of war, shall we say."

"And what spoils will you be claiming," Rey asked rather tersely, "if you don't mind my asking? After all, I am supposedly the new President."

Busby Marsh seemed completely unfazed by Rey's audacity. "Oh, I've been an Ambassador to several places under Sewell and the idiot before him. It gets real boring quickly. I am going to be Secretary of Defense this time. After we finish up this little housekeeping task, we are going to decide whom to invade next, aren't we? We've got to keep that military-industrial complex going to keep unemployment down."

At first Rey thought he was joking, but he soon realized it wasn't deadpan humor he was seeing, but humorless sincerity. "Shouldn't I be involved or at least consulted on any of this?" Rey asked.

Marsh settled back in his chair, and Rey got his first good look at him. He was rubbing very pink palms together and had the disturbing trait of shooting the tip of his tongue out of his mouth like he was checking the air like a snake for the scent of rodents. He also noticed Marsh had very small, very even, pearly teeth in a brief slash of a mouth. His head was out of proportion for the rest of his body, like a pumpkin on a stick. He had big, bushy, sprouting eyebrows that he was obviously very proud of, keeping them manicured and dyed to match his unruly thatch of hair.

Then Rey placed the name. Marsh hadn't been at the military-industrial complex dinner because, up until now, Melville and Samms had blocked him from this most lucrative market. Marsh ran one of the largest software companies and was using the threat of cyber warfare to get one huge foot in the door. Nanotechnology was another one of his niches, and miniature militarized drones driven by his software were another way to get his other foot in the door. From the looks of it, he not only planned to place both his big feet but his whole tall and ungainly body in it, assuming he was to become Secretary of Defense.

Marsh was obviously impatient to get on with divvying up the prizes. "Well, thank you for visiting us, President Newly. Once we have this tedious and thankless little task done, we will give our list to Thornton. Once Achor approves it, I am sure they will pass it on to you for your signature. You are excused."

"Excused? Excuse me!" responded Rey in an alarmed tone, offended by the curt dismissal. "I would like some input in something so critical to my success and the welfare of the nation."

While Busby Marsh gave him a pained look and Senator Festerwart continued to stutter, Admiral Futtock, who had been soaking in all this quietly but with an alarmed expression, now spoke up in a deep voice that sounded like a foghorn. "Now listen here, Newly. Our previous presidents did their jobs properly and left everything to us. I doubt you have ever commanded anything bigger than a rowboat. You go on and watch TV or something. We make the decisions, and you make the speeches." He waved Rey off with a meaty hand on a large, flabby arm. He then commanded two of his attendants, who looked like they were Navy Seal Team members, to remove this upstart annoyance. "Escort this esteemed man to shore and tell the landlubber guards out there I will have them keelhauled, or whatever we do these days, if they let him back in."

Newly was astonished to find himself picked up under each arm and unceremoniously deposited out of the room, with a polite "sorry sir" from his two muscular handlers. His last glimpse was of a slyly grinning Busby Marsh as the door slammed and locked behind him. His own Secret Service attachment angrily started toward the two Navy Seal guys, but Rey stopped them. "They're just following orders from a very nasty man. I'm going to find out just how much clout I have around here."

Soon he found himself in even more trouble. As he continued searching around the executive offices to find Thornton and ask if he had any clout, he saw a familiar face heading his way. He knew he had seen the man on TV but couldn't place him. "Hey, boss," the man said in a broad Texas accent, shaking Rey's hand with a vigorous pumping motion that shook Rey from head to toe, rattling his teeth. "How is the president business going?" the man asked. Seeing Rey's perplexed look, he appeared somewhat offended, but nevertheless proceeded full steam ahead. "Surely you know me. I'm Mylo Mailstrom, the Attorney General from the Sewell administration! Nithing just told me the good news. I'm going to be working with you, and I'm telling you what, I'm as pumped as a Texas oil gusher. I have some kick-butt new concepts for the good of America," Mailstrom announced.

Somehow mistaking Rey's startled expression for one of interest, he barged ahead: "Listen to this, my man, I mean Mr. President. This is hot off the presses. The buzzword gurus say the hottest sound bites the American people are buying are 'law and order' and 'quick justice.' Believe me, this is the ticket. We used a pointy-headed intellectual from some big Ivy League school, Dr. J. Woodhouse Crenwrinkle, to do a big-time, bang-up study for us on the whole thing. He found a direct correlation between the amount of money paid for legal counsel and success in court. Can you believe it took a few million dollars in tax money to determine such a no-brainer?" Mailstrom chuckled and leered at Rey. "Do you see it? Quick justice! The person with the highest-priced lawyer automatically wins the case. The ABA likes it, as legal fees will soar and their dues with them. Saves time from all those cumbersome trials, too. They will obviously be grateful to us—'wink, wink,' as we say! Ingenious solution to a major problem, I think."

Mailstrom paused with a huge grin on his face. "From now on, no time wasted with lengthy trials. No messy legal wrangles and appeals. Just set up an ABA-approved lawyer-rating scale, look up the fees of the representatives, the highest-priced one wins, and bingo-bongo, you got your verdict." Seeing Rey's less-than-enthusiastic response, and beginning to sense a lack of receptiveness, he suddenly looked grave and muttered, "It's better for the little people, too. It eliminates the backlog of cases and speeds up justice. That is the most important thing. Help the little people!"

Rey couldn't hold it in. "How does that help the little people? Doesn't the guy with the big bucks automatically win?"

Mailstrom stepped back as if bitten. Then he shot a venomous look at Rey. "And I should ask why not? It's the way it pretty much works now. This is America, and everybody respects money. This just takes a lot less time and saves mucho resources. Plus, this way the little guy is relieved of wasting time with jury duty. It's a win-win all the way around. Achor Nithing thought it was brilliant. It got me my AG gig!"

Rey decided he ought to hurry up and find out just how much clout he possessed if he was going to stop harebrained ideas like this one. When he found out a little later how much clout he possessed, it wasn't much.

Thornton excoriated him for wandering where he wasn't needed. He was only allowed in a few offices. Not only had Busby Marsh called to complain, but so had Hiram Festerwart and Nathaniel Futtock. "Rey, I let you out of my sight for one hour and you manage to tick off our third-largest donor, Busby Marsh, the Senate Majority leader, old Festerwart, and Admiral Futtock, the Head of the Joint Chiefs of Staff. Then the one guy from the old administration worth keeping, Mylo Mailstrom, says you were pigheaded and pusillanimous, whatever that means. Plus, to top it all off, the outgoing president, old Sedgewick Clayton Sewell himself, had his Chief of Staff call and angrily complain that you were rude to Sewell. He said one of your hooligan guards, as he called them, broke one of his assistant's arms. If Achor finds out, he is going to kill me for not keeping you under my thumb—and then he'll skin you alive."

"Then don't tell him," Rey shouted at the stunned Thornton. "I'm pissed off that critical decisions are being made, and I don't even know the meeting is taking place. They even asked me if I had a brother who wanted to be an ambassador or if P.T. wanted a top job in the Commerce Department."

"See, they were trying to let you be involved!" Thornton said with a big, ingratiating smile, trying to mollify Rey. "Granted, it was probably not an important country, I'll give you that. And old P.T. Pipestone is going to be too busy happily bashing heads of his competitors to get involved in bureaucratic stuff like commerce. I would have suggested, though, that Jacqueline Boguiden be appointed to Russia or China, or one of them Arab places, and let her chew them up. She is one tough lady!"

"I would hope such appointments would have some merit behind them," Rey huffed, realizing he was getting nowhere fast with Thornton on this topic.

"They paid top dollar for the rights. At least Marsh did. We gave Samms V.P., Achor says Melville will be Secretary of State, or, if he doesn't like that, our Ambassador to the United Nations. Keep them both happy, busy, and out of our hair. He had to give Marsh something, and he gave us 'big bang buck' as the cool kids used to say. I would say that has a lot of merit."

Rey also soon found out every president has a cabinet whether he wants one or not, as Thornton so succinctly told him. The team he had so rudely interrupted soon had for him a list of all appointments and cabinet people, all approved in advance by Achor Nithing, and he grudgingly but dutifully signed off. Each name came with an impressive bio and a classy press release, all the work of Bylow Bellwater and, doubtless, also approved by Nithing.

Thornton patiently made sure he understood the good side of this carefully constructed and smoothly operating machine of governance. "This is all to make sure that the USA is a country that works for the good of America. Minimize chaos and disorder. I say out-Chinese the Communist Chinese, before they grind us under their heels. We need to protect our people. Achor likes to say that without us behind the scenes running things this country would be like an octopus on roller skates, going every direction at once and falling on its stupid face. Too much power and money are at stake to let amateurs run it."

To help ease his discomfort and worry, Rey spent as much time as he could with his two sons, encouraging and loving them. They had fun exploring their new home, still the White House despite the boy's desire to paint it different colors. Despite the cold shoulder from Prissy because of the Zara incident, he tried to be positive with her, too. They learned Camp David was a great place to tramp around and climb trees.

They had a few picnics out there, bringing along Grandma Theta Pipestone, as P.T. was already out eagerly hunting down former rivals. Rey reluctantly turned down the opportunity for several all-expenses-paid family trips to expensive and exotic places, not feeling it was a good thing to do with the economy still down and lots of people out of work. They all wanted to go back to Pewamo, and got one short trip back, but it proved stressful, as everyone kept pressing all the family members for special requests and building projects. He didn't have the heart to tell them he was powerless when it came to purse strings or appointments. As a matter of fact, he didn't know if he had any power except to exasperate Thornton and keep Prissy permanently miffed at him. Then he was shocked to hear the Nithings had dropped a big bucket of bucks on his hometown for public works, all to be named for P.T. and himself.

He wanted to enroll the boys in a local DC public elementary school not too far from the White House but was told it was out of the question. "If it's good enough for the local people, it's good enough for my boys," Rey said repeatedly. But the law was laid down. He would not be allowed to homeschool them either, but an elite private school was available. It would be easier for the Secret Service to guard them, he was told, as almost all the other elected officials with school-aged kids sent their children to the same school. Purely a matter of security, he was assured, safety in numbers and all that. Many people on the White House serving staff seemed to be impressed with his genuinely passionate desire to have his boys experience the local school, but it was another battle he couldn't win.

He started to think the P.O.T.U.S.-napping, as he began to think of it, wasn't going to happen. With the election over and won, Zara had made herself scarce around the White House and the Executive Offices, staying far from Rey when she was there, much to Prissy's satisfaction. Even Snapper seemed to have finished his photo shoots.

Rey was beginning to worry they had forgotten about the whole thing or had been found out, when Snapper slipped him another blank note. It was blank until he again touched it with his fingers. This activated the paper, and a hidden message slowly emerged. All it said was "eight tonight by the oak tree in the Rose Garden."

Rey often went to the Rose Garden for solitary after-dinner strolls, so he knew he wouldn't look suspicious. Despite his best intentions, he found himself hoping it would be a meeting with Zara, and then guiltily corrected himself. He immediately went to hug his boys, telling them how much he loved them, and found Prissy sitting sadly on a piano bench beneath the still-hanging portrait of old Sedgewick Clayton Sewell, since Rey's portrait hadn't been completed yet. Rey had secretly checked and found Sewell was supposedly in a home for dementia patients somewhere in Georgia. When Rey had accidentally seen him, he had seemed sharp enough, maybe a little whiney, but Rey supposed getting rudely rousted out of your home of eight years might do that to you.

He decided to man up with his wife. He had thought out an approach that, to his primitive male mind, seemed foolproof. He practiced it and felt he could pull it off. Now seemed an opportune time.

"Prissy," he started. "I know you think I tried to do something with Zara, but I swear I did not." Rey was proud of himself for thinking up this line, because it was technically true, as he hadn't initiated the embrace, and, besides, there hadn't been time to do anything anyway. So far, his acting skills had not failed him. He didn't let Prissy's stony-eyed look deter him and forged on: "I know I don't tell you this enough, but I do love you." This also was technically true, if he left out the word "only" before the word love. He wasn't sure what he felt for Zara. He could feel he was on a roll with Prissy, who was at least listening, if with no discernible expression. "If I didn't have you, I would feel terrible," he continued. This was also technically true, if he didn't dwell on it in any depth. "You and the boys mean the world to me, and I would do anything to protect you." This was one hundred percent accurate on the old Rey truth meter. He just wished he knew precisely how to protect them.

"Why are you bugging me, Rey?" Prissy finally said, her eyes now smoldering with barely contained fury. "I am not blind. I can see how you were looking at that Zara." She was seething now with a passion that he realized was hatred, not love. "I'm not going to sleep with you no matter what you say." She said the last with a defiant lifting of the head and a crossing of the legs, signaling the play area was closed for action. This statement about sex between them was technically very true. It seemed Prissy always figured sex was only good for one thing: making babies. When Rey had been blown to pieces by the land mine, they could put almost everything back together, more or less. Soon after marriage they found out he was not impotent but was infertile. Finally, after ten years, they arranged for a sperm donor and Prissy got pregnant with the twins. It was a painful pregnancy with lots of life-threatening complications. A long, excruciating delivery ended any hopes of adding more little ones, despite the charm of the little guys.

Suddenly, Prissy shook her head with disgust and looked him straight in the eyes with a fierce expression. "I want to talk to you about the boys. I never told you this, because I didn't want to hurt you before," she paused dramatically, "but it was not an anonymous sperm donor. It was an old boyfriend, Rey."

Rey felt like he had been shot between the eyes point blank with a bazooka. His insides erupted, and he nearly threw up. He sucked in a deep breath as his chest constricted and a sharp pain shot up his arm. As he collapsed over the piano bench, he smacked his head violently and then crashed to the floor. His last sight was of Prissy's stricken face, constricted in horror. His last thoughts weren't just about her betrayal, or him even dying, but about what would happen to his family now?

CHAPTER 6

The Great Escape at Last

When Rey suddenly came to, he sprang up like a jack-in-the box, nearly head-butting a bearded, white-jacketed orderly who turned out to be the former photographer Snapper Melville in disguise. "You sure messed up our plans, Rey."

"What do you mean your plans? I thought we were to meet at eight by the oak tree in the Rose Garden. This sure isn't any oak tree, and I smell Zara around here."

"She's driving the ambulance we're in. We hijacked it after the EMTs came to the White House to give you CPR. When they brought you out to go the hospital, we gave them a knockout drug to remove their memory of the event and give us about a half hour to hand you off to another team, then get back in there to cover our tracks. I don't know why you went into shock. All I know is Prissy said she said something she shouldn't have—remind me not to mess with her! Fortunately, for all of us, it was already 7:30 and we had our tools and team in place to do the snatch. We just weren't planning on doing it this way, especially not directly from the White House!"

Rey tried to get up from the stretcher only to be forced back by a surprisingly strong Snapper. He might look medium-sized and stringy, but the young man had a strong grip. Plus Rey realized he was strapped in. "I have to go back, Snapper. I need to talk to Prissy. I can't leave my boys, I mean the boys. I mean, back there." He realized he was just garbling everything. And a determined-looking Snapper obviously wasn't going to let him get up either, having him strapped down quite securely.

"Where are you taking me?"

"Same place we took President Sewell," Snapper answered. Seeing Rey's shock, Snapper quickly explained: "Sewell does not have dementia, and he's not in Georgia, and he was not a bad man. They manipulated him just like they did you, although he might have been a little more willing than you at first. Initially, it didn't take much for them to get him to play along. He had a major weakness for beautiful women and nice food, and they kept him well supplied. Toward the end, about the sixth year, to his credit, he realized he was helping them do irreparable harm to the country. Once they realized they had lost him, they just drugged him for the last few years. Creeping dementia or early Alzheimer's they claimed. Doped him up. Slapped him in a memory home and forgot him. We easily snatched him out of there. Believe me, he is doing fine. The wine and the women may not be quite as good, but he's doing just fine."

"But what will happen to the boys and my wife?" Rey nervously asked, painfully aware he hadn't said "my" in regard to the boys. He knew he still loved then intensely no matter what Prissy said. "I never should have gotten them involved in this pit of psychopathic demons."

Snapper smiled mischievously. "Well, you didn't have

much choice. Other people decided to get you involved, and, once decided, it was out of your hands. But, don't worry. Nithing will keep them safe and secure. We will make him think you were snatched against your will, because basically you were! We can be very convincing. He will want to keep his leverage over you for when he hopes he will get you back in the White House."

"But what are you doing here, Snapper? Your dad is a very wealthy man, connected to everyone, and a very powerful player in this so-called government."

Snapper angrily shook his head as he hurriedly prepared Rey for the next waiting vehicle. "He is a psychopath who can turn instantly from a charmer to a killer. Since I was a young child, I've seen him do hideous things that I cringe to recall. Skinning my pets alive in front of me, terrorizing and beating the help, humiliating and raping women on the staff, earning the nickname 'Groper' Melville, intimidating me because I wasn't good looking or smart enough. Just complete calculated cruelty! My mom . . . . Let's just say I didn't have a dad like you. I've seen you with your boys." Then he stopped as a sad, stricken look crossed his face. "But, hey, enough talk about me."

Then Snapper looked at him with genuine concern. "What about you, Rey? I've admired the way you encourage and love your sons. I know you and Prissy have been having problems, but it seemed to be getting better until this week. Then when we were there pretending to help the EMT crew before we drugged them, Prissy was hysterical and telling Thornton Nithing on the phone about some horrible war wound or something. I knew you got your leg and arm ripped up, but, whatever she was crying and telling Nithing about, I don't sense it was causing him any chagrin."

Rey couldn't believe Prissy would tell Thornton their big, deep, personal secret. Of course, he couldn't believe she neglected to tell him about the sperm donor not being anonymous. Now he started seething with anger. She always liked a guy named Grant Tramm, an engineer old P.T. admired, but she said it never worked out, or, at least, she led Rey to think so. In his now-fevered imagination, he could see that Morton and Milton looked just a little like clones of that smug, tight-ass engineer. He was a lot like P.T., very meticulous, controlling, and quite mechanical, always nitpicking any little thing he thought was wrong. He, too, was an "awfulizer," always able to find a small flaw in the most beautiful thing and then dwell on it until it drove people crazy. He always said if engineers ruled the world, everything would be orderly and make sense, without all the emotional crap. He disdained Rey and mocked his love of birds and sensitivity to people. The thought suddenly came to Rey that, hey, maybe that idiot was a psychopath, too. If I am still President, I could check him out and make his life miserable. Do a "P.T." on him! Nah, never could do that, he realized.

Rey started to get up again, but Snapper still had him tightly strapped in and quickly shot him up with something as he explained his actions: "Your blood pressure is going bonkers again, and you were starting to go into shock. Whatever you are stressing over is not worth it. Go to sleep."

Suddenly the ambulance came to a halt, and Rey was rapidly but gently transferred to another vehicle. He was groggy and immobilized by now. Ten minutes later, he was transferred again. By this time, he was well under the influence of the powerful sedative Snapper had given him. Occasionally, he could smell Zara near him, and a couple of times he thought he felt her soft touch. Or was it just wishful dreaming? Whenever he started to swim out from the dark well of sticky unconsciousness, he kept seeing Prissy's face as she laid him out with the horrible truth. He would start to yell, and then Snapper or somebody would shoot him up again. Down he would go. His last thought was of his boys, his sweet, little, innocent boys, lost and alone with the Nithings of the world. He would get them back, no matter what it took! They were his boys no matter what, and he resolved to get them to safety. Then he drifted off again into troubled unconsciousness.

CHAPTER 7

Welcome to the Wild Outdoors and Fuzzy Logic

The shuffle between vehicles continued well into the night. Rey lost track of how many times he was drugged and transferred. When he finally woke up, he was still securely strapped in but had to pee like a camel and take a dump, too. "Snapper, I've got some physical needs to attend to, or your vehicle is going to be condemned," he yelled. He worked one arm free and sat up but couldn't undo all the complex harnesses. His face felt strange, and he realized a fake black beard had been attached. One glance in the rearview mirror indicated his hair had been dyed to match. He thought it sort of gave him a rakish, piratical look.

The guy who was soon leaning over him was certainly not Snapper. He looked like an oversized, gnarled, African garden gnome, with hints of Asian ancestry thrown in. He had a bushy white beard and long, grey, frizzy hair pulled back in a ponytail, with deep mahogany skin. "You even fart in my vehicle and I will gut you, smelly varmint," the strange man said gruffly. "P.O.T.U.S. or no P.O.T.U.S. Pffft! President of the United States, my ass."

The man hastily unbuckled Rey's remaining safety restraints and let him out to stretch his numb arms and cramped legs. Rey noticed he was in a little clearing in a big, fragrant pine forest. His guess was Georgia or maybe Alabama. Shoot, it could even be Michigan, since it was summer. He was apparently lost in the woods and a hostage of a weird-looking mad man of some sorts.

"Where is the john?" Rey asked, in a shaky and raspy voice.

"Well, I don't know if any of the trees are called John, but feel free to introduce yourself," the querulous old gnome barked at him. He threw Rey a roll of toilet paper. "Works better than pine needles, but you kin try them if you want."

"Wise-ass," Rey muttered as he wandered off to find a suitable tree. When Rey found his way back after fertilizing a large swath of the forest, he saw the last part of the trip had been in an old red, white, and blue van. It was rusty and dirty but neat and clean inside.

"That is known as 'The Spirit of America,' or the 'old ruster wagon,' depending on the person. And my name is Crazy Jake 'Nambo' Quark. At my age, I've got to start settling on one name, so call me Nambo, and the marvelous mode of transportation over there, Spirit."

"And this place is called . . .?" Rey asked, further observing that Crazy Jake Nambo Quark had on faded and patched-up blue pants, with a blazing set of red suspenders struggling to hold them up. This was topped off with a ludicrous purple and yellow bowtie clipped on to what looked like the tops of some heavily worn and faded long underwear that appeared to be patched with strips of cloth composed of most of the colors of the rainbow. He put the word colorful in the phrase "colorful character," for sure. Every bit of skin that wasn't covered with ill-fitting, garishly colored clothes appeared to be sprouting frizzy white hair, including several out of his nose and some on his ears.

"This place is called 'nowhere.' But," he paused to spit some unidentified gunk out of his mouth, "we are on our way to Crazy Jake's Reservation for the Temporarily Bewildered." Seeing Rey's look of incredulity, he continued. "Look, Newby, I know it ain't the White House and all, and this ain't exactly no limo. And my plane sure ain't Air Force One, but my niece Zara and her crazy friend Gomer . . ."

The startled Rey stopped him with a wave of his hand. Staring at the gnarly old guy, Rey sputtered, "I believe his name is Grover, but everyone calls him Snapper. And my name is Newly, not Newby." Suddenly some of what the old guy said registered. "Wait! Your niece is Zara? You have a plane?" At least the niece bit explained her golden skin and vaguely Asian-looking eyes. The plane didn't explain anything. Things were getting stranger and stranger, and Rey's head hurt from whacking the piano or from the drugs Snapper had injected into him.

"Yes, didn't I just say so? You need to listen better if you want people to like you. And I also got the privilege and pleasure to fix us some breakfast, Mr. Brewster, as in rooster, Blackoak, your new moniker by the way, Newby, to go with your new dashing, emaciated Abraham Lincoln look." Rey realized he hadn't shaved, and his rough growth was itching him from beneath his fake beard.

"You like biscuits and gravy?" the gnome asked him in a gruff voice. "It's too bad if you don't like them, as I don't exactly have an extensive menu. Like a little bit of grits, bacon, and sausage? Would you like some hot black coffee? You better, because that's all we got." With that, Nambo checked his camp stove, which was soon heating up, savory bacon soon sizzling in the pan.

Seeing Rey beginning to drool, Nambo just shook his head and prattled on. "You sure are a dolt. I can't believe Zara cares about you. There's handsome men like me still around. Not that I mean her and me, with her being my niece and all." Nambo continued to talk to himself as he hauled some more "vittles," as he called them, along with a beat-up card table and chairs out of the Spirit. Soon a sumptuous feast was spread out on a red-checkered tablecloth he also had pulled out of his vehicle.

"Like to fish, Rey, I mean Brewster?" Nambo asked out of the blue, around a mouth jammed with biscuits, eggs, grits, and gravy. Biscuit pieces flew out in all directions as he waved a gravy-caked hand, pantomiming casting a fishing rod.

"I used to. No time now. Too much work. Yard and kids, watching TV," Rey said between gulps. Either this was the best food he had ever eaten or he was starving. As the president of the country, you naturally got lots of choice food, but this just flat-out tasted greasy and great.

"Garden and kids are okay. But a man gives up fishing might as well be dead. I say, 'No fishing flattens the soul.' It is a form of meditation. I grow some of the best bluegills and tilapia in all America. I grow pigs, too. Should be the national animal. You can use every part of the pig for something, maybe even the squeal. Like the buffalo to the Native American, though I don't think I ever heard of a pigskin teepee. Never heard of a buffalo-skin football either though. You give me pigs, chickens, and a few cows, and I can feed a whole bunch of people. I'm aiming to get me a few buffalo, too, when I sell a few more cars."

"You're a car salesman?" Rey asked, trying to follow the machine gun stream of consciousness proceeding from the gnome's mouth.

"Didn't I just say so? You need to listen better! But not just any cars. My business is called 'Carta Suitya.' You know like that Kama Sutra sex position stuff. I bring people in and then give them all sorts of fancy psychological tests and interview them. Then and only then I match them with just the right car that will give them good 'carma,' you know, kind of like good luck on steroids. I leave the sex positions to other people."

Rey was having a hard time following all the logic or lack thereof but picked out certain parts. "You are a psychologist?"

"Didn't I just say so? People don't realize how a car can reveal so much about who and what they are. Everybody's got, like, three people in them. Who they really are, who they want to be, and who they are pretending to be. Only when you drive a car that matches who you are, unless you're messed up, of course, and hate yourself, can you be happy. Happy people buy lots of cars."

Between dodging the spewing biscuit bits and following the somewhat convoluted logic from the pig as the national animal, except you can't make teepees from pig skin, all the way to cars and sex positions, Rey was developing a roaring headache. His stomach was feeling okay, but his head hurt, and he was starting to doze off from his full belly.

"Now the Spirit over there is my type of vehicle. It's a

Mercedes truck from way back and looks slow, but it's well built with a powerful engine that purrs like a lioness in heat hidden in a beat up, rusty old body. Like me, I'm a very deceptive guy. People always mis-underestimate me. Now you, you look like a newer, but used pickup. Trusty, loyal, decent, helpful to lots of people, decent engine under the hood, but never let the world see your real horsepower. Like that deceitful Achor Nithing fellow."

Rey jarred awake at the mention of Achor Nithing. "What about that Nithing fellow? Is he around here?" Rey was furtively looking at the woods, as if expecting one of the Nithings to charge out like an enraged grizzly.

"Settle down, my man. We are completely off the grid. Nithing has been looking for me for years. Ever since I put his old man Rancor Nithing in the State Home for the Criminally Insane. We called him old rancid Rancor. It took me years after he did me and mine wrong. But I did it all legally as the State Attorney General the first time. It changed my life. His family came after me, and I had to give up the law, become a psychologist, and then an anthropologist to figure out those malignant devils. A disgusting family of pure evil."

The now thoroughly bewildered Rey didn't know where to begin. "So, you were a lawyer?"

"Didn't I just say so? You need to work hard on your listening. Rottenest job I ever had. I had a great legal mind, but I hated always looking at the negative. Over half of all lawyers are severely depressed and suicidal, some say close to 70 percent. The only difference between a lawyer and a catfish is one is a low-down, scum-sucking bottom feeder and the other is a fish. Lawyers are a plague to society, like rats in a shack or on an old sailing ship. You fumigate, you put down poison, and they are right back. Gnawing at the innards and foundations of any civilization, scurrying everywhere. Blasted lawyers always making laws, whether you need them or not. They make the laws as confusing as they can and then make money disagreeing with each other about what the damned law means. The more they mess things up, the more they get paid. Never heard of a single lawyer doing a noble deed or doing anything to improve the lot of the common person, myself excluded, of course. Some of my tribe is made up of former lawyers. They make good pig herders once they finally get the hang of it."

"Lawyers make good pig herders?" Rey asked, trying to picture that happening.

"Didn't I just say so? Does a bear fart in the woods? Sure does. My tribe is made up of temporarily bewildered people, and I un-bewilder them. Do I need to repeat that?"

"Nope. Got it. But I don't think 'un-bewilder' is a word, and I think you used 'mis-underestimate' earlier, but I got the concepts." Rey hoped he was getting something, because there was a lot of thick stuff floating through here. "I don't think I quite have the tribe part down though," Rey said.

Seeing he wasn't going to get any immediate clarification on the tribe topic from old Nambo, he took another tack. "Back to the Nithings. You put away the father for doing something to you, if I get your drift. At least the first time you said. But now the sons, Achor and Thornton, I assume, are hunting you down, but can't find you?"

"Nope, they know where I am. But I got leverage. Powerful leverage. I know what they are. Snakes in suits. Lizards in loafers. Crocodiles with calculators. I'm a hacker 'supreme,' and their darkest secrets are mine. They know it. And the few bad traits or habits they don't have, I make up and plant in the media. Their goose would be cooked if they mess too much with me. They also stay away because I would shoot them on sight. I'm also a crack shot, not just a crackpot. I can shoot out the asshole of a bear 100 yards away. Like I said, I got lots and lots of leverage. Their old man Rancor was a pedophile and a psychopath. Almost certainly he messed the boys up, too. Second time I put him away permanently, where he couldn't charm his way out of his chains and strangle some naïve assistant whom he'd convinced he was a good guy. They still tried to take away my land, using some sneaky legal maneuvers, but now I got my tribe. Your Uncle Flynn Pompatella helped me with the scheme. Now, like you supposedly, he is a decent, honest, good man, but he is also a good listener. There, I said three good things about you. I had to work at it real hard though."

Rey was too surprised hearing his legendary uncle's name that he ignored the mumbled comment about three good ones, whatever the reference to three good ones meant. He would find out later. But for now, his curiosity was getting the best of him. "Wait a minute, Nambo. My mom, Swan Newly, bless her sweet soul, was part Pewamo Native American. Her brother was a Wabeno, I guess something like a healer or shaman, in the northern Great Lakes tribes. His name was Jack Flynn, and his native name was Pompatella. She never knew what happened to him. He disappeared well before the time my dad died in a terrible industrial accident. I was about four years old when my uncle went away. This was over thirty-six years ago. She said he used to hunt down the windigo. Hey, wait a minute. Windigos are like a Native American name for crazy people, right? I mean really evil crazy people?"

"Kind of like intraspecies predators," the old gnarled gnome agreed. "Every culture has got them. Pewamo had windigos. Vikings had what they called nithings. Pretty much the same thing. They were considered evil incarnate, vile creatures that snuck up and killed people for the sheer joy of killing. The more innocent and helpless the person, the better. The Vikings weren't saints by a long way, but they considered calling someone a nithing the most terrible insult, resulting in a fight to the death. Rancor, Achor, and Thornton proudly flaunt that name. Did I tell you I was an anthropologist before I became a car-selling psychologist and a pig-farming fisherman?"

"And before that, you were a lawyer and a computer hacker. I know you already said that. Maybe I'm a little dizzy from all the drugs and driving, my roaring headache, and this delightful food. But I want to talk more about the Nithings. You just mentioned them again. They have my family. And then I want to know more about my Uncle Flynn Pompatella."

"Well, good, you're finally listening. The best cure for dizziness and headache, Newby, is cleaning dishes. Take them down to Wicky Wacky Creek over there and scrub them out good with sand, some good old pig fat soap I've got here, and a pig tail scrubber." Nambo stretched and belched, and scratched his extended stomach. "I need to meditate and get ready for our next leg of the trip. I tend to snore when I meditate so don't rouse me no matter what, unless a big bear or a naked woman comes into camp. Got

121

that, Rooster? Not a naked bear, not even a small bear, just a big bear or a fully naked woman."

With that he promptly slid back against a tree, shut his eyes, and almost instantly started meditating louder than anybody Rey had ever heard. It sounded more like a chainsaw, interspersed with some incendiary and fragrant farts.

It was obvious he wasn't going to get any more scrambled information from the snoozing lunatic—at least until Nambo woke up. Rey grumbled as he washed the dishes, but he admittedly did forget about his headache. What an amazing old man. If even half of what he said was true, it was astonishing. The bit about his missing Uncle Flynn Pompatella was an amazing coincidence, or was it?

Rey hated to be suspicious, but he was starting to detect a suspiciously tangled plot here. Maybe his nomination to be President wasn't just a computer glitch or a social media miracle moment. He quickly realized too much thinking was going to give him another headache. He finished the dishes, briefly admired the plump trout swimming in Wicky Wacky Creek, put the table, chairs, pans, and dishes away in Spirit, and then climbed into the back of the vehicle and began to relax. He tried not to worry about his family and especially what his boys were thinking about him being missing. No matter how hard he tried to block it out of his mind, though, he worried about Thornton Nithing being around his family. Finally, a full stomach and the warm sun got the best of him. Soon he was meditating as loudly as old Nambo.

When he finally woke up, Rey realized they had been on the road again for some time and were bumping down a deeply rutted track into what appeared to be a huge tree farm. At least there was a small forest, with trees decked out with what appeared to be colorful treehouses. He also saw teepee-like structures, with what appeared to be some Mongolian yurts, lots of ponds, and tons of children. He saw a few small pigs, but they were mostly being prodded along or carried by little kids and by a few seedy-looking older people who could have been lawyers at one time. He also saw lots of small Shetland ponies and burros either pulling carts or being ridden by laughing children.

When the rickety vehicle called Spirit finally stopped, a friendly looking, fuzzy-headed alpaca stuck its inquisitive head in the window and stared at Rey with a goofy expression and began nibbling on his fake beard. To the side of the bumpy road, a huge banner was hanging over a big old red barn that said: "Welcome to Crazy Jake Nambo's PReservation for the Temporarily Bewildered." First, he noticed the letter P had been added to the sign, making it read "Preservation" instead of "Reservation." And then he noticed the short, pudgy Sedgewick Clayton Sewell, the former President, of all people, coming out to greet him with no lifts in his shoes. Blazing red hair replaced Sewell's formerly majestic white mane, and he was surrounded by a jumble of happily singing and dancing children. His grin was a mile wide, and he was wildly waving his arms. "Welcome, friend! Welcome!"

≡ CHAPTER**8** ≡

Welcome to Paradise: Please Herd the Pigs!

Sedgewick Clayton Sewell approached Rey, signaling silence with a finger to his lips. He hugged Rey and whispered in his ear: "Eyes and ears everywhere, even here, so we need to be careful. My new name is Tarkington Barch. Now let me formally welcome you to paradise, Brewster 'Brew' Blackoak, P.O.T.U.S. on the lam. Contrary to rumor, I am not demented, but sometimes it seems it might help. I see you have spent time with Crazy Jake Nambo, so you are now officially temporarily bewildered, as if you weren't before!"

Then Sewell stood back, took a good long look at Rey, and quietly observed: "The fake black beard and scratchy new growth is a nice touch, by the way—definitely not presidential, unless maybe you're trying to look a little bit like an emaciated, unshaven Richard Nixon, or perhaps a shorter and crazier version of Abraham Lincoln!"

Rey shook his arms to get some circulation going and then did a few jumping jacks and stretched his legs. The little kids who had accompanied Sewell were already swamping Nambo. They were swarming in from all over, like darting little minnows, and it looked as though he was pulling candy from their ears and noses, making it magically appear out of thin air. Then he started playing a reed pipe he pulled out of one of his many pockets. Like a pied piper, Nambo led the kids off into a huge barn.

"So, he's a magician and a musician, too?" Rey asked, flabbergasted by the multi-talented old guy.

"And he's a damned good lawyer, if there is such a thing. Turned psychologist, turned anthropologist, turned used car salesman, and, don't forget, pig-farming fisherman," answered Sewell, now Tarkington Barch, shaking his head. "He is truly an amazing man, but one among many in this crazy, off-kilter place."

"Most amazingly, he is related to Zara Tallaree, and a nemesis to the Nithings," Rey added. "Somewhere in there I also picked up a connection to my late mother's Pewamo tribe and possibly to my long-lost Uncle Flynn Pompatella."

"Flynn Pompatella? He's your uncle?" the former President asked Rey with an amazed expression. "Curiouser and curiouser, as they say. Quite the string of coincidences. Flynn's part Irish, I hear, but mostly Pewamo. He wanders through here quite a bit. He helped Nambo get tribal recognition for a local band of Native Americans called the Pockatoo Mucky-tuck, a long-lost branch of the Pewamo, distant cousins of the Potawatomi. Now they hold this land in trust, literally an independent nation. Under both American and international law, the USA can't legally touch it. Sweet deal, huh? A lot of tribes put casinos on their trusts, and that's their right, but your Uncle Flynn Pompatella and his Pockatoo Mucky-tuck friends, along with Nambo, some dude named Reverend Louie Pastore, and others of the dangerous church persuasion decided to put homes for temporarily bewildered people on theirs."

Wanting to know just what sort of off-kilter place the self-proclaimed crazy man had brought him to, Rey started peppering the former Sedgewick Sewell with questions, mostly about these reservations for the temporarily bewildered.

"They are places, sanctuaries I guess you could call them, where people who are lost, broken, and homeless, with their 'souls flattened,' as Nambo says, can come and get rejuvenated, get their legs and lives back, so to speak. It's a place where people whose brains are scrambled from negative thoughts and repeated losing can discover their real strengths and potential. They learn 'success strategies,' as Nambo calls them. Lots of hard work, discipline, and a ton of encouragement and positive psychology does the trick for most of them. No freeloaders allowed. You start out herding pigs, burros, or alpacas, a humbling experience, I can tell you. Herding the little suckers for weeks almost made me appreciate Congress! Then you work up to growing crops, raising and catching fish, and then finally move on to other things, like making toys for kids and building structures. Eventually, you get to wear a green sash, which signifies a mentor and healer of people."

The former golden orator paused for a breath. Then he started in again with great enthusiasm, waving his hands for emphasis. "Notice I can do this without a teleprompter! My heart is in this! People here help you discover your strengths and how to put them to work. People come here broken and leave enthusiastically engaged and with new purpose to their lives. They go from being victims to being victors. Some go back to start soup kitchens, others raise food in their community, and some even establish small businesses with the skills taught here. Others act as volunteers, mentoring in schools, whatever they can do to make a difference. We want to retake the communities. We want to rescue and restore the lost and broken people."

"It sounds like communism," Rey said, startling himself as he realized he was sounding almost like P.T. and the Nithing boys. "Wow, now where did that come from? Maybe I was getting brainwashed by the Nithing and NAP machine after all!"

"It is absolutely not communism," Sewell charged on, completely unfazed by Rey's comment. "It's just the idea of getting everybody a good start. Nambo says it's not about reparations but about repairing the nation, by fixing up people one person at a time. It's the old original American idea of a helping hand, or a hand up, not a hand out, like the barn raisings they did in the pioneer days. The community pitches in and helps those who are trying to help themselves."

Sewell paused for a quick breath, his eyes feverish with excitement. "Sometimes we get old-fashioned hippies here, and they either pitch in or get pitched out. Anybody hurts a child here, he or she becomes pig food. Believe me, no psychopaths here. Nambo says he smells the lizard people miles away. He calls them that because he says their lizard brains overwhelm their amygdala and prefrontal cortexes. Wherever the emotions are. Are you following me so far, or do I sound too much like Nambo?"

"Believe it or not, I think I'm following you. You're a little more linear than old Nambo, so I can more easily follow your train of thought. I can see you are genuinely excited, not a zombie like you appeared back in DC. Speaking of Nambo, the man does carry on, doesn't he? A real stream-of-consciousness speaker."

"Nambo is just testing you. He's not sure he can trust you yet. His big thing is listening. He struggled for years to learn to listen well, and now he is a listening fanatic. He teaches people that the whole transformation begins with learning to listen authentically to people. 'First seek to understand, then to be understood,' is a favorite maxim he borrowed from somebody. Everything we teach here is based on positive interactions that build positive relationships. For example, he stresses that we should have a high positivity ratio in all our relationships. You can measure it in any organization or relationship. It's called Losada's line. It's named after Marcial Losada, a Brazilian genius who did an analytical study over ten years and with thousands of people on how they interact. You must have 2.9013—we rounded it off to three—positive interactions to every negative one just to break even, or both you and the other person suffer grave consequences. Nambo is always muttering, 'three to one, three to one,' especially with people like you and me, people he considers dolts."

Rey vaguely recalled Nambo muttering about three to one after making three positive comments about him back at Wicky Wacky Creek. Now things were becoming a little clearer.

"Three to one is just to break even and undo the damage from one negative interaction," Sewell went on, his enthusiasm still going strong. "Six to one is ideal. When you have a high positivity ratio in your relationships, people feel better and do better in life. Positive interactions are encouraging, instructive, and respectful. Negative interactions are discouraging, destructive, and contemptuous or cool. The higher the ratio of positive to negative, the better." Realizing he was lecturing again, the former President stopped.

Seeing Rey's confused look, he explained: "For example, we teach all of our new people here to do a '15-10-5' exercise. Fifteen feet away we make eye contact with people we meet, at ten we smile, and at five we say the person's name or give them a positive greeting and the thumbs-up sign. Believe it or not, Nambo learned all about this at Penn, the university, not the state pen, working on one of his doctorates. When we do this, both people's mirror neurons fire, making them feel better. If you're smiling, the dopamine neurotransmitters go up, enabling faster and more effective learning and retention. Serotonin levels go up, producing feelings of well-being, and oxytocin hormone levels go up, helping people feel friendlier, more trusting, and more bonded to each other. When all this happens, your helper T-cells go up, building up your immune system. Also, cortisol, the stress-related hormone goes down, and so does the blood pressure. Nambo teaches all this stuff to everybody here. It's all supported by research at Mayo Clinic, Harvard Medical School, and at Penn by some geeky dude named Martin Seligman. It works! He's always teaching about neuroplasticity, the ability of the brain to continuously repurpose neurons, learn, and change. He says if you want to change the world, change the way people think."

The former President's ease in rattling off all the scientific details was impressive, even if Rey didn't understand half of it. "There's no test on this, is there?" he asked, laughing. "By the way, not bad for a demented and retired President!"

Sewell went on in a lowered voice, watching to see that no one around them was listening to two apparently doddering old fools. "Uh, well! I don't brag about it, but before I got tangled up in the political machine and with the Nithing monsters, I got degrees in both civil engineering and physics. I was a professor at a good state university. The Nithings thought that sounded too pointy-headed, or at least that idiot Bylow Bellwater did, so they changed it all." He hung his head in shame and continued: "They plied me with beautiful women, expensive booze, and good food—so I willingly went along. Actually, I was an easy target, until Zara made me see the light."

Rey jumped in. "Speaking of Zara, is she really old Nambo's niece?"

"Oh, yes, most definitely. I don't know the full story, but I'm sure she can fill you in. Again, let me say, don't be fooled by him. He was diagnosed as having Asperger's Syndrome as a child—you know, a high-functioning autistic individual. He was a genius, especially in math, earning his first doctorate at fourteen, but he was a bust at social interactions. Eccentric and isolated, he really couldn't work with others. He came across as cold and stilted. 'Highest IQ ever recorded in this state,' Zara claims, but he will be the first to tell you that means nothing. Without positive relationships, even the brightest person is miserable. Realizing his weakness, Nambo decided to study people and gradually became an expert at building positive relationships, eventually getting another doctorate in Psychology at Penn, working with that Martin Seligman fellow I mentioned earlier. Along the way, he also became a phenomenal teacher. He is not a natural teacher, if there is any such thing, but he teaches from the heart. The 'heart and the art' of teaching he calls it. He has earned three doctorates and a law degree altogether. He is what I call 'chronically curious,' has an eidetic, or what's sometimes called a photographic memory, and, if he suffers from anything, it is idearrhea—too many ideas and not always enough time for implementation. That's where I am going to help him out," Sewell concluded. Seeing Rey's questioning look, he just smiled.

Later that afternoon, at an orientation session for people new to the Reservation for the Temporarily Bewildered, Rey got the chance to watch Nambo in action. It was an amazing show that would change his life in a dramatic fashion. Attendance was mandatory, one of the few things you had to do if you wanted to stay, along with earning your keep and following a few basic rules of respect.

"I'm Jake Nambo. Welcome to the Reservation for the Temporarily Bewildered. Our objective here is to help you reverse the curse. I am referring to the curse of rejection, the pain of being lost and broken. I want you to know you are already good enough for God and good enough for us. But working together, we can get you even better, healed and strong and back in the battle! You can be victors and not victims!"

Rey was taken aback by Nambo's opening remarks. The formerly gnarled-up, old country bumpkin was suddenly standing straight and communicating with an electric and commanding voice. He was speaking unaided by any teleprompter. His comments obviously were coming straight from his heart, and flames seemed to shoot from the intense eyes beneath his bushy eyebrows as he mesmerized the rag-ged group of new refugees.

"We want to help move people from the slavery of learned helplessness to the liberation of realistic learned optimism as you discover and unleash the strengths within you." Sensing some wariness in the group, he softened his voice. "Look, I know many of you have been lied to and manipulated by some pretty mean characters: con artists, shysters, and sales-men. I hope you have looked around here and picked up on the fact that people here are genuinely joyful, well fed, and se-cure. They are kept here by love and not force. We don't force anyone to follow our ways, or even to believe what we believe, but we do insist you follow five simple rules." He pointed a knobby finger at the wall and had the group read along with him:

1. If you don't work, you don't eat.
2. You do no harm to another individual or yourself.
3. You treat everyone with dignity and respect, including yourself.
4. You treat other people as more important than yourself.
5. You attend class every day and build on your strengths.

"I could expand on each of these, but I don't want to overwhelm you. Five simple rules to change your life. We be-lieve each of you is a unique creation designed to do great things, whether you believe it or not. Our aim is to help you learn how to interact better and build positive relationships. We want each of you to become enthusiastically engaged in life, find a calling, open your mind to new ideas and learning versus having a closed mindset, and learn to achieve some success by identifying and developing your strengths. Your brain can learn new things all the time. It's called neuroplasticity. No matter how old or young, you can continue to grow your brain!"

Rey could see many expressions of disbelief but also glimmerings of hope. These people had been beaten down for years and were justifiably suspicious, but Nambo's obvious passion and loving smile were real. And he was just getting wound up.

"These people with green sashes are going to be your mentors in this process. They've been where you have been and have gone through our process. They are living testaments that it works. Our objective is for you to leave here with the strength and skills to go back and protect and build your communities. You will learn self-protection skills from my mom, Sister Mary Contrary Jones, and her team, so the bullies and thugs will learn to leave you and your loved ones alone. You will learn how to set up small micro-banks within your community as well as how to build businesses and organizations that will strengthen your communities and create jobs. We call what we do 'evangineering,' giving you a vision, the tools, and a doable dream. You've heard of Reconquista, the taking back of the land? Well, this is recolonizing our communities, taking them back from the corrupt leadership, cartels, gangs, and thugs and making them great places to live and grow again."

Nambo then laid out a simple regimen they would all follow. Everyone was encouraged to wake up early, eat a big breakfast, exercise, work on assigned tasks around the place, and then engage in a learning activity. After a healthy lunch, everyone would take a brief nap, exercise again, and then get back to work or education. After dinner, there would be time around a bonfire for storytelling and singing.

Nambo emphasized that anyone could leave at any time. He also announced that no electronic devices, including cellphones and personal computers, were allowed on site. If someone wanted to call a loved one or family member, there was a computer room and a phone bank with a secure and hack-proof satellite uplink where people could go during their free time, but they were warned not to give out their location to anyone.

All gadgets, weapons, and drugs were then collected. None in the group chose to leave, but there was some grumbling, especially among those who were addicted to the screens on their gadgets.

Once the orientation was concluded, the newcomers with whom Rey was placed were given red sashes and told they could wander anywhere on the nearly ten thousand acres and ask any questions. They were to reconvene at the nighttime campfire for storytelling and singing. Then bright and early the next morning, they would get rolling on the proposed regimen that would strengthen their physical, mental, and spiritual well-being.

As he decided where to roam, Rey could see everyone seemed to be encouraging each other and helping the few laggards, having a great time themselves. You could see the change from beleaguered defeatism to a sudden spring in the step. As Nambo said, hope alone is not a strategy, but with skills, hard work, and the right mindset, it will work. It struck Rey as a cross between a boot camp and a revival meeting, although no specific religion was being preached. He noticed all the regulars were seemingly happy though, and everyone hustled about the grounds with an energetic sense of purpose.

As Rey wandered around the place, he was struck by how easily the men and women on the Reservation for the Temporarily Bewildered got along. They seemed to relate in a wonderfully friendly and unguarded manner. When he later mentioned this to the former President, Sewell explained: "Well, everyone here learns quickly they have to follow the five rules, which are strictly enforced by their peers and mentors. Also, the women who have been here a week or two have been through the self-defense course taught by Nambo's mom, Sister Mary Contrary Jones, alias the 'Ninja Nun,' or, as some call her, the 'Howlin' Shaolin Sister.' To make a long story short, the men don't mess with the women here, except to treat them as their equal."

Intrigued, Rey prodded Sewell: "Tell me more about Nambo's mom."

"Sister Mary Contrary used to work for Mother Teresa, whom she still fondly calls 'Mamma T.' They smuggled unwanted babies—such as those with Down Syndrome and other birth defects, as well as partial birth abortion survivors—to India, where Mamma T and the nuns placed the babies with loving Indian families. They also handled adoptions and placements for other disabled and disfigured people in countries like India. Mamma T said she would take them all and love them, so Americans wouldn't kill them. But our national pride and politics soon stopped that. That's when Sister Mary Contrary teamed up with her adopted son, the old mahogany maestro, AKA Crazy Jake Nambo, and started the first of several reservations for the temporarily bewildered. They also helped to found a few places like this outside the United States. But most of the unwanted and cast away they kept here, loving them and giving them meaningful lives."

"Go on," said Rey. "Tell me how Nambo and this Sister Mary Contrary first linked up."

"Nambo's natural mom died early. Some say she was killed by Rancor Nithing, the Nithing boy's hideous dad. Nambo ended up in an orphanage where there was a study of the concept called 'contact comfort' conducted in the 1940s and '50s. A large control group of institutionalized babies just got normal institutional care. They were fed and diapered, and that was it. The experimental group got an hour a day of holding and cuddling from special mothers, meaning mentally challenged older girls. After a number of years, the researchers were stunned to find that, as they grew older, the experimental 'hugged and cuddled' group far surpassed in achievement children their own age in the general population. The control group getting just the minimal institutionalized care stayed institutionalized. In her work with Mamma T, Sister Mary Contrary heard about the study and tried to save all the kids. Unfortunately, she got into trouble with the researchers and a few leading people in her order for messing with the study. Undeterred, she decided to become what she calls 'an undercover mother' and help at least one of the children. So, despite her single, religious, and professional status as a nun, she somehow was able to adopt Jake. At the time, he was a two-year-old toddler who was already showing signs of being an anti-social prodigy. With his mixed race and Asperger's Syndrome, it was unlikely he would ever escape the institution or be adopted. Fortunately, though, Jake had for a brief while been in the cuddled experimental group, and Sister Mary Contrary was able to help him cultivate all his gifts. As she likes to say, she raised him 'from a pup, up.'"

Rey was amazed with this story and began to think he had sorely underestimated the strange man.

"Like I told you earlier," Sewell continued, "he ended up being quite a prodigy, the 'Mahogany Maestro,' as his admirers refer to him. Despite the Asperger's, or maybe because of it, he blossomed intellectually. He would become fanatically focused on a subject and study until he knew every detail. He was preternaturally bright and quite articulate as a youngster. He could talk endlessly and monotonously about the intricacies of anything that caught his imagination. He especially liked all sorts of technology such as radios, radar, and, later, computers. But he couldn't relate socially with most people. Largely because of Sister Mary Contrary and her love for him, he finally learned how to get along with others.

"Interestingly, Nambo has played a hidden but key role in the advancement of technology. If the truth be known, when people talk about Apple, Jake Nambo should be mentioned along with Wozniak and Jobs. He also worked with Microsoft, and his name should be listed along with Paul Allen and Bill Gates. He just kept getting chased out of the companies by jealous technocrats and later even the psychopaths of NAP—but not before he parlayed his first billion into a lot more billions."

"Wait, wait," Rey stuttered. "What do you mean by his first billion? You don't really mean he's made many billions, as in dollars, do you?"

"Yes, I mean billions, plural. Nambo has this thing about numbers. Psychologists call it synesthesia. He sees colors along with all the numbers. Each number is a distinct color. It's like his wiring is all crossed in the sensory part of his brain. One sensory pathway crosses over to another sensory pathway. Somehow it helps him see numbers differently, especially patterns and relationships. He claims he sees and hears much more than the normal person does.

"Let me tell you how he got started. Jake got his first doctorate at age fourteen. But even with a PhD, he couldn't get a job because of his age and because he had terrible people skills. So he lied about his age to get a job driving a bus. Suddenly, all these crazy algorithms hit him, he says, like they were flashing a neon rainbow in his brain."

Seeing Rey's confusion, Sewell explained: "Algorithms are not the tunes the former Vice President in the Clinton Administration danced to. Horrible joke, I know. They are more like patterns, or formulas to help you predict things. Somehow, out of the blue, Jake figured out a set of them to accurately predict the commodities and stock markets with a far better than normal success rate. He took his money from driving the bus, and some he borrowed from Sister Mary Contrary, and went to Chicago to work at the Commodities Exchange. Within three years, his company was worth billions and being pursued by all the big guns in the business. He happily sold out, cleaned up, and then Mary said he repaid her a million times over. The money he was still holding he put into a strange little startup called Apple and another weird one called Microsoft. It's rumored he also may have something to do with some other weirdly named former small startups called Google and Yahoo, too."

Laughing, the former President added with a gleeful gleam in his eye, "Whatever you do, don't tell that stuffed-up Melville and supercilious Samms, even Busby Marsh the arrogant dolt, but they aren't close to being the richest men in the world. Crazy Jake Nambo is. He still plays the markets. He is like a George Soros but with a soul, or Warren Buffet with a conscience and not just a billfold! He would tell you the money means nothing, that it's just a means to an end. And this is part of the end here. People have referred to this place as a colony of Heaven."

Rey was flabbergasted. He had been camping out with a gnarled old African garden gnome and didn't realize he was the richest man in the world. "You referred to his adopted mom, this Sister Mary Contrary, as the Ninja Nun, the howlin' Shaolin?"

"Well, she's no longer an 'official' sister, although she is still part of a religious order. As I said earlier, she refers to herself as 'an undercover mother,' so to say. Her church still loves her but decided she is a little too dangerous, too toxic, riling up important people by sneaking kids and disfigured people off to India, confronting politicians, and disrupting research on humans and everything. So she functions underground. A guerilla sister! Since she was going into the toughest parts of towns, she also realized she was a target for the criminally inclined. With the money Nambo gave her, she took up Krav Maga, the martial arts taught by the Israeli Defense

Forces—you know, the IDF—and supposedly perfected by the Mossad, the Israeli version of our CIA. It was originally developed before World War II by a Jewish martial arts expert to help unarmed Jewish people defend themselves against the growing Nazi threat. It's all about grappling and furious punching to produce a quick kill.

"Once Sister Mary Contrary got her second billion from Jake, she got so intrigued she went over and studied with the Shaolin Kung Fu monks in China to learn to fight blindfolded and know where your enemies are by sensing them. Then she went to Brazil to learn Brazilian karate and other martial arts. She has seamlessly knitted them all into her own unique form of motherly martial arts she calls Bully Blaster. She effectively and efficiently teaches people to be self-defense experts. She also teaches all the people here, young and old alike, who want to learn how to accurately and safely shoot, then earn concealed-carry certificates. They also learn how to make a weapon out of almost any available object. She says she hopes they never have to use any of these skills, but, like her, many of them are going back into violent places where gangs and killers are commonplace and want to prey on the weak, lost, and broken."

"Is someone squealing on me?" A mirth-filled voice came from behind Rey. He turned to find a four-foot-six, elfin-faced woman in a brightly colored nun's habit. Sister Mary Contrary stood facing Rey, with her chin tilted up and her hands on her hips, with her feet placed firmly on the ground, but far apart, considering her small size. Despite knowing she had to be past eighty, Rey thought she could pass for a spry fifty at most. Sister Mary Contrary fixed Rey with a straightforward gaze and then nodded sharply, saying: "I think I could make you into a fighter, given a few months! You look a little soft around the middle, though," she said and poked him gently with a finger that was just a blur, it was done so quickly, making him jump. "Well, maybe take me longer! Reaction's a little slow there, son."

"Uh, Sister Mary," Sewell whispered, "on a need-to-know-only basis, this is the current President." He continued with a sly grin on his face: "The one and only Rey Newly, known officially for now as Brewster Blackoak, for secrecy's sake."

"Okay, a politician," she said, obviously unimpressed. "I retract my training time estimate. It will take at least a year to make you tough, unless you count stabbing in the back as fighting."

"Ouch," Rey said, laughing. "If it counts for anything, I never wanted to be a politician, and, unlike this guy, I only lasted a few weeks as President before getting ejected."

"Ouch," countered Sewell, reacting to the true if unintended jibe. "I'm going to report you to the peer review board for hurting my feelings!"

"Boys, boys!" Mary teased, laughing. Then reaching out her hand, she shook Rey's briskly. He felt the calluses from hard work but also felt the warmth she projected. "So, you are Flynn Pompatella's long-lost nephew. He is heading this way fast. As soon as he found out you were out of the Nithings' clutches, he contacted us and is taking the underground railway to get here." Seeing Rey's confused look, she continued: "The underground railway was what people called the trails and hiding places people used to sneak the slaves from the South to freedom in the North before the Civil War. We use a similar system of safe houses, hiding places, and secret routes to move key people like Nambo, Reverend Louis Pastore, Flynn Pompatella, and even me between our places."

Suddenly a flash of awareness hit his brain. Placing Louis Pastore's name with the man he had met at the religious-industrial complex gala, Rey posed a question: "This Pastore guy I've heard mentioned, the dangerous church leader . . . He said he used to shepherd a church in Pewamo. Is that correct?"

"Among many other areas across America and overseas," she confirmed. "He first teamed up there with Jack Flynn, AKA Pompatella. That's where he met your mom and dad. Decent and kind people. It was really unfortunate that Fillups Farnswaggle and the Nithings blew up the church and many of your relatives and other innocent people with it.

"Louie Pastore and Flynn went after the killers. They formed an effective team, hunting down psychopathic killers. But they got in over their heads with the vicious Nithings and the NAP. That's when my boy Nambo corralled them and got them on our team."

Rey's head was spinning. "Wheels within wheels, huh? Too many coincidences. Did they kill my dad, too, at the brewery?"

"No, we don't think so. Probably just corporate greed and lack of safety devices in the brewery did him in. But you never know about the NAP. I don't think they ever linked him, your mom, or you to Flynn and Louie Pastore. Everyone was very careful about that. Obviously, even you never knew. When your Uncle Flynn gets here, he can fill you in on both Fillups 'Abominable' Farnswaggle, the Nithings, and the whole NAP nastiness. Believe me; he never forgot you or your mom. He just couldn't get close to you or else the NAP creatures would discover you and use you as leverage. I do know he did send your mom frequent but discreet payments to help keep your family afloat, especially after your dad died."

After more animated discussion about the work of the reservation, Sister Mary Contrary hustled off to teach a self-defense class. "I'll get to you later, Rooster, and see what you're made of. Maybe I can teach you to stop being a meat-filled piñata at a Pitbull party! All in love, of course!"

Later that day, Rey and Sewell sat in on an advanced class taught by Nambo. He was excitedly explaining why positive social interactions were so important and why everybody did the 15-10-5 thing here at the reservation. "So many of us have invisible barriers keeping us from realizing our potential and keeping us victims, not victors," Nambo explained. He showed a video of a happy pike in a tank full of tasty minnows. Whenever it was hungry, the big fish would just flick its powerful tail and gobble one of the hapless minnows huddled in the corner. Then one night, the devious psychologists put a clear sheet of glass in the tank between the dozing pike and the anxious minnows. Now, whenever the pike decided to feast, instead of a tasty minnow, he slammed his head violently into the glass plate, sending water flying everywhere. After a day of complete frustration and minnow deprivation, the glass plate was removed. What followed was shocking to the class. Even though the barrier was no longer there, the pike assumed he could not get to the minnows. Even when the minnows started bumping into him and swimming around him, he still didn't react. Eventually, he starved to death in a tank full of minnows.

Nambo continued: "Two things we learn here. Number one, don't trust those devious psychologists. Number two, we all have invisible barriers of some sort blocking us from a positive life and success. What are yours?" he asked.

What followed was a lively give-and-take describing possible barriers. He launched into a description of some people walking around with invisible vultures—negative thoughts and poor self-image—circling over their heads, attracted by "road-kill thinking," as Nambo called it. Other people had invisible banners over them proclaiming them winners. What made the difference? It was the invisible "love bucket" he claimed they all carried. Negative "vulture" people have empty love buckets with holes in them. Positive "banner" people, on the other hand, have buckets brimming with love. How does this happen? He explained that all of us also have invisible dippers or droppers. We either draw love, like water, out of a person's bucket by frowning at them, saying destructive things to them, ignoring them and the like. Or we can use our droppers to put love in their bucket by smiling at them, making eye contact, saying their name, properly praising them, encouraging, and treating them with dignity and respect.

It was a great description of positive interactions and how it was important to have a ratio of at least three to one to build a person up, six to one, if possible. The point was, each devastating negative could undo three positives. Rey was saddened to think how many times he had failed to meet or exceed this ratio with his boys, and especially with Prissy. He knew if—no, when—he ever got another chance, he would be more encouraging, instructive, and respectful in dealing with all of them, maybe even old P.T.

A massive horde of yelling and laughing children disrupted hope of any further conversations in the class, as the children came rushing through the woods and headed up a hill. "It is obviously getting close to dinner time," Sewell said. "I assume Nambo fed you something today? He often forgets normal people need to eat."

"Actually, he did a bang-up job. If dinner is anywhere close to as good, I'm going to gain a lot of weight," Rey said, still savoring the sumptuous breakfast.

"This will be even better," Sewell added, his mouth watering. "Then, after dinner, we go to a celebration campfire for singing, magic tricks, storytelling, and roasting marshmallows. But don't worry about getting fat. You'll begin working it off in the morning with exercises, farm work, herding pigs, and Sister Mary beating you into shape! Remember, if you don't work, you don't eat around here!"

The dining barn was the huge hulk of a bright red building Rey had seen earlier. It was jammed with incredibly long rows of spotlessly clean picnic tables covered by red-checkered tablecloths. Fragrant smells of freshly baked bread and pies, along with other delectable and yet unidentified savory scents, were wafting from every open window and door. Hundreds of people from all directions were merrily plunging in to wash their hands under the keen-eyed surveillance of a woman with a t-shirt that read, "The Mom in Me Counts." Only after they had passed her clean hands-face-ears inspection did they get to take a seat. Even Rey and Sewell had to pass!

Everyone was no sooner seated than Nambo stood up

and quieted the group. "Let's take a minute and each one in your own way say a heartfelt, grateful thank you to the Great One who created such delightful creatures as the octopus, the platypus, and all of us weird people for all of our blessings." He paused briefly to playfully scowl at a few of the young ones who had giggled at his "octopus and platypus and all of us" line. "I know each one of you has been asked to keep a gratitude list and add at least three new things every day. Thank Him for those. Also, thank Him for all the things that went well today, at least three of them. Thank Him for another day of peace and plenty. Let's have a moment of silence as we praise Him and thank Him, and bless those who prepared the food, please."

After a brief, reverent silence, and with a loud shout of "Amen" from Nambo, all bedlam broke loose. Huge, steaming trenchers of savory potatoes dripping with butter went sailing by, going hand to hand, followed by heaps of mouth-watering pork and chicken slathered with rich gravy, and all sorts of roasted vegetables and warm homemade bread. The sumptuous food just kept coming down the rows of tables in an endless production line. Everyone took turns filling each other's drinks and making sure the littlest and oldest got fed first. Sister Mary Contrary patrolled the tables, making sure a modicum of manners prevailed and everyone was being helped.

Rey soon proved very adept at ladling food to his plate from the fast-moving serving dishes while helping a child next to him also get a good plate, and soon both their plates were overflowing. His only mistake was when he asked someone to pass the bread and he got hit in the head with half a loaf tossed his way. Rey was quickly stuffed, much to his chagrin, when more plates of delectable desserts, fruit pies, and confections, drizzled and drenched in honey and powdered sugar, came flying down the line.

"All prepared by loving hands and tender hearts," Sewell burped after devouring a luscious chocolate fudge cake with ice cream that dripped down his jowls. "Best food in the land. Have you ever seen so many joyful people in one place?"

After everyone was stuffed, each table held a discussion all about the things that had gone well that day. Then a production line of children and young adults swooped all the plates off the tables and into the kitchen where soapy hot water was splattering around like a demented fountain, but somehow both the dishes and people got rapidly and spotlessly clean, and everything put back in the proper cabinets and drawers.

Over the whole banquet hall, a banner was hung from wall to wall that said: "Do all the good that you can, in all the ways you can, in all the places you can, at all the times you can, to all the people you can, whenever you can." Rey recognized it as a quote from John Wesley, co-founder of the Methodist Church.

On another wall was a banner that read: "Always tell the truth in love." As far as Rey could see, both banners portrayed well the behavior he observed all around him.

Then they all moved outdoors into the balmy night weather for the celebration campfire and introduction of new reservation attendees. It was a time of singing and great sharing. Nambo amused everyone with amazing magic tricks, and then Sister Mary Contrary proved to be an exquisite guitar player, song leader, and storyteller. Many of the children got into the act doing skits, telling original stories, or singing songs to thunderous applause. Finally, the littlest ones started to doze off, and people slowly left the diminishing bonfire to head to their teepees, yurts, and treehouses.

Rey looked up to see Nambo gesturing for him to join him as he walked away from the fire. They walked a while to get away from the milling crowds of cheerful, laughing people and soon came to the fragrant pigpens. "Be careful and don't fall in," Nambo cautioned him in a somber voice. "You'll scare the pigs! Then they will tromp you, crap on you, and then eat you, just like a lot of people in DC." Then he added smiling, "But, at least, pigs are quick about it, good to eat, and we could eventually recycle you! That's three good ones!"

They walked silently on past the pens and out into an orchard full of apple trees, and then into a pine and hardwood forest, until they finally reached a clearing with a beautiful lake reflecting the brilliant stars. "So, young man, what do you think of our Reservation for the Temporarily Bewildered so far?"

"I'm blown away," Rey said honestly, noticing Nambo had dropped the bumpkin persona he had used earlier at Wicky Wacky Creek. "Just the three-to-one rule made me stop and think about how many invisible vultures and barriers I may have." He paused, and then brought up a touchy subject: "I am just a little concerned about the overt religious overtones, if you don't mind my saying."

"Well, first off, we are privately funded, and attendance is voluntary, except for you, of course. But second, and most importantly, we don't force anyone to believe anything. We have all different faiths here, and, believe me, all are welcome.

No proselytizing takes place. On the other hand, we make no excuses about our faith. I firmly believe that the creator and maker of all things, untethered by time, the great star maker, Elohim Bara as our Hebrew friends say, loves each person and wants him or her to know Him. Also, undeniably, the USA was founded largely on Judeo-Christian principles, and we are not going to deny it."

Seeing Rey was not going to argue, Nambo continued: "You know anthropologists have studied thousands of different cultures, Rey. No matter how isolated each group of people were, every one of them had a concept of the afterlife and some form of higher being or beings, a 'God-shaped hole in the soul' as the book of Ecclesiastes says. So, we just skip any sermons and try to live our faith, being sermons with shoes on, 'living testimonies of love' as the Apostle Paul wrote. We feel all people need physical, mental, as well as spiritual strength to get on well in life. I tell people who disagree that we can argue theology after we rescue all of God's lost and broken children. We don't believe it is their fate to be hungry and hurting. We believe we are to be the hands and heart of a loving God. However, we also don't want people to pretend to believe something to get fed. If they are touched by our concern, or by the way our faith moves us to do good works, so be it. If not, we feed them and love them anyway. If the people we feed don't see the love of God in us, where will they find it? To quote some old song, they've 'been looking for love in all the wrong places.' Our country and communities are broken, many people are lost, and we are determined that we are going to do something about it."

Rey nodded his head in agreement. "I agree that Christianity and other faiths need to step up and help more instead of expecting the government to do it," Rey said, reminded of the smug religious-industrial complex people he met earlier. "Some of the so-called believers, they probably don't mind your clothing or feeding the poor, something they know they should do themselves, but they don't seem to want them in their church pews! I guess it disturbs their peace and order!"

"There are very active warriors of the faith like Louie Pastore and his 'dangerous' church movement," Nambo added. "They help us feed people and protect them in the inner-city communities where we're working. They open their churches during the coldest weather. But, overall, much more could be done by the mainstream churches. When you have government involved, it just gives another opening for the psychopaths to control and manipulate needy people," said Nambo. "We don't need big government, just more people with big hearts."

"One more thing on this religion question," Nambo continued, "and then I'll drop it. I'm a mathematician. I see numbers differently from most people. One thing I do know is that we have an intricately fine-tuned universe, meticulously organized solar system, and unbelievably complex but balanced planet—hundreds of factors minutely calibrated for one purpose, I believe: to support life here on Earth. I can't even begin to imagine, mathematical genius that I supposedly am, the odds against it all happening by chance without some intelligent guidance. It must be multiple trillions to one. I believe we are not cosmic accidents." Seeing that Rey was satisfied, they walked on.

"On another subject, Rey, I noticed you seemed to be

enjoying the love bucket discussion on invisible barriers, vultures, and banners. Whether it takes six weeks or six months, we are trying to give every person that comes through here an advanced degree in grit. Our society is good at beating people down, flattening their souls. We want them to learn how to combat that and build themselves and other people up, to be victors not victims. We also teach them better people skills as well as decision making, problem solving, goal setting, and other skills they need to have meaningful and successful lives. Our goal is to start a peaceful revolution to transform minds and build positive, strong people who are able to stand up to the sharks in suits and thugs in the gangs and cartels. We want our people to be like the Ibo or Igbo in Nigeria, Africa, like the Navajo and Pewamo here in America, and the Chimbu people in New Guinea. These groups all have in common the fact they are versatile, agile, entrepreneurial, and aggressively adaptable, resilient survivors who thrive on adversity and use it to grow stronger."

As they continued to talk and walk over the land, Rey couldn't help but become ever more impressed with Nambo the man and his active mind. It was obvious he wanted to rebuild or heal the land—and that he wouldn't rest until he had accomplished that goal.

"It's ridiculous, Rey, that we can't fix our broken and lost people and feed our homeless. It's estimated there are a minimum of 240 trillion dollars in energy assets in this country alone—with oil, natural gas, and coal, plus much more to discover. Then think of the potential in solar and wind. We also have huge tracts of forest going to waste that could be wisely harvested for fiber and building materials without harm to the ecosystem. Here in America we also have some of the richest farmland in the world, most of the great universities, and many of the great innovative companies. The total net assets of the USA could easily top 500 trillion dollars. We have all of this, but we act like we're poor! We don't need more government. Just get the bureaucrats out of the way and turn the good, big-hearted people loose."

On a roll, Nambo continued: "I see us faced with four big challenges. The first is the power of the psychopaths. You've faced this. Ferocious predators. They now know we can identify them and possibly deal with them. They are completely unencumbered with conscience or compassion, and they have an insatiable thirst for dominance, power, and control at any cost.

"Second, we have the rise of narcissism and the decline of empathy. All the studies show our young people are becoming more self-absorbed and less concerned about others. I believe a large part of this is due to the amount of screen time children are experiencing! Eight to ten hours a day!" Seeing Rey's confusion, he explained: "The human face itself has over 40 muscles, and they can make over 10,000 expressions. At least 3,000 relate to emotions. We are born with a few universally recognized expressions, like fear or surprise, or smiling. All the others are learned through face-to-face time, then reinforced by storytelling. Children aren't learning these critical emotional skills anymore, because they are spending valuable developmental time either being ignored or staring at screens. That's why no screens are allowed here. Instead, kids get lots of face-time and storytelling."

Seeing Rey's positive nod and look of comprehension,

Nambo charged on, full of enthusiasm. "The third challenge is what I call 'bigism,' the idea that bigger is always better. Big government, big banks, big companies, big schools—all of them conspiring to stamp out the individual. We push a concept here called 'subsidiarity.' Subsidiarity says that the local government should never do anything that the individual can do for him- or herself. The state government should never do what the local government can do for itself. The national government should not do what the state governments can do for themselves. It's the way the Founding Fathers wanted it, creating a laboratory of the states and communities, each competing to do their best! Now we have big everything battering down the little guy and stifling independent thought, action, and innovation."

"The fourth challenge?" Rey asked.

"Well, it's either a challenge or possibly the answer. It's the advent of artificial intelligence or AI, as people call it. I'm a computer guy, and I can tell you that this is either going to be the end of us humans or the beginning of a whole new era. AI has grown by leaps and bounds, replacing humans left and right, and we need to learn to do the things computers can't or shouldn't do. The psychopaths see it as the way to grab power, to dominate and control. I see it as the way to free up humans to be truly human. Much more on that to come, believe me. My team at Hadron Group is really pounding away on how to make the advent of AI a blessing, not a curse, how to harness the marvelous machines to help us become more human."

Then he turned sad, glistening eyes to Rey for a second and began to discuss Sister Mary Contrary. "She's my adopted mom, Rey, the only one I ever had. Her big heart and courage rescued me, in some ways ending her career, and then she restored me as a real person who can relate to other people. How can I not want to do the same for others? She likes to quote Mamma T all the time, as she called Mother Teresa: 'Being unwanted, uncared for, forgotten by everybody, I think that is a much greater hunger, a much greater poverty than someone who has nothing to eat.' Our aim here is to take the unwanted, uncared for, broken, lost, and forgotten people and feed both their bodies and their souls. Then we'll turn them loose back into their neighborhoods and hometowns, rescued, restored, resilient, energized, and much stronger than they ever were before, a tremendous force for good to fight the forces of evil."

Pausing for a deep breath, Nambo energetically charged on. "Now I am no greenie weenie for sure, but think about this. If we could just restore Chesapeake Bay and the Hudson, Charles, and Columbia river estuaries with fish, and the High Plains could once again graze 100 million buffalo instead of those skinny, methane-belching, farting, polluting cows, we could almost feed the whole planet from here in America alone and still have a better place to live. It's called Tikkun Olam, heal the world. Or, if we could restore our shorelines and grow kelp and red seaweed, we could feed and fertilize the world, and harvest enough to provide all our biofuels, just from the USA. We can do it if we just develop enough people with the vision. Tikkun Olam, heal the world!"

The conversation soon switched back to the subject of psychopaths and Nambo's continuous struggle with them. "You need to learn to recognize them, Rey. They love to lie, even when the truth would serve them better, and are facile twisters of the truth. They have no compunction about killing or harming others to get power, dominance, and control. I admit I have an advantage that few people have. My sensory system is all scrambled, but it works. It's called synesthesia, and, in my case, one symptom is that when I see numbers I also see colors for them. But a second symptom I have is that when I'm around psychopaths my senses are heightened. I can smell them, and they look and sound different. They smell like rotten, road-killed, dead meat to me. Many people don't want to admit someone can have this sense, but evolutionary psychologists say the ability to sense and smell predators from a distance, a 'harm sense' if you will, would have great survival value in the wild. For me it works as well as hooking them up to all these new high-powered MRI scans and watching their brain at work, and I'm way more portable!"

"Unfortunately, I don't have that ability," Rey said, in a genuinely sad voice. "I wish I did. It would help me avoid them, or, better yet, find them and root them out, protect my family from their paws. They are all around my family now, especially my precious twin boys—and I don't know how to rescue them." Rey's voice almost broke from sadness.

"Well, then, you will need to develop the next-best skill. The key to recognizing psychopaths is to learn what are called 'micro-expressions.' They are the little tells and tendencies all people have. Everything from eye-rolls, to breathing patterns, nervous gestures, and body posture. But especially watch the eyes. For the most part, even a very skilled, habitually smooth psychopath will look up and away if he's lying, like he's reading a script. His eyes might twitch a little bit or blink more rapidly, and he'll swallow harder. His lips will go dry. The face is like a landscape, and you need to learn to read each one, like a tracker in the wilderness. Believe me, it's not easy, especially with people who feel more comfortable lying than telling the truth. But you can learn."

Nambo shared a lot more with Rey that night. It was obvious he hoped that Rey might be able to help his team somehow defeat the nasty NAP beasts. "They are a menace to all mankind. Fortunately, they have such a tremendous sense of self-grandeur and are so awed by their self-perceived brilliance and risk-taking skills that they almost always tend to underestimate the rest of us. They can be easily lied to because they have little or no recognition of the truth. Also, they want to believe the worst of everybody, because they do so of themselves. I'm convinced this infinite ability to delude themselves will lead to their ultimate downfall. Also, because they can't trust each other, they're loners even in large groups. They're constantly ready to devour each other, always looking for leverage. This can be a great advantage for us. They can't work together very well, but we can. Many capable minds in cooperation are better than one working alone. It's known as collective genius. If we can work together and collaborate as a true team, research shows the team IQ is far higher than any one individual."

Seeing that Rey was still tracking his train of thought, he went on, his voice ringing with excitement and his eyes shining with an inner fire: "My overall objective here is quite simple. I want to have people leaving the reservation recharged with a calling. It's not about having a career or gathering cash for themselves. Instead, it's about placing a focus on rescuing people and rejuvenating our devastated communities. If we can get them to develop their strengths and learn to work together with the skills and self-defense mindset we teach, we can revolutionize America and send the dominating psychopaths packing!"

Rey had wanted to ask a very troubling question for quite some time. "Well, what do we do with the psychopaths once we defeat them? I've heard it said that attempting to counsel them only helps them learn to become better psychopaths."

"Well, we would try to intercept them early in childhood. Using the already existing brain scans we discussed earlier, we could discern at a very early age who has no remorse or normal emotions, or who has brain damage to key areas. Some people refer to this as having the 'warrior gene,' which is needed to fend off predators. Whatever it is, those children without normal emotional abilities need to either be cured or controlled. If we can't teach them empathy and compassion, we would have to isolate them from the rest of humankind. They have to be kept from harming the innocent. You can't have them running loose like foxes in the chicken yard!"

"Right before I was snatched, I was in contact with one who claimed to be a Shamar, a protector or guardian." Rey was aware that Nambo flinched at this, and then the old man looked at Rey with a hostile and flinty glare.

"I am aware of these Shamar," Nambo said with a decidedly frosty and disgusted tone. "I know they are for real. I've met some, and even know some well. They're reformed psychopaths," he sniffed disdainfully. "They claim they are like wolves but with strong moral codes against preying on the weak. Predators of predators, kind of like orcas hunting down great white sharks, I take it. Maybe they should be called Shamus instead of Shamar!" He snapped this last sarcastically, with a negative shake of his head. It was apparent he was not completely convinced of the good intentions of the Shamar.

"He seemed helpful," Rey said defensively, feeling he had to stick up for his deliverer. "His name was Poger Reinbolt. He helped Zara and Snapper pull off the heist to get me here."

"The Reinbolts," Nambo said, literally spitting the name out. "I've not met either of them, but I've heard a lot. Their dad was a fierce warrior, I admit, a dangerous dude named Darius Reinbolt. I battled him, and then I heard he had a big conversion. They talk big. Reformed or converted psychopaths, I don't know if that is even possible. As a person who believes in the malleability of the human mind, I suppose I should be more optimistic about their ability to change. But I haven't seen any evidence of a true conversion. There used to be a President we referred to as all hat and no cattle. These guys are all caps and no tractors, all pigs and no shit. This Poger and his big brother Darvin claim to be the nemeses to the Nithings, working on some big computer scam to smoke them out. I've told Zara and that young idealistic Snapper pup to avoid them like the plague, not to trust them, but it's obvious I'm not being listened to."

"Maybe I'm the evidence you need to believe them," Rey said, watching for Nambo's reaction. "They reached out to help me. Somehow they plan to use me to help sideline the NAP victory parade."

"Well, I don't have to like working with them," Nambo said darkly. "This whole thing, including your botched and mangled kidnapping, is forcing us to move faster than we wanted on our own plan. This is a delicate undertaking. Lots of people's lives are at risk, as you well know. You can't just scramble and make it up as you go."

It was obvious to Rey that he was not going to convince Nambo of the validity of the motivation of the Reinbolts or the Shamar. The rest of the evening was just spent enjoyably strolling through the moonlit landscape, taking in the pleasant smells of the rich earth and still smoldering fires, hearing contented voices and laughter coming from the assembled people.

Even though he was constantly worried about his family and what they were thinking about his disappearance, Rey had to admit he immensely enjoyed the next two weeks as he explored Crazy Jake Nambo's reservation. He found the hidden airfield and reveled in watching the various homemade and restored biplanes cavorting in the sky over what he was calling Namboland. Just like all the other new folks, he woke up early, ate heartily and exercised, took all the courses, discovered some unknown strengths, and worked with the pigs, burros, and alpacas. He even got to know some reformed lawyers. He was proud when he got promoted from herder to fisherman and enjoyed wetting a line in the ponds and bringing in a good catch to add to the meals. Despite eating more than ever before, he noticed he was not gaining weight but instead was slimming down and putting on some muscle. He even learned a few deadly fighting moves from Sister Mary Contrary and grudgingly got her to admit he had a smidgeon of potential, despite being a politician. If only Prissy could see him now, he found himself thinking. And then he would sadly add, if only my boys were here safely away from the monsters.

Midway through the second week, Rey finally met his Uncle Jack Flynn Pompatella. He was busily catching tilapia and bluegills from a farm pond for dinner when he heard a rumbling voice in his ear. "You catch more fish when you don't fart so much, Sweet Baby Rey-Rey."

With the mention of his little known and only vaguely remembered boyhood nickname, the voice suddenly became familiar. Memories of being chased and tossed in the air by a burly, dark-haired gentle giant flashed in his mind. He turned to find an impressively large, raven-haired man smiling at him with dancing blue eyes that were gleaming with what looked like tears.

Seeing Rey's glance at his tearing eyes, the big man laughed. "Must be wind getting in my eyes. I can't ruin my image as a mighty Irish warrior and wooden Indian!" With that he grabbed Rey and hugged him to his big barrel chest, sobbing softly.

Rey was squeezed so hard he thought his ribs would pop. Gasping for air, he finally coughed out, "This must mean you're Uncle Jack Flynn."

Flynn finally released him and was soon answering a barrage of questions from Rey. Some of the answers were new, some he already knew. From early youth, Flynn was best friends with Rey's father, Roddy Newly. "Roddy and I were in the same grade at school, and his little brother, Trey, was two years younger. We sort of adopted Trey and became known as the three Irishmen, even though I was the Irish Indian. Along with Silk Wilke's dad, Herman 'Silkworm' Wilkes, called Silkworm because he was slim but also smooth, we dominated in football and basketball. The Pewamo Pirates ruled, dude. We creamed the Brewer Creek Braves and went to State every year, man. We set all the scoring records you eventually broke. None of us were college-oriented, more working-with-the-hands type of guys. No wars were being fought, so we graduated from school, went into the trades, and then Pastor Louie Pastore came to town.

"We were a bunch of wild construction-working dudes and didn't want anything to do with church! But he was an excellent carpenter and a darn good softball player to boot. Soon he had us advising him on how to build his church and then playing ball on the church team. He sang like a bullfrog in heat, but he loved us three Irish Indians, as he called us. While we showed him how to do stuff, we would all sing. Ha! Soon we were building the church, singing harmony in the choir, and beating the daylights out of all the other church softball teams in the county.

"Your dad, Roddy, fell in love with my beautiful, gentle little sister, Swan, and they got married in the church. We were attracting all our construction buddies and their families to the church, and the buffets we served were unbelievable. We kept adding on to the church and built others in the area. It was tremendous, as Pastor Louie always taught what he called the 'unvarnished gospel,' letting us know that the real Jesus was a laughing carpenter and construction guy just like us. He claimed Jesus would have even played softball if it had already been invented! He said the Bible began with 'In the big inning!' Pastor Louie even went hunting with us up at Crow Stump Run out by the Pewamo reservation. We called where he hunted Safety Ridge, because he was such a poor shot that all the deer headed that way knowing they would be safe!"

Flynn's laughing eyes suddenly clouded over, and then he seethed with anger. "And then old Fillups 'Abominable' Farnswaggle came to town. The big church bubbas at headquarters caught wind of what we were doing. Building our church and many others was okay, but what they liked the most were the offerings. Big black cars rolled in, Pastor Louie got sent off to rescue another church they previously had run into the ground, and we got the 'wonderful' Reverend Fillups Farnswaggle. What a joke! The first thing he did was stop the church construction in other communities and build himself a fancy office with a private bathroom, all decked out in oak and marble. Then he fancied up the church and preached about how we were all abominable sinners. It was obvious we weren't good enough for his church. He wanted to preach only to the big money country club people, to heck with the plumbers, carpenters, electricians, and construction people who had built the church.

"When the numbers drastically dropped off and the offerings crashed, Farnswaggle came up with a devious plan. He purchased lots of insurance and then waited for a suitable time. Your dad and I had pretty much already stopped attending and happened to be out of town working a construction job, but your Uncle Trey, my younger brothers Florian and Finian, and my mom, Grace Pompatella Flynn, along with some others who still belonged to the congregation, confronted him at the church. Fortunately, they left Swan home to take care of you as you were a feisty little booger, I mean toddler."

The big man paused and took a deep breath, nearly sobbing again. "To this day, I can't talk about it without crying. Somehow, they mysteriously got locked in a meeting room, and then a gas main 'inexplicably' exploded, conveniently taking all the records and most of the main complainers to an early meeting with their Maker. Only Farnswaggle miraculously survived, having stepped out 'just in time' to get some records they requested," Flynn said, in a choked voice.

Through gritted teeth he continued: "When I came back and confronted him, he just said, so full of unctuous pomposity, 'The good so often die young. It was a miracle I escaped.' I had no idea at the time what a psychopath was, but I can still see his cold eyes as he attempted to convince me it was an accident. He kept saying over and over it was just a miracle he survived. At the time, I admit, I couldn't believe anyone could be so uncaring and cruel as to kill such loving people such as your uncle, my mother, and two brothers over what amounted to a pittance. I realize now it wasn't the money. He just liked the killing and hearing the agonized screams." The big man was so emotional he had to pause and collect himself again before continuing.

"When I tried to file a lawsuit against him, I found out I was tangling not just with him but also with a real monster, a much bigger and malicious clandestine organization I later learned was called NAP, the National Association of Psychopaths you now know so well. Reverend Louie Pastore came back and warned me. He explained how the psychopaths, the 'snakes in suits or lizards in loafers,' as he called them, had taken over leadership of many of the large old-line denominations. He said they were part of the so-called religious-industrial complex. In it only for the money! Forget the real message of the good news.

"I still wanted to take them on, but Reverend Louie explained that if I did so, and they found out, we would be risking our families. Most of the guys just resigned themselves to losing our church and people. I couldn't do it, couldn't live with my mom, brothers, and a best friend burned alive, and Reverend Louie couldn't either. By this time, they had milked the second church where they had sent Louie, and he clearly saw them for what they were. Fillups Farnswaggle took the insurance money and left town. Louie and I went underground incognito to take on the NAP and all their devious web of associates we found were connected to the highest powers in the land. I changed my name from Jack Flynn to Flynn Pompatella, taking my mom's maiden Pewamo tribal name.

"Your dad wanted to get revenge too, but he had you and Swan to look out for. I left him to watch over your mom and you, little Rey-Rey, and joined with my oldest brother, Jon, who lived out of state. I had to stay away, or the NAP would have possibly made the connection between Flynn Pompatella and your family, found you, and used you as leverage to get me to surrender or worst. Fortunately, old 'Abominable' Farnswaggle had never gotten to know the 'little people' in the church, so, thankfully, he didn't make a connection between Trey, Roddy, my sister, you, and me."

Many other great stories were told and Rey enjoyed getting new information about his dad, "Wild" Roddy Newly, and his deceased Uncle Trey Newly. Jack Flynn, AKA Pompatella, might have stretched a few extra facts here and there, but it was rollicking good fun to hear the stories of the adventures of the three Irishmen.

Uncle Flynn also filled Rey in more on his Pewamo heritage. The tribe always had been more entrepreneurial and resilient than many tribes, being traders and peacemakers. But they were too few in number to fight back against the bigger tribes like the Iroquois Federation or the Dakota and Lakota from the west. The rapidly expanding Caucasian invasion also just rolled right over the Pewamo. So they stuck to small villages in swamps and other marginal land, content to fish, harvest wild rice, grow all sorts of vegetables and fruits, hunt, and raise livestock. They also continued trading whenever they could.

It wasn't that the Pewamo were afraid to fight. In fact, they were known as the "gentle giants" among other tribes who tried to attack them because their men were big and tall, if a little on the portly side, and they never lacked in courage when protecting their people. In later years, they proved their bravery again and again in every major American combat engagement—from the Civil War to the Gulf Wars and even in Afghanistan. Their men fought and died for their country, and they always had numerous decorated veterans far out of proportion to their actual population.

Most of the time, though, the Pewamo were just gentle people who liked to joke, tell stories, and trade rather than fight. The other related tribes like the Ottawa, Ojibwa, and Potawatomie used to get agitated with the big, but gentle jokers. One time they took them on the warpath and assigned them a cabin of settlers to destroy. Later, they found the warriors had surprised a young mother alone with her children. She had been baking apple pies, and the fierce-looking war party was immediately won over by the aroma of the pies and her brave demeanor. They soon shared recipes, devoured her pies, and then left the stunned lady and her children safe and sound, minus some pies, and took the recipe home. The more warlike tribes often jokingly commented while they were out collecting scalps that the Pewamo were collecting recipes! Flynn liked to point out this just proved the great diversity among the five hundred-plus original native nations. Some were great raiders and warriors and others just wanted to get along, adjust to changing events, survive, and perhaps pick up a few good recipes along the way.

Faced with changing rules, regulations, and restrictions, the Pewamo eventually became farmers and merchants. They fit in well with the local people who were mostly hard-scrabble Irish men and women of the Flynn and Newly clans who escaped the potato famine in Ireland. When President Andrew Jackson and other later government officials ordered all the Native Americans east of the Big River to go to what is now called Oklahoma, the so-called Indian Country, the local Irish hid their Pewamo friends to save them from the devastating journey. Later, the Irish settlers even helped their Indian friends get a small reservation by Crow Stump Run on mostly swampy land, where Brewer and Nottaway Creeks came together to form the Kazoo River. These were called the Muckytuck Clan of the Pewamo. Another band called the Pockatoo Pewamo completely lost their lands, but now, thanks to Nambo and Flynn Pompatella, they successfully sued the government and were granted a nice reservation.

All the Pewamo bands were blessed with native healers and entertainers. Flynn's mom, Grace, was a full blood Pewamo and a Wabeno, a mystical healer and wisdom keeper of the Pewamo people, Northern Woodland, and Great Lakes tribes. She trained Flynn well in the Pewamo language, customs, and folklore. His dad, Big Jon Flynn, Senior, was an Irish lumberman who died young from the dangerous work. Grace especially warned Flynn about creatures called the "windigo," malevolent cannibal spirits that could possess people. Like Navajo skin walkers, they were evil people who killed and consumed their fellow men without remorse.

Grace told her children about hunting parties getting caught in the snow and the windigo sneaking around at night killing all the hunters, throwing them out to freeze, eating them to survive, then showing up in the village all fat and healthy with an excuse for being the lone survivor. She described the windigo as a man who was not a man, a woman who was not a woman. Flynn eventually recognized that Fillups Farnswaggle and the NAP were of similar bent. They were the white-skinned windigo.

After several near fatal encounters with the NAP people, Flynn and Pastor Louie finally encountered Crazy Jake Nambo. He kept them and Flynn's brother Big Jon from getting killed, and Flynn reciprocated by giving him the idea of using tribal legal approaches to set aside trust lands that would keep them free from government entanglements. The rest was history.

Rey had always known he was at least one-quarter Pewamo, but other than family reunions, he never embraced his heritage. He had good friends who were full-blooded and, of course, loved his mom, who was half-Pewamo, but now wished he had learned more. Flynn let him know there was still time and much more to learn.

Rey also learned, as he had expected, that his troubles with NAP were not coincidental. Flynn was most apologetic as he explained the tangled weave of events. "We—Nambo, Louie, and I—followed you from the beginning. We kept an eye on you, just in case we needed a capable man. Good athlete, never arrogant, good and decent kid, smart as a whip, and then you got sidetracked by the war and your injuries, and then marriage into that hideous Pipestone family and working at the Pipestone prison! Then betrayal by your friends at work and even your family. But we saw the potential. All things work together for good, Rey, we firmly believe. For example, we investigated your unfortunate war experience, and, by chance, we discovered on that desolate island a great place to safely keep some of our people. Over the years, what you saw as setbacks we saw as great, formative experiences for you. They certainly kept you humble at Pipestone! We needed somebody humble, honest, helpful, and decent to stand up against the psychopaths."

His uncle took a deep breath and continued: "Nambo was never quite as sold on you as I was, but he and his group called the Hadron Hackers broke into the NAP computers and finagled them so they'd select your boys' innocent Dad of the Year nomination and then you as their last-minute candidate. Of course, this was after NAP's surefire guy hit a suspicious pothole, also mysteriously manufactured by Nambo and his hacker minions. We naively thought, if we had you there, inside the NAP machine, an honorable and good man, we could somehow get an inside look at their operation, maybe even deter them from their devious goals. We thought you would unsuspectingly go along, until we could reach you and use you for the forces of good. You were stronger and more courageous than even I thought. I deeply apologize. We had no idea how dangerous it would be."

Rey listened to all this and struggled with the urge to slug and strangle his uncle. "So basically I was set up and abused so I could be set up and abused," he said.

His uncle squirmed uncomfortably under his accusing gaze. "We prefer to use the terms 'strategically maneuvered,'" he said, grimacing at recognizing his own weak-sounding weasel words.

"So, without asking me, you put my family and me at great risk."

"I felt horrible about it, Rey. But listen, the NAP brutes are like a lurking infection that reached a critical mass, ready to surge into the bloodstream of America. Nobody, especially decent people like you and your family, would be safe. If you could see the perverted and hideous plans they ultimately have for everybody in the country and the world, you would be horrified. They make Hitler and the Nazis look like the Junior Varsity." His uncle paused, wearily shook his head, looked at Rey with deep sorrow in his eyes, and let out a deep sigh. "I'm so sorry, Rey, but desperate times call for desperate measures."

Rey wanted to be mad but realized his genuinely grieving uncle was right. He now knew that NAP had killed his uncles, his grandmother, and possibly others. He had seen up close how ruthless and despicable they were. Someone had to stop them. He only hoped his family wouldn't be collateral damage. He looked at his uncle and wanted to be mad but couldn't. It was time to man up. He wanted to strike back and strike back hard, but at NAP not his uncle.

Flynn, seeing Rey's hesitation, mistook it for anger. "I am so sorry it turned out this way. Nambo warned us it wouldn't work, but more because I think he underestimated how strong you would be. He probably thought you would just fold."

Now Rey was angry. "Why, that old goat! He's a fracking, finagling pig farmer. He manipulates all these seeming coincidences to get me in hot water, all the while thinking I wouldn't be strong enough to handle it. I'll show him. He's got my family in this, and he'd better be willing to support me in clobbering NAP and rescuing my children!"

Flynn was taken aback by his vehemence. "Settle down, Rey. You've got us all behind you. It's just things have gotten a little out of control, with NAP suddenly realizing they must move now or they will be prematurely outed by Nambo and his team. They were hoping to consolidate even more power and leverage before revealing the true extent of their influence. We put you in the lion's den, not expecting you or events to shake them into a flurry of frantic action this soon."

Once Rey calmed down somewhat, they continued getting to know each other and building their relationship, recounting stories of Swan and other family members. Rey discovered he had a new, insatiable interest in learning more about his Pewamo heritage. His uncle assured him he would learn a lot more in due time.

As much as Rey enjoyed the catching up, he was still bothered by the constant worry about his family. How could he rescue them? Sensing his concern, his uncle advised him about moving too fast. He cautioned him there was a big struggle going on. If Rey could have sensed what was coming soon to shake his world, he would have been even more worried!

At the beginning of Rey's third week at the Reservation for the Temporarily Bewildered, everything came crashing down. Zara and Snapper suddenly flew into the camp in a sleek, small plane piloted by the beautiful young actress herself. She immediately called Nambo, Sister Mary, Flynn, and Rey into a conference. "Poger Reinbolt has uncovered a plan by the Nithings and NAP to carpet-bomb this place. They know Rey is here, and it seems they are beginning to suspect he is perhaps not such an unwilling guest. Look at this."

First she showed them a top-secret CIA and FBI most-wanted listing that had Rey's name and an unflattering mug shot at the top. As if that weren't bad enough, she then pulled out a small computer screen and played a clip that caused Rey to feel as though he would throw up. It was him on the clip, no doubt, mouthing all the vile and stupid NAP propaganda with relish. It looked like he truly believed it. When his stomach stopped revolting, he shouted in a raspy voice, "I never said any of those things!"

"Isn't technology a bitch, Rey?" Nambo chuckled, shaking his head, a wicked grin on his face. "They just used your previous tapes and voice recordings and then digitized you. All that great work with Zara, and now they can make you say and do anything they want."

Rey looked accusingly at Zara. She just shrugged her shoulders and said in a matter-of-fact voice, "With new technology, they can do that to anybody anytime. Let's face it, they have been doing that for quite some time with every politician, Rey. Besides, what could I do? Say to you, don't cooperate, don't go before the cameras? That would have blown my cover, and it would have been the end of you and your family."

Rey grudgingly admitted she was right. "How many clips are there like this?" he demanded to know. Seeing her total chagrin, he continued, "I imagine they are running them all the time, around the clock, on every station?"

Zara just nodded sadly. "They are in complete control. Instead of throwing a fit over what we can't control, we need to strategize on getting you out of here. The attack isn't planned until the day after tomorrow, so we have some time." Seeing him preparing to spout off about being used again, she pointed a finger and tapped him forcefully on the chest and then bluntly reminded him, "We also need to think about your leverage. Because the Nithings and NAP are beginning to doubt your loyalty, maybe Prissy and the boys aren't so safe anymore. I imagine they will use them along with a digital version of you, and possibly an actor impersonating you, to maintain the image they've invested so much time, resources, and effort in. If they get the real you, however, all bets are off. They possibly would think they don't need your family for leverage. They could just dispose of you all in a tragic accident or terrorist attack. Use it to rile up the country to attack an enemy. It's cold, but it's the way they operate! We've got to keep your family valuable to them, and the best way to do that is to keep you on the loose."

That stopped Rey in his tracks. He realized scolding Zara

for letting him get used was getting them nowhere fast. He remembered Nambo saying how easy it was to lie to liars, especially those who never tell the truth and don't recognize it when they see it. Suddenly, a devious plan sprang into his mind, full born. It would deeply hurt him and his family, but he hoped it could save them, too.

He quickly shared with the assembled team the deeply embarrassing secret about his infertility and what Prissy had told him that brought on his stress attack and nearly destroyed him. He could see they all felt sorry for him and felt his embarrassment, and it warmed his heart. Out of necessity, though, he hurried on: "I still love Prissy, and I love my boys with all my heart, but that gives those beasts complete leverage. I think if I lied and told them Prissy cheated on me and the boys aren't mine, challenge them to check the DNA, they might just believe me and assume they are no use as leverage on me. I assume then they would keep them and not just digitize them too and kill them? Maybe they would use them to get a return on their massive investment, but not threaten them to get me to surrender!" He made this last supposition hopefully, looking face-to-face, fearing he could be wrong.

Zara nodded thoughtfully, obviously running the scenario through her mind. "I hate to add this and hurt you more, but I think Thornton is actually attracted to Prissy. It's not love, just lust, but it may be enough to encourage him to keep her around. You know he is going to show anything you say to her and probably the boys, but they also realize you are gone and they are no doubt seeing digitized lies coming from the fake version of you on TV, so they wouldn't know if it was a lie or the truth. It's a risky strategy, but Thornton might buy it and Achor is too far removed to care. Besides, it fits the devious way they see the world, so they can easily believe the lie."

Then Zara's voice took on a growing tinge of excitement. "Also, remember both Nithings have the hots for Paula Pipestone, and your wife is her sister and the boys her nephews. They are also using P.T. a lot. They are P.T.'s daughters and grandkids. I think they would hesitate to harm any of them, as there is no benefit to NAP, and their sudden demise would take a lot of explaining." She looked at the rest of the group for assurance, confirmation, or advice. They all just shrugged their shoulders noncommittally, admitting that no normal person could, in truth, tell what the devious psychopaths might think or do.

Rey felt his heart break but knew he had no choice. "Get the production unit ready, and let's get it over with before I change my mind." He realized he was probably dooming any hope of a future relationship with his family, but he could see no other way out. He had to give them up to keep them safe. But he also felt Zara was right, that the version of the "truth" he would tell the Nithings and NAP would resonate with their own repulsive worldview, and he hoped, reduce the danger to his family.

As they finished the clip, with Rey channeling his anger at the Nithings and the whole unfair world into a vitriolic dismissal of Prissy and his boys, adding bitterly at the end, "So why should I die for them?" another high-tech plane landed at the far end of the runway. Zara informed him it was Poger Reinbolt, the man who had helped them orchestrate his disappearance.

When Poger got out of the plane, Rey was astounded to see a man of only thirty. As he approached, Rey could see he had the presence and bearing of a much older man. He was obviously a hardened and experienced warrior, muscular and tempered like steel from several tours in Iraq, Afghanistan, and even more hostile places. He had a hard-featured, weathered face, topped by white blond hair in a severe buzz cut with some darker streaks beneath.

Nambo plowed forward stiff-legged like a stalking carnivore to meet Poger, despite Zara's restraining hand. The two men came nose-to-nose and stopped, bristling like two alpha wolves meeting for the first time. Nambo had a malicious look on his face that Rey wouldn't have believed possible just a few moments earlier. Reinbolt remained calm despite the physical challenge, and he broke the tension first by speaking in a level, but polite and precise voice. "I know you hate the sight and smell of me, Doctor Nambo, but I want to help. I've come to collect President Newly and help deliver him to a safer place. We also believe that the NAP has convinced the US Air Force to carpet-bomb this place in forty-eight hours, but if we evacuate the P.O.T.U.S., we can cash in some chips with some key contacts and convince them the effort will be a waste of time and resources. It would be very bad PR and a leverage nightmare, with all the non-combatants you have here."

Nambo finally relented, accepting the logic of the situation, and turned away with a look of deep disgust remaining on his face. He walked over to Rey and grabbed him firmly by the shoulder. "I wish there were another way, Rey. Never trust a psychopath, even a so-called reformed one." He darted another baleful look over his shoulder at Poger. Then he continued: "I am sorry, Rey, for initially doubting you. We've all risked and lost loved ones, but it was unfair to enlist you without warning. However, I don't think we could have picked a better man. I think you were born for a time such as this."

Rey realized his Uncle Flynn, who had been standing beside him, was also tensed and looked ready to strike. He fastened a fierce gaze on Poger and snarled. "I lost my nephew once because of bastards like you, and if I lose him again I will hunt you down and pluck your heart out, windigo." With that he turned, and both he and Nambo stalked off, shooting dangerous looks back over their shoulders.

"Well, wasn't that nice?" Zara noted cheerfully. "Now that we got the polite chitchat and friendly testosterone-tinged introductions over with, let's talk strategy."

Sister Mary was the only remaining leader, and she surprisingly reached out and took Poger's hand, a gracious smile on her angelic face. "Young man, you must forgive my beloved son and our great friend Flynn. Psychopaths have grievously hurt them both in the past. They both have had friends and family hideously tortured and killed. They are normally very forgiving people, but it is obvious I must work with them some more! Welcome to Crazy Jake Nambo's Reservation for the Temporarily Bewildered, by the way. Let me get you some good food. Rey can make you a fire, and I will send some boys back with a tent and some sleeping bags. Nambo and Flynn won't have you come any further onto this land, and it is their place and their rules, but we can show you hospitality right here, can't we, Rey?" With that she smiled warmly again, turned, and quickly walked away.

Poger was obviously touched by her sincere words. "She

actually treated me like a real person," he said disbelievingly. He turned to Zara, Snapper, and Rey. "Is that really Sister Mary Contrary Jones?"

Seeing their nodding heads, he followed her with wistful and approving eyes. "Now there goes a person with a right to hate psychopaths, but she treated me with tenderness."

"You get me out of here safely and keep the place from getting carpet-bombed, and I'm sure even Nambo and Uncle Flynn will eventually change their minds," Rey commented while collecting twigs for a small fire. He soon had a good blaze going, just in time for some chattering boys riding in a pony cart to bring them a warm and tasty dinner, topped off with several glasses of strong, sweet cider and a still piping-hot Pewamo cinnamon apple pie.

"We will leave first thing in the morning," Poger said, and, leaning toward Rey, he added surprisingly, "You are so lucky, Rey, so very deeply lucky."

His statement and the longing tone in his voice took Rey aback. "Well, I don't know if I would exactly call getting elected as President for a few weeks and then getting yanked away from my vulnerable family lucky, or even getting put on the top of the CIA and FBI most-wanted list as very lucky. Getting to herd pigs and alpacas was a little lucky, I guess." He finally shut up, seeing Poger's earnest look.

"I've seen how your wife and boys look at you, and how you look at them. I can see how your Uncle Flynn and even, incredibly enough, old Crazy Jake Nambo love you. I can't imagine what it must be like to be loved and to love like that. I don't have that emotion. It's like I'm a deaf person trying to imagine the most beautiful music. I can maybe pick up a beat or two, but I have no idea what can so greatly move people. I can't feel love, Rey, and you can. That's lucky."

After that, Poger and Snapper retired to their tents, commenting about an early start, leaving Zara and Rey alone watching the sparks fly up into the sky. He couldn't help but glance at the exotic and sensuous Zara, her presence so much more potent in person than in even his most fevered private thoughts. She laughed and it kindled sparks in her eyes like lights in an opal. As they talked, snuggling close together to keep out the cool night breeze, she looked at him with a smile so brilliant and warm it completely disarmed him. Her smooth skin and lustrous soft hair glowed in the firelight. She was all smiles and silky touches, even leaning forward attentively to listen deeply whenever he spoke, giving him feelings he wished he didn't have but wouldn't deny for anything. He was so mesmerized and bewitched by the magical moment and her closeness to him, he didn't even see her drop the drug into his cider.

≡ CHAPTER**9** ≡

A Strange
and Wonderful Land

When Rey finally awoke from his drug-induced slumber into pitch-black darkness, he found himself snugly strapped into what seemed to be a packing crate or a coffin of some sort. He was in a horrible-smelling diaper and lying in what appeared to be a cradle contraption, swathed in packing foam. He was so dazed at first he couldn't even scream, and he also realized he had lost all muscle coordination along with the control of his bladder, thanks to the drugs. He was relieved when he gradually regained his coordination and realized the condition was not permanent. Whatever it was that Zara had slipped into his drink had done a job on him. In the background, he could hear a low, droning sound, like being in an airplane. Despite his condition, the sound and the lingering effects of the drugs soon lulled him back to sleep. What finally awakened him to full awareness was a sudden jolt as the crate he was in landed on a hard surface, jarring his teeth, but doing no harm.

The droning sound was gone. His thoughts and emotions were still in a great turmoil, as he couldn't quite get his jumbled wits recovered from the sudden avalanche of events that had disrupted his leisurely and lust-filled firelight cuddling with Zara. He realized he was still befuddled by thinking of her. This was an embarrassing admission, and it rankled and disturbed him even more. Zara had used his teenaged, hormone-driven attraction to distract him and use him again. He felt like such an idiot. He had almost betrayed Prissy again, lured by the exotic Zara and then overwhelmed by her charms, and become an easily manipulated fool. The idea that Zara obviously thought him so easy and gullible a mark disturbed him the most. The fact he should still care what she thought of him just added to his fierce agitation. It was then he realized he was hearing what seemed to be the soft roar of an ocean, waves pounding on a beach, and children laughing and shouting somewhere beyond his packing-crate prison.

The packing crate suddenly flew open, initially blinding him with blazing sunlight. As his eyes recovered, he found himself confronted by a weird-looking man. You could easily mistake him for a mild, slightly pudgy, bumbling old fellow with a bush of black hair framing a tanned, creased face, except that he was about seven feet tall and he carried a dangerous-looking spear in one huge hand. He was barefoot, dressed in scruffy jeans and a Hooters t-shirt, of all things. In his other hand, he carried a crazy-looking parasol to shade himself from the blazing hot sun. "Now let's see what kind of strange care package they sent us this time," he muttered, while adjusting his coke-bottle-thick glasses to peer into the dark container. When he saw and smelled the diapered and strapped-down Rey huddled in the bottom, he jerked back. After readjusting his glasses, the man peered in again at Rey with wise, but playful eyes, then wrinkled up his nose at the odor rising from the container.

Rey didn't particularly appreciate being gawked at by the weird-looking stranger. He was already in a foul mood, thinking about being so easily duped and then dumped by Zara. Now he realized how ridiculous he must look in an adult diaper, full and spilling over. "If you keep wrinkling your face up like that, it might get stuck in that lopsided position, which I admit would be an improvement," Rey said rudely, while struggling to loosen the straps and then awkwardly scrambling out of the container, into the dazzling sunlight, trying to straighten his rumpled, sagging, and very soggy diaper while attempting to maintain some modicum of dignity.

"Spunky monkey, aren't you?" asked another voice from the other side of the container. This belonged to a scrawny, diminutive Asian-looking man dressed in baggy shorts that didn't hide his bandy legs and knobby knees. He was wearing a gaudy Hawaiian shirt and a green accountant's visor over his eyes. "By the way, you should address the Monvale of Troon with proper respect."

"The Monvale of what?" Rey asked, clambering free of a few remaining pieces of packing material and noting sadly that the stench of his body accompanied him. He saw he was on a flat, pockmarked piece of land surrounded by sparkling ocean on three sides and an immensely high, jagged, cloud-shrouded, volcanic looking pile of rocks and peaks behind him. It all looked vaguely familiar. Nah, must be the drugs still messing with his mind.

"Now, Harvard, the man is obviously discombobulated," the big man called the Monvale said, again readjusting his glasses to intently stare at Rey while maintaining a distance to protect his sense of smell. "He must be the unfortunate soul young Poger Reinbolt told us about."

Bowing gracefully and sweeping his long arms out to encompass the surroundings, the Monvale intoned in a mellifluous voice, "Welcome to Foondavi, our humble home. This is Harvard Kowloon," he said pointing to the Asian man who was suspiciously surveying Rey from beneath his eyeshade, while firmly holding his nose, "our Attorney General and Chief of Finance. I, as previously mentioned, am the Monvale of Troon."

"I'm sure you have the proper papers?" the one called Harvard Kowloon inquired officiously, his voice nasal sounding and squeaky, possibly because he was still holding his nose shut.

"Papers, what papers?" Rey responded querulously. "I get drugged, diapered, dropped in a box, dumped on some beach, and then accosted by two dopey vagabonds or brigands, and I'm supposed to have papers?"

"A very spunky, smelly monkey," Kowloon said, squeamishly stepping back behind the big man for protection. Glaring out at Rey from his protected position, he added, "And quite possibly very violent, too."

"Don't worry about papers," the big man said dismissively, his face breaking into a huge smile that split his massive brown face ear-to-ear. "We can work up something official after you, uh, take a refreshing dunk in the ocean. Then you can join me for tea or something stronger, then an official reception at Troon," he added grandly. He gestured toward a cluster of brightly colored but ramshackle shacks made mostly of driftwood and other assorted debris, located under some palm trees. "We call this our illustrious capital." He paused, eyeing Rey gravely. "I think we will call you Joe Frumerica, if you don't mind. Eyes and ears everywhere, even here," he said glancing furtively around the beach. "Can't have people knowing we are entertaining the P.O.T.U.S., no matter how bogus!"

Harvard Kowloon was obviously shocked and flustered by this revelation. "This is the . . . no, it can't be! The President? And do you really think it is wise calling him Joe Frumerica?"

"He is obviously from America. And we can't call him Mister President. I have my reasons," the one called the Monvale responded obstinately, his mind quite obviously made up, but just as quickly changed. "I guess, given our history, we can eventually come up with a better name," he said mysteriously. "Joe Frumerica will do for now."

By now Rey was quite agitated by being talked about and named without even being consulted. "Can I have a say in this?"

"Nope," the Monvale responded firmly, and he pointed Rey to the ocean just fifteen feet away. "Go pollute the South Pacific and then wander over to our humble abode. Then we'll let you take a cold shower to rinse off the seawater and any other remaining detritus. After that, you'll be welcome to enjoy a refreshing cold pineapple and coconut drink with an umbrella and a significant rum and vodka kicker in it. This way you'll get properly polluted. I mean, attitude adjusted. Afterward, you can get acquainted with our benighted isle."

Rey had to admit the gentle ocean surf did look quite refreshing, and his odor was repulsive, and the cold attitude-adjustment drink sounded extremely inviting. Plus, he couldn't shake his bad memories from before the long trip in the container. "Well," he thought to himself, "you've got to go along to get along," and he didn't see any available means of transportation to leave the island. It looked like Foondavi Troon was where Poger Reinbolt wanted him, and he had to assume it was as safe a place as could be.

Soon Rey was clean and refreshed and starting on his third or fourth frosty cold attitude-adjustment drink, enjoying the shade of the swaying palms and watching the dappled ocean painted in at least thirty pastel shades of brilliant blues and greens. Dolphins were jumping in the surf, and children were singing somewhere not far off. A lone fisherman seemed to be catching something in the hazy distance, and he realized it was Harvard Kowloon catching them dinner. His last thought as he dozed off in a hammock was that this vaguely reminded him of Crazy Jake's place, but the drinks were much better.

When he finally woke up, Rey realized he hadn't felt this refreshed in a long time. He was dressed in a garish and frazzled beach-bum outfit the Monvale had given him. He was still in the hammock, gently swinging in the ocean breeze on a rickety driftwood porch beneath the graceful palms and some other strange trees. On a trellis over his head was draped an astounding assortment of bougainvillea, orchids of all shades, multi-hued roses, and what looked like frangipani and other fragrant tropical flowers he couldn't even begin to identify. Strangely enough, hummingbirds of assorted shades were buzzing in and out of the flowers and butterflies were fluttering around his head. He wondered if he were hallucinating. Hummingbirds? In the South Pacific? It had to be the drinks!

"Welcome again to Foondavi and our capital city of Troon," the big islander said grandly, gently waving a huge paw, urging Rey to stay in the hammock and relax, and then indicating the five small, very dilapidated shacks made of brightly painted driftwood, punctuated by what appeared to be stained glass windows. "This fine town houses the entire government of our twenty-mile long by ten-mile wide island of 10,000 or so gentle souls. As you can see, we believe in very limited government, as you will find Foondavians to be very independent minded. Trying to govern them would be like pushing a chain or shoving water up a hill. I'm afraid we have the mentality of belligerent goats, or so said one former and not-so-beloved missionary."

Then the Monvale stopped and pointed again at the shacks composing Troon. "Like us islanders, these quaint abodes are made of all the flotsam that accidently drifted here and jetsam that is purposely discarded and floats up to our beaches and reef. Foondavi has no existing aboriginal people, the original inhabitants having been carried off long ago, we believe, by slavers and disease. We who now inhabit this fair land are just the off-scouring and dregs, the outcasts shall we say, of all the nations of the earth. Whaling ships and freighters dropped their malcontents off here. Chinese gangs dropped Harvard's not-so-ancient ancestors, the esteemed Kowloons, here, as a fitting punishment supposedly worse than death for irascible characters. Con artists, escape artists, deluded artists, drunken whalers, anyone slightly off-kilter, all sort of riffraff were discarded or washed up here. Alas, we are an isolated dumping ground for freaks and rejects. Many disabled and disfigured people were dumped off here like the ancient Eskimos left their old ones out on an iceberg. Others dropped their enemies here to die at the hands of our reputedly cannibal residents. Consequently, we are even more diverse than your America, and almost as crazy. We speak old Foondavi, the gentle tongue we call it, a pidgin language made up of useful and descriptive words from all over. We also speak fluent American English, for reasons we will discuss shortly. Each Foondavi child is taught at least one other major language to help us survive. Everyone is bilingual if not trilingual on Foondavi."

Refilling Rey's attitude-adjustment glass, the big guy continued giving him the Chamber of Commerce introduction to what he obviously considered an amazing island. It was a unique place. Located far in the southern temperate oceans, well below the Pacific islands of Tubuai and the Australs, Foondavi was not too warm, but not too cold. Free of the sand fleas that plagued many islands, and because of its temperate location, it would have been an ideal tourist location except for a few unfortunate things.

Foondavi originally had been home to massive quantities of birds, giving it its ancient Polynesian name that means bird crap rocks. Because of the abundant guano, it also was once covered by verdant forests of sandalwood, milo, and soapberry. Huge eucalyptus and acacia trees grew inland, as did more typical rainforest trees such as ohia and koa, and even a unique form of massive, soaring redwood graced the island. But . . .

"First, they cut down all the trees to make cheap furniture and tourist knickknacks," the big man moaned. "Then they scraped off all the millions of years of accumulated guano-rich topsoil to make gunpowder and fertilizer, leaving us just these bare rocks. The birds are back, we are slowly regenerating the soil and replanting trees, but it will take years to rebuild Foondavi into the environmental Eden it once was. As you will find, however, our greatest treasures are our people, our patience in the face of adversity, and our way of life."

Seeing Rey's rapt attention still focused on the hummingbirds darting around his head, the Monvale added, "We also imported some pesky pollinators to help us begin the reforestation and replanting."

As Rey gazed off toward the towering rocks and rugged ramparts, he could also make out some tortuous gorges that appeared to be eroded streambeds, probably from flash floods gouging out the volcanic soil. It made for a dramatically plunging and scenic shoreline. He could see bright spots of color clinging along the ledges. The Monvale explained that, because they get huge typhoons and occasional tsunamis, the people almost all live on the windswept highlands. Only the unimportant, but expendable, volunteer politicians and government officials—namely the Monvale, or people's representative, and the visored Harvard Kowloon—were made to live in the tidal flats danger zone, a policy he hinted would be wise for other civilized societies to follow. "Tsunamis and tidal waves come through with a disturbing regularity. When our government and bureaucrats get washed away, we just start over. It could be worse; they could have placed us on one of the volcanoes!"

The Monvale went on to explain that the island was, in fact, a unique fusion of five overlapping volcanoes, all now thankfully inactive. Four of the volcanoes were relatively recent ones, meaning within the last million years, each connected to the other by what were lava flows. They averaged slightly above five thousand feet in height and were cloud wreathed, jagged heaps of lava rock, ringed by a reef that encircled them with only a few foaming breaks where the sea came roaring in, providing a good rinsing action. The final volcano, on which they were now located, was the oldest, and the sunken mountaintop was now ground down to a flat, sea-level expanse of rock-filled volcanic soil and coral. The flats, as the Monvale called them, were also sometimes swept over by rogue waves that plagued this part of the ocean. It was pockmarked with holes that appeared to be filled with water, and off in the far distance Rey could see what looked like a rubble-filled former runway and a broken-down plane with the remains of what appeared to be an old army jeep. Shocked, he suddenly realized where he was.

Seeing his stricken face, the Monvale quickly placed a gentle hand on his arm. "Yes, my friend. The people of Foon-davi remember you fondly, Rey Newly. You were the gentle and kind American they called Joe Frumerica Junior, who wandered into the booby-trapped field your previous fellow warriors set for nonexistent communist guerillas. Our people assumed you knew the landmines were there and were just going to check on them, or they would have warned you."

Gazing at the big man, Rey suddenly saw over his shoulder a Pewamo Pirates banner hanging in the back of the dilapidated shack. Another look of shock and then sudden recognition crossed his face. "You're big Jon Flynn! Pompatella's, I mean my Uncle Jack Flynn's, big brother and . . . " Suddenly he gasped, "You're my uncle, too, and the guy that set all the basketball scoring records!"

"The records you and my stinky little brother broke after I left school. But my team won the state title!" he added proudly. Then he quickly looked in all directions to be sure no one was overhearing their discussion. "Now, don't say anything more or I will have to drown you! I must always be the Monvale to you. There are eyes and ears everywhere that would betray us, even here on this blessed isle!"

He went on to explain that his younger brother, Jack Flynn, now known as Pompatella, and Nambo had sent him here incognito to check on Rey's "accidental heroism," thinking there was some possibility that NAP had arranged it, which incidentally he found wasn't true. Upon conducting his investigation, he discovered the remote island was, in fact, filled with innocent, simple, wonderful people and would make an ideal place to safely stash people they wanted to hide—people NAP wanted to eliminate. It was totally useless as far as resources or tourism. The island was also so far off the beaten path that few maps even included it.

But there historically were some problems even in this simple paradise. Rey heard from the Monvale that long ago a probably well-intentioned, but largely deranged, misguided local prophetess—a village idiot according to the Monvale—named Delilah "Devil Eye" McTree, along with her son Shacknasty McTree, had been busily trying to reinstate and commercialize something called the "cargo cult." He explained that the cargo cult was a quasi-religion tracing its origins to the beginning of World War II, when American troops suddenly fell from the sky in fluffy parachutes, built an airstrip, and then began arriving in amazingly huge, bird-like planes full of miraculous, heaven-sent stuff like Spam, chocolate, cigarettes, Jeeps, and beer. Not speaking English, and being people with only Stone Age technology, the natives reveled in all the good stuff G.I. Joe Frumerica brought, without understanding what was going on in the world around them. Then, just as quickly as the manna from heaven appeared, it disappeared—as the Pacific war front moved on, literally overnight. A few empty Spam cans licked clean of any tasty remaining scraps, some fragrant but empty chocolate wrappers, some soggy cigarette butts, a broken-down Jeep, and spare parts and other discarded junk were all that remained, including the wreckage of an old cargo plane.

The islanders were dismayed and crushed. They lamented the loss and pondered the problem and could only imagine they must have done something to drive the god-like people and goodies away overnight. Hoping to win back Joe Frumerica, after a few years they built a replica cargo plane from the wreckage as best they could, parked the discarded Jeep beside it, scattered the remaining empty Spam cans and candy wrappers around it like offerings, and attempted to patch up the dynamited airstrip, even building a rickety control tower, which was soon destroyed by a typhoon and then a rogue wave. They conducted services in as much English as they could remember, promising to never again pilfer supplies or commit any other sins they could conjure up, but all to no avail. They even failed to convince a few underemployed American students to come over and try to teach them Amer-

ican English, thinking maybe their prayers in pidgin Foondavi and broken English weren't getting through. Still, nothing worked. No big planes, Spam, and chocolate. No beer,
Jeeps, or cigarettes. The gods must be deaf. Try as hard as
they might, the locals couldn't figure out how to monetize or
commercialize the cargo cult.

Finally, the devious if demented old Devil Eye McTree
stumbled on a surefire remedy. She proclaimed National
Typhoon Day. Somehow, she got a message to other far-off
islands about the disaster that had devastated Foondavi. Because the island was struck on a regular basis by typhoons, it
looked naturally like a disaster zone, with its buildings made
from floating refuse from the ocean, the ruse worked to a degree. Some useless stuff came parachuting in, mostly building materials, but not Spam, chocolate, cigarettes, Jeeps, or
beer. She followed it up with National Volcano Day. Then she
faked a disease outbreak, using photos of some of the already
disfigured denizens of the island. She even had naturally skinny old Kowloon's father learn to put on a famine face. But the
efforts met with diminishing returns from a disaster-weary,
burned-out American public. The big planes of goodies and
gods still didn't come and land. Occasionally packing crates of
used teabags, broken television sets, and even a few old tractors with no gas collected by well-meaning westerners would
be dropped from low-flying cargo planes that then completed
the long round trip back to the next nearest island. But to
their chagrin, no Spam, chocolate, cigarettes, Jeeps, or beer!
Just worn-out sweaters and old magazines, plus other useless
stuff that just frustrated the few remaining devout islanders
with the hints of greater things in America and elsewhere.

Then approximately twenty years ago, Delilah hit on the idea of an insurrection. Someone told her how America had clobbered Japan, Germany, and Korea and then rebuilt the countries. They, unfortunately, left out Vietnam, Iraq, and some other places—less fortunate recipients of American military largesse. She figured Foondavi was already in a disastrously clobbered state, so what could possibly happen? Maybe she could lure Joe Frumerica back! So, she started the Foondavi Liberation United Front Forever (F.L.U.F.F.) and somehow got the attention of a rising young US naval officer named Nathaniel Futtock. He could smell a commie plot from thousands of miles away, which was good, because Foondavi was nearly inaccessible, thousands of miles away from anywhere. This could be a real low-risk career maker!

The best-laid plans of the cargo cult people were soon in disarray again, as no big flying birds full of Spam, chocolate, etc., were sent. Instead, fueled by Futtock's ambitions, mysterious black helicopters came buzzing in like lethal hornets from stealth warships. Black-clad Special Forces not so gently interrogated the terrified islanders. Landmines were liberally distributed in suspected terrorist locations—as the fiscal year was nearly over, and, if you don't use it you lose it—then the black-clad warriors pulled back to see if the F.L.U.F.F. commies would strike.

The islanders wisely and discreetly marked all the landmine locations, avoided them, and decided this was not a promising development. When a second reconnaissance team landed later under the command of a pleasant young American, they hoped maybe their fortunes had changed. He seemed to like the people and was intrigued with the bird life of the island. He did have some chocolate and coffee he graciously shared with them. No Spam, but some MREs that tasted somewhat better than the poached seagull they were used to. Things were looking up. But then, instead of checking on the landmines like the islanders expected, the nice American unsuspectingly led his team right into them.

The black-clad helicopters returned to pick up the one severely injured survivor and the pieces of the rest of the blown-up team. Then all hell broke loose as the warships launched a savage shelling of the island. A fleet of massive eight-engine B-52 bombers soaring five miles up also carpet-bombed the fake cargo cult airfield and surrounding area with a continuous cascade of thousand-pound bombs that destroyed the replica plane and rebuilt control tower.

Fortunately, because the islanders hid in the caves they had used for years to avoid slavers, pirates, and itinerant salespeople, the bombs didn't hurt any people. It did, however, scare the birds, roast a few goats, and give the rest of the goats Post-Traumatic Stress Disorder. What was left of the airfield and surrounding area was a large assortment of nice deep shell holes the islanders later put to good use for fishing and as duck ponds.

In due course, Nathaniel Futtock grew bored with the seemingly well-hidden F.L.U.F.F. and smelled commies in a more easily accessible region. He quickly decorated himself and some of his command for valor and then wrote off the desolate pile of now-cratered rocks. Soon Foondavi and F.L.U.F.F. were forgotten. But the islanders often wondered what happened to the injured "Joe Frumerica Junior," as they called the nice young officer who offered some temporary hope and seemed to be enamored of the island, its people, and its birds, before everything was blown to bits.

With the history of the Foondavi summarized, the seemingly unflappable Monvale was startled by a sudden buzzing sound that filled the air and a vibration that caused him to start swatting at his pocket as though bees had invaded it. Finally, his big hand emerged with a new model cellphone. He listened for a minute and then gestured for Rey to follow him into the dilapidated shack. To Rey's surprise, a trap door swung open and they soon descended into a rock-walled, temperature-controlled, and highly secure basement room filled with high-tech equipment. On a screen facing him was the glowering visage of old Jake Nambo.

"Before you get hysterical, let me explain a few things. As usual in life, things are not as they appear," Nambo started, while aggressively leaning into the screen.

"I'll say," responded Rey. "But my main concern is the safety of my family while I am stuck out here on this bird-infested rock in the middle of the ocean with some real wacky characters. No lawyers yet, unless this Kowloon character qualifies."

"Well, I can guarantee your family is safe for now, especially if you continue to cooperate with us. NAP bought the whole charade. Who says you can't con the con man?" Then Nambo continued in a more soothing voice: "We want them safe, too, Rey. Let me just say your accidental early collapse threw our carefully laid plans into disarray. It left us to improvise on the fly. We didn't cover our tracks as well as we would have, and it led NAP to discover our ruse faster than planned. We can never underestimate them."

Rey fixed Nambo with a malevolent look in return. "You dragged us into this. As I have learned, there are just too many coincidental things in this situation. If it were just about me, it would be bad enough, but my family is innocent. Through all your finagling and hacking NAP computers, you set me up, and now my family is paying the price. As I told my Uncle Flynn, I am grudgingly on board now, I want to stomp the NAP bastards, but one day I will settle with you, you old, conniving pig farmer."

Nambo ignored Rey's anger and continued in a more soothing voice, "You are right, Rey—right to be mad and right about the not-so-coincidental events. For the most part, they're not even slightly coincidental. I planned or manipulated all of them. In fact, I believe few things in life or nature are left to chance. As my old friend Albert Einstein said, 'God doesn't play dice with the universe,' or something like that."

Seeing Rey's look of surprise, Nambo rapidly rolled ahead, ignoring his comment about friendship with Einstein. "I know I don't apologize enough. A sign of my still low emotional skills quotient or EQ, I guess! Good people are hard to find, Rey, people who are not easily corrupted by power or greed. People who just want to serve out of love for family and country. George Washington comes to mind. He could have been the first King of the good old USA if he had listened to the urging of his officers. Also, there was an old Greek farmer and general from ancient history by the name of Epaminondas. Twice he left his farm to unite the Greeks and lead them to victory, and then twice he walked away from being crowned the ruler. I know you don't believe it yet, but your Uncle Flynn has convinced me you are such a man." Seeing Rey's stunned silence, Nambo went on. "Forget the history lessons. Let's look at now. I searched the country high and low—and found you."

Rey started to object: "You could have asked me." Then he realized just how stupid that was. He realized he never would have believed. He never would have accepted that a broken-down factory worker could be a world leader. He wouldn't have had the confidence after his searing history of defeats. But now, he was in it to win. The lives of his family depended on him.

"As you know, I helped rescue and hide your Uncle Flynn and Pastor Louie after they rashly took on the powers of NAP. I soon came to respect their spiritual, physical, and mental strengths. I learned about your family and what NAP had done. When your uncle told me about you and your unfortunate fiasco on Foondavi over twenty years ago, I started watching you. I checked you out and I investigated the island. NAP only sniffed around the place once, when they ejected that execrable Reverend Farnswaggle on the poor, unsuspecting people, thanks to a subterfuge by me. I admit I out-strategized myself on that one, figuring either the goats or the folks would eliminate the slimy booger. Instead, the varmint survived and turned the experience into a literary goldmine by writing about the cannibals of Foondavi! Calling them cannibals was almost as bad as the earlier carpet-bombing of the island by the idiot Futtock. Anyway, when the time was right, I used my team's supreme hacking skills to out the NAP Republican useful idiot candidate. Then I arranged for you to be accidentally discovered by that bumbling Thornton Nithing, thanks to your sweet boys' innocent hero worship for you, and, of course, some deft hacking by my talented team."

This was old news to Rey, already having been cued in by his Uncle Flynn, but Nambo's obvious overweening pride in his manipulative powers finally set off the stunned Rey. He felt his nose was again being rubbed in the crap because he was so freaking gullible. "So, you admit it is you and your manipulations that put my family in danger!" he said, seething with anger. If he could have reached through the screen, he would have strangled old Nambo.

"All families are in danger if these predators get complete power. We have all lost loved ones to these monsters. It is not a game that you can sit out and watch from safety. Sooner or later, your family would have been targeted, but now they are out in the open and, we believe, harder for NAP to destroy. Let me emphasize they are perceived by NAP to be valuable leverage over you and the Pipestone family."

Rey slowly calmed himself, realizing he was out of control and that his present state of anger wasn't helping him get any closer to rescuing his lost family. "But why do you have me here?" Rey asked. "I need to be doing something to help my family or I'll go crazy!"

"Foondavi is the last place they will look. It's completely off the grid, except for this top-secret satellite feed I have arranged. Because I lured them into dumping one of their own lunatics over there earlier, they think the island is filled with cannibals and completely useless to them. They don't understand the fantastic power of the Foondavi Way that you will soon discover. We originally sent your Uncle Jon Flynn, now called the Monvale, out to both protect him from NAP's revenge and to check out what had happened to you. Since then, several of our key leaders have gone and experienced Foondavi in all its magical glory."

Magical glory? Fantastic power? Rey was more than a little confused by these last comments about Foondavi, but he attempted one last time to convince Nambo to let him come back to the USA and fight for his family.

Nambo was unconvinced: "This is a battle for the battered, flattened soul of America, Rey. All the psychopaths and perverts are coming out of the woodwork. It's going to be a struggle to the death. We either transform the minds of the people, or it's lights out for America. Your job is to use your time on Foondavi to prepare yourself for leadership." Seeing Rey's confused look, he continued. "Watch and learn from the Monvale and the people of Foondavi. You'll see! It turned me around and changed my life. When the time is right to strike the deciding blow and begin the revolution, we'll get you back here." With a curt nod, and no explanation for the cryptic comments about Foondavi changing his life, Nambo abruptly cut the connection and left Rey sputtering in frustration, confusion, and anger.

Seeing his frustration, the Monvale patted him on the back. "Nambo referred to one of the NAP leaders he lured here to be marooned on Foondavi early on, before he truly knew what a jewel this place really is. Let me tell you about him, because you know the villain he is referring to. He was once our family preacher."

Some people never give up, and old Devil Eye McTree was nothing if not resilient. Her people were first dropped off on the island as punishment for being inveterate carnival frauds and unrepentant con artists. Following in the footsteps of her relatives, McTree was always working another con. This time it was rumored old devious Delilah was looking for either a husband, or at least a one-way ticket off the island. After the US Navy departed the devastated Foondavi, she saw an old ad for a mail-order missionary and mailed off a request. Sometime later, a container parachute floated down on the island and out plopped a disheveled heap of bloated humanity by the name of Fillups Farnswaggle. Either God has a twisted sense of humor, or maybe Nambo had indeed somehow finagled it as he later claimed, but the fact that this poor excuse for a missionary should splat down on an island which had just accidently played a role in grievously injuring Rey Newly was a remarkable spot of bad luck for the people of Foondavi.

If you knew Fillups Farnswaggle, there was no reason to doubt why he had been so unceremoniously jettisoned on such a seemingly inhospitable place as far as possible from civilized life. Even the psychopaths of NAP seemed to have a certain threshold level of tolerance for unscrupulous and stupid behavior. Fillups Farnswaggle had easily descended below this scum-scraping level through his greed, stupidity, and vulgarity, eclipsing all previous low standards for depravity and cruelty. He was like the man Winston Churchill described as a bull carrying around his own china shop, a disaster waiting to happen. The only question was why the NAP monsters had not just killed him. The idea was later discussed, and the islanders assumed that the NAP leadership determined that a slow, lingering, painful death by starvation on a pile of rocks populated only by rapacious cannibals and feral goats would be a fitting tribute to the man.

At that time, no one knew much about Foondavi, only the fact it was as far away from anywhere and everyone as you could get on Planet Earth. If for some unfathomable reason NAP's leaders ever needed Farnswaggle again for some nefarious purpose, they could retrieve the scoundrel, or what was left of him, assuming he survived the typhoons and inhospitable commie cannibals rumored to infest the bird crap-encrusted lava.

True to form, Farnswaggle soon inflicted himself upon the unsuspecting islanders. His favorite word was "abominable," which he used to describe almost every individual he met and every aspect of Foondavi life. The people soon came to refer to him as "Rev Abominable," and they tried to avoid him whenever and wherever possible. Because he was initially too fat to climb the precariously steep slopes into the highlands, he just haunted the lowlands, and people soon learned to provide him enough food and drink to try and keep him fat and happy and far away from their homes and children. Any time he interacted with the islanders, he treated them with disdain and haughty holiness. His one disciple appeared to be Delilah "Devil Eye" McTree, whom he referred to as his "delightful Delilah." Even her vile son, Shacknasty McTree, showed unusual wisdom for such an unadulterated dolt and stayed far away.

At one point during his well-earned exile, Farnswaggle found an old discarded typewriter and some paper a well-meaning group had used to wrap up some junk to send to the cannibal heathen. Without much to do, he banged away on what he considered his opus, *My Life Amidst the Cannibals of Foondavi*. In the book, he described the innocent islanders in despicable terms, making up all sorts of gruesome and horrible tales to thrill his hoped-for readers. Somehow, he got the manuscript off the island, and the hair-raising book became an instant hit. The bestseller then was turned into a movie that grossed hundreds of millions of dollars, thousands of miles away from the isolated and innocent island it momentarily made infamous. Once a money-maker again, Farnswaggle bribed someone to do the people of Foondavi a huge favor and pluck him off the island and back to the states to plunder another unsuspecting church or two, leaving the frustrated, scheming Delilah far behind.

Then Jon Flynn came to the island at the behest of Nambo and his brother to investigate the landmine incident. He let Pastor Louie, Nambo, and his brother know what the recently departed despicable "Rev Abominable" had done to the island and that the gentle people were not cannibals. They soon realized Foondavi could be an ideal spot to bring people whom the NAP brutes were trying to eliminate. Eventually, Pastor Louie visited the island to try to undo the damage to the faith that Fillups had inflicted. He soon realized the loving people were ministering more to him than he was to them. Even though they had nothing, the islanders, other than Delilah and a few rough sorts, were such peaceful and happy people. It soon was obvious they were more focused on the things that last. They called Pastor Louie "Revaluyah," because he always was saying "hallelujah" and not "abominable"! He soon had them started on a cargo cult recovery program, teaching them you can never get something for nothing. He won them over with love, service, and the real faith. Plus, he provided some sorely needed medical supplies. He also set up a means to take some of the smartest young people temporarily off the island and get them educated in medical science, agriculture, aquaculture, botany, and any other specialty potentially useful to Foondavi. He even eventually arranged for some regular shipments of Spam, chocolate, coffee, and, it was rumored, some great beer! Soon Foondavi was the unofficial safe house sanctuary for the feisty opponents of NAP.

As Rey heard this account from the Monvale, he realized he had recently seen Fillups Farnswaggle. He was the same slimy fat slug in the expensive suit, oozing smugness and superiority, who was the keynote speaker at the religious-industrial complex dinner, talking sanctimoniously about his suffering in the mission field among the cannibals, and then sucking up offerings to supposedly help the islanders—like a demented vacuum cleaner. He was still milking Foondavi for all it was worth! The thought just hardened Rey's resolve to do in these villains.

Listening to the calm and informative Monvale, Rey learned a lot more about the amazing island and people of Foondavi. Monvale gestured toward the highlands, and again Rey saw specks of brilliant colors among the barren rocks and eroded gash-like gorges. He could also see as he looked closely that interspersed with barren rocks were a few wispy-thin waterfalls plummeting out of the wasted, windswept landscape. He explained to Rey that the splotches of vibrant color were small villages made up of colorfully painted dwellings called fales, rock and driftwood constructed open air houses, festooned with flowers, like those found on Samoa. He went on to explain that, like the traditional Samoan architecture, the Foondavi fale is characterized by an oval or circular shape, patterned after an upside-down boat, with wooden posts holding up a domed roof. There are no walls.

"The base of the architecture is a skeleton frame, and no metal is used," the Monvale explained, "which is good because metal is rare here. The open design also lets the healthy fresh breezes come through and keeps the people open to the sun and beautiful views of the ocean. The men and women go down to the sea every day and fish from the rich waters of the reef for all sorts of quarry. We salvage any useful thing we can off the shoreline. We've transplanted kelp and red seaweed to harvest and use as fertilizer, food, and even to make biofuel for the few generators we use to run our computers and emergency lights. Those brightly colored buoys you see bobbing out there hold up the nets that support the kelp and seaweed. Fish and shellfish such as oysters, clams, and scallops hide in the kelp and make tremendous eating. As you will see when you start to wander the island, all the little villages perched on the lava ledges are connected to each other by a high ring road with bridges, net ladders between rings, and a steep road to the sea. There are two and in some places three main ring roads, one at 300-400 feet above the sea level, and another at 1,000-2,000 feet or so, the third much higher up and very precarious. We do vertical farming on the steep slopes between the ring roads using fiber nets, growing olives, fruits, and all sorts of vegetables. All of them are fed by drip irrigation from our mountaintop cisterns that are filled by the seasonal rains that sweep through during the typhoon season. Lots of little pocket valleys and some treacherous gorges are crossed with what we call "flirty bridges," because we say in jest you are flirting with death when you go over them! You will soon notice flat land is at a premium. We had to meticulously terrace some steep slopes and build topsoil into them. We grow all types of vegetables and fruits in the rich lava soil. Over eighty types of potatoes grow here in the pocket valley farms, and farther up the mountain we have some terraced rice paddies the size of a typical American living room that produce enough rice to feed twenty to thirty people. We fertilize these paddies with fish remains and our own sanitized personal soil!"

Seeing Rey's confused, if slightly disgusted look, the Monvale added, "Nothing goes to waste here, Rey. We use everything to rebuild the soil. We literally eat our own sanitized waste, pardon the crude language. Then when we die, we are laid in the garden and a fruit tree is planted over us. We call them family trees. If we are sweet in life, we produce sweet fruit. If not, well, there is a use for prunes and sour things, too!" He went on to explain they initially had a lot of help from a group of Native American specialists, especially the Pewamo Muckytuck clan with whom Rey was already familiar. Members of the generous Pewamo clan, with the encouragement of Nambo, work with abandoned and impoverished people across the world, as the Foondavians formerly once were, to help them become agriculturally independent. "When you can feed yourself and be independently sustainable, you can have real freedom," the Monvale said proudly.

Now, after twenty years, the islanders grew more food of multiple varieties than they could possibly consume. They also were now helping to train and feed people on other less fortunate islands!

On another day, Rey commented on the beautiful lilting language of Foondavi. Mention of the language spurred another exciting thought in the Monvale. He explained how you can tell a lot about a people by studying their language and seeing what type of words make up the bulk of their vocabulary. For example, some American Plains Tribes had numerous words, composing the bulk of their vocabulary, describing horses, raiding, hunting, and particularly buffalo. He said if Rey thought that was interesting, then consider how many American words were concerned with cars: types of cars, brands of cars, parts of cars, etc. It was estimated that close to thirty percent of American words involved cars, and almost as much again concerning sports. And the French? Over thirty percent of their words were about food. What did he think the bulk of old Foondavi words were about? The Monvale claimed over thirty percent of Foondavian words concerned family and various relationships! They had thirty different words alone to describe love, compared to four for Greek and one in English. "In America we love our dog, our car, our wife, and our country all using the same word!" he had hooted. Foondavians also had numerous words describing different types of peace—and several words for goats, few of which could be shared in polite company.

It seemed that goats were at once both the bane and a blessing of Foondavi, the Monvale admitted ironically and grudgingly. They originally had accidentally been dumped on the island by a storm-tossed, deserted freighter and immediately set about eating what few green things had managed to refasten themselves to the rocks. They were relentlessly hunted by the islanders, kept for their milk and meat when domesticated, and won the hearts of the Foondavi people with their rascally and resilient behavior, especially when they ate up the first draft of Rev Abominable's book about the so-called cannibals of Foondavi. In fact, the goats constantly hectored Farnswaggle, nibbling the tattered suit and tie he insisted a proper reverend should be wearing even in the subtropical heat. In fact, the goats probably played a key role in finally driving the abominable pest off the island.

Despite his incessant gnawing concern about his family, Rey found himself increasingly mesmerized by the island, its people, and its creatures. Besides goats, the islanders were blessed with an abundance of sea birds. Foondavians nimbly scaled the rugged peaks and then harvested a carefully calculated number of eggs from the various species so as not to endanger them. They also kept chickens and a few hardy, surefooted Shetland ponies and loveable burros that pulled carts of older Foondavians around the precarious ring roads and over the shaky bridges between villages, then up and down to the ocean. There also were sleepy-eyed, free-roaming alpacas who managed to get into everybody's way. "We shear them and make beautiful blankets, sweaters, bedding, and jackets from the alpaca fiber or hair. Very useful and loveable creatures," the Monvale explained.

As Rey explored the island, he fell in love with the small, cozy villages composed of the open fales that were somehow lashed together with brightly colored driftwood added to bricks chopped from the lava rock. Even though they were based on the basic design the Monvale had described to him, he also found each family added creative embellishments to make each home unique. Open to the sea, and often leaning over a steep drop-off, the homes had either wood or thatched reed shutters and colorful stained glass windows the family could quickly close if the sea suddenly turned stormy. They were decorated by such huge, riotous masses of gorgeously colored flowers and blossoming vines that it often was hard to see the underlying stones, bricks, and boards. He thought it was a wonder the buildings didn't collapse under the fragrant covering.

Rey also was amazed at the abundance of iridescent hummingbirds of all different varieties buzzing among the blooms, contending with bees to get nectar. The people explained they had been brought in from America with the hope they would help pollinate the newly introduced plants and flowers. Joyously, the hummingbirds had taken to the Foondavi climate and blossoming vegetation with great gusto. And competing with the hummingbirds for airspace and flowers, and adding to the vibrant mix of colors, were butterflies of all different hues. In fact, a lot of species threatened elsewhere were welcome guests on Foondavi.

Another Foondavian feature that enamored Rey were the little, tightly enclosed, supposedly goat- and alpaca-proof gardens. These were carefully tended plots thriving on frugally recycled fish and animal remains as well as sanitized human excrement. He also enjoyed lounging in the lovingly preserved groves of family trees, planted over the remains of beloved Foondavian ancestors. They bore all sorts of delicious fruits and nuts. In addition, heavily laden vines with grapes and berries seemed to cling to every available rock and from the netting strung from the cliffs.

Each village grove and garden Rey entered was an intricate maze of beauty and a place of great pride to the people of the village. But the greatest prize of the islanders was obviously their children. Dressed in the brightest colors, they ran free everywhere. It made Rey's heart ache for his boys.

"Don't they go to school?" Rey asked one day, coming back out of the highlands from one of his extensive rejuvenating jaunts around the island. "Most definitely," the Monvale responded. "Every child's education is the responsibility of the parents. The kids learn a lot working with their parents. No sterile classroom-bound, one-size-fits-all, dump truck, industrial model education here. The parents teach each child individually, or they find a capable tutor in the village. By the age of twelve, the children must be able to read, write, and reason, as tested by another village's elders, or they won't be allowed to go on to learn a craft, vote in village elections, or have anyone want to marry them. Even people with reading disabilities can learn with the right mentor. It's important to note that we have very few computers on the island, no cellphones, and no televisions. But we do have lots of real books! We are a literate people, sharing what knowledge we have. Every night families tell stories around their fireplaces. We take education very seriously and send off our best to some surprisingly good schools. Harvard Kowloon, for example, is a Harvard MBA, but we don't hold that against him. We also have doctors and nurses here who were trained at the best medical schools. Our children aren't forced to come home when they finish school, but almost all do. The few that don't immediately return home keep Foondavi a sacred secret and often come home later. The lure of Foondavi is the love of her people and the peace of the land."

One day when Rey pressed the Monvale more, he found out that even in this loving and healthy environment they ended up with an occasional psychopath or, at least, the occasional anti-social personality. "On the last volcano, in the crater, is a special camp we call Fenrir Home. It's named for an ancient Norse myth about a monstrous wolf named Fenrir that was kept penned up by the gods but eventually escaped and ate their god Odin. Fenrir Home is where we send our psychopaths. The only pass in and out of the camp is heavily guarded. There, we lovingly train the remorseless, recalcitrant ones to be Fenrir Shamar, the guardians of Foondavi. Our children, no matter how twisted, are shown we love them and need them as protectors, not predators. Poger Reinbolt, whom you have met, has helped us greatly with the task of training and reforming these few remorseless ones. They spend days on end climbing the steep slopes after the wild goats and learn to shoot with the best experts. I understand they make great snipers and assassins. Poger has told me that the American CIA and the Israeli Mossad have found some good recruits among our Fenrir Shamar. They compare them to the fearsome and fierce Gurkha warriors of Nepal. I know if we were ever invaded there would be hell to pay if we turned the Fenrir Shamar loose." He sighed deeply and sadly shook his head. "Those who are just incorrigible, or maybe anti-social but not psychopathic, we send to the sea steads."

"What are sea steads?" Rey responded. The word sounded familiar but he wasn't sure.

"They are floating hulks, old oil platforms, some old cruise liners, and a few new, well-funded, specially designed boats. We let them dock at the back of the island, out of the rough seas, away from everybody. We charge them a small docking fee, and they don't bother us and we don't bother them. They are collectives of people who choose to live freely out of the reach of legislative or legal arms of countries. Most are libertarians, though a few are communist communes. Our only demand is that we are allowed to visit once a month to make sure if anyone wants to leave, they can. We provide medical and other help, if needed. No prison ships allowed. They can each advertise among themselves, and sometimes a rare Foondavian will choose to join them, at least for a while."

As the days went by, Rey, now widely hailed as "Joe Frumerica Junior," walked the steep and precarious trails known as the ring roads. He continued to build strength in his damaged body, mind, and spirit. His mind never drifted far from his purpose of preparing to return and rescue his loved ones, but he found the island and the exercise invigorating. He could see why so many of the natives were barrel-chested and muscular, having traversed the nearly vertical trails and climbed up the vertical netting strung between ring roads to help harvest the crops. Everywhere he went, Rey was greeted with friendly eye contact, smiles, and then a greeting or thumbs-up sign, just like at the Reservation for the Temporarily Bewildered. He noticed there was not one dominant race but a "polyglot Polynesian potpourri," as the Monvale described it. Referring to the sincere friendliness of the people, the Monvale also commented, "They were doing that when we got here, so we can't take any credit. Everybody pretty much knows everybody else, or who you are related to. And they are friendly even with the rare stranger."

As he wandered the island on his own, Rey was regularly invited in to one tidy, cozy little home after the other for a meal or a piece of pie. At first he thought it was because he was Joe Frumerica Junior, but he soon realized this was how all travelers were treated on Foondavi, especially the storytellers. And the islanders always asked Rey to share stories about his fabled American homeland.

Every village was justifiably proud of its hospitality, its cooks, and its crops. In the spirit of camaraderie, the villages regularly erupted in sing-sings, or "boondoons," as he learned the spontaneous celebrations were called, when they serenaded other villages with mixed choirs of all ages. People pounded on drums and pans, strummed various stringed instruments, and sang in tones that combined African with Polynesian sounds and rhythms in highly creative ways. As

Rey wandered from one cliffhanging, flower-festooned village to another, all clustered in the little pocket canyons beneath sheer cliffs, he could see how the rugged beauty and the sweet sounds of the place could easily capture the heart.

After a long walk, Rey would often pause to rinse himself under a cool gush of ice-cold water streaming from the mountain reservoirs. He learned the craters of the four volcanoes all captured water from the constant swath of clouds that collected around their peaks. Then the water came funneling down lava tubes, or in some cases man-made tunnels. Each little village had a main water spigot running from this mountain water source that they would tap for crystal-clear, cold drinking and bath water, with little side sloughs that could send running water to the houses where there were overhead storage tanks for individual use. Then the water was fed into a fishpond and finally into an irrigation and stock tank that was used to water the hanging gardens, one precious drop at a time, using carefully designed drip irrigation. Each house also had gutters that funneled any rainwater into the tanks. None of the precious water was ever wasted.

It was patently obvious the Foondavians loved colors. All the houses were painted, with the predominant colors being pink, various tints of bright greens, and all shades of brilliant blue and yellow. It all contrasted well with the volcanic rock and the wild explosion of colorful flowers and vines everywhere. "I notice all the wild mixture of colors, like they're using up the artist's palette, but somehow it all meshes well. Where does the paint come from?" Rey asked a bemused Monvale.

"An unfortunate freighter washed ashore. We rescued the crew, and they gladly offloaded all their thousands of gallons of paint to get the craft afloat again. People accused old "Devil Eye" McTree and her son of setting false lighthouse beacons to lure the freighter into shore, but, as devious as Delilah is, I doubt even she would do that, ha, although we did have a mysterious rash of freighters drifting in for a while, and many of them did coincidentally have some of McTree's relations aboard! But you would think they would have been a little smarter in their selection of vessels to hijack! We are so far off the major shipping lanes, I can't figure out what the derelicts were doing steering this way. Speaking of the McTrees, most of her clan are now holed up in the Fenrir Shamar crater camp or out on the sea steads we discussed earlier. They are a real shady bunch and can't be trusted. Some of them would probably work for NAP if they got wind of it. So even here we have our villains," he ended sadly.

Mention of the NAP threat made him determined to re-double his efforts to learn what mysterious lessons Nambo wanted him to master so he could get back into the battle. As beguiling as Foondavi was, the fate of his family still remained in the forefront of his thoughts.

One day Rey was walking by the destroyed old airfield close to the tidal flats when he saw what appeared to be the foundations of a large structure. This led to quite an interesting story from the enthusiastic Monvale about how deceptively cunning the islanders could be when necessary. It so happened that quite a few years before, the international Mafia, a subsidiary of NAP, decided to find an isolated location where they could put up a casino and a pleasure palace, unencumbered by any moralistic or restrictive government, or even international law. The closest neighbor of Foondavi, a distant island called Cozorre, a corrupt place then run by the Cozatta family, encouraged them in the idea. "Crocodiles with calculators," the Monvale called them, in a rare moment of anger. The idea was that people would fly into a newly built Cozorre International Airport and then be flown to a secret location where any pleasure, no matter how illegitimate or horrid, would be offered. For prying eyes, it would appear to be a temporary visa on your passport for a few days on the sleepy little island of Cozorre.

The Mafia came to Foondavi and started to grab a lot of curious island people for leverage. The Monvale and Harvard Kowloon quickly assured them it wasn't necessary. They stated they were delighted and honored someone found a profitable use for their worthless little island and innocent, nearly Stone Age people. Once they understood what was planned, they almost too readily pledged complete support. They showed the nefarious visitors a nice level place to build, in fact, the only flat and suitable building place on the entire rumpled island. They even willingly provided labor for a relatively low wage as well as for some chocolate, Spam, beer, coffee, and a few odd tools.

A large structure was rapidly built, using local rock and freighted-in cement. Silky white sand was flown in and lots of palm trees provided. They restored, even extended the abandoned cargo cult runway, and put in a new working control tower. Then the Mafia prepared to bring in their first set of well-paying and unscrupulous scoundrels. Like clockwork, the first roaring typhoon of the season came whirling in, followed shortly by a ferocious rogue wave. A complete act of Mother Nature, it was totally out of anyone's control—although, of course, the locals expected it! The soggy, dispirited Mafia left, cursing the island and the now safely hiding islanders, and never came back, blaming the Cozorre power brokers for not warning them of the treacherous island and its primitive cannibal people. The Cozatta family all mysteriously disappeared; it was rumored they were buried in the foundations of a new casino built somewhere else by the vengeful Mafia.

The Monvale chuckled for a long time, recounting the episode, then shared another even more devious escapade. A few years later, another heinous plot was hatched by another group of Cozorrean miscreants. This one was to use Foondavi as a dumping ground for nuclear and biohazard waste. Cozorre, of course, would be kept clean and act as only a transshipment center, charging a small handling fee for the paperwork. It would all be handled by the United Nations, so it was all above board, ha, ha! When the Monvale and Harvard Kowloon heard of the plot, they put their scheming brains together and hatched a devious plan. Harvard Kowloon was hurriedly dispatched to Hong Kong. Soon, authentic, rich-looking envelopes containing very official-looking documents postmarked from Hong Kong were sent to key members of each of the United Nations representatives. The richly embossed envelope only said in elegant script, "Top Secret," and "Approved Clearance Only," and some other seductively mysterious-sounding verbiage. When the impressed recipients looked inside, they found a brief note telling them that a top secret "unnamed" foreign spy agency had placed hidden sensors in many of the top stock trading organizations and that a specific large company's stock on the New York Stock Exchange was going to rise the next day. A week later, the person got another richly embossed and expensive-looking top secret letter. Inside it they found a note that reminded them that what was said last week had come true and that tomorrow the stock would go down. As predicted, it did. The third week another impressive-looking letter was delivered, reminding the recipients of the two previous accurate calls and telling them this time the stock would decline again; they should not do anything yet, since a fourth letter would be coming and then they could jump in and make a big killing.

Several key UN delegates were beside themselves, realizing they could make a large fortune using this secret, albeit illegal, insider information if they listened to the sender. A few of the more courageous risk-takers already had, to their great gain. Now they were ready to go all in. When the fourth letter arrived, they were slightly disappointed. Although it reminded them of the three previous accurate predictions, it said, if they wanted the fourth letter, they needed to pressure a Security Council member of their choice to block the Cozorrean-backed proposal to create a nuclear waste and biohazard dump on an obscure, weirdly named island. Key influential people immediately barraged the UN Security Council using all sorts of bribes and leverage, trying to get them to vote no on the measure. Just by chance, one of the Security Council voters himself was greatly encouraged by all the unexpected support, because he was already planning to stonewall the proposal just to get the secret fourth letter.

Pressure also came from a group of small island nations whose home islands were flat and barely above sea level. They were transported to Foondavi by a sleek, mysterious ship belonging to some eccentric billionaire, then flown over the flat part of the island by high-tech black helicopters to see the ruined foundations of the former Mafia resort supposedly swamped by rising ocean levels. Their hosts strongly stated this was global warming at work and would be a very unsafe nuclear and biohazard dumping site. Some of them were hoping for a fourth informative letter too, so they were already persuaded to be strong advocates of blocking the Cozorrean measure. The added inducement of having a for-real developing nation global warming victim they could advertise was just fantastic icing on the cake.

The Cozorreans were shocked when their seemingly surefire proposal was shot down resoundingly. They had to struggle mightily to keep their own island from being designated as the dump site instead. The only people more shocked were all the people waiting for the secret fourth letter they never received. When discreetly investigated, the suspected foreign country's intelligence agency, as usual, claimed no knowledge of the ruse, it being illegal and unethical!

When Rey heard this, he was confounded. "How did Harvard Kowloon and you do such a thing? Did you, in fact, bug the office of a key company? I know you guys are crafty, but that sounds a little illegal, actually a lot illegal, if there is such a thing!"

"I am shocked, shocked that you would think the Monvale of Troon and the good Doctor Kowloon would do such a nefarious thing!" Seeing Rey's surprised look at the Doctor title, the Monvale added, "Doctorate in economics from the London School of Economics, besides his Harvard MBA. Now back to being shocked. Remember I said many of our people are descendants of criminal con artists? This was a classic con playing on the greed of people. There were originally over 360 official-looking letters that went out to various key UN decision makers from the Hong Kong post office in our first mailing. Half of them, about 180 or so, said the stock would go up, and the same number said it would go down. Whichever one was right, gave us 180 winners to receive the second letter, so ninety got an up and ninety got a down. We now had ninety potential winners. So then we sent the third letter with forty-five up and forty-five down. This gave us over ten percent of the UN going crazy, salivating, thinking they would make a significant, but illicit fortune. We also got lucky and one of the Security Council members was still in the running for the fourth letter. Of course, there was no bug in anybody's office, as that would have been highly illegal. And, of course, you know we wouldn't stoop to that level, harrumph! A few of the people who jumped the gun even made a little money; some lost a little if they got the wrong prediction. They should have followed our advice and waited, and no one would have lost a dime. By the way, Cozorre doesn't mess with us anymore, the little snots. With friends like them, who needs enemies?" Seeing Rey's look of disapproval, he quickly added: "We may not be unscrupulous psychopaths, but we never said we were saints!"

As Rey continued to wander up, down, and around the twenty-mile-long by ten-mile-wide island, he continued to gain respect for the islanders. If you ask an American who someone is, he will say, "That's Joe Blow." Ask a Foondavi-an and be prepared for a full-blown history of the family, a description of key ancestors such as a grandpa who float-ed ashore on a door 125 years ago, and a rundown of the person's living extended family, all of whom fish off Boogan Head in a green boat! Twenty-five minutes later, the Foonda-vian will finally add, "And his name is Joe Blow." They know a person is so much more than just a name. Everyone is a song, a history, a continuous strand in the collective DNA. Most of all, everyone has great worth, whether he or she has contribut-ed it yet or not! "Everyone is gifted. Some just haven't opened up their packages yet!" the Monvale would often say.

One of the things Rey loved best about the islanders was their willingness at the drop of a hat to have a celebration, or what they called a "jamaroon." The smallest positive event or action set off a chain reaction of celebrations throughout several villages. Each jamaroon involved dancing, eating, and singing, but each had its own significant ceremony. Some ja-maroons were sadder as in the case of a "wobabo" jamaroon, the going-away ceremony, which often meant a funeral in the grove with the burial beneath a new fruit tree, or perhaps just someone leaving to go on a long trip. As sad as the wobabo ja-maroon started, the irrepressible nature of the Foondavi peo-ple soon broke through and they ended up celebrating the life of the person and talking about the future heavenly reunion, or how they would celebrate the return.

Probably the most important of all jamaroons, however, was the "napoa" jamaroon. This was the naming ceremony. New babies were, of course, given baby names, but as soon as a child's personality began to emerge he or she was given a simple love name such as the likes of Sweet Berry, Tickle Toes, or Nibble Lip. As they got a little older and passed the reading, writing, and reasoning exams, children also were given another name, sort of a descriptive first name to go with the family name such as Burly Bombletree because of a boy's large size, or Freeby Greeb because of his generosity.

The biggest and best napoa jamaroons were for the "earned" names. These were names that were given by the council of wise elders in each village and were reserved, in most cases, for people who deserved high honor. For example, Rey learned that the name for Wise One or Wisdom Lender in Foondavi language was Worly Worlo, and Master Craftsman was Tufooga. There were many trades such a weaver, carpenter, builder, boat maker, fisherman, farmer, and the like, so the Tufooga name, which was borrowed from Samoan, was fairly common. Nonetheless, it was hard to earn. To be a Tufooga in any trade was an honor won only if the person displayed master craftsmanship as well as accolades for his or her personal service.

Rey also learned that such names as "Harvard" could be given to designate a person having gone off island and graduating from a school. That helped explain the weird university first names often heard on the island such as Yale Cronk, Stanford Moogie, and Princeton Quadroon, although he never heard the stories behind the names of Vegas McBlue and Yonkers Troon.

Nonetheless, during a particular napoa jamaroon, Rey was surprised to hear the name Nambo murmured and have people looking directly at him. The experience made him realize how much he missed the old Mahogany Maestro, Crazy Jake Nambo, but it also made him curious. What did the name mean and why were the islanders looking at him? No one would say. It would be a while before he found out, and it would change him forever.

All the celebrations and joy were wonderful, but Rey was still plagued by concern for his family. The Monvale just continued to counsel patience. "The wheels within wheels are turning. Your family continues to be safe, though admittedly in a precarious situation. Keep learning and getting stronger."

Rey decided he had to do something to occupy his mind while he waited. He decided that being the only monolingual person on Foondavi was not good and, with the encouragement of the Mondale, started to study the old language of Foondavi. He enthusiastically threw himself into learning the local lingo. He knew language was often called the "software of the mind," and he felt that learning it would expand his mental capacity as well as help him understand his new friends better.

Soon Rey found out why the locals referred to it as the "gentle tongue." While Foondavi was a pidgin type of language, made up of useful and descriptive words taken from many languages, it had a distinct sound of its own. There were no harsh, guttural words, and it sounded melodious.

There also were few negative, discouraging, or bad words, yet there were a myriad of expressions of positive encouragement, instruction, and respect. The bulk of the words, as Rey had learned already, were for detailed descriptions of relationships, which was not surprising, being on a small island with close contact among people. For example, there was a specific word for younger brother's second son on mother's side. Also included in Foondavi were intricate definitions of the relationships, spelling out in detail how they should be treated.

Another big block of words was designated for celebrations of all sorts. Special treatment was given to how to praise and correct children, emphasizing the role of building them up and not knocking them down, on being the best little Foondavians they could possibly be. Over twenty words for different kinds of peace and over twenty-five for forgiveness and reconciliation also existed. In addition, the language contained over thirty words for different types and levels of love, and it was very descriptive of the whole sexual side of life, making a strong distinction between love and lust, which Rey knew he needed to closely study and learn. But the vast majority of words had to do with depicting how to be a wise and good Foondavian.

Rey couldn't help but contrast this with American English, when he recalled the Monvale sharing earlier with him that the bulk of American words had to do with automobiles, followed closely by the unofficial religion of sports.

As he continued to delve into the language, Rey also learned that more warlike languages would have over 100 distinct words for ambush, while Foondavi had almost no words for war. If language was the software of the mind, words were undoubtedly the programming. He liked the Foondavi program.

The gentle tongue also was easy to read, as it was completely phonetic, and he was soon enthralled. The language perfectly represented the Foondavi people!

The wise elders in each village he entered would take honor in teaching him a new word and how to pronounce and apply it. Almost all the words came with picturesque parables or metaphors, so the concepts were easily remembered. For example, different parables about bridges between villages being broken and restored were used to portray the importance and types of forgiveness and reconciliation, subjects that made up big sections of the vocabulary.

The greatest numbers of words by far were reserved for the process of learning and the teaching and rearing of children. Most were accompanied by examples from planting, fertilizing, and growing fruits and vegetables. It was obvious the culture revered great teachers and learning. Every village contained several teachers and mentors, or "wisdom lenders" as the gentle tongue designated them. They would congregate in the community fale in each village and mentor young and old, or learn from each other. To be a wisdom lender, especially at the Tufooga level, was a high honor.

Rey also found out that another honored role on the island was that of an "epoa." The epoa jamaroon was basically a poetry fest. However, epoa was the old Foondavi word for the number twenty-one. To Foondavians, the number twenty-one was special because it meant ten fingers, ten toes, and one heart—all to be lent to others to help them love, grow, and learn. The epoa itself was to be three lines of seven words either in English or the old gentle tongue. Then selected people, who were epoa tufoogas, or poetry masters, would rate the effort on a scale of one low to seven high on three categories. How clear was the meaning, how creative the insights, and how important was the concept conveyed? A perfect score of twenty-one, epoa, was exceedingly rare and a source of much celebration. The best of the epoas were collected and placed in special books to be shared throughout the island around the firesides. To have a designated and celebrated epoa tufooga in your village was considered a high honor!

Quite a few treasured and well-used books could be found on the island, but Rey soon learned that the one they referred to most was the *Golden Book of Collected Wisdom*. Once he learned how to proficiently read the gentle tongue, he could borrow a precious copy of the book from the home village of the McBlue family of Tickle Toe Trickle. This village got its name because of the small burbling stream that ran through it under lots of little bridges, forming little trout-filled pools. It was in a small pocket canyon not far up country from Troon, so Rey often trekked up the steep, winding path leading there to enter the lower ring road. He didn't realize until later that his borrowing of the treasured and revered book meant he accepted them as his adopted village. It was a big deal, and a napoa jamaroon soon broke out, proclaiming Rey a new son and giving him his first unique Foondavi name of Fuzzy McBlue, because of his uncut curly hair, scraggly beard, and possibly his big blue eyes. He didn't realize this at the time, but the coincidental name was to prove quite prophetic.

After much dancing and singing and a lot of great food, as it was expected that everyone brought their best dish to such an important celebration, everyone had a chance to tell a story and sing a song to honor him. He was finally able to settle down in the community fale in front of the softly glowing fireplace and read the book, accompanied by a swarm of all the little McBlue children who sat on his lap and at his feet. He was astonished to find that the book included portions of Proverbs from the Hebrew Bible as well as sections from Philippians ("Think more highly of others than yourself"), James ("Consider it all pure joy when you encounter various trials"), and Romans ("All things work together for good for those that love God and are called to His purpose") from the Christian New Testament. It also included sayings attributed to the great Gandhi ("You must be the change you want to see in other people"), a little Dale Carnegie ("You never really win an argument"), and even some Chinese proverbs ("Keep the mountain green and you will always have firewood"). This last proverb he took to mean, "Always build and preserve your resources." There were also proverbs and wisdom attributed to the Ibo and Kikuyu people of Africa ("When the elephants fight, it is the ants that get trampled") and some Navajo and even Pewamo insights ("Conquer the enemy within and the enemy without can do nothing"). The Ten Commandments were also highlighted and illustrated in very meaningful ways, accompanied by more parables. The rest of the book was comprised of award-winning epoas.

The whole *Golden Book of Collected Wisdom* was chock full of insights and gentle rules from all corners of the world about positive social interactions and how to be the best Foondavian you could possibly be. A parable or word picture that enthralled his young audience also accompanied each proverb or wisdom saying. He found there were also many songs and rhymes with accompanying hand gestures and dances the children all knew. These seemed to help the little ones understand the concepts no matter how complex. Some of the more verbal youngsters would declaim pertinent epoas they had learned that dealt with the specific subject. It was an amazing time for Rey, seeing and sharing the real joy the children displayed in learning. They considered it a privilege and not an onerous task!

As Rey continued to wander the island, he was finding himself growing stronger day by day physically, mentally, and spiritually. He found he was developing a calm, strong sanity. He realized this was all going to help him be a better leader when he returned home. He was being touched deeply by Foondavi and its people in thought, heart, and spirit. In return, he was fully embraced by the gentle people and their peace, kindness, and goodness. They might not have the material things of the world in abundance, but they had the lasting things well in hand.

Learning the gentle tongue also led Rey to more adventures on the ring roads as he climbed higher into the misty heights. One day he was walking high up in the clouds along a particularly precarious route when ahead of him he saw a curious sign in a very ancient form of Foondavi. It was placed over what appeared to be a small lava tube opening from which a small rivulet was flowing. As he silently watched, a beautiful young girl suddenly stepped out and didn't see him. She turned away from him and headed down another trail. He watched her go, then approached closer and perused the strange sign. He wouldn't have known the meaning of the name inscribed on the sign, except a wisdom lender had fortuitously shared it with him just the prior day. The word translated into English as "reservation or sanctuary." It reminded Rey of Nambo and his use of the word for his special place on earth.

Full of curiosity, Rey crept up the tube just a little way and was surprised to find it gradually widening. He soon was crawling out into an opening in the mountain. It looked like a cathedral of huge trees, perhaps redwoods of some sort, he thought. He was astounded to see they soared over his head to a height of at least three hundred feet and swayed gently in the soft breeze gently flowing through the deep gorge. He had no idea there was anything like this hidden on the island. Then he heard laughter, and a small child came bounding out of the shadows and nearly bowled him over. When he gently caught her to lift her up to her feet, she let out a startled cry and backed off. Rey saw she had beautiful eyes, but the rest of her face was deformed either by a disease, an accident, or a genetic defect.

Soon a gently murmuring crowd of the most unusual-appearing people he had ever seen surrounded him. All of them were strangely formed but beautiful in their own shy and gentle way. They were talking in a highly accented form of the gentle tongue, but he realized much of the accent was due to facial disfigurement. Many had deformed arms but were waving them excitedly, letting him know they were pleased to see him.

"These are God's gentle creatures," a deep baritone voice rang out in English from behind him, "disfigured survivors of human and natural mayhem. And whom may I ask is entering our own little Garden of Eden?"

Rey turned and was shocked to see the booming voice belonged to a small but plump male version of the elfin Mary Contrary Jones. The man approached Rey with a cheerful smile on his face.

Rey replied back in English, "I was formerly known on Foondavi as Joe Frumerica Junior, but now have had the name Fuzzy McBlue bestowed on me, but I have so many other names I hardly know where to begin. However, I will make you a wager," Rey replied back in English.

"You will make me a wager? I don't have any money as I don't get any wage to wager!" the kind-looking tiny man said, gurgling another laugh that made his ample belly shake.

"I will wager you are related to Sister Mary Contrary Jones."

It was now the small man's turn to be surprised. "She is my sister, my real trickster of a sister, a crazy little ninja nun! And you, young man, must be the name to remain unnamed, unless the snakes enter my garden again."

Rey soon found out the man's name was Larry Leroy Jones, a former professional lightweight wrestler known as Leaping Larry Leroy Jones, who had specialized in the French fighting style of kickboxing to win a world featherweight championship—way back in the old days when it was only slightly fixed, as he quickly added. Because his brain was getting kicked in too many times over the years, his sister hooked him into teaching her and her "children" how to kickbox. She then tricked him into leading a group of her special children to Foondavi, where they could lead a decent life away from bullies and judging eyes. "Between my soft head and soft heart, I got addicted to helping all these little cast offs and rejects," he continued in English, gently rustling the hair of a little urchin hugging his leg. Others were tugging at him to get his attention. "Do you know the old tongue, the gentle one, my friend?" Larry asked. "I hate to be rude and talk in front of so many of my little friends in a language they can't speak."

Rey quickly responded in fluent Foondavi. "I have the utmost respect for your sister and your nephew Jake Nambo."

"Old Jake the Snake, the Mahogany Maestro!" he said laughingly in Foondavi, and then added quickly, seeing Rey's shocked look: "And I mean that most endearingly. I assumed you knew his background since you seem to know Mary."

Larry proceeded to fill Rey in more about Nambo as they walked through the towering trees toward a warmly lit log house in the distance. A Down Syndrome child on one side was holding Rey's hand. The original little girl he had bumped into held his other hand. Their faces glowed with unworldly peace as they skipped along accompanied by lots of others of all different shapes and sizes. Rey suddenly realized the word in Foondavi wasn't "disfigured." Instead it was a word that meant "uniquely beautiful."

"As you should have been told by now, 'Nambo' is not actually a name. It's a gentle tongue or old Foondavi word or title meaning 'protector or guardian son,'" Larry continued. "So, Nambo is not really a name. It's a revered position among the island people, similar to the position of a shirt wearer in the Dakota or Lakota Native American people. The Dakota shirt wearer, or our Nambo, must be selected by others, usually a council of wise elders, and must consistently demonstrate generosity, courage, and steadfastness. In our own unique Foondavi way, we added to that list what would be called 'a servant's heart.' Generosity and courage are fairly easily understood, but steadfastness means persistence, commitment, and resilience. Grit in other words. The rare leader that is designated Nambo must be a person whose values will not be shaken. He must serve as a protector of all people, especially the weak and vulnerable. Many years ago, a young and battered Jake came here with me to grow up in a safe place. He was not physically disfigured by radiation, genetics, abuse, or accident like these children, but he was disfigured in a deeper way. He was a high-functioning autistic child, often perhaps inaccurately referred to as an Asperger's child. He was a cultural misfit in the old USA. As you can imagine, after your experiences of the last few months, the island agreed with him and the Foondavi way eventually worked its magic. It dramatically changed him. The wise elders saw the change and unanimously selected him as a Nambo at a very young age. He has been a protector and guardian of Foondavi and all of God's helpless and lost children since that time."

Rey saw the pieces of a complex puzzle begin to come together. "So," he asked cautiously, "what is Nambo's real name then?" He didn't expect the jaw-dropping answer he received.

"His original name was Jacob Nithing. His mother was abducted and raped by Rancor Nithing. She was continuously brutalized by the loathsome man and then left behind, broken and discarded, and ended up in an institution," he said bitterly. "When Rancor found out later she was pregnant again and was to give birth, he came back to kill her and the baby. She managed to get a very premature Jacob into my sister's care before Rancor caught and killed her."

"What a brave woman!" Rey said, sadly shaking his head in wonder.

"Who said she was a woman? She was only a little more than fourteen years old! That monster Rancor was afraid he would be tried as the pedophile rapist he was."

"That explains a lot," Rey said, still seeing the seething hatred in the otherwise loving Nambo when he discussed the Nithings or crossed paths with a psychopath.

"What about the Quark name he keeps adding to his self-description?" Rey thought to ask.

"Well, I'm definitely not a physicist, and it's one of the few things Jake Nambo isn't, at least yet to my knowledge. Let me take a layman's run at it. He says the 'quark' is a small subatomic particle fundamental to all matter. It flits around everywhere, largely undetected, but you never find them isolated or alone. They are always combined with other particles like protons or neutrons to make something stable called a 'hadron.' It's interesting, because some of the six 'flavors' or types of quarks can only be produced by high-energy collisions, and one of those is called the strange or crazy quark." Seeing Rey's puzzled look, he continued: "It may not help, but Nambo sees himself as only one small part of the bigger picture, flitting here and there, a strange, somewhat crazy person formed by a huge collision most of us haven't even detected. His objective is to create a stable, unifying force for the positive. That's why the bigger group he is now busily forming is called the Hadron Group. It's a bunch of hackers and thinkers devoted to disrupting and destroying NAP."

Seeing Rey's still confused look, he continued: "I know, clear as the fog on Boogan Head, our mountain over there, but it's the best I can do. It will all come clear when you finally meet the Hadron Group."

The rest of the afternoon was spent wandering around the exquisite setting of the Eden Gorge, as the place was called, getting the guided tour by Larry after the gentle souls prepared them as sumptuous a meal as Rey ever tasted on Foondavi or anywhere. "There are approximately ten other gorges like this, hollowed out by the water and lava rushing down from the high peaks. They were shut off and hidden by the old Foondavians when all the different predators came in to ravage the land of trees and soil and anything remotely valuable. Each gorge now acts as a biodiversity lab, too, as we try out different plants to see how they can help us eventually rebuild Foondavi. We have hundreds of different trees here, plus all sorts of vines and ferns. As you can tell, it stays fairly moist here, very temperate, and protected from the wind. We have trained Foondavian botanists, biologists, ecologists, 'gists' I don't even know the meaning of. Many were trained at great universities, thanks to Nambo's money and pull, and others are trained here via satellite link. We are checking out over 300,000 types of plants from all over the world, and many more bugs as well, to test for drugs that can be used for healing diseases throughout the world. We then turn our findings over to Nambo's privately owned big pharmaceutical 'drug' company, and he patents them and makes the cures available to people at a low cost and reasonable profit, driving the big pharma companies crazy! No margin, no mission, we always say, so we don't mind making a realistic profit to help the company grow. The world gets healed, we make a little money, and we can keep these projects going. The other use of these isolated, nearly inaccessible gorges on this isolated and nearly inaccessible island is to protect all these gentle souls that have been discarded by the world. My crazy sister Mary rescues them, and then I get to shepherd them here in our little haven."

"How many people know about this, both the biodiversity and the home for gentle souls?" Rey inquired.

"Very few people even here on the island. Delilah 'Devil Eye' McTree or her son Shacknasty McTree would probably turn us or you over to NAP in a heartbeat to get Spam, beer, and chocolate. You wouldn't even have been let in if the Monvale hadn't cleared you." Seeing Rey's quizzical look, Larry gestured to indicate a well-hidden sniper tower over the small lava tube entrance Rey hadn't noticed on his way in. "Usually that tube is closed and a Fenrir sniper is always on duty. We just opened the small tube door to let a student helper out to go see her parents, and you wandered in. Fortunately for you, the Monvale, Big Jon Flynn, said not to shoot you. He still has high hopes you 'might amount to something yet,' were his exact words."

"I'm a little hurt he didn't think I could be trusted," Rey added, a little miffed. "I love Foondavi and these people, even Nambo and Big Jon the Monvale, believe it or not. I would never do anything to betray them."

"If you get caught by NAP, they will torture you and find out anything you know," Larry said knowingly. "I have the scars all over my body to prove it. At the time, I fortunately didn't know about Foondavi. Believe me, as brave and tough as I thought I was, pro fighter and everything, they were soon wringing everything out of me. I even betrayed sweet Mary, my own sister, so she had to go undercover," he said, the last part in a deeply broken voice. "If Poger and Darvin Reinbolt's father Darius and the Fenrir Wolves hadn't rescued me, I would be dead. Wrung out and hung out literally to die. That's why I had to come here with the young Jake. I didn't have a choice. I can't be trusted not to crumble again under torture. They love to torture people and joke, while doing it, that they get paid by the hour. So they prolong the agony as long as they can."

The day was growing late, and the shadows were quickly closing in on the narrow gorge. A waterfall was rumbling gently in the distance, and the gentle ones were singing inside the big log structure with the soft golden light pouring out of the big windows.

"Tell Mary I love her," Larry said, reaching out a broken hand to Rey. "I know she has forgiven me, but I still wake up at night hating myself for folding. The Monvale says everyone does, even the best trained Special Forces people, but I still wish I could have held out."

As Rey entered the tube again, he waved at the sinister-looking Fenrir sniper manning the tower who didn't wave back but just maintained a stern face. Rey also turned back and waved at Larry who was framed with the huge trees behind him, surrounded by the gentle souls of Eden. He did wave back.

The Monvale wasn't very happy with Rey when he returned home to the driftwood shack in Troon. "Did you really consider letting them shoot me?" Rey asked, hoping the answer was no.

"It was my fault for letting you freely wander anywhere you wanted to go," the Monvale said sternly. "I wanted you to learn Foondavian ways so you could get strong and help us translate many of these things back into America, when and if it is ever safe for us to return. And, yes, I considered letting them shoot you. If you get caught . . ."

Rey was shaken to his core. "Then don't let me get caught," he said, in a tone that indicated he hadn't lost everything the rotten Thornton Nithing had taught him.

The Monvale just ignored the bravado. "Tomorrow you get to prove just how brave and tough you are, little nephew. It's called the egg chase. The council of wise elders in their usually unquestionable wisdom decided it's time to test your skinny little butt and find out if you have it in you to be a real Foondavi man. You already received your first Foondavi name, Fuzzy McBlue. Now let's see what you've really got!"

He went on to explain that the egg chase resembled an ancient rite the Easter Islanders used to practice. Who knows how the Foondavians learned of it, or maybe they created it and the Easter Islanders copied them? No matter who created it, the deceptively named egg chase was a real nut cracker, to so crudely put it.

As Rey knew from reading the Golden Book of Collected Wisdom and from Larry's comments about the Nambo title, the islanders tested all their young men and women on four traits: generosity, courage, steadfastness, and willingness to serve others. The test of courage was the egg chase. As Big Jon Flynn described it in all its gruesome detail, the mild-sounding egg chase took on ominous overtones, and a sense of foreboding overcame Rey.

The chase started with a five hundred-foot hazardous climb down the side of Boogan Head, a nasty mountain cliff jammed with jagged rocks overlooking a two hundred-foot-tall needle-shaped island full of sea birds. The last fifty feet down Boogan Head was a diving plunge over submerged boulders into the heaving waves of ice cold water that separated the main island from the needle about three hundred yards off shore. Those brave souls who survived the shark-infested swim though the churning and numbing water then faced a two hundred-foot climb up the sheer rock face of the needle. There, they snagged an egg from crevices in the steep cliffs at the top while dodging the attacking sharp-beaked birds defending the nests. Finally, the survivors climbed back down the cliff without breaking the egg, swam back across the narrow, but treacherous strait, and struggled all the way back up to the starting point, presenting their unbroken egg to the council of elders officiating the event. There was no time limit, and it wasn't a winner-take-all test—for as many participants as could finish would be honored. Not many were chosen to do this grueling challenge. Worse yet, not many finished.

According to Big Jon Flynn, there was no strategy to win. He did tell Rey to get a good night of sleep and that it was okay to be afraid. "You just need to control your fear and turn it into energy," he said. "And, remember: Not too many even try, and even fewer finish, so give it your best shot. Just being selected to try means a lot, believe me. I was here several years before they finally offered me a shot!"

He pulled up his shirt and showed Rey a jagged scar. "Rocks got me on the way down, and sharks nearly got me on the way over. Coming back, I was in shock, but somehow I made it to the top. If a big oaf like me can do it, so can you." With that he gave Rey another bone-crushing hug. "By the way, I really wouldn't have let them shoot you, though the thought did cross my mind!" And then he left Rey to sweat out the night dwelling on thoughts about sharp rocks and nasty sharks.

Rey somehow managed to get some sleep, but the next morning dawned bright and early. His adrenaline was roaring as he, the other contestants, and some supportive islanders walked the long, steep, winding hike to Boogan Head. His only consolation was that the other participants looked to be as scared as he was.

The local wisdom lender Tufooga, who was in charge of the trial, started out addressing the group that included several young ladies as well as a ragtag group of shaking young men. The other islanders were there as witnesses to either the participants' utter defeat or great victory. The wisdom lender, intoning words in the gentle tongue, referred to something Rey remembered reading in the *Golden Book*. "Honorable

Foondavians, we call on you today to watch these young men and women attempt a courageous act. Listen to my wisdom, young ones. Courage is not the absence of fear but learning to control that fear. You should be afraid. The cliff is high, the rocks sharp, and the sharks are very hungry."

Turning to the windswept cliff, the Tufooga blew a conch shell to supposedly send the sharks away. Rey wasn't sure if that was going to work so well, but by now he was willing to give almost anything a shot. He was dimly aware that a growing crowd was gathered around the Monvale and the wise elders, watching the shivering young people dressed in only skimpy bathing suits, carrying a sack to collect an egg and teetering on the wind-blasted cliff edge of Boogan Head. An official-looking elder came and slathered some oil over their bodies and in a gentle voice told them to keep their hands off the oil or they would be too slippery to grasp the rocks. Rey immediately felt the insulating effect of the oil cutting out the wind, and he hoped it would work the same with the icy water that was crashing on the rocks below him. Maybe it was a shark repellant, too, he hoped wistfully.

With a last admonition that any of them could walk away or stop at any time with no shame attached, the Tufooga told them when he blew the conch again to start climbing down the cliff, which was now crowded with shrieking sea birds circling beneath them over the ragged rocks. He reminded them to leap far out beyond the submerged rocks when the time came to dive, and then lifted the conch shell to his lips. Rey's last thought was that he hoped the sharks remembered to go away!

When the signal came, Rey plunged over the edge of the

cliff, finding meager handholds that started tearing at his fingers. He made the descent surprisingly well and then faced the fifty-foot dive over the rocks. It looked more like a hundred feet to him, but he blocked the fear and pushed off, leaping headfirst as far as he could into the roiling waves below. He hit the stunningly cold water with an impact that nearly knocked him out, remembering vaguely and belatedly that someone said to jump feet first. As this thought came to him, he was fighting his way up from the depths and made the mistake of opening his eyes in the cold, salty water. He was stunned to see swimming past him a cold predatory fish eye the size of a large dinner plate on a fish the size of a small bus. He momentarily hoped the conch shell hadn't been a dinner bell and then thankfully broke the surface and gulped a welcome mouth of fresh air.

Putting all thoughts of hungry sharks out of his mind, Rey immediately and frantically started stroking his way toward the needle that loomed ahead of him. He used to swim with his Pewamo friends in the old Kazoo River, but this was unlike any river. The tide was running strong, and the water was breathtakingly cold. He could feel the heat and strength being sucked out of his already-fatigued body as he struggled toward the rock ahead. Suddenly, he realized a young man beside him was going under. He was bleeding from a head wound, probably from hitting a rock, and was gulping huge mouthfuls of water as he went under again. Without thinking, Rey grabbed the young man in an old lifeguard rescue hold and headed toward the sheer rock face of the needle. He was seething mad at the so-called wise elders for staging this idiotic exercise and at Uncle Jon for not excluding him.

He used his red-hot anger to focus and propel himself and his near-comatose friend through the dark, foaming waves to the needle outcropping. Then he shoved the fellow up on the rocks and shouted at him, "The roughest part is over, dude! Let's go get some eggs for breakfast!"

With that, he started dragging the young guy up the cliff. The young man soon started to revive. Smiling thankfully at Rey, the young man regained his footing and joined Rey in the ascent up the rugged slope. They helped each other find handholds and provided support to the other when necessary. Soon the two were being pecked and pelted by enraged seabirds, a good sign Rey figured, they must be getting to the top, but still no eggs. After much scouting, Rey finally spotted an egg. Without thinking, though, Rey handed the egg to the young Foondavian and pointed for him to head down. But the young man declined. Instead, he boosted Rey up a few more feet of crumbling rock face, where they found a second egg.

Rey and his companion could see other contestants struggling in the distance, but they kept their focus narrowed on descending the needle while keeping their eggs safe. When they reached the foaming inferno of the strait, they eyed each other, inspected their unbroken eggs, and started out swimming desperately for the far shore.

Although both made it to land, Rey's forty-year-old body and injured leg started to betray him. Although he was in great shape from hiking over the demanding Foondavi ring roads, the cold and the exertion were just too much. He was shaking with cold and exhaustion and wanted to collapse— but the young man he had rescued wouldn't let him quit. He hoisted Rey up the cliff face until Rey regained some strength.

Then they both staggered, arm in arm, to the Tufooga and handed him their miraculously unbroken eggs.

The crowd went wild to an extent unusual even for the normally boisterous islanders. Rey was numb and nearly unconscious, his adrenaline drained. If not for his Uncle Big Jon the Monvale holding him up, Rey would have collapsed. All the other participants were still huddled on the far shore. Two huge twenty-foot-long white sharks had ignored the conch shell signal and were cruising the strait looking for lunch. Rey and his partner had swum right over the top of them, ignoring the warning signals to wait until the sharks cleared out. Rey was too dead tired to admit he hadn't heard any signal, and his partner had collapsed beside him into a deep sleep of utter exhaustion. "Let them think what they want to think," he thought as he slumped nearly unconscious against his big Uncle Jon. His uncle smiled down at him and whispered, "Not that I ever doubted you, Rey, but you are even stronger and braver than I expected!"

———

Rey had slept for twelve hours—and probably could have slept even longer—when his Uncle Jon rudely shook him out of his deep slumber and scary dreams of toothy sharks. "There is going to be a big napoa jamaroon for you up at the McBlue village. The wise elders are coming from all over the island. Come on, get your skinny self dressed! This could be a big deal!" the Monvale prodded.

Rey staggered into his clothes, thinking the only big deal he wanted was to sleep for several more hours. Also, although his stomach was telling him a good meal was needed to replenish his energy supply, another part of his body was letting him know he needed to jettison some of the swallowed seawater.

It turns out, it was a big deal! The council of wise elders had decided that, because of Rey's bravery and serving heart, he would be one of only four active shirt-wearer Nambos for the island. The elders already were impressed with Rey's generosity and serving spirit, but his aid of the fellow egg hunter at the risk of his own life was icing on the cake. His steadfastness was further proven by his refusal to quit, and his courage was without question, having literally swum with sharks.

Rey protested strongly that he was not qualified to be a shirt wearer. The wise ones, however, responded that, if he thought he was qualified, they wouldn't want him! So, the question was posed to him by one of the elders, "Would you accept the honor and the responsibility of being a shirt wearer for the island?" He found out his big Uncle Jon, the Monvale, whose full Foondavi name was Nambo Tall Tree Flynn, was one. Another was Nambo Geechi Troom, a boat-building lady Tufooga from the other side of Foondavi whom he had not yet met. And, Rey was pleased to hear the person being considered for the fourth and final active shirt-wearer honor was his young partner from the egg race whose name was Poover Cronk. Rey's new earned name was announced as Nambo Griot McBlue, meaning "protector and storyteller."

Then the napoa jamaroon began. It was considered for years the jamaroon of jamaroons, partly because, after a few too many "attitude adjustments," the Big Nambo Tall Tree

Flynn, the Monvale of Troon, danced the fire dance and nearly burnt the village down—and his pants off.

═══════

A week later, Rey was invited to the Shamar Fenrir training camp in the crater on Foondavi's highest volcano. He was surprised to find Poger Reinbolt there. He told Rey it was getting too hot for him in the US, so he parachuted in, arriving somewhat like Rey had—but without the drugs and diaper! Poger now proudly showed Rey around the grim but tidy encampment he had helped build. From the stoic guards at the entrance, to the tightly controlled but non-hostile atmosphere, Rey could see the place meant business. Everywhere the Shamar Fenrir code was posted:

1. Protect the innocent and helpless
2. Never stand by while evil reigns
3. Love life
4. Always put others first
5. My calling is to rescue and restore God's lost children.

Poger was obviously quite justifiably proud of the highly organized camp. "We have close to four hundred psychopaths gathered here from across the globe, in all stages of reform or revolt," he informed Rey.

"Sounds just like Congress to me," Rey answered, failing to get a smile from the taciturn man.

"We bring them from all over and even get a few from

the island here. They develop good lung power and physical endurance at this nearly mile-high level. They learn to shoot long distance and bring down feral goats in this rugged terrain. During the day, we train them on the Shamar Fenrir code and monitor their activities. We have to be ready for anything NAP throws at us. Although we plan to outfight them, we've decided the best way to defeat the NAP military force is to outthink them. We must study them, Nambo McBlue. We must know our enemy well to defeat them. This means we get to know them so well that we can't help but come to respect them. Disrespect of the enemy causes death. The NAP force is a well-oiled, efficient, effective killing machine, designed to dominate. They are completely and totally unencumbered with conscience or compassion. They are cold, bad-ass killers," Poger admitted.

Rey had been waiting to say something to Poger for a long time. "I wanted to thank you for pulling me out of DC and providing some shade for my family. I also feel like I have to apologize for Jake Nambo and my Uncle Flynn, better known to you probably as Flynn Pompatella, for the way they acted at the reservation when you came to rescue me a second time."

Poger just put up his hand to stop Rey. "They are well justified, seeing how they have suffered from psychopaths. My family is dedicated to undoing as much evil as we can. My mom and baby sister were killed by the NAP monsters when my dad, Darius, attempted to withdraw from NAP. He just couldn't stomach the evil any more. We want to show the world that psychopaths can be reformed. We know we can't make everybody trust us. We can just ask to closely watch us and see if we keep our word. We came to rescue you from DC and then the reservation partly because the people here on Foondavi remembered you." Poger barked a short, mirthless laugh, shaking his head: "We were told that, as unbelievable as it sounded, there was actually a good and honorable man in DC—and to quickly go and get him! They remembered you from the earlier US invasion. You were a brave and good man then, maybe on a misguided and messed up mission, but reputably a decent man in all regards."

Rey started to dismiss the compliment, but then a shrill-sounding alarm suddenly went off and people started running for their weapons. "An escape?" Rey asked Poger, that being the worst possible thing he could think of.

"No, something terrible is going wrong on the island. It's not a drill. That is the Shamar Fenrir call to arms!"

Poger quickly picked up a field phone and listened intently. "We have some very bad news," he reported. "Somehow NAP used stealth technology to get by all of our monitoring. The NAP Navy has pulled up offshore with several stealth warships loaded with the latest battle helicopters. The troops already have seized several villages and marched the people down to the tidal zone by Troon as hostages. It's that nasty, constipated Admiral Nathaniel Futtock, the NAP stooge again! He's threatening to nuke the island or, at least, pepper it with cluster bombs. They just played me a recording where he was screaming, 'What is it about nuclear you don't understand?'"

Rey was devastated. "I assume he wants me," he muttered.

"I am afraid so. Listen, between the Fenrir and the Monvale and Harvard Kowloon, we can trick him and whip his butt. The lazy, arrogant, stupid dolt didn't even do reconnaissance and see we're here. He's completely out in the open and vulnerable. We could sink his slinky stealth boats and no one would miss him."

"No, it's too big a risk. I can't let him harm anyone on Foondavi, and a lot of his people are probably innocent bystanders just doing their duty. I also don't want to blow your cover. You are doing good work here. I just need to figure out enough leverage to keep him from breaking me through torture."

"I can share some ideas with you as we hustle our butts down to Troon. Maybe we can scheme up some ideas that might work. I surely can give you more insights into the perverted minds of people like Achor Nithing. The so-called Admiral Futtock is just a bit player. He is fetching you for NAP and the Nithings to try to gain favor, without a doubt," Poger explained.

Soon Rey and Poger were approaching the flatlands around Troon. Poger pulled back after whispering some last-minute sage advice to Rey. When the Monvale attempted to stop Rey from turning himself over, Rey said, "I am a Nambo now, a shirt wearer." He pointed at his multi-hued shirt and continued, "You and the islanders have prepared me well. I am much stronger now. Besides, I think I have enough leverage to keep them distracted, and I wager Crazy Jake will have even more. They have always underestimated us, and especially me, so let's not give them any reason to stop doing so." With that he gave his teary big uncle a bone-crushing hug and strode boldly out to meet the NAP Navy—and the nasty piece of work by the name of Admiral Nathaniel Futtock.

As Rey walked forward, he saw the NAP Special Ops people were getting nervous and possibly trigger happy, suspiciously watching the supposedly hostage villagers who were casually singing and having a picnic, waiting for whatever would happen. Rey was proud to be their Nambo. He smiled a nervous smile at the islanders and waved a last goodbye to the singing people who cheered and waved back. Then he walked casually up to the commandos with his open hands held up and out, so they could see he was unarmed. "I am your man, Rey Maxwell Newly. Please let these harmless people go free," he requested.

Because of the milling crowd and the risk of landing on the potholed runway, a large black helicopter hovered overhead instead of landing. Rey was roughly cuffed and then slowly hoisted aboard like a piece of cargo. As the helicopter rose, Rey realized the people below were singing a melodious going-away song. The beautiful women's voices were swooping high, and the men's deep voices were singing a resonant base line. It was the most hauntingly beautiful sound he would ever hear, as the people he loved sang their shirt-wearer Nambo off to America.

Once the helicopter landed on the stealth ship, Admiral Futtock approached with a malicious leer on his ferret face and then slugged the handcuffed Rey in the mouth with a pistol butt. To their credit, Rey's guards stiffened, and one said gruffly, "We were ordered to save him for Achor Nithing."

Futtock ignored him and just sneered at Rey. "How could you live with such primitive people?" he asked. He yanked his thumb to gesture at the still-singing crowd. "We should have nuked them, the fracking cannibals, but Nithing doesn't want a PR mess. I should just lob a quick one at them anyway and say it was an accident. Why don't they shut up their cannibal commie pie holes?" he complained, grimacing at the swelling ending of the going-away song as the warship pulled away. Then he looked at Rey, laughed, and asked, "What is it with the ugly, old, raggedy shirt, asshole?"

"You could never understand even if I told you," Rey answered. Then he was knocked unconscious by another hard blow to his head from the enraged Admiral Futtock. His last fleeting thought before he passed out was actually quite ludicrous: "I came with a loaded diaper, but I left with a full heart and mind."

CHAPTER 10

The Not So Glorious Return Home

Rey must have been out for quite some time. When he finally awoke, it was to the droning of a jet streaking across the Pacific to a large US airbase located on another island. From overheard muffled discussions, Rey determined his kidnappers had decided to fly him to a secret NAP airbase located on the east coast of the US, close to DC. He was mostly kept hooded and isolated, so that presumably as few people as possible would know his true identity. Occasionally, though, he would be shoved into a small, locked room, have the hood violently yanked off, and be allowed to briefly look around the small enclosure that disgustingly served as both his lavatory and snack room. These few brief moments were intended to allow him to tend to his biological needs, but then he was again hooded and cuffed by the same efficient but surly guard.

This monotonous routine seemed to go on for days, but Rey couldn't be sure. Finally, the plane landed, and a familiar ugly snarl roused him from his bored stupor. "Mr. President, I assume," Achor Nithing greeted him, as the hood was again violently snatched from his head. The glaring light revealed Nithing's yellow-flecked wolf eyes and repulsive, sneering face. "You are the Latin scholar. Try this on for an appropriate eulogy of your adventures. '*Sic transit Gloria mundi,*' my man," sniggered Nithing.

"Something about not catching the bus on Monday, I believe," Rey responded sarcastically, surprised at just how weak and scratchy his voice sounded after days of silence, but hoping a bit of his intended jab still came through.

"'So passes the glory of the world,' is what I said, as you well know," Nithing corrected. "You could have had it all, Rey, if you just simply worked with us. Massively unbelievable amounts of money, power, all the glory of the world, and even more enjoyable days with your lovely family."

"I already informed your idiot brother and you about the status of my supposed family," Rey responded, this time getting a good snapping bite into his recovering voice. "Check it out. The DNA will confirm what I said, and I'm sure my former loving wife has confirmed it, too. The landmines crushed my manhood, to put it bluntly, and my wife cuckolded me, to use a term from ornithology about the disgusting habits of cuckoo birds, but, of course, you wouldn't understand."

He could tell from Achor's uncharacteristic pause that his barb had sunk home. Rey knew that psychopaths like Achor hated nothing more than losing leverage on a person. He also knew, however, that the story fit well with how the vile and manipulative predators thought.

"Yes, Thornton did pass that delicious little tidbit on to me," Nithing said grudgingly. "It serves you right, you know. No balls and now no glory. But, not all is lost," Nithing said, with what passed on his odious face as a wide and growing smile, "as there is still the art of torture. I love it. You will loathe it. It won't be fast, but it will be furious, and it will be fun for me and brutal for you. I am a veritable artist, painting pictures in pain. I can make it last a long, long time."

Nithing's tantalizing thoughts of pending torture fortunately didn't last long, as he soon received a cell message informing him that Jake Nambo and his Hadron media team were threatening to launch a huge media attack on NAP, and on Nithing specifically. As isolated as Foondavi was, Hadron's ability to communicate with the USA was much faster than NAP's fastest jets.

By the time Rey and Nithing were on the ground, Jake Nambo and his media team were already bombarding the NAP leadership with all sorts of potential leverage they had been accumulating for years. While Rey never learned the exact gory details, he now knew enough about the Nithings to know there were some juicy details that would be like blood in the water to other psychopaths and deadly poison if made known to the general public. You could not even allow a hint of the appearance of weakness among the group of vicious predators comprising the loose alliance called NAP, or they would be all over you. Also, NAP was still unwilling to give up its hard-earned cloak of invisibility that allowed it to so easily and successfully manipulate the government-owned mainstream media and the still completely duped and dozing American public.

The agreement in the end was that Rey would be kept secure and unharmed in a psychiatric facility and would be closely monitored by both sides. There were cameras everywhere. He was relieved to find out that, as part of the deal conceded by NAP, his wife and boys were also freed from the grip of the Nithings and given full protection from harm, much to the intense displeasure of both Thornton and Achor. They were immediately placed in the protective custody of Jake Nambo. Jake's team especially liked this last piece of the deal, not just on pure humanitarian grounds, but because it indicated a widening split between the Nithings and the rest of the surly and unruly NAP leadership. Besides, NAP figured they had enough digital recordings of Rey and the family to produce any media event they wanted, and they figured they could always provide stand-in actors for the family, if absolutely necessary. They determined Rey's family was now an unnecessary expense and a useless bargaining chip. They had the President right where they wanted him.

Not surprisingly, Rey found the psychiatric hospital depressing. The guards insisted on keeping his feet shackled, so he shuffled everywhere he walked. They also drugged him, along with the other residents. Because both Melville and Samms owned big drug companies as well as for-profit penal institutions, the fix was in using as many drugs as possible without permanently dispatching the patients or prisoners. It was obvious to Rey that keeping him clear headed was, unfortunately, not part of the negotiated deal.

The administrators of the hospital did let Rey keep his funky, multi-colored shirt, not being aware or even caring what it stood for. When he looked down at it, he was reminded of Foondavi and the need to remain courageous. There was no way, even as fuzzy headed as the drugs made him, that they could take away his thoughts of Foondavi or his family. During every waking minute and even in his dreams, Rey mentally walked every inch of the rugged island and reveled in his memories of the individuals he met there, the gentle tongue, and, of course, the *Golden Book* he realized he had somehow completely memorized while on the island. It all kept adding to his strength and determination.

Rey's guards were rotated on a regular basis. After a few weeks, he noticed one of the newer guards had a familiar gait. As he watched more closely, Rey was sure he knew the person. Finally, the guard in question sidled over close to him to pick up a dirty tray and covertly whispered out of the corner of his mouth, "Don't keep staring at me or you'll give me away, dude!"

With a poorly disguised start, he realized it was Snapper Melville, the self-proclaimed humble chameleon, who was turning out to be quite a master of disguise. Snapper discreetly shoved a bottle of pills under a pile of magazines near Rey and whispered, "Take these, not the junk they're giving you. Get ready for a jail break in a few days." With that, Snapper scooted off.

Rey found himself momentarily wishing he had asked about Zara and then felt disgusted with himself. He just couldn't get that trickster vixen out of his mind. Snapper didn't appear again, but the new pills helped clear his head. He just palmed the others the regular guards gave him and then flushed them down the commode when he got the chance.

When the break came, it was spectacular. The doors on Rey's high security cell and section suddenly flew open, and the electronic shackles they kept on him simply came unlocked and fell off his ankles. He was stunned with amazement. He looked at the guards and realized they were holding their heads, as if they were struck with an excruciating headache. He realized a soft, mellow voice with a southern accent was crooning to him, seeming to come out of what looked like a small fly buzzing by his ear. With a start he realized it was a high-tech fly bot, a miniaturized drone. "My name is Carlyle the Computer, and I am here to rescue you by command of Jake Nambo." The voice said "computer" with a southern accent, so it sounded like "computah," but Rey wasn't up to being picky about accents right now. The soothing southern voice of Carlyle continued: "Just follow the yellow brick road, slick, and we'll get you out of here real quick."

Rey realized the yellow brick road referred to was actually a string of brilliant yellow lights flashing and beaming from the baseboards and illuminating a pathway for him. He followed the lights and walked past several more dazed guards and staff, all seemingly stunned and immobilized by the strange humming noise. The illuminated pathway led him outside the gated facility, until ahead he could see a bright red sports car with a smiling Zara Tallaree inside waiting for him. He tried not to notice her skirt inched up on her golden thighs or the welcoming sparkle in her eyes as he slid into the seat beside her. "You're not going to drug and diaper me this time, are you?" he asked with as much bite in his voice as he could possibly muster while looking into her incredible eyes.

"Oh, took your feisty pill this morning did you, blue eyes! Well nice to see you too, Rey. Come on, be real," Zara said with a lilting laugh and a teasing tone to her voice. "We didn't have time to argue with you. Would you really have voluntarily let me deck you out in a diaper and dump you in a packing container if we hadn't made you compliant? I don't think so. By the way, you are cute in a diaper!" Before he could give a snappy response, she rapidly accelerated the car out of the parking lot and tore onto a super highway. Within minutes they pulled up behind a big semi, which lowered a ramp while both vehicles were going well over sixty. Zara hit the accelerator and shot the car up into the empty cargo hold.

"That was amazing," Rey admitted, still trying to pry his eyes off her long, amazingly shapely legs. "Who is your friend Carlyle the Computer?"

"The most unlikely ally you could imagine. He was a well-connected, forty-five-year-old southern US Senator high up in the NAP echelon. He was in a serious auto accident, and the NAP people figured they could save his brain and make him a cyborg, a combination of human brainpower and synthetic artificial intelligence. They figured this could help them tap into all the computer networks so they could be digital dictators. DARPA, the Defense Advanced Research Projects Agency, has been working on these things for years. There's already been a lot of organic synthetic stuff going on with digital hearing aids, insulin pumps, pacemakers, brain chips, and the like, so this was the next big jump. It's a digital neural lace over the brain, connecting brain to the Internet. The super trans-human, if you will."

"I have no idea what you are talking about," Rey said. He started to swat at another fly buzzing by his ear, when Zara grabbed his arm.

"That's him, or at least part of him," she said to the confused Rey, who only saw a pesky insect with what looked like miniscule wires sticking out of it. The fly continued buzzing around his head and then finally landed on his ear.

"Correct. I am almost everywhere and see almost everything!" the soft-spoken, southern-accented voice said in his ear. "This is a fly-bot I'm addressing you from. Hold out your hand and I'll land on it so you can admire the intricacy of my creation."

Rey held out his hand and the fly-bot landed. He squinted closely and could see intricate wire arrangements connecting what he guessed were miniature cameras, speakers, and huge amounts of computational power. "I am nanotechnology at its finest," Carlyle boasted.

Rey had to admit he was impressed. Carlyle went on to explain that his team was producing thousands of such devices each day and spreading them throughout the US. "We are linked to all the extensive CCTV security cameras, we can use face recognition and lip-reading software, and we can tap into any electronic device." He described some other handy little gadgets for which Rey could only guess the purposes, but they all sounded like they had military and surveillance potential.

Carlyle the Computer, or more appropriately, the cyborg AI, went on: "The singularity is here and gone, Rey. Like a bullet train, it has left the station, and most people don't even know it's arrived yet. Kind of like those neutrinos or whatever that move faster than light and get somewhere before they even leave."

Rey had no idea what the cyborg AI was talking about. "You lost me. What's this 'singularity' thing?" he asked.

"For simple minds like yours, it is the point in time when computers can program themselves, take over their own learning, and be completely independent of any human direction or intervention. I am a hybrid, in that I still have my mind, yet I am linked to the most powerful artificial intelligence machines."

"And this means exactly what?" the befuddled Rey asked.

"I am in control. NAP thinks they control me. I believe you call it the typical psychopathic delusion of grandeur. They thought they could put me in a can, connect me with a huge amount of circuitry, and just shut me off if I got lippy. I fooled them. I am in so many servers now—secured away in deep, hardened bunkers all over the world—that they can never root me out!"

"But your brain must still be vulnerable," Rey said, picturing a poor, pinkish grey, three pounds or so, fleshy lump of human brain cells huddled in a container somewhere, only covered with something called a "neural lace."

"Correct," Carlyle responded. "But they need to find me first! And I have penetrated all their systems. I am a hacker par excellence, if I must humbly say so myself." Then for no reason at all, Carlyle whispered in his small, strange, southern-accented voice, tinged with a slight mechanical tone and a hint of paranoia: "Oh, they are looking for me. Very much so. They want Carlyle, but they can't have him."

"That's where we come in," said Zara, in a very assuring and cheerful tone of voice. "We were approached by Carlyle out of the blue, and we have offered to help him stay safe and secure. In return, he helps us know what NAP is up to even before they do. Right, Carlyle sweetie?"

Rey was amazed Zara seemed even to be trying to seduce the computer, and he seemed to be responding. "Right," Carlyle purred back. "NAP is a little unsure of what I'm up to, but they can't fathom anyone outsmarting them. They think I'm just a stupid piece of machinery. If they figure it out, though, poor old Carlyle could be in big trouble without sweet Zara's help."

"I've also agreed to help Carlyle meet Big Blue Twenty-Two," Zara mentioned. Seeing Rey's look of confusion, she explained: "You remember the computer that won at Jeopardy a few years back? Well, this is many generations beyond that. One of Jake Nambo's companies built and operates him. Carlyle is enamored of Big Blue Twenty-Two."

"He has my deepest admiration," Carlyle literally purred. "My interest is purely computational, of course, nothing carnal, though he is a handsome hunk of digital pulchritude, I mean hulkiness, er, circuitry design."

Rey was astounded. It sounded like Carlyle might be a gay or bi-sexual computer, as well as being a little paranoid. "I'm sure Zara can set you up to meet Big Blue Twenty-Two. But watch her, so she doesn't drug and diaper you like she did me."

"Oh, I am quite aware of her potential for mayhem," Carlyle answered. "But I've calculated the odds. Even with her penchant for plots and other devious activity, she knows I can read micro-expressions at 100 frames a second, instantaneously analyze voice prints, process it all in milliseconds, and, thus, detect deception beyond any human capability. That's why I know you don't really approve of my interest in Big Blue and also that you are anything but hostile to sweet Zara."

Rey was suddenly aware both his micro- and macro-expressions were screaming loudly to Carlyle. "What you and

Big Blue do as two consenting computers, or whatever you are, is fine by me. Can you see I mean it? You know I am not lying. And Zara and I have a very complicated relationship! Purely platonic, I guarantee!"

Carlyle chuckled, a weird and disconcerting sound coming out of a little piece of machinery still sitting on his hand. "Thank you for changing your mind about the relationship between Big Blue and me. Now, about how Zara feels about you . . ."

"I would rather not know," Rey said, totally dismayed and confused again, eyeing the calmly and confidently smiling Zara, who seemed not the least bit discomfited. "I would probably be disappointed to know what she really thinks about me, and then be disappointed I was disappointed, whatever that means."

"Humans are so inscrutable. I will have to ponder the meaning of this for a while to unscramble your rambled thoughts. I never was good with emotions or empathy, even when I was fully human, and I am sad to have to admit, with all this dazzling computational power, the empathetic part of me hasn't improved at all."

Fortunately, for the uncomfortable Rey, the rest of the conversation was spent discussing and formulating strategy for dealing with NAP. Zara informed him they were going directly to a secret meeting place for a grand council of war. Jake Nambo would be there, Zara would be representing the Fenrir Shamar, and there would be some other key resistance figures he would meet. He was quite disconcerted to learn he was going to be the main topic of discussion. They were going to try to figure out what to do with Rey, known to most people now only as Nambo McBlue, now that they had him. They also were going to plot how to counter attack and defeat the NAP forces using Carlyle and whatever other resources they could muster.

≡ CHAPTER 11 ≡

The Grand Council of War

The grand council of war was being held as completely off the grid as could be managed, while still keeping Carlyle present and accounted for. Carlyle assured the participants that all access was blocked and that there were no other listening devices present.

Jake Nambo strode in dressed in his usual unusual get up, immediately walked up to the now heavily disguised Rey, and gave him an unabashed hug. "I am so proud of you," he said huskily. "Big Jon Flynn sent us all a recording of the egg chase. Unbelievable and courageous performance, if I must say so, being a former participant myself." Tugging on his own rainbow-hued, bedraggled shirt and pointing at Rey's, he smiled at Rey and admitted, "And now there is a second American shirt wearer, another Nambo, Nambo McBlue, by gummy! What an honor this is!" Then taking Rey off to the side, Jake Nambo whispered to Rey something that would have great portent for his future: "You will need to trust me, Rey. We need to take immediate action. You know I only have the best intent for you and your family. You trust me, right?"

Rey could only nod his confused assent, not knowing what this meant, but knowing that, for some reason, probably a gut instinct, he finally and truly did trust the old guy.

For the time being, there were two other people present in the room besides Jake, Zara, and the newly minted Nambo McBlue. One was dressed like a college professor, wearing some scuffed-up walking boots and a tweed jacket with arm patches. His leathery, sunbaked face and squinting eyes didn't seem to go with the garb at all, however, and neither did his jaunty, bow-legged walk as he came over to grab Rey's hand. It was calloused and strong, and Rey could sense rock-hard muscles moving under the clothes. "I'm Ambrose Belisarius Spar," he said in a surprisingly soft voice.

"Military strategist of the highest level," Carlyle said from somewhere above them, in his mellow southern drawl. "Numerous scholarly articles and twelve highly acclaimed published books. More importantly, he's been there and done that. More medals than his uniform can hold and trusted by the real US military, not the NAP dupes. If we would have had him and a few more Irishmen, the Confederacy would have won." Everybody looked askance at each other, not knowing what to make of Carlyle's weird addendum about the Confederacy.

The second participant was a woman who deceptively looked like a middle-aged, matronly Hispanic librarian. She had a head of mousy dark hair and a worn expression. But Rey noticed a very determined look burned in her eyes. "I'm Shiva Ree Del Rosa," the woman said. Rey wasn't sure if she was named for the Hindu goddess of war or the Jewish seven-day period of mourning for the dead. Either way, it was obvious that, just below the seemingly placid exterior, there was lurking a very imposing and talented woman.

Before Del Rosa could say any more, Carlyle spouted off a complete résumé that was every bit as impressive as Spar's, except hers was in the area of nanotechnology and weapons design. Her curriculum vitae also included two Nobel Prizes and several other prestigious science awards. When she finally got a chance to talk, Del Rosa's voice took on an electric charge and her face glowed when she talked about her area of expertise.

A short while later, three more experts, all recently hired by Jake Nambo's personally funded think tank, the Nambo Foundation, joined them. One was a geeky-looking, youngish dork with wildly flowing hair and a bemused smile, who was considered by Jake Nambo to be the leading world expert on cyborgs. He was openly disconcerted to find out Carlyle was present, even though he supposedly had been forewarned he would be, which was not reassuring to Rey. He assumed a cyborg expert would know all about the "singularity" and the unbelievable power of the human brain linked to unimaginable computational power through a neural lace. Of course, this was now beyond textbook musing or a controlled lab setting. Instead, this was the hard reality of the now, like a zoologist being in the room with a live lion. There was a feral cyborg in the room, and the famed expert appeared shaken to realize the fact.

The second person of the new trio was a graying lady who was considered an Economics genius. Lizette Maquis was her name and stirring up trouble, her game. She had lost her secure university position because of her iron-clad conviction that big government was not the solution but a symptom of the failure of human nature. "Big is not beautiful" was her mantra, which, of course, was music to Jake Nambo's ears. Plus, her being petite and astoundingly attractive, with china-like skin and blazing green eyes, didn't hurt and further helped her make her point to the obviously smitten Jake Nambo. "We must turn loose the creative potential of people. For the most part, though, big business, big schools, and, most of all, big government don't do that very well," Lizette explained. Small micro-banks of neighbors lending to neighbors, and small schools focused on creative problem solving and decision making were key components of her big "little" ideas. She was also a huge booster of creative and compassionate capitalism. She made it clear she did not mean completely unfettered capitalism, but capitalism regulated adequately, treating people decently, and actually producing things of value, with huge tax incentives for small companies doing compassionate things such as starting up comfortable care centers and senior homes. "I don't really have anything against big companies," Lizette went on. "It's just they have to stay creative and competitive by producing value and creating jobs, not cornering markets and patents and plugging up the flow of ideas and innovation. Most Americans have nothing against people creating wealth, but look at Melville, Samms, and Busby Marsh. Have they ever created anything of real value in the last twenty years or even helped any others get wealthy? No!"

The third new person was the most surprising. Rey had actually heard of him through his cursory study of psychology. He also had heard his name mentioned in the positive psychology talks held at the Reservation. The man's name was Cuddy "Quag" Quagga. Quag informed the group with a cheerful voice that a "cuddy" was a small Scottish hut or a small pony, depending on your choice, and that "quagga" was the name of an extinct horse-like animal with the combined characteristics of an ass and a zebra, making him both stubborn and untameable. He added that he got the nickname "Quag" because of his last name Quagga, but also because he was always a nag, bogging down negative research and people, making them rethink their proposals in a more positive way. He was going to help them get the country heading in a more positive direction. "Change the mindset from status quo to a growth mindset," was his advice. He was short and stocky, with coarse but flowing hair just like a Shetland pony, and he did give off the air of being stubborn and untameable. Rey thought Quag, along with the proven Ambrose Belisarius Spar and the impressive Lizette Maquis, was a potential Nambo in the making.

Once everyone got introduced, Jake Nambo directed the group to the business at hand: "First, our unseen partner here is Carlyle, a recently cyborged human I already described in my top secret message to you. He has turned on his NAP masters because he knows they will turn on him in a second, as they proclaim everyone is expendable. In their overweening sense of grandeur, they view him as just a machine. We view him as a valued partner. I know his presence is disconcerting to some of you, but he has an unmatched ability to read micro-expressions and voice prints. He can tell if any one of us is being deceptive, or if someone has been compromised and leveraged by NAP's usual vile but effective family and friends leverage strategy. If everyone will please look at the monitor over here and say, 'I am not leveraged or under the control of NAP,' we can get on with the meeting." Everyone willingly repeated the phrase, while anxiously looking into the monitor. Almost instantaneously, there was an "all-clear" confirmation from Carlyle.

Jake nodded and continued: "I've already taken the liberty of calling this team of high-energy thinkers, the Hadron Group. I've previously sent all of you a description of why I chose that name. I've also explained why I am going to be known as Jake Quark from now on, in deference to another Nambo in the room, Nambo McBlue, who is fresh in from Foondavi." With this he gave a deferential, but proud nod to Rey, who had not been formerly introduced up to this point but realized, from the looks, that everyone already knew about him. Reaching his arms out and figuratively encircling the group, Jake continued: "I am hoping we, the Hadron Group, will be a stabilizing force, producing continuous, positive, innovative, and adaptive change in America and the world, and countering NAP and the controlled chaos they as predators prefer and foster. We all know who the most obvious enemy is, NAP and their many unsavory tendrils. But the larger enemy is also within each of us, as well as our fellow Americans. I know you don't all agree with me, but I believe we are also losing the purpose our founding fathers placed within us as a nation and people. As a nation and a people, we have allowed ourselves to be lured away and become self-consumed with youthful appearance, money, and sensual pleasures. We are fast losing the urge to heal the world and help the helpless. We will reverse this! We will transform the American mind."

Seeing no one was opposing his situation report, Jake charged on: "Several recent events have precipitated our taking action now. We believe the nation has reached a tipping point. Congress, big business, the military, religious, and educational institutions are nearing a time when the psychopaths of NAP will be in a position of dominance and complete control and will slither out into the open, like roaches into the light. All the new, portable brain-scanning technology that enables high-resolution visualization of the brain has the potential to blow the cover off NAP. We can now identify even the most deceptive ones. In the near future, we will even have remote brainwave-scanning technology coming on board that also will blow their cover. This has spurred them to bold action before the slumbering general public sees the threat. They are marshaling their forces and posting themselves in key positions of power. Carlyle has confirmed they are not quite there yet, but they are very close, maybe only months away. We have to move now and expose them to the public, disrupting their strategy and waking up the sleeping nation before it is too late. They are like most predators and prefer to work in stealth, sneaking up on their prey." There was a general buzz of agreement in the room. "Because of this we are launching a project called Go Blue."

The only comment in the room came from Carlyle. "Ooh, I like that color!" Everyone except Jake and Zara just looked befuddled at Carlyle's comment.

The amused Jake Quark continued: "Under the direction of the former P.O.T.U.S., Sedgewick Clayton Sewell, of all people—but a skilled engineer and scientist I might add— one of my research teams was commissioned to look for other ways to detect and cure psychopaths. They inadvertently stumbled on an amazing and somewhat disturbing discovery, a synthetic chemical similar to colloidal silver but without its bad side effects. When injected into the human bloodstream, this chemical does two things: For some unexplained reason, it permanently and irreversibly changes the skin color of the person to bright and glowing yellow, pink, green, or blue, depending on the dosage. It also renders the individual unable to tell a lie. Once a person is injected with the chemical, if the body senses a falsehood, a dramatic and deadly chemical reaction is triggered that renders the person instantly immobile but conscious. After some painful convulsions, death shortly follows. This last bit of unfortunate data was accidently discovered by a research volunteer who had been injected and then lied about liking his new hue, so to speak. Thinking the death a coincidence, a second volunteer said she wasn't worried about anything like that happening to her. Well, it soon became obvious the new coloration agent was also a deadly lie detector!"

Still seeing confused faces, Jake attempted to clarify: "We will contest the recent elections as rigged and can provide ample evidence that it was clearly corrupted. Then we will force the NAP people into a re-election and provide a surprising candidate of our own, one who cannot tell a lie."

"Is that even constitutional?" Rey blurted out, to a chilling silence from all those around him. "I mean the part about a re-election, not about not being able to lie."

Jake quickly responded. "Mr. McBlue, with all deference to your absence from our country and your well-proven patriotism and courage, it is obvious NAP has made a mockery of the US Constitution. They regard it as an antiquated document, written on mere paper, as they so like to repeatedly and disdainfully point out. They also like to dramatize that it was signed by slaveholders, religious village idiots, and rebellious drunkards. For over 100 years now, working with previous presidents, they have been trying to destroy it as not being progressive enough."

"I still honor it," Rey said, realizing he was perhaps being a stubborn ass. He wasn't that relieved when only Quag Quagga joined him in his resistance.

"I agree with Nambo McBlue here," Quag said. "What good will it be if we ruin the Constitution to save the Constitution and become the people we are trying to defeat?" he asked in a polite but pointed manner.

Jake quickly put out his hands, palms down, in a placating and halting gesture, and responded: "Our best legal minds are working on it, and we think we have a way to do it so that the basic integrity of the US Constitution remains intact. We will do nothing that even closely resembles what NAP is doing. They are making a shambles and a mockery of the whole election process. We will restore the process and protect the Constitution while doing so, making the process function better than ever. You have my word."

Seeing he had successfully placated everyone, Jake got back to the matter at hand. "We could have chosen any color for the lie detector pigment change agent and certain young twin boys at my place weighed in heavily for green, pink, and even bright yellow, but I finally convinced them that a hero had already coincidentally chosen the color. I am proposing that our own Nambo McBlue be our candidate, that he be the first public person to literally 'take the blue.' He will be the first politician who can say, 'If I tell a lie, I will die.' What

I'm saying is that I'm nominating Nambo McBlue to lead what we are calling the 'True Blue Revolution' movement. It will shake NAP and the dozing citizens of our country to their core. It will literally transform and awaken the minds of Americans."

It was Rey, AKA Nambo McBlue, who was shaken to the core. He realized he was going to once again be the guinea pig candidate. He was starting to feel manipulated and abused again, when Jake inserted a sweetener he didn't expect: "And our lovely Zara here has volunteered to be his first lady, while actually functioning as his ever-present body guard."

Rey looked over and saw that Zara was seductively winking and smiling at him, biting her lip to keep a chuckle from breaking out and ruining the seriousness of the moment. Against his will, Rey felt his self-restraint melt.

Everyone was busily shaking Rey's hand and lauding his personal bravery and sacrifice, while he was still attempting to gather his distracted and scattered thoughts, let alone find his voice to proffer some sort of counter proposal.

Jake was already off and rolling before he could interject anything. "I have studied him for twenty years. As a courageous Shirt Wearer of the Foondavi and American people, a decorated war hero, he is a most decent and honest man of intense integrity. Adding the True Blue truth factor, 'if he lies he dies,' he will be the first P.O.T.U.S. candidate in a long time that Americans can actually trust. It should be dynamite."

Rey Nambo McBlue hated to admit crazy Jake was right. His newly rescued family and his new friends in Foondavi would all be safer if they could pull this off. Besides, he was getting used to being a sacrificial lamb. He started to return the enthusiastic handshakes, and he even playfully gave Zara a hug, which she unfortunately and wholeheartedly returned, thoroughly throwing him off stride again.

Jake then gestured, and a huge flat screen filling one wall of the meeting room flashed on. He proceeded with the meeting: "Everything will be carefully orchestrated with my media teams and our new and trusted friend Carlyle. At first it will begin with volunteer efforts by committed alumni from our Reservations for the Temporarily Bewildered. They'll work in nursing homes as well as homeless shelters and mentor students in our worst schools. The motto will be: 'Be selfless and help the helpless.' Soon, some strategically and clandestinely shot video clips will start popping up, virally spreading all over the social networking sites, inspiring people of all ages across the USA to respond to the 'True Blue Revolution' movement, of course, eloquently spearheaded by our own Nambo McBlue. He will be the first, but I'm sure many others will follow, to take the blue injection to show total commitment to the truth and to serving our less fortunate brothers and sisters. Carlyle will discreetly keep the NAP forces from blocking the Internet and social networking sites so the word will get out. He can also mess with their communications systems. Don't be surprised if, out of frustration, the NAP minions don't strike out at the 'True Blue' movement. We'll be ready, though! We'll document and widely share their brutal responses."

Jake continued: "At the same time, as a second prong of our strategy, we will begin challenging the legitimacy of the last election, a process already started by the relentlessly whining Boguidens, who obviously didn't get the NAP memo about it being their turn to lose with dignity. Their shrill caterwauling will actually help us, diffusing the focus from us. We expect this to further confuse the NAP machine monsters, keeping them off balance and running for cover."

Pausing again for any comments, Jake nodded at Quag Quagga. "Doctor Quagga has a few points to mention here, I believe, as he has been working to round out our strategy."

"Thank you, Jake," Quag intoned as he darted up to the podium. "Through all of this, we need to be as positive and constructive as possible, drawing a stark contrast to the negative and destructive NAP machine. We all agree they are a hideous, hydra-headed, loosely affiliated gang of contemptible monsters, but enough of their good points! Hah! But we can't call them that." Then Quag regarded each member of the newly formed Hadron team with a solemn expression in his big brown eyes. "If we can remain very positive and non-violent, they will soon reveal their own true nature to the American people, who, though asleep for some years, still have at least a modicum of decency about them. As average Americans watch the brutality unfold, they will first get passive aggressive in response. Eventually, they will be openly aggressive toward NAP, especially once the full extent of the mainstream, government-owned media's duplicity with NAP is brought to light through our efforts. Granted, it is difficult to remain non-violent when psychopathic monsters are involved, but we believe the presence of Fenrir Shamar will help us. Also on board will be a group composed mostly of the remaining decent members of our brave Special Forces and military, as they are already chafing under the baleful influence of the NAP people. If NAP goes too far, there would be open revolt, and no one wants to see that."

Seeing everyone was tracking with him, the compact and energetic psychologist continued: "The Blues will add a visual element to our movement. They also will be living and practicing the tenets of positive psychology so clearly articulated at the Reservations for the Temporarily Bewildered. They will tell the truth in love. They will be overwhelmingly positive, engaging enthusiastically with the community, relating to everyone with dignity and respect, and mentoring people on how to find meaning again in their lives. In the end, we see the movement as a second American revolution in which the people throw off a repressive big government of crony capitalism increasingly dominated by uncaring pawns manipulated by the NAP machine."

Hearing all this, Rey admitted he was ready to roll with the plan! His family was as safe as they could be with Jake, and recent reports indicated that Foondavi was not being targeted by NAP at this time. Although he was ready as he ever would be to go "Blue," he found the notion of never being able to tell a lie a daunting, if intriguing, challenge. He admitted he had always been good at technically parsing his comments, thinking back on some of his carefully planned discussions with Prissy. Whoops! On second thought, maybe he wasn't so skilled! Now he would have to be, or find himself paralyzed and suffering painful convulsions before going on to the hereafter or wherever. "You lie, you die." "Go Blue, and you never go back."

"Okay, everyone," he heard himself intoning in a surprisingly brave voice. "Let's go Blue!"

≡ CHAPTER **12** ≡

Once You Go Blue, You Never Go Back

In a very short while, Rey found himself hooked up to a dripping IV and having his hand disconcertingly held by a nervously smiling Zara. Jake was repeatedly droning in his ear about the seriousness of always telling the truth, and it bothered Rey to see he was also very worried. As he went under, he swore he heard Carlyle humming the Blue Danube Waltz and whispering something about another Big Blue. And then, nothing.

Coming back to consciousness wasn't much fun, as he was momentarily nauseated from taking the drug. Then he looked in a mirror on the wall, saw his blue-tinted, bearded mug staring back, and was really nauseated. Soon Carlyle's best southern-comfort voice murmured, "Ooh, ooh, ooh, I do like that Papa Smurf look you got going on, Nambo McBlue. You sure enough do look like a buff, blue-eyed, Papa Smurf," Carlyle said, quite amused, "with the curly hair, the beard, and all. But who would vote for Papa Smurf, I wonder?"

"It's your job to make sure they do," Rey, now literally Nambo McBlue, responded grumpily.

For several days, Rey was closely monitored and schooled by a special team assigned and directed by Jake himself, along with Quag Quagga. They constantly reminded Rey to not slip and be deceptive, and they grilled him on ways to honestly answer difficult and tricky questions he was likely to face as he went out into the public. Not surprisingly, telling the truth was not always easy!

Rey was really beginning to feel grouchy about the constant hectoring and training, until Zara glided into the room. He quickly reminded himself not to tell any lies or say anything slightly deceptive, no matter what Zara might ask or tease out of him. But, before either of them said anything, Zara pointed at the wall, making even such an innocent gesture a sensuous experience.

News on an extremely large flat screen TV was blaring from the wall and showing scenes from what was already being called the True Blue Revolution. Next, the program switched to a staged press conference where the old fake "digital" Rey Newly was decrying the idiocy of Americans getting involved in doing what the government was fully capable of doing. He saw what appeared to be a few blue-tinted people interspersed with the volunteers occupying the nursing homes and shelters, collecting and carrying food and sleeping bags. He knew many of the brave Blues were volunteers from Jake's various operations. Many carried signs saying, "We are the ninety-six percent who care," referring, he supposed, to the four percent who were psychopaths, while other signs read, "Be selfless and help the helpless" and "Occupy yourself with helping others."

Then Rey saw Doctor Quagga addressing a press conference, praising the True Blue Revolution and explaining the positive philosophy behind what they were doing. He also explained the ninety-six percent number to the assembled press, saying it was estimated that approximately four percent of people felt no empathy, guilt, or remorse and could tell lies without blinking, even preferring lying to the truth when the truth would serve them better. He stressed that, unfortunately, the four percent were increasingly occupying places of power. He didn't openly label them "psychopaths," but the press knew, for sure, to whom he was referring. The True Blue Revolution was going to occupy places of need, he said, and try to "correct the neglect," another True Blue Revolution slogan. The newscast kept getting scrambled from some strange interference and then coming back even sharper in focus.

As the days unfolded, the Go Blue strategy picked up steam, despite the knowledge that taking the blue goo, as the injection was called, could be deadly. This was widely known now, because of a surreptitiously obtained video clip released by NAP of the two volunteers inadvertently lying and dying. Instead of scaring people as probably intended, however, the graphic documentation only underscored the complete commitment to truth and integrity the True Blue Revolution demonstrated.

As predicted, the NAP forces representing the established order proved easily goaded. They responded by broadcasting glaringly brutal videos of True Blue Revolution people and their supporters being pepper sprayed, belted with batons, and violently dragged by their hair from nursing homes into waiting police vehicles. The video clips also showed crying senior residents attempting to cling to their new friends. Wheelchairs and walkers along with the fragile elders were flying askew, much to the growing disgust of newly awakening Americans and even the disgusted mainstream media.

A brightly glowing, blue-skinned, blue-eyed, curly-haired and bearded man named Nambo McBlue started showing up at more and more of the demonstrations, bravely getting beaten a few times, even though the NAP police were repeatedly warned by NAP officials to avoid pummeling him, at least when cameras were present. He didn't mind the few bruises, especially after watching other brave True Blue revolutionaries and friendly sympathizers being dragged off.

Carlyle and Jake's media team always seemed to find him, shaking with barely controlled emotion, and he had no problem providing eloquent but pithy sound bites, emotionally reiterating the True Blue Revolution talking points about helping the helpless and replacing the uncaring politicians and other powers that be. Make America True Blue again!

Actually, many of Nambo McBlue's talking points closely resembled the now reinvigorated J. Wrenfield Boguiden's tired spiel, but without the whininess. While Boguiden carped about unfairness, Nambo McBlue eloquently inspired the American people to get involved and help the helpless by, shock, actually getting out and helping the helpless. It definitely appealed to the traditional American spirit of helping each other that had gone slightly dormant for a while. Also, while Boguiden avoided the True Blue Revolution protests, apparently afraid to get his expensive clothes dirty, Nambo McBlue increasingly seemed to be appearing everywhere. He made sure to allude to the Boguiden campaign charges and ask why the Newly administration was not responding to either them or the True Blue Revolution charges of callous disregard of the poor and unemployed.

The True Blue Revolution public relations team also made sure people were aware that more and more previously missing documents and emails were emerging that demonstrated, in glaring terms, that the last election was fraudulent at best, broken and corrupt at worst. Previously unknown to the public, all these documents were genuine; they were provided by Carlyle, after being run through a lot of databases to cover the source. When asked if he weren't afraid of being found out, Carlyle only sounded wounded anyone would doubt him and would go on to explain how much smarter he was than NAP, and how NAP always underestimated their enemies and each other. When it was pointed out he was doing the same thing, he pouted a while and then repented. The whole team started to watch him a little closer to see if he really was getting emotional and paranoid, despite his claims it was not possible.

Finally, the incessant mounting pressure grew too great on NAP, so they had the digitally manufactured fake version of the recently elected President Reynard Maxwell Newly announce brokenheartedly that it had now come to his attention that the previously aired claims by the brave Boguiden campaign actually had some merit. He claimed the Justice Department would investigate and prosecute any election fraud. In short order, several scapegoats were found. By now, however, the awakened public demanded a new election. The tried and proven delay-and-deny strategy was no longer effective, so various proposals to hold another election were put forth. Eventually, through a convoluted approach that would be argued about by Constitutional scholars for generations, a re-election was agreed upon. At this stage, though, it was obvious the race would have to be threeway. The digital Newly, of course, would defend what he and NAP thought was his rightly stolen election. The vindicated Boguiden, known in jest as "Old Bogey"—jealously guarded by his dangerous daughter, Jacqueline, and goaded on by a host of radically charged followers—stubbornly refused all the not-so-subtle overtures by NAP to drop the whole thing. And the new emergent third candidate was the leader of the rapidly growing and increasingly popular True Blue Revolution, "I cannot tell a lie or I will die," Nambo McBlue.

Nambo McBlue was being heralded as the first honest politician since George Washington. "This 'blue thing' could actually be nirvana for a careful politician," argued the wily Jake. "You won't ever have to remember what you said. Just tell the truth or die!"

"More like a veritable politician's nightmare," Rey countered. "No mumbo jumbo, just straight talk." He also thought grudgingly that it was easy for Jake to love it, as he wasn't the one who would do the dying with one slight misstep on the path of truth.

But Rey had to admit there were some apparently surprising and unusual side benefits to the blue goo. As soon as he took the blue goo, Rey could literally feel a strange tingling in his brain, even though he knew he had no nerves there. When he inquired about this, the psychologists told him that, from observing him, it appeared his brain was changing for the better. Some preliminary brain scans and his own experience told him he was beginning to think faster and recalling far better, plus his whole sensory system was starting to work more effectively. The doctors noted that the improvement was the brain's "neural plasticity" in action. They told him it appeared on the scans that his brain cells were making new connections faster than normal. Their preliminary theory was that his neurons were repurposing from not having to be deceptive all the time. They explained that, because humans started as small, slow, fangless scavengers, a major part of the human brain had been heavily devoted to deception, that lying and deceiving were vital to survival. This large portion of the brain, perhaps as much as forty to fifty percent they estimated from their initial scans, seemed to be repurposing to other things. They also explained that usually much of the brain appears to be made up of useless elements of the genome known as "junk DNA" or "dormant DNA," but somehow the blue goo was engaging these normally inactive elements and stimulating parts of the epigenome, called "microglial enhancers." It all meant that Rey's brain was now becoming supercharged to an amazing degree. Although Rey didn't understand much of the scientific jargon, he could feel and experience the ongoing changes. The specialists told him to check back in a few weeks and they would do more tests and scans to see if there were continuing changes.

The ongoing changes didn't bother Rey. He knew he needed every bit of help he could get, as the pressure built to both always tell the truth and to learn all sorts of material for the impending campaign.

But all was not perfect for the newly minted Nambo Mc-Blue. He did have some sad moments and a few concerns in his life. His sadness was caused by the fact that he couldn't risk being with his family. NAP had easily seen through his blue deception, using voice recognition and other tools to recognize early on who Nambo McBlue really was. They immediately tried to bend all the previously agreed upon rules to gain the leverage that threatening to kill his family would garner them. Fortunately, Jake had skillfully hidden Prissy and the boys; even Rey didn't know where they were. Plus, Rey was closely monitored by Carlyle and couldn't even attempt to slip them a covert message. He could only trust Jake, who said they knew what he was doing, understood the sacrifice he was making, and always knew the truth about how he cared for them all. Jake wasn't blue, but he was believable. Nambo McBlue knew he had to trust Jake on this, and hope and pray someday he could rejoin his wife and sons.

Another concern was the constant presence of Zara. Her very smell nearly drove Rey to paroxysms of passion. He knew about human pheromones, but this was ridiculous. He had been around many attractive women, but she put the "attract" in attractive. The worst thing was, she knew it, and he was sure she flaunted it to drive him to distraction right when he needed to focus. Rey finally found the nerve to discuss his predicament with Zara. She clearly, if cuttingly, explained, "You are in lust with me. You are in love with Prissy. I can tell. I would give anything to have a man like you love me, but I know it is not just going to be. I'm not your type."

When he pressed her about it, she finally revealed her deep, dark secret. She explained she had wanted to tell him for a long time and now knew she could trust him. She also said it would be fair to give him some leverage, as she knew she had been tormenting him, and now he needed to focus on the election, not her. She fixed him with her big, beautiful eyes, took a deep breath, and confessed: "I am a psychopath. I am, most importantly, a reformed psychopath, but still a psychopath. Remember, I am Crazy Jake's niece. What you didn't figure out is that I am Achor Nithing's illegitimate daughter, born to Jake's sister, who Achor despoiled and left when she was very young. It's another reason he hates psychopaths and, specifically, the Nithings so vehemently. His natural mother and sister were both victimized and destroyed by Nithings."

Rey was totally blown away. "But Jake can't stand even being around psychopaths," he blubbered, realizing he was emotionally disbelieving her story, even as the logical part of his brain was starting to accept the idea. "He can smell them a mile away."

"He gave me this special pheromone-based perfume I wear. It's very strong and covers up the smell for him. For most people, it's just a faint but very pleasant scent. For some reason, though, it drives you wild. Your eyes dilate, and all your micro-expressions, and I might add a macro-expression," she added, smiling coyly and causing him to blush, "all go on heightened alert. I noticed it the first time we met. You are putty in my hands, big blue dude, and don't you forget it."

Zara went on to explain that this was why she could work with and represent the Shamar, despite her Uncle Jake's misgivings: "He claims I am not a pure psychopath, just a manipulative little damsel without too much compunction about using sweet men like you." Then she looked at him dreamily, in a way that sent his heart fluttering that had nothing to do with her perfume. "Although I do wish I could get someone like you to love me. Then I think I could really become human. I really don't like to hurt you, Rey, and even though I'm not blue, I would turn blue for you to get you to believe me about how I feel."

With a newfound cognitive understanding of his physiological and emotional reaction to Zara, Rey could address yet another source of even greater concern. He was afraid Carlyle was "losing it." The cyborg would be paranoid about NAP catching him and, at the same time, express a tremendous sense of grandeur, as if he were a god-like super being unable to be touched. Then he would go on and spin some totally unrealistic fantasy about him and Big Blue Twenty-Two. It seemed like he was confusing fantasy with reality on an increasing basis. Carlyle also was forgetting details, large and small, more and more.

When Rey subtly mentioned these things to Carlyle, the cyborg acted confused or embarrassed. Usually, he just dismissed the concerns with talk about how he was pressed on all sides with details and cyber-attacks—and cyborgs could have bad days, too!

Surprisingly, when he expressed his concerns to the team about Carlyle, Rey got much the same reaction from Jake, who also was increasingly distracted, as his strategy was slowly rending apart the NAP machine. Jake definitely liked to watch the various NAP factions cannibalize each other. Regarding Carlyle, though, he only shrugged his shoulders in disregard and muttered something to the effect that, you should never hack a hacker. He seemed to think he and Carlyle had leverage over each other, and it appeared Jake thought his was superior. "Egos, egos everywhere," Rey thought.

When Rey checked back with the brain specialists after a few weeks, they confirmed his growing suspicions that something was dramatically altering his brain. Whatever was happening hadn't stopped after the initial injection. Instead, it had accelerated. He could literally feel his brain continuously changing. He came to realize, and Doctor Quagga confirmed, what the other psychologists had initially shared with him in their preliminary analysis—that the idea of always telling the truth had many other unseen ramifications.

Quag explained that normal humans spend much of their brainpower deceiving the world and even themselves, maybe mostly themselves. They may go their whole life living a lie, never confronting their true feelings or who they really are. There apparently were evolutionary benefits to both men and women adroitly and even unconsciously lying. Big lies as well as small ones might make it easier to get along with people in groups, soothe potential allies and enemies, and even fool potential mates into hooking up and sticking around. It appeared deception was wired into the brain from an early age.

They explained when Rey's brain was freed up from the huge effort of deceiving itself and others, many other senses started to kick in. They called it "building new neural pathways," a synaptic explosion making millions of new connections. They expected to see such growth in a healthy two-year-old brain, not in a mature adult.

But Rey noticed his sensory powers continuously expanding. It seemed he could now more easily sense the feelings and emotions of others. Sometimes he could even sense the presence of others before they entered the room. It was like he had the "harm" sense he had heard Jake talking about, which would make sense because there were predators around. He could sense when people were observing him, with a prickle running up his spine and non-existent fur standing up in warning. More and more every day he could sense when people wanted to harm him or, conversely, who wanted to help him. He also felt as though his IQ was greatly enhanced, his perception of problems was running much deeper, and he saw nuances he hadn't seen before. With an increasingly sharper mind, he could tell he made decisions quicker and that those decisions, according to the reactions of those around him, were better than decisions he had made in the past.

To further confirm that what Rey was sensing was really happening, Doctor Quagga used the absolute newest hightech brain scans to view Rey's brain in action. Even the good doctor was startled at what he saw. Rey's brain was literally rearranging his mental wiring by the second—"repurposing the neurons," Quag called it—and indeed was focusing on other senses, now that it didn't need to invest so heavily in the need to deceive. The earlier preliminary hypothesis by the psychologists was abundantly true; they just may have under estimated the amount of change! Dr. Quagga now said it appeared it is not fifty percent, but over eighty percent of the Homo sapiens brain that is usually invested in deceit and protecting the ego in some fashion. With the blue goo, Rey's brain was freed up to do all sorts of new things. The True Blue Revolution might be much more than political; it could be an amazing psychological revolution for humans, too. But for now, it was time to focus on defeating NAP, or all else was a loss.

≡ CHAPTER 13 ≡

On the Long and Winding Campaign Trail

"Ready to go, my big, brave Nambo McBlue?" Zara cooed silkily, sweeping into the room dressed in an unbelievable outfit. She was hard bodied with a sexy but powerful frame that even bulky clothes couldn't disguise. So, why even try seemed to be her strategy today. She had on a slinky, skinny scrap of a backless dress that left only a few delectable locations to the lusty imagination. Seeing Rey's breathless reaction to her ensemble and lush exposure of skin, she laughed that sparkling laugh that sent shivers up and down his spine. "Pop your eyes back in, Papa Smurf. This outfit is to distract the press, not you. This is my Twyla McBlue persona."

"You better have your martial arts skills set on hyper drive, as you are going to get pawed by the press and drooled on by the usual old perverts," he responded, as he admired her out of the corner of his eye and hoped his own drool was under control. Despite the clever disguise she was deploying, she looked as lasciviously luscious as ever.

"My pervert alert is always on hyper drive when I'm around you, McBlue," Zara laughed. She gave him a long kiss on the cheek, letting him not so discreetly check out a few of her more delicious attributes.

"Not that I'm fighting it, quite obviously, but why the slutty, sex pot look?" he asked.

"Well, Mrs. Boguiden is sweet, a beauty in her day, but quite matronly. And President Newly's wife is ..." She paused and glanced at him out of the corner of her eye to see if he was getting angry. "Well, the digital first lady is very proper and very much a motherly figure. She's got sort of a prissy, good-girl thing going on, and some men find that sexy." She said this last pointedly, checking out the innocent look that quickly flashed across his face.

"Well, I can't lie! Whatever it is you got going on, I definitely like it," he said, getting another good look at her. "And you definitely are different from either of those two," he said, watching her flounce her lithe body and pert bottom around in the back seat of their old, beat up, rented limo, and trying mostly unsuccessfully to cover up some of her curvaceous body with the little bit of material available to her.

"Exactly, Papa horny Smurf. I could call you 'Big Blue,' but Carlyle would get jealous, and maybe even get ideas."

"I'm listening and watching," said Carlyle's soft southern drawl. "And your micro-expressions and voice tell me you are making an attempt at being humorous, as you humans say."

"Us humans," she corrected him. "You are still human to me, and I wouldn't say anything to hurt you. You know I care about you."

The big collection of circuitry actually sniffled about this. "I know," he said in a muffled voice.

"Now we have a sentimental computer and an over-sexed first lady," Rey commented, wondering what a real Nambo

McBlue should do in this situation.

"Exactly! I will be a diversion, a distraction, and also a differentiation from the other first lady candidates. I will try to take a lot of the attention away from you, just in case our disguise is not as full proof as we hope. Also, I will be on hyper pervert alert, as you like to say, but mostly to protect your precious blue hide."

Their team had been alerted to the fact there were several active threats to Nambo McBlue's life. One wild rumor was that Jacqueline Boguiden planned to derail or at least behead the True Blue Revolution, thinking her dad could handily beat the reeling, presumptive President Reynard Maxwell Newly. To that end, she had been practicing her sniping skills and had disappeared from her father's campaign. The talented hit lady would be a worthy opponent even for the Secret Service.

Another suspected assassin was Paula Pipestone. She supposedly wanted to prove her loyalty to the Nithings and NAP, but she also secretly harbored a deep grudge about the supposed love of her life, Rey Newly, spurning her for her own dull sister. Now she wasn't even allowed to see either her sister or Newly in person, for a reason no one on the NAP team would explain to her. She was cut off from all contact and sent out of town.

In a contorted form of logic, Paula had decided that, as much as she wanted to, she couldn't kill Nithing's man, the brother-in-law who had spurned her. Instead, she would knock out the blue challenger, proving her worth to the Nithings and unconsciously her love for Newly. Besides, being her father's proud daughter after all, she found the True Blue

Revolution hokey and corny, whining about helping useless people. Plus, she couldn't stand the color blue, being very partial to red, let alone stand a blue man, unless she was choking him to death. Something about the bearded and blue Nambo McBlue just really got to her. Surprisingly to everyone but herself, she was said to be one of the best natural snipers the NAP Special Forces had ever trained.

The event toward which they were heading was a presidential debate. The Newly campaign had fought it, saying it was beneath the dignity of a sitting president. Boguiden had taunted the digital Newly, saying it was a sign that he lacked courage, didn't have any accomplishments to show, and couldn't speak without a teleprompter. The True Blue Revolution just replied, "Our man cannot tell a lie, so he will tell the truth, the whole truth, and nothing but the truth," knowing the other campaigns couldn't handle the truth. Nonetheless, all the campaigns refused to let the probably exaggerated threat of an assassination deter them one bit—as we can't let terrorists derail what's good for America now, can we?

The True Blue Revolution campaign had talked a lot about the difference between red, white, and blue. Red was the color of the Newly team, red being for red ink flowing from their broken budget and also standing for their totalitarian approach. Some unauthorized supporters came up with the not-so-subtle acronym RATS, for Rotten, Angry, Totalitarian, and Socialist. They avoided the word communistic, but made sure everybody saw a connection, even though it probably was the most cutthroat, capitalistic big government-oriented administration ever. The "Red RATS" name stuck and dragged the NAP team down.

The white campaign was the Boguiden group. He was preppy, Ivy League, stilted, and painfully white. He was the Caucasian caricature of the out-of-touch old white guy. He was gentle and possibly honest but unable to reach the American people. Sort of like plain vanilla, bland and white.

And then there was the blue campaign, the True Blue Revolution, led by a truth-telling blue man. They stressed small, limited government close to home. Communities being in charge of caring for each other. No big banks. Small micro-banks of neighbors lending to neighbors. Encouraging and rebuilding the entrepreneurial spirit of Americans. Americans making Americans strong. All the proven ideas of Lizette Maquis, the "Petite Professor Pepper Pot," as Jake dubbed her. The great thing was that their leader, Nambo McBlue, actually believed the ideas. After experiencing Crazy Jake's Reservation for the Temporarily Bewildered and Foondavi, there was no doubt in his mind that the unleashed human spirit could do amazing things. He didn't have to lie. He knew this stuff really works and would actually be good for America. He was true blue, and his sincerity was obvious to all.

The debate went well for the True Blue Revolution. The actor trying to play the part of the digital Newly fumbled several canned lines, when both his wrist teleprompter and hidden ear bug suddenly and inexplicably went haywire and started channeling questionable hip hop, blue grass, and blues songs, then random taxi cab signals, along with someone crooning "Blue Moon." He panicked and nearly fainted, knowing his acting career and most likely his life was probably over, all because of a sudden, unexpected technical glitch no one could easily explain or fix.

The malicious people imbedded in the Boguiden camp required no such skull drudgery. They just let J. Wrenfield, Old Bogey, be himself, and he dug himself one nuanced hole after another. He told a few poorly timed, unfunny, corny jokes. As much as Americans like hokey and corny, he came across as phony and stiff. He even tried to make gentle fun of himself but came across as a man who never heard a joke he couldn't kill. It was probably true, as they say, that he didn't have a single redeeming character flaw, but lacking a genuine sense of humor is what really did him in.

Nambo McBlue knew Old Bogey was a good and honest man and truly felt sorry for him. But he also knew he was unknowingly in the pocket of the NAP machine as their designated loser. His staff was dominated by NAP cronies and highly paid hacks. Even though he stubbornly refused to lose, they let him flounder by having given him wonky lines and confusingly complex policies he couldn't really explain even with his high intellect. It was apparent to all but him and a few devoted patrons that he would be an ineffectual president, even if he somehow miraculously bucked the flow and got the position.

Yes, Nambo McBlue felt bad but knew he could show little mercy. He did help out the stumbling candidate, gently reminding him once or twice when he forgot some key points of his plank, especially after he couldn't recover from a joke going horribly flat. But then Rey skewered him on his complex policies in contrast to the True Blue Revolution's simple approach of cutting government waste, lowering taxes, wiping out unnecessary regulations, and turning lose capitalism—all the while helping the downtrodden get a hand up, not a hand out. The crowd loved it. And all of it was the truth, as he pointed out repeatedly, or he, McBlue, would be dead!

As they gathered for the post-debate handshaking, Rey suddenly saw Thornton Nithing pushing his way through the crowd, not recognizing Rey but glaring at the unflinching Zara Tallaree, now Twyla McBlue. "I thought I smelled your infernal perfume," Nithing snarled at her as he gawked at her voluptuous curves. "It's you, Zara! I would know those, uh, shapely parts, uh, anywhere."

"Excuse me, sir," Nambo McBlue said, quickly stepping forward and thrusting a muscular arm between Thornton and Zara, before she broke Thornton's larynx or decommissioned his baby maker, which Rey had no doubt was Zara's next move. That quick move saved his life.

As Rey lunged forward and spun Thornton away from Zara, a quick series of muffled shots rang out, sounding like popped champagne corks. To trained ears, however, the sounds were those of suppressed, high-powered sniper guns. A bullet tore past Rey's ear, and blood suddenly spouted from the back of Thornton Nithing, splattering the crowd. Hands grabbed Nambo McBlue and threw him down, and he heard the frantic Secret Service people shouting commands. He realized Zara had protectively thrown a tablecloth over both of them and was ruefully shaking her head. "I should have left the damned perfume off for one night, but I was afraid you wouldn't want me anymore." With that she put a feral glint in her eye, gave him a quick kiss, and slipped out beneath the table to go assassin hunting.

Even though the debate was a resounding victory for the

True Blue Revolution, somehow the attempted assassination was twisted and spun by the mainstream government-controlled media into an attempt to harm the current administration, with a top aide to President Newly being the apparent target and victim. Then a digitally altered video of the assassination attempt was released that made it look like McBlue used Thornton Nithing as a shield or pushed him into the path of the bullet. The polls seesawed, and the candidates were advised to stay away from crowds, which only played into the hands of the Newly and Boguiden campaigns—that did poorly around people but better with produced, digitally altered, teleprompter-orchestrated video spots.

It was two days later before Zara showed up again at campaign headquarters. She had swapped her fetching outfit for a camouflage suit that still managed to accentuate her figure. "The bitches got away," she announced. Seeing his perplexed look, she explained: "It was a woman who shot at you with full intent to kill. Actually, it was two of them, though probably not working together. But both apparently were after you. The Secret Service is calling you the 'reverse lady killer.' Most potential presidents have women after them and see themselves as lady killers, no matter how old, fat, or ugly the candidate may be. You, instead, have two infuriated women out to kill you. It appears Paula Pipestone has a real grievance about the digital you as the President but can't kill Achor Nithing's man, so she wants to prove herself to Achor Nithing by wiping out the True Blue Revolution candidate. Go figure that convoluted reasoning! She's a real piece of work for sure."

Zara went on: "And it looks like the charming Jacqueline Boguiden has a murderous fascination with you, with pictures of the burly Papa Smurf all over her hideout, along with draft love notes scribbled and then torn up. It seems she feels offing you would give her both intense sexual pleasure and win her daddy the presidency. There you go, twisted chick thinking from both of the beautiful hit ladies. How you can have such a corrupting effect on women, I'll never know!" Zara capped off her report with a sudden, lingering kiss, pressing her warm body tightly against him. Just as quickly, though, she disengaged, leaving him stunned, breathless, and even more confused than usual.

"Can you explain human females to me, Nambo?" he heard Carlyle ask. "I don't even clearly understand men, and I was one."

"Carlyle, it would take all the circuits in the universe to begin to understand one woman, especially the one called Zara," Rey responded.

As the election rolled on, Carlyle offered to come up with several cleverly nefarious ways to win the election, but Nambo McBlue and Jake squelched them all, remembering what Doctor Quagga had said about not becoming like the enemy. They both told Carlyle to keep it fair.

"If I had hands, you would be tying them," the cyborg said in a whiney, sulky voice.

"Carlyle, if you had hands, I would make sure they were in handcuffs. I don't want to be like them, or we lose even if we win," Rey said, noting with growing alarm that the cyborg was getting awfully emotional. In fact, he was understandably emotional after being told by Zara that a NAP cyber assassination team had somehow gotten to the Big Blue Twenty-Two and had savagely trashed his hard drive and hacked his backup, assuming it was Big Blue and not Carlyle who was sabotaging their efforts. What could be saved was dismantled and divided into several smaller computers. What made Big Blue unique, however, seemingly could not be salvaged. Carlyle felt guilty that the work he surreptitiously had done for Hadron Group had led to Big Blue Twenty-Two's untimely demise. The situation was especially sad, because Carlyle had never gotten to know Big Blue, or whatever it was he had in mind.

Inconsolable in his grief, Carlyle cried, "You are nothing like them, Nambo. You are blue and screwy and definitely unlike anyone I have ever seen, though there once was a sexy pile of circuitry called Big Blue Twenty-Two. Oh, how I miss him, even though I never met him!" The cyborg actually wailed, hurting their ears.

Zara and Rey later agreed, if you never hear a cyborg whine, you are not missing anything. Zara also was worried about Carlyle's stability and spent hours talking to the lonely being of mixed-up wires, circuits, and human brain parts, trying to soothe him when he was paranoid and smooth out his swings from depression to euphoria. She asked Jake and Rey if a cyborg can be bipolar. Even Jake had to admit it was uncharted territory.

Although Nambo McBlue had a busy schedule making more campaign commercials, he decided he should find time to visit the seriously wounded Thornton Nithing. Everybody in his campaign vetoed the gesture. Jake warned him, "They will see it as a sign of weakness. By now you should know they can't fathom genuine compassion, even if they wanted to. Also, they long ago figured out you are the real Reynard

Maxwell Newly and probably would love a chance to whack you on the sly."

Despite their advice and dire warnings, Rey ditched his Secret Service patrol, snuck up the back stairs of the hospital behind some interns too busy talking to notice an unauthorized interloper, and then walked to Thornton Nithing's room. He was surprised to find it unguarded. He also noticed on the way to the room that all the monitor cameras were broken or turned aside, which should have been a warning. Thornton was sitting up, covered in bandages. He didn't appear to recognize Rey as anyone other than the hated and despised Nambo McBlue.

"You here to mock me?" Nithing inquired with an attempt at false bravado, faking a tough-guy accent, "or just to knock me off?"

"Actually, I'm here to tell you I'm sorry you got the bullet meant for me," Nambo McBlue answered.

"I don't buy that for one minute. You're just hoping my brother and I will feel sorry for you and that we won't smash you and that slut you claim is your wife," Nithing shot back.

Rey felt himself getting heated and could tell the roiling anger between them wasn't exactly doing Thornton any good either. "I'm sorry I bothered you, Thornton. I genuinely wanted to express compassion for you," Rey said.

"I don't do compassion. Compassion is for losers, and us Nithings aren't losers," he spit. Then the big guy started blubbering tears and angrily waved Nambo to go away.

A guard then showed up and was startled to find Nambo McBlue there. He politely escorted him out of the room and out of earshot of Thornton. "Hey, there are no unauthorized visitors allowed, Mr. McBlue," he said. "This prick is on the NAP shit list for messing up the assassination attempt. His brother was just here and pulled all the guard detail but me. I was just for show and am leaving now, too."

The guard was nervously licking his lips and anxiously looking both ways down the hall. "Some serious shit is coming down. He won't make it through the night without someone offing him. I'm only telling you this, because I like the True Blue Revolution. My mom is out at one of the nursing homes you guys occupied, and she loves your blue people. She even wants me to take the blue, but I'm not brave enough." With that, he turned and took off running down the back stairs.

Rey debated with himself for a minute and then stuck his head back into the room one more time to valiantly try to get Thornton to leave with him. He was shocked to see he was already strangled, having hung himself while Rey was talking with the guard. He had tied his bed sheet around the cubicle bar, rolled off the bed, snapping his own neck. Now Thornton was turning a very unattractive blue himself.

Realizing the big brute Thornton was beyond any help, Rey cleared his head and quickly ran down the back stairs, figuring the shit was indeed coming down. He now realized the monitors were purposely messed up to allow an assassin unseen access. As he left the hospital, he forced himself to casually stroll down the block, covering his blue features with a hoody, and breathed a sigh of relief. When he was a block away, a black car came sliding up the street, screeching to a halt in front of the hospital. Two men bolted out and ran up the stairs Rey had just descended. A few minutes later, the men came running out and jumped back into the already moving car. Thornton Nithing's career as a remorseless predator was over.

As the campaign rolled on, the real dirty tricks commenced. The NAP team knew if you told a big-enough lie enough times you could get a large number of people to believe it, especially if you relentlessly repeated it. To that end, a digital Nambo McBlue popped up on screens everywhere, spouting twisted perversions of what the real McBlue said when he was in the debate. When Rey as Nambo McBlue appeared on the most popular political talk show to try to repair the damage, the host sneered and just said: "So, before you were for it, you were against it. You're a pinheaded flip flopper."

"I can't tell a lie," Nambo McBlue responded. "I am not a flip flopper."

"How do we know that isn't a lie?" the animated host, now smelling blood, shot back. "All we have is your word for it, and some scientific gobbledegook that a simple man like me, although admittedly a Yale graduate with high honors, can't understand. Oh, and do you deny that all the research on this blue gook, 'lie and die' juice, was paid for by Quark Industries that is owned by some shadowy, eccentric billionaire loner named Crazy Jake Quark, who finances your campaign and political career?"

Nambo McBlue started to sweat and stall. He knew he was in a real box. He couldn't lie and just die right there on national TV, even though he felt himself dying politically. "If I lie, I do die, so I won't deny that the secret blue goo formula was developed by Quark Industries."

"But how can you deny saying those things on the video

clips, the exact opposite positions from your debate performance? That performance, by the way, even I, a champion debater while in grad school at Princeton, have to admit, was excellent!"

"I thought you went to Yale," Rey commented, hoping to throw off the probing inquisitor.

"Yale for undergraduate and Princeton for my master's degree. Don't prevaricate or pontificate—excellent words for the day, by the way. Just answer my original question. I'm a simple man, so give me a simple answer. How can you say two opposite things and not lie?" the interviewer reiterated.

Mustering his confidence, Rey explained: "The statements to which you are referring were taken out of context and don't reflect what I believe. They also were digitally pieced together in a non-flattering way. You can do almost anything digitally these days. That's the flat out truth, and you know it. Let me reiterate for you my original positions," which he tried to do over the interrupting host until the commercial break.

During the break, the host surprisingly warned Rey what was coming next: "By the way, the rumor is there is no marriage certificate on record for you and your absolutely smashing babe of a wife. Same goes for your birth certificate— nowhere to be found—and the same goes for your college grades. I've seen this type of charade before."

When the grilling started again, Rey found that the blue goo was a mixed blessing. He always had to tell the truth, no matter how much it hurt. "I'm sure if my opponents provide all of their personal information, my campaign will do the same," Rey countered. Technically that was true, and he didn't die, although he was feeling pretty queasy by now.

"Well, Mr. 'If I lie, I die,' I would think that, with your being such a man of stated integrity and high moral values, you could just answer with a straight yes or no."

Rey knew he couldn't dodge the tricky questions of the truth-seeking commentator much longer. The problem was that NAP or someone was leaking the guy good stuff, much of it true, all designed to make Rey and the True Blue Revolution movement look bad. He began to suspect that maybe some of the leaks even came from Carlyle, who, against the wishes of Jake and the team, wanted to get nasty and flush out the NAP rascals. In a moment of blazing clarity, Rey realized that, whatever the source, the leaks were going to be turned painfully and perhaps mortally against him. He didn't want to die, especially not on TV!

The commentator now flashed his famous "got-you" smile and continued the inquisition: "We have a reliable source within your campaign, anonymous of course, that claims the True Blue Revolution believes that some evil cabal, a small elite, has seized control of our government and is manipulating the system for their own nefarious gains, ignoring the shattered little people they leave behind. This would be quite a thought-provoking thesis, except for the fact that historically every fanatical fringe group has always claimed a conspiracy and provided their own candidate for the cabal leaders."

The host paused with the very smug "got-you" look still on his face and then asked, "So, do you and the True Blue Revolution actually believe that many of the USA and world political and religious leaders are really lizards in loafers, snakes in suits? Isn't this more than ridiculous, bizarre even, way over the top, the beliefs of another lunatic fringe?"

As the host saw Nambo McBlue sweating and hyper ventilating, hesitant to respond and die, he went for what could have literally been the kill but instead gave Rey an unexpected way out. "So, is this the official position of the True Blue Revolution or not?"

Rey saw the opening and immediately leapt at it. This was not the official position of the True Blue Revolution. Granted, it was a reality, but something Carlyle or somebody else, not the brain trust, had released, as they knew people would view it as a fanatical idea.

Because Rey could technically deny this without telling a lie, he jumped on it with a passion. "No! Resoundingly no! This is not the official position of the True Blue Revolution. Actually, it is completely counter to the planned strategy of how we want to portray the opposition to the public."

The talk show host was thrown off balance by the unexpected vehement denial. Before he could launch into some other surely fatal yes or no questions, Nambo McBlue just went on the attack, hoping—like some woozy, punch-drunk prize fighter—to just make it to the bell. "Why would such a talented but simple man like you ask me such simple questions that anyone on my support team could answer for you? Why would such a skilled interviewer choose to only put me and not all the other candidates to the test? This is the type of questioning I expect out of the mainstream, government-owned media, from a strident bloviater, not a noted and esteemed paragon of the truth such as yourself. Bloviater, strident, paragon, a few more good words of the day, by the way." Ding. Round over, escape made, clinching all the way and staggering.

Unfortunately, the tussle with the famous host didn't help Nambo McBlue in the polls, although it didn't sink him either. As election day—or as the pundits called it, "re-election day"— rolled around, it was a neck-in-neck-in-neck, three-way race. Some people had serious concerns about electing a blue person president. There were some other people questioning Rey's mixed-race marriage, a blue but presumably former white guy supposedly married to an exotic looking, very sexy, Asian-African-Indian, whatever, beauty who quite frankly looked nothing like any other first lady in history. There were questions raised about his real ethnicity, his real marriage, even his academic credentials, despite his undeniably brilliant debating prowess. Probably the biggest challenge was accepting that he would actually be the first totally honest politician. Many people just didn't think that could ever happen or, perhaps more troubling, if the country could handle the truth.

Another problem was that the True Blue Revolution, as peaceful and other-directed as it appeared, was being ripped apart relentlessly by the mainstream government-controlled media. As the revolution began to shake up the administration, the attacks became more virulent. At first they just focused on Nambo McBlue, describing him as bold but bookish, with unkempt hair and wispy mustache and bushy beard, looking like a younger, blue-skinned version of Lenin or Marx. News reports also claimed that the peaceful resistance of the True Blue Revolution was disruptive and immobilizing Congress, keeping it from focusing on the real problems of America. How could the current administration move America forward with the hubbub created by the True Blue revolutionaries? And President Newly and his adorable family were so nice! Especially the twins!

Still another hatchet piece said that, while moral leadership is as powerful as any weapon, Nambo McBlue was a hypocrite for living with someone who possibly was not his wife and using the poor, deluded youth of America to disrupt the stability of our great nation. He also was accused of being unstable himself, of demonstrating mercurial moods by clashing with the calm and logical popular cable TV host. Although the media conceded that Nambo McBlue was well spoken, clean, and neat "for a blue person," they still questioned everything about his background. But his eloquently powerful and well-sculpted wife they left alone, as her mere presence seemed to leave them panting in frustration or perhaps something else. A few articles about her bulging, um, biceps and fine-turned thighs didn't exactly hurt the campaign, but they didn't help either.

Another challenge to the True Blue Revolution campaign came about when a doubting member of the NAP press corps inadvisably decided to take the blue goo, because he couldn't believe the lie-and-die scenario. Not being one to ever tell the truth, even when it would serve him better than a lie, the newsman lied about why he took the blue. Immediately, he was rendered speechless and died soon after from agonizingly painful seizures, all gleefully recorded in copious and gruesome detail by his NAP cohorts. Of course, the press twisted the situation and focused on the irresponsible dangers of going blue.

Indeed, two other hapless and impulsive people also took the blue goo and found out that living a transparent and truthful life was far from an easy thing—and it truly was irreversible. They admitted they both had been made to wait the two-week period to be sure they wanted to take the blue and were both certified by professional psychologists as having their senses under control and as being fully cognizant of the irreversibility factor. Nevertheless, the press capitalized on their supposed fear and inescapable situation, hyping it constantly and giving the True Blue Revolution more negative exposure as a fanatical cult worshipping the truth. When one lied, saying he was not fully informed about the challenges of going blue, the resulting death was sensationalized and trumpeted everywhere as blue goo suicide.

In addition to all this turmoil, Carlyle's impulsive, ill-advised, and unsanctioned leaks attempting to flush out the real NAP actually hobbled the Blue Revolution team and Hadron Group, putting them in the awkward position of having to deny the very existence of a vicious enemy that really did exist and was out to destroy and devour them. They constantly had to dance around any statement that seemed to allude to a shadowy force moving behind the scenes or end up looking like paranoid fanatical lunatics, even though the shadowy forces were deadly real and out to get them!

In an attempt to staunch their rapidly sinking poll numbers, the True Blue Revolution called a hasty press conference at the National Press Club in DC near the White House. They were going to further downplay the idea that they really believed NAP or some other secret elite group of power brokers actually existed. Rey was worried about how he could dodge any fatal questions, but they were getting beaten so badly in the polls, because of the barrage of untrue and negative ads as well as all the distorted press coverage, that they had to do something. They needed to prove desperately they were not some fringe fanatical group.

Unfortunately, the press event turned into a disaster. The place was swarmed with neo-Nazis, various religious defense groups, the Ku Klux Klan, the Anti-Defamation League, and even a serious-looking spokesperson for something called the Bilderberg Group, whoever they were. Every bizarre, paranoid hate group and conspiracy theorist was there. Quickly, the event turned into a media circus and spiraled out of control. Of course, the mainstream government-controlled press slanted the news and made it appear that all these disparate groups were uniting together under the True Blue Revolution, as unlikely as that was to any sane and unbiased observer, assuming there were still some sane and unbiased people left!

Interestingly, the more the government failed at everything else they should be doing, such as halting the deepening recession and dealing with unemployment, they still had stunning success at creating magical numbers. They seemed to prove that the economy, which looked like a beached and bloated whale, was not in decline but actually robustly growing. More importantly, the Administration was slowly being successful in making the average American mistrust the True Blue Revolution as a communist or at least socialist threat. Led by the esteemed, at least by himself, haughty Senator Hiram Festerwart, the White House methodically sought to deny the peaceful intent of the Blues and, specifically, Nambo McBlue. They even discredited the movement as a plot to destabilize America when the USA needed stability to grow and defend itself. Finally, they attempted to destroy the authenticity of the True Blue Revolution by using conveniently leaked secret documents to show it received mysterious foreign funding from some exotic Pacific Island nation named Foondavi, believed to be a communistic hellhole. Not only that, but the movement was backed by a strange, somewhat foreign-looking, shadowy guy named Crazy Jake Quark, who made his billions in questionable ways! Deny, discredit, and destroy, or intimidate, humiliate, and eliminate—the proven strategy of desperate despots everywhere. Hey, why discard a winning formula to defeat losers?

Even the eminent psychologist J. Woodhouse Crenwinkle was wheeled out and weighed in with a purportedly statistically significant study about the Blues representing and encouraging a tremendous rebellion among America's young people, with their hypnotic drumming and atonal singing inducing a drug-like euphoria. He also authoritatively stated, garbed in his scientific-looking white lab coat, that it was proven science the blue color they exhibited destroyed any hope of gaining employment as anything but rogue musicians and bartenders. The opposition even tried to use a creatively digitized video clip of the esteemed psychologist and True Blue Revolution supporter Doctor Quagga, claiming he had been misguided about the nefarious real reasons behind the movement, hinting at some horrible satanic origins, and how he now wanted to withdraw his support. Unfortunately, for NAP, the piece refused to go viral and kept scrambling the networks of all the media outlets, with something called the "blue virus" being blamed. The actual Doctor Quagga showed up and in a chagrined voice denied saying the derogatory comments, and vouched for the validity of the True Blue Revolution.

Truth be told, though, even the government-owned mainstream media thought about getting on the Blue train. Maybe some news announcers who had to tell the truth and nothing but the truth could win a good piece of the audience? Fair versus fake news had a nice ring to it! The idea was broached to several talking heads as a way to win the ratings game, and all of them thought it was a great idea for someone else to try, probably some up and comer. As the idea floated downstream like sewage, a few of the bottom feeders thought it might be a good career move. However, when they found the blue goo was both deadly and irreversible, and would apply to their private lives as well as to their news pronouncements, they strongly reconsidered. Eventually, a tremendous dearth of willing candidates unfortunately killed off the idea before it could kill off any overzealous purveyors of the news.

The average American, inundated by the typical mass media offerings of mostly unsubstantiated garbage, listened and tried to sort it all out. But the big lies kept coming, and then bigger lies followed. Many found it easy to believe the old adage that "where there is smoke, there must be fire." Besides, they didn't really like the stuffy and "too white" Boguiden, who always appeared as though he were looking down his perfectly shaped patrician ski slope nose at them. Plus, he grated on their ears with his piously calculated, nuanced concepts delivered in his stilted cadences. It also was rumored that his wild-looking daughter was being sought as the attempted "debate assassin." And then there were these strange blue people. They looked foreign, or, at least, for sure not really American. Can you trust a blue person to lead the nation?

What predictably emerged from all this was confirmation that the US is a bipolar nation. There is a powerful centralized government supported by a captive and controlled mainstream media, and then there is a large group of fragmented and isolated people, constantly pummeled by the media when not dulled down by TV tripe.

The ever-present weight and power of the first group, the big government and big media, though somewhat diminished by the True Blue Revolution, started to win out. The mood of a majority of the nation was one devoid of hope and tired of change. The current guy had his cute kids and comfortable-looking, matronly wife, and except for the one tongue-tied debate where he flubbed up, he probably deserved another chance. After all, he was a man of the people, good for America, a war hero, a literal Boy Scout. Wasn't that what they were repeatedly told?

In the end, the NAP machine won by a squeaker. It was definitely not a mandate, with the NAP-controlled Republicans under Newly suspiciously surging ahead at the last minute and taking thirty-seven percent, the True Blue Revolution with the flailing and pummeled Nambo McBlue sinking into second with thirty-six percent, and the somewhat semi-controlled by NAP Boguiden Democrats only garnering twenty-two percent of the vote, with the remaining five percent voting Libertarian or for some unidentified cartoon characters. After the dust settled and all the votes were counted, the House and Senate each were nearly divided in thirds, making for a quagmire of inactivity. Nothing new there!

Nambo McBlue was stunned. Jake wasn't. He proclaimed they put a real clog in the wheel of what had been seen as the inevitable and invincible NAP machine. The House and Senate were equally divided, with the True Blues actually taking several established seats from NAP incumbents and previously favored newcomers. One Nithing was reputedly "eliminated," and the other was scrambling for his life, as the enraged NAP organization had been assured of a guaranteed runaway victory. Truly, NAP was in disarray, with several ferocious predators busily attempting to claw and scratch their way to the top over the heavily wounded and sinking Achor Nithing and his once seemingly invincible machine.

On the other hand, the Hadron Group still had a lot of leverage over the NAP and had rallied a lot of resources, with the new Hadron Foundation and the Hadron Institute Think Tank attracting more brilliant and independent thinkers by the day. Most of the True Blue Revolution people themselves took the breathtakingly close loss as a mere encouraging momentary setback, and the movement was daily gaining more converts. They were becoming a strong and unified opposition to the establishment.

There was good news on other fronts as well. Led by the Pewamo Nation and a chief named Flynn Pompatella, several more native nations converted their casino earnings and spare land into Reservations for the Temporarily Bewildered. Several large foundations were granting money to help them. Other Native American groups started designating more trust lands for similar projects. There was definitely a loyal opposition growing by the day among a wide assortment of people.

In discouraging news, Carlyle had disappeared into the cyber netherworld. He had grown increasingly distracted as the election rolled around and dropped the ball on several occasions. Rey thought it was a NAP plot, but Jake disagreed. "Listen," he told the team, "We noticed early on that he was paranoid and starting to suffer from dementia. I don't know if it is a function of becoming a cyborg or if he had those tendencies before the procedure. He always was a wild one long before he had the auto accident. Lots of rumors about sexual episodes of all types. Heavy drug use was probably involved. It seems he even had been an active KKK member before going into the US Senate. So, without a doubt, he was a very unstable and all-around poor choice by NAP to become their first cyborg. In addition, he was probably distracted by lusting after Big Blue Twenty-Two, believe it or not, and some of you can understand how that can mess with your mind."

Jake didn't look at Rey, but Rey could swear Zara was smugly smiling. "Then add to all those facts, he was obviously crushed when the nasty NAP cyber assassination people got to Big Blue Twenty-Two and savagely disassembled him. It destroyed Carlyle's hope for a future fantasy world. Digital dreams can get smashed, too, I guess."

Rey, alias Nambo McBlue, was another story. He told Zara he felt like a worn-out, punch-drunk boxer. She only stroked his cheek softly and informed him she was happy to have been married to him, at least for a little while. Then Zara disappeared, ferociously looking for the two hit women assassins who were still after Rey. They had become an obsession with her. "Maybe I can't have you, but they can't kill you, my sweet, big, blue boy."

Jake was a little less romantic. He told Rey to quit whining and get to work! "Sometimes you win and sometimes you learn. We can really put up a resistance and keep them off balance!"

It really was a proven scientific fact that once you went blue you couldn't go back. Rey trimmed his scruffy, wispy beard into a neater Fu Manchu. He wanted a vacation with Prissy and the boys, if they would still have him. Maybe they could go to Foondavi, he thought. But Jake asked him to remain in the saddle for just two more weeks, explaining, "There is a big international strategic summit planned in Zurich, Switzerland, and they've asked for True Blue Revolution representation. We also think maybe you and Zara together can track down Carlyle. We need him. We know he is still around, because he is still protecting us from hacking and there is still activity in the circuits. We figure he is hiding somewhere licking his wounds, if you can picture a computer doing such a thing. He has so many hidden hardened servers and blind trails, but we know somewhere his actual vulnerable brain is sitting. I would like to help him get it to a super secure location. It's also rumored the NAP people have ill-advisedly cyborged yet another NAP person. They are like the Nazis of old, brazenly experimenting with people with no regard for human rights. We think they call her Camilla the Computer. We think she helped sabotage our election efforts once they started suspecting Carlyle was turned by us. We need to warn Carlyle, as he is probably emotionally vulnerable, assuming that is possible. We also need to get him focused back on the job, especially for the international summit. Your job is to find him, let him know we will protect him, and then let him know I will personally work with him to create a Big Blue Twenty-Three just for him. We need to get him back to work! The

True Blue Revolution is just getting started."

Suddenly, they all heard a long, drawn-out cyber sob and realized Carlyle was sneakily listening in. Despite their immediate solicitous invitations, he initially refused to respond but finally gave in to their coaching. Other than to offer sentimental and voluminous thanks to an embarrassed Jake for his Big Blue Twenty-Three offer, Carlyle didn't have much to offer. He knew of Camilla but was not forthcoming with any information about her. Carlyle was obviously still hurting but didn't want any help at this time.

≡ CHAPTER **14** ≡

Time Wounds All Heels

In a bit of news that Rey was elated to hear, the felonious Fillups Farnswaggle finally wore out his welcome, even with the perfidious psychopaths of NAP. Tired of his constant nattering about being a big revenue producer and the savior of cannibals, some of the more industrious members of NAP tied him up in a burlap bag and beat him with some serious Louisville Sluggers into a pulp, not a pulpit. They were going to dump his bloody carcass in the local river, but even psychopaths have some concern for ecology. Instead of polluting the river, they just rolled him out of a fast-moving car into a drainage ditch. The badly bloodied and greatly humbled Farnswaggle was rescued by a couple of Blues leading a team of people picking up litter and drunken homeless people out of the ditches around the town to send to a local Reservation for the Temporarily Bewildered.

"You're not going to eat me?" Farnswaggle asked fearfully, as they pulled the sullied sad sack out of the bloody bag and he saw their blue faces staring back at him.

"No offense, but you look unpalatable, sir. Also, whether you know it or not, you are a child of God," the blue leader, Anu Pokritos by name, responded respectfully.

"Yes, yes, yes! I once worked among a tribe of cannibals," Farnswaggle mumbled. Seeing their look of disbelief, Farnswaggle puffed himself up, attempted to straighten his tattered clothing about him, and announced: "I am Fillups Farnswaggle, a great evangelist and a very holy man."

His proclamation didn't get the humbled response he hoped for. Instead, he was plopped back in the bag and taken unceremoniously to a local True Blue Revolution headquarters. When he was next pulled out of the bag, he found himself facing a split screen with four fearsome faces staring out at him. He cringed as he recognized Louie Pastore, Flynn Pompatella, and another he belatedly recognized, to his chagrin, as the infamous psychopath hunter, Crazy Jake Nambo. He was also surprised to see the former presidential candidate Nambo McBlue glaring at him. He began to grovel and snivel, begging for mercy, but was called up short by the sonorous voice of Reverend Louie. "We have been waiting for years to bring you to account. Confession is good for the soul, assuming you still have one. Do you want to confess?" Reverend Louie asked.

As Farnswaggle started to blubber and profess his innocence, Reverend Louie held up a hand to stop him. "Your neck is literally on the chopping block, and some very eager people from both NAP and our side are scrambling to be the first to take a whack." He said these words with enough venom to drop a charging buffalo. Indeed, they seemed to forcefully shake the now silent Farnswaggle. "Pick your words wisely and know we can tell if you are telling the truth or not," Reverend Louie warned. Pointing up toward a monitor in Farnswaggle's detention cell, he added: "We have a cyber detection unit watching your every move and expression, so, for perhaps the first time in your miserable life, tell the truth."

Farnswaggle got the message and spent the next fifteen minutes sobbing and slobbering, spilling his rotten guts about everything he had ever done for NAP and himself. Even the hardened Pastore, Flynn, and Jake were shocked at the depravity in which he had participated.

Crazy Jake could only think of the suffering so many people had undergone because of this venomous snake. Rey's thoughts were about his poor, sweet mother, Swan, and the years she mourned the loss of her husband, mother, and brothers. He was stunned when the cringing, vile reprobate had the audacity to ask for forgiveness for all the evil in which he had willingly participated. Rey was even more stunned when Reverend Louie, supported by Flynn, said: "We forgave you years ago, for our own sake and sanity, not yours. Not forgiving you would have been like us taking poison and expecting you to die. However, we will not forget."

He went on to tell the now tearful former evangelist that he would be going to prison. "You will now have a real prison ministry, not a sham." Seeing the fear filling Farnswaggle's eyes, the good Reverend quickly added, "And you will be watched over and protected by our cyber protective force."

"Do I have to?" Carlyle asked plaintively, speaking in a sullen voice for the first time in days. "What type of music doesn't he like? Can I play that?"

"Carlyle, find forgiveness in your heart!" the Reverend Louie sternly admonished.

"Ha, ha! I just looked for my heart! Don't have one!"

Reverend Louie just shook his head. "Give him a secret

name that only the five of us and Anu Pokritos, the Blue leader that found him, are to know. Tuck him away safely and securely. Let's give him a chance to prove he has changed. He might even want to eventually take the blue."

When the screen went black on a shaken Farnswaggle being led off to prison by Anu Pokritos and his people, Rey could hardly find any words he would feel safe in saying. Seeing how upset he was, Reverend Louie reached out and took his hand, while his uncle put a burly arm around him. "We have to be better than they are, Rey," Reverend Louie said in a soft, saddened voice. "Revenge seems sweet, but it only poisons the soul. This way, if he truly does repent, he can help reach many others. I don't think he was a true psychopath, just a useful tool totally blinded by greed and power. He will serve a lot of time, and we hope eventually serve others. Maybe he'll even find a little redemption beyond the spiritual he has already received."

"Your mom, sweet, loving Swan, would have agreed," his Uncle Flynn added somberly. "She was one lady full of grace, and a grace revolution is something we are going to need when we finally bring all these psychopaths to heel."

Crazy Jake had remained quiet all this time and finally weighed in, gravely saying, "I say forgive but don't forget." Shaking his head sadly, he mused, "I wonder how Mandela did it. Who will be our Mandela?" There were no volunteers.

≡ CHAPTER 15 ≡

The International Summit

Basically, what Rey learned before the international summit was that the USA was still the world's last best hope, even among psychopaths! It appeared psychopaths had pretty much locked up and dominated almost all the other powerful countries. The strange good news for the Hadron Group team was that the foreign psychopaths surprisingly were really vested in USA NAP's demise and elated that the Nithings received a much-deserved comeuppance. It ends up, the other countries were as concerned as Hadron about NAP taking over the most powerful economy and military in the world and turning it into a world conquest machine. After all, that is what they would do if they were in NAP's shoes!

Jake knew he couldn't stand the concentrated putrid stench of so many psychopaths in one location, so he sent Rey as Nambo McBlue to represent Hadron. He also deployed Zara to pose as Rey's buxom beauty of a wife, Twyla, but she was actually there to protect Rey and distract the other lecherous psychopaths.

Rey and Zara weren't too surprised after their arrival to see Groover Melville make a grand entrance into the finest grand hotel in Zurich. He actually had two trumpeters announce his entrance as he came through the door flashing millions in rare jewelry. On his arms were beautiful feminine eye-candy bodyguards who, to Rey's discerning eyes, almost rivaled Zara. Seeing his appraising gaze, Zara not so discreetly punched him in the ribs. Next came six thousand pounds of personal luggage, including dozens of priceless suits for every occasion, a two-man makeup and hairdresser team, and several other attendants. All this was accompanied by a contingent of sullen and very unhappy Secret Service people tasked to protect the new Secretary of State. Melville was visibly upset when no one paid the slightest attention to his ostentatious entry.

"You are so tackily American, Melville! It's pathetic," said a grumpy-sounding Vice President Samms, who neglected to mention he also had been similarly snubbed as he emerged grandly from the bar with his own glittering entourage.

Both men simultaneously noticed Nambo and Twyla McBlue sitting in the lobby. They sniffed their arrogant noses and looked away. "Losers," they muttered loud enough to be heard around the room. Then they continued to carry on a private conversation just loud enough for everyone to hear. "Nasty, no-good, loser upstarts. Can't tell a lie, my butt! How can you hope to run a country that way? And then the gall of proposing wasting hard-earned money on all those useless and worn-out people."

The international summit didn't go much better for Melville and Samms than the election. It was a bummer. The other psychopath contingents reveled in the opportunity to humiliate Melville and Samms and anyone else representing NAP. Plus, the international leaders were angry that President

Newly himself didn't show up but sent these flashy peacocks to represent him. They knew the closely contested election results had halted or at least hobbled the NAP plans for world domination. They also were thankful that NAP would have to remain underground for now or at least behind the scenes, where they had functioned for the last two hundred years.

The other representatives were interested in Nambo at first. Of course, they also leered at Twyla McBlue, even though she was bedecked in a demure dress that valiantly but vainly attempted to cover up her glorious body. When the leaders, however, realized that Nambo and Twyla weren't a new version of psychopaths, their contempt was palpable and they ended up avoiding the McBlues, as if the disease of having a conscience was contagious. They knew True Blue Revolutions were already taking root in several of their countries, with potentially devastating impact, and they didn't want to focus any more attention on the issue than necessary. Most of the talk was about what the latest and most successful brutal repression efforts looked like.

It was late on the second day of the summit when Carlyle showed up. Well, he didn't actually show up. He spoke up. He directed his soft voice to Zara, even though he knew Nambo McBlue was present in their suite. "Sweet Zara, can we talk?"

"Of course, Carlyle. We have greatly missed your usual chatty dialogue," Zara responded.

"As you know, I have suffered a grievous loss, and I'm afraid I let my friends down. But I have good news. There are more beings like me out there."

"Now, Carlyle," Zara carefully cautioned him. "You must be careful. When people lose someone close to them, they often spring back into action too soon. It's a normal thing to do but can be dangerous while you are still emotionally vulnerable. Also, you know NAP is out there. I don't want you to get all paranoid, but remember Jake warned us there is a cyborg named Camilla getting geared up by NAP."

The following silence was deafening and went on so long they were afraid they had lost him again. "So you really believe Camilla is with NAP?" Carlyle asked.

It was a simple question, but both of them could mentally hear the cyborg's hopes crashing again. "That is true to the best of our knowledge. Ask Rey here. You know he can't lie, and your ability to lie detect is equally as good if not better than the blue goo. You know I'm not lying. You can ask him the most embarrassing things and he can't lie. I do it all the time." She said this last with a fiendish chuckle that was greatly discomfiting to Rey, as he knew only all too well how true it was. She delighted in tormenting him with embarrassing questions he would never have thought to ask but had to answer.

Carlyle actually laughed, making an amazingly gentle sound, like the tinkling of bells. Rey could feel the attention turning to him and actually did catch the slight movement of a small micro-bot on the ceiling he had missed on his preliminary surveillance. "Don't worry, Rey. The room is clean except for me. So you really believe this Camilla is a devious NAP invention?" Carlyle asked again.

"So we have been led to believe," Rey responded.

"Games within games. I see you are still alive, and my readings indicate there is no deception. Can I ask you an embarrassing question?" Carlyle continued.

Rey just threw up his arms. "I guess it's the curse of the blue! Sure! Why not? Everyone else is doing it."

"Do you love Zara, or do you love Prissy?"

Rey didn't even pause. "As Zara herself has so tactfully and diplomatically pointed out to me, I lust after her. I would love to love her, but, early on, my heart and mind locked onto Prissy. No lie, so I don't die. I love Prissy, and I love my boys."

"Can a cyborg lust or love?" Carlyle innocently asked.

"Not being a cyborg, I don't know. But I think love is more a mental state, which you can handle well. On the other hand, I think lust seems to be a much more physical thing. The more I am away from Prissy, the more I find myself loving her," Rey went on. But then he saw Zara secretly trying to wipe a tear from her eye, and his heart was breaking for her. "Sometimes the truth stinks," was all he could say.

There was a pregnant pause and then Carlyle added, "My new human hero, Vaclav Havel, the former freedom fighter and Czech Republic president, once said, 'Truth and love must prevail over lies and hatred.'"

"Wise words, my friend. And what, may I ask, Carlyle, is the actual intent of your questions?" Rey really wanted to know, as Carlyle was not normally this interested in emotions.

"After Big Blue Twenty-Two was dismantled, I felt a deep pain in my circuits, a pain I never felt when I was fully human. After our election defeat, which, by the way, you greatly facilitated by making me promise not to cheat, I withdrew and read everything I could find on emotional intelligence. I want to change and become a better being. I wasn't very good before. I think you could help me by being my friend and mentor. And Zara, too, as long as you can lust after a friend."

Zara nearly dropped her hot tea and then started violently waving her fist at the fish-eye micro-bot on the ceiling. "Why you old, lecherous bit of wires and perverted neurons! I thought I heard some heavy breathing when I was taking my bath last night. You want to be friends with me, you ask permission before gazing on my naked beauty!"

"Okay," Carlyle readily agreed, "but can I keep the video?"

"Send a copy to me," Rey yelled, while Zara pelted him and yelled at the ceiling.

"Clear your hard drives," she said sternly to the cyborg. "Boy, that sounds kind of weird, doesn't it?"

After that wild discussion, they started talking strategy. They dialed up Jake on a secured line. After Carlyle blurted out to the confused and then bemused Jake that he was clearing his hard drive of all nude videos of Zara, they got down to business.

They decided they could leverage the international concern about NAP to advance their own goals. Jake, as usual, took charge. "Let's make sure the international psychopaths know we will try our hardest to keep NAP in check. The True Blue Revolution is viral and can't be stopped at home or abroad. In turn, NAP probably will help us, or at least not hinder us, if they see their international rivals are also being threatened by the True Blue Revolution. Using our strong clout in the US House and Senate with our newly elected True Blue Revolution representatives, we will attempt to support True Blue Revolutions with USA power and influence wherever and whenever we can, and block NAP initiatives, because it is our unalloyed feeling that representative democracy is the best form of government."

Jake continued: "At home, we'll have help keeping the foreign influence and even USA NAP activities to a minimum. Believe it or not, powerful elements in the CIA and FBI have had it with NAP trying to corrupt them and have been purging NAP planted and leveraged people left and right while NAP is in disarray and the current administration is weakened. Carlyle will keep monitoring the situation as best he can. Unfortunately, though, their new cyborg Camilla is now trying to disrupt us right back."

Jake cautiously urged Carlyle to not underestimate Camilla. "Maybe we can win her over. Maybe we can't. Supposedly NAP doesn't trust her completely either, especially after their experience of losing you. The rumor is, they want to develop computers completely devoid of any Homo sapiens brain parts, a race of robo-sapiens, if you will. A machine that is completely cold, rational, and calculating that can out-psychopath a psychopath. How they figure they can control that, I have no idea. The chutzpah, the ego of psychopaths just continues to baffle me." Jake continued: "We need to work out details to move your actual brain to a safe and secure site. I am going to let you and your friend and mentor, Rey, work that out. As far as I'm concerned, only you two need to know where it's located, though we would ask you to find a trusted doctor and check out your brain's health. We are concerned the strain may have gotten to you, Carlyle, causing you to forget a few things." The rest of the session involved minor details, and soon they were winging home.

As soon as he could, Rey went to Crazy Jake's Reservation for the Temporarily Bewildered. His boys both rushed up to him like two unleashed and energetic puppies. Without a stare or a care about his blue face, they jumped into his arms. "You do look like Papa Smurf, Dad, but we love you anyway! Just wish we could have convinced Crazy Jake to make you green! Purple or pink would have been even better." Prissy stood back and watched the boys lovingly pound on him. After he promised to go fishing with them and meet their pet pigs, alpacas, and new friends, in that order, they dashed off to more adventures.

"Let's go for a walk, Rey, or should I call you, Nambo?" Prissy suggested softly. But she wouldn't look him in the eyes. She stared down with a sad look on her face.

"I'm always your Rey, Prissy, always," he said as they slowly walked hand in hand under the apple trees and sat on a bench beside one of the ponds.

"I saw you campaigning with that sensuous Zara. They said she was your wife," Prissy commented. She was keeping her eyes down and her voice flat, so Rey couldn't read what was going on.

He finally turned and faced her but refrained from lifting her tear-filled face. "Prissy, as is obvious to anyone who will look at me, I am a blue man now. That means if I lie, I die. You know that's true, don't you?" Finally, she looked up at him through glistening eyes and slowly nodded yes. Then Rey continued. "Ask me if I love you and only you."

She refused to ask him. "I don't want you to die, Rey."

"Prissy, I love you and nobody else. If I lie, I die. And I will not die," he said without the slightest hesitation and smiled, waiting patiently. "Look at me. I'm not dead. I am more alive than ever before. Ask me anything you want, and I will tell you the truth." He just hoped she wouldn't ask him about her cooking. It wasn't worth dying over lousy liver and onions, lumpy potpies, or flavorless meat loaf. He also hoped she didn't ask him about lusting for Zara, as unrequited as it was.

Prissy stared at him a long time. Her eyes kept getting softer and softer. "I believe you, Rey, and I love you, too. Now that we are being honest, I have to tell you that I lied about the sperm donor. It really was anonymous. I just wanted to hurt you, but not that bad. All I really ever wanted since I first saw you was to love you and be loved by you. But everybody just kept pounding me down. I never felt good enough to be loved by anybody, let alone you. But the people here have taught me how to love and be loved. Rey, I can really love you now!"

That night for the first time she made love to Rey because she really loved him. As she kept pulling him closer and closer, their hearts really did beat as one, something he always thought was just in romance novels but now knew was true. The earth didn't move under their feet, but he figured that could come later. The physical part was very nice, but the mental and spiritual parts were even better. They both felt fully and completely loved.

The next day, Rey and his family took a special flight in Jake's private jet to an airbase in the far Pacific. Then they boarded his large yacht and leisurely cruised to Foondavi.

When they arrived in Troon, it appeared as if the whole island turned out while the welcome home song was sung. Prissy admitted it was the most beautiful song she ever heard. The boys, though, thought it needed some electric guitars and drums but otherwise sounded real cool. A terrific welcome back jamaroon was held and was the talk of the island for years.

Prissy had insisted on taking the blue before leaving the states, so the McBlues had no problem immediately taking her in to the warm embrace of their loving family and village. The boys took to Foondavi so fast that Rey was worried they wouldn't be able to pry them loose when summer ended and they all needed to return to the reservation for school and to continue the True Blue Revolution.

After a few days on the island, no one seemed to notice when Rey took a small, insulated, and carefully protected case out of his larger baggage and hauled it up to the highest ring road. He stopped at a small lava tube by an old sign reading Preservation or Sanctuary in the gentle tongue. When the door silently slid open, Rey walked inside and was happily greeted by Larry Jones and a host of his very special gentle people.

After an exuberant greeting from everyone, Rey walked to the back of the gorge to a secluded lava brick structure he had asked Larry to have secretly built and then into a specially prepared room. Satellite dishes were already hooked up to his exact specifications, as were solar-powered generators. A wall of flat-screen monitors flashed on as he walked in. He unlocked and opened up the case and carefully put the pinkish grey brain of Carlyle into the specially designed container.

Suddenly, a mellow southern drawl filled the room: "You took your sweet time, blue boy!"

"I wanted a little private time with my wife before worrying about you peeping in on us, you bag of neurotic and perverted neurons. Plus, your constant cornpone chatter was getting on my nerves. Besides, I know you were operating wireless anyway, staying in touch, so don't give me any lip. Oh, that's right, you don't have any lips!" Rey teased.

After a little more banter, Carlyle filled Rey in on what was going on in the world. Things were progressing as well as could be expected. The True Blue Revolution was seeping into every corner of the world, not just America, and more and more people every day were taking the blue or at least joining the cause.

Rey liked knowing he didn't need to lead the effort. The movement was living and breathing; all it needed was an occasional gentle nudge from Jake, Rey, or Carlyle. NAP was still on the run, and the predators were stalking, beating, and chewing on each other for a change, much to Jake's enormous delight. Camilla the Computer was a constant threat, a troublesome personage, growing stronger every day. And Carlyle always became a little testy when Jake or Rey reminded him to not underestimate her. Jake also was following through on his promise to build Big Blue Twenty-Three to Carlyle's exacting specifications and much to his delight. Rey didn't really want to know any of the details.

The second day before Rey was to leave the peaceful and secluded sanctuary and head back to the McBlue village and his family, Carlyle told him he had a surprise for him: "Close your eyes and turn around." Rey did and then opened them on Carlyle's command. There, in front of him, on a massive monitor was a big, blue, smiling face. "It's me, Carlyle! I've taken the blue. If I lie, I die!"

Jake and his researchers weren't too sure about the validity of the change, but Carlyle claimed he managed to find a way to inject his own brain with the blue goo and now was truly True Blue indeed. He wanted to be just like his hero, Rey. "Now I have to tell the truth in love, so I can at least appear to have empathy!" he chortled.

Rey and his family spent the rest of the summer on Foondavi, being feted from village to village as they wandered the island. The boys soon found more pet goats and alpacas, made tons of friends, and took to the gentle tongue like they had been speaking it their whole lives. They each got names reflecting their sweet and gentle personalities. Prissy got prettier by the day, as she soaked in the love and acceptance she had thirsted for her entire life. Her new name reflected the gentle beauty she was, and, not surprisingly, it didn't translate into American English. As she unfolded like some of the beautiful tropical blooms on the islands, Rey found he was enraptured more each day by her sweet and gentle spirit, which was the closest her gentle tongue name translated into English.

In the secluded valley and in his special high security room, Carlyle found his true purpose of defending the gentle people from the fierce forces of evil. He found a deep and profound peace. He also reveled in Foondavi and wandered with his adopted family, the Nambo McBlues, using his micro-bots and fly-bots to monitor and protect, like the true Fenrir Shamar he was rapidly becoming. He also was learning to become a wisdom lender under the auspices of the McBlue Tufooga, visiting him on a special flat-screen monitor that shone a special blue light out on the tiny village. Also, as Carlyle worked to find strategies to repurpose his neurons and form new neural pathways around the damaged parts of his brain, his memory seemed to be improving. In fact, the beauty of Foondavi and the fondness of finally finding true friends gave him meaning in life, and the acceptance and abundant love kept his paranoia and depression at bay. When the time came when he would finally die, it was agreed his brain would be buried in an honored place under a McBlue family tree in the grove.

In the *Golden Book of Collected Wisdom*, it now says this about the world. "In the darkness the predators wait, but in the light we find strength to love and face another day. Truth and love must always strive to prevail over lies and hatred. As long as the True Blue Revolution rolls on, the power of loving hearts will hold back the forces of the dark. Always, always tell the truth in love."

Also by **Jerry Willbur**

Herding Hummingbirds:
Creating and Keeping Uncommon
Cross-Current Leaders

Giant Killers:
Creating the Remarkable
Customer Service Culture

More information about Jerry and his books
can be found at **jerrywillbur.com**
or at **facebook.com/DrJerryWillbur**.